The Things That Are Caesar's

The Things That Are Caesar's

BUD NORMAN

Affiliated Writers of America/Publishers
Alexander & Fraser, Inc.
Wichita, Kansas

ISBN: 1-879915-13-8

Library of Congress Control Number: 2003112478

Published by Affiliated Writers of America
An Imprint of Alexander & Fraser, Inc.
507 Barlow
Wichita, Kansas 67207
316-706-7875

Manufactured in the United States of America

DEDICATION

To Mom

The Things That Are Caesar's

CHAPTER ONE

"Tragic Prelude"

John Brown stood defiant on the Kansas plains. Two mighty armies were poised for battle on either side of him, while behind him a tornado fanned the flames of a rampaging prairie fire, but the great man showed no fear. With outstretched arms he held a rifle in one bloodstained hand, a Bible in the other, and righteous wrath blazed behind his long white beard. John Brown's wild eyes seemed to stare far past Frankie Livengood, through the limestone-and-marble walls of the Kansas capitol, beyond the state's sea of golden wheat, into America's coming cataclysm.

Frankie Livengood slouched against the oaken doorframe outside the governor's office, his soft hands stuffed in the coat pockets of a frayed brown suit, wishing he could smoke a cigarette. He squinted at some minor detail of the mural.

Although Livengood had worked in the capitol for most of the previous twenty-five years, and seen the second floor's famed mural hundreds of thousands of times, the image of John Brown continued to fascinate him. By now he was aware of many flaws in the painting, such as the long white beard that Brown didn't grow until leaving Kansas, and the way the tornado appeared to be fanning the flames in the wrong direction, and he had also learned several disturbing facts about its subject. The beloved abolitionist once messily slaughtered a family of non-combatants near Osawatomie, for instance, and Livengood had read convincing arguments by historians suggesting that Brown was simply a lunatic who likely would have killed people even without the benefit of a good cause. Somehow, such flaws only enhanced Livengood's fascination, and the way he saw it, both painting and subject had turned out very well.

Livengood would often pause from his work to relish the artist's rough but heartfelt style, or to contemplate Brown's role in erasing the stain of slavery from the fabric of American life, or perhaps to reflect on Kansas' bloody birth into the Union, thus putting the more petty politics of the moment into perspective.

On other occasions, Livengood would look at the painting merely to postpone some unpleasant chore. This was one of those occasions.

On the opposite side of the door, Gov. Chuck Bentley was about to announce to the statehouse press corps that he would not run for a second term, meaning that Livengood, officially the legislative liaison for Governor Bentley and unofficially his administrative second banana, now faced two unpleasant tasks. He would soon be subject to the inevitable humiliations of another job search, and even worse, because it was immediately at hand, he had to hear the damned speech.

The speech had seemed a grating enough collection of cliches, euphemisms and outright obfuscations when Livengood had written it, and he could predict that in Governor Bentley's bellowing twang it would sound even worse. Still, when the clop of Bentley's cowboy boots announced his entrance into the office, Livengood took his place behind the pack of reporters and assumed his most respectful and attentive expression.

"My fellow Kansans," Governor Bentley began, with what he considered a dramatic boom. "I come before you today to declare that I will not seek the nomination of the Republican Party for re-election to the office of governor of Kansas. If nominated, I will not accept. If elected, I will not serve. Having achieved my most cherished goals for this administration during the past three and a half years, I feel it is time for me to return to the hard work I love so much on my farm. I thank the people of Kansas for honoring me with the position of governor of this great state, but the position I have always valued most is that of husband and father to my wonderful wife and beautiful children. Now I will assume the position on a full-time basis."

Livengood's vast experience with political rhetoric prevented him from succumbing to a disgusted guffaw or two, but he could not resist enumerating to himself a few of the myriad flaws in the speech.

To begin with, there was hardly reason for Governor Bentley to address the possibility of being re-nominated, much less re-elected. He might as well have announced his plans in the event of being made God.

The governor probably had achieved his own most cherished personal goals for the administration, Livengood conceded to himself. After all, Bentley had lived in the governor's mansion, flown in the governor's plane and shown up with the governor's title at his high school reunion. If one were looking for significant achievements on behalf of the public, however, the Bentley administration had not been successful even by Livengood's thoroughly diminished standards.

As for all that hard work that Bentley would soon return to on the farm, Livengood could only wish that he had his own huge hunk of heavily subsidized western Kansas ranch land where he could do such hard work as cashing USDA checks and barking orders at the underpaid farm hands. The way Livengood figured it, that would probably beat having to beg yet another bullshit politician for yet another ulcer-inducing job.

And it's too bad, Livengood silently ranted to himself, that Bentley's wonderful wife wasn't the mother of his beautiful children. If not for the first Mrs. Bentley running around the state talking to reporters about how Governor Bentley had ditched her at a certain age, even after she'd undergone the harrowing breast enhancement surgery he had insisted on, Bentley might have had a decent shot at another four years of living in the gubernatorial mansion, flying in the gubernatorial plane and making his gubernatorial boasts at the high school reunions. The thought slightly sickened Livengood, but not so much as the prospect of unemployment.

Livengood did enjoy one inner chuckle at Governor Bentley's promise to "assume the position on a full-time basis," but the satisfaction quickly disappeared. The governor told the assembled reporters that he had enjoyed working with them, and that they were welcome to drop by the farm for a chat any time they happened to be in Wallace County, but that he wouldn't be answering any questions right now, leaving Livengood with the task of defending the Bentley administration. This would be a very hard day on the job, indeed.

The television reporters had no idea who Frankie Livengood was, and for the sake of balance they all ran off in search of a rare Kansas Democrat to provide a sound bite as inane as Governor Bentley's, but the handful of radio and press reporters quickly pounced. The reporters more or less liked Livengood, because he provided the most reliably colorful on-the-record quotes in the statehouse, but they were annoyed by Governor Bentley's refusal to answer their questions and were eager to begin kicking at the corpse of his administration. Their questions came at Livengood as a cacophony of insinuating tones, with allegations about the governor's family life overlapping with accusations about the revenue surplus expenditures melding into charges about the tax cut veto. It was all the noisier to Livengood's ears because he could not honestly deny the criticisms implied in any of the questions.

So Livengood waved his palms at the reporters and said, "Whoa, whoa." He offered them a quote as bland as anything Governor Bentley might have said himself, then insisted the rest of the interview be off the record. After negotiating terms that would allow the reporters to identify him as a high-ranking staff member, along with enough clues for anyone who might be hiring a political aide to figure out who he was, Livengood proceeded to attribute the demise of the Bentley administration to bad luck and the bad advice of a certain unnamed advisor. Livengood explained that he had an ethical obligation to withhold the identity of that advisor, and would not relent no matter how the reporters badgered him.

Yes, Livengood admitted, the governor's ex-wife had certainly damaged his standing in the party, particularly among its more religious members. But what was a high-ranking staff member such as Livengood to do about that?

It was true, Livengood conceded, that the decision not to return the revenue surplus to the taxpayers had damaged the governor's standing with the economic conservatives. It was also true, Livengood acknowledged with a sage nod of the head, that the subsequent tax cut veto had worsened that damage. In both cases, Livengood said, the certain unnamed advisor had swayed the governor despite the sound advice of certain unnamed high-ranking staff members.

As the other failings of the Bentley administration were addressed by Livengood, with the blame for each one ambiguously shifted elsewhere, the reporters ran off one by one in self-important hurries. Soon the only reporter left was Dan Dorsey, still wearing the same patient grin he'd shown throughout the interrogation.

"That was a fine speech you wrote, son. It put me in mind of Cincinnatus returning to his plow," Dorsey said. "The part about 'assuming the position on a full-time basis' was a nice touch, too."

Livengood shrugged. "I try."

"Too bad about that bonehead advisor talking Bentley into investing the surplus and killing the tax cut," Dorsey said. "Folks probably wouldn't have minded so much about Bentley dumping his wife if you'd put a few extra bucks back in their pockets, even with her getting the boob job and all."

"Yeah, well, maybe," Livengood said, sneering each word. "I suppose we could have cut a check to everyone in the state for just enough to buy a new bowling ball, but instead we made investments that'll be worth two bowling balls on down the line. So sue me."

Dorsey smiled triumphantly, having confirmed his suspicions about the identity of the unnamed advisor. After thirty-eight years of covering state government, long enough to have attained the titles of Bureau Chief of the Sunflower News Service and "dean of the capitol press corps," Dorsey was not easily bamboozled even by the likes of Frankie Livengood. Besides, Livengood was the only person Dorsey had ever known who could have talked Bentley into such politically suicidal decisions, and Livengood was certainly the only one who ever would.

Although Dorsey could have complicated Livengood's job search with this information, he was not inclined to do so. He knew that none of his readers were likely to give a damn about some otherwise unnamed high-ranking staff member, for one thing. For another, he retained a certain fondness for Frankie Livengood.

All of the other statehouse reporters had gradually become younger than Livengood, and regarded him merely as a reliable source and a dissipated old hack, but Dorsey could still remember the fresh-faced and smart-assed Frankie who had come to the capitol as a teenaged page twenty-five years earlier. Livengood was now 38 years old, of average build only by virtue of living in a state where slightly overweight was the norm, with question mark posture, bags under his squinty eyes that seemed to sag with the weight of the world, and just enough boyishness left in his face to inspire suspicions of immaturity, but Dorsey's perception had not changed.

Still grinning from the enjoyment of his good-natured attacks, Dorsey noticed that Livengood was frowning deeply. Following an awkward pause, Livengood blurted out that, "I hate this life, Dan."

The outburst rattled Dorsey. Although he had grown up in a stereotypically expressive Irish household Back East, Dorsey had lived so long in Kansas that he was now uncomfortable with such raw expressions of emotion. Knowing that Livengood was a lifelong Kansan, of stoic Kansas stock, Dorsey could scarcely imagine how low his friend must be feeling to make such a statement.

Not knowing what else to say, Dorsey followed an old instinct and suggested that a drink might help. He offered to buy the first round.

"Jesus," Livengood said, staring out the window, seeing nothing. "This life is killing me."

CHAPTER TWO

"An Evil and Wicked State"

Frankie Livengood was too far lost into the darkness of his own thoughts to see, but the office window he gazed through afforded a clear view of Jesus' name being invoked in prayer.

Edna Dimschmidt, a tall, wiry woman of 44 with a fiercely pious face, and Ellie Whimple, a tall, wiry woman of 30 with softly blank features, kneeled to pray together beside a statue of Abraham Lincoln. Even the few passersby took little notice of the scene, and this being Kansas, it didn't warrant any stares. But those who did bother to eavesdrop on Dimschmidt's conversation with The Almighty were treated to a rousing and deceptively consequential prayer.

"Oh Lord our God," Dimschmidt said, loudly enough to ensure the attention of the nearby pedestrians, if not The Lord Himself. "We beseech Thee, dear God, to guide us as we enter this temple of an evil and wicked state. We ask Your protection from the temptations of money, power and secular glory that this building represents. Lead us, Oh Lord, in the effort that brings us to this seat of Pharaoh, this hall of Caesar. Bless us, oh Lord, in the discussion we are about to have with Representative Patterson, and help us that we may persuade him to support Your servant Hampton Hibbert, a righteous man, in his godly campaign to conquer this unholy place and lead this sinful state to Your perfect grace. In the name of our savior Jesus Christ we pray. Amen."

With that, Ellie Whimple offered a quiet, "Amen," and the two women rose and strode up the capitol steps.

Frankie Livengood hid behind his hat as he passed Dimschmidt and Ellie on his way down, escaping to the sanctuary of a nearby tavern.

In the soothing dimness of the bar, Frankie Livengood and Dan Dorsey cursed the world. They had downed three shots of whiskey apiece, then chased each one with a beer, and the alcohol had loosened both their tongues and the terms of their social contract, allowing them to commiserate freely.

"You know what really pisses me off?" Livengood asked.

Dorsey admitted he did not know, specifically, but said he was willing to learn.

"It's not the damned politicians I have to work for," Livengood said. "It's the damned voters who elect them."

Dorsey said that he heard that.

"I mean, we run a fool like Bentley on the slogan that he's going to 'Run Government Like a Business,' and when we do just that, the public wants to hang us. They scream for budget cuts, and when we do it, they start feeling sorry for the poor-ass people getting cut. Where the hell do people think those cuts are going to come from? Take out what the feds have mandated, what's set in stone with the highway bill, and all the sacred cow stuff, and there's really not much of a budget there to begin with. Hell, cut it any thinner and it's going to start affecting white people. Middle-class white people, Dan. I'm telling you, it's just not politically viable."

Dorsey nodded, Livengood continued.

"The wisdom of the people—ha! These, these 'people,' as you call them, they come into my office every day hollering to high heaven for the government to get out of their lives—as if I even give a good Goddamn about their pathetic lives—and then they storm in the next day wanting to know why we haven't solved every little problem they've got.

"And they'll go on and on about how the government can't do anything right, and then they'll turn right around and want to know why we haven't stamped out sin in Kansas yet. Well, hell, Dan, sin's a big problem in this state. I've seen the studies. Stamping it out would probably take a tax hike, and that sets up one hell of a dilemma for a Republican."

Dorsey said he heard that, too.

"And that's just the damned Republicans I'm talking about, the so-called conservatives. My people. Don't even get me started on the damned Democrats, the so-called liberals."

Waving his palms at the very idea, Dorsey said he certainly wouldn't want to do that. He signaled the bartender for two more shots, two more beers.

"They hate me, Dan. They hate me," Livengood said. "They hate the government, so they hate me. You don't know what that's like."

Dorsey sarcastically agreed, noting that, "Everybody loves the press."

"Yeah, yeah, everybody hates everybody. I know that. But I'm telling you, Dan, *everybody* hates the government. I'm not just talking about the nut jobs who think I'm working on Project 666 for the United Nations invasion force—and I'm not saying there's no such plan, mind you, just that I never got the memo—I mean everybody. The liberals think I'm a Nazi. The conservatives think I'm a commie. Even the people who don't give a damn about politics enough to be anything still give a damn enough to hate my ass."

Dorsey could offer only a sympathetic shrug.

"Hell, I'm no Nazi. I'm no commie. You know me, Dan. I'm just a damned Republican, that's all. If they don't like it, they can vote for a damned Democrat. And I'll tell you something else, I'm no anti-Christ, either."

"Not that I ever noticed," Dorsey said, swallowing the fresh shot in one gulp.

"Some of these hopped-up turbo Christians we've got around here, they may think I'm the anti-Christ, but Jesus, I'm a Christian, too, you know. I believe in the virgin birth, the resurrection, the Father, the Son, the Holy Ghost, Matthew, Mark, all those guys. I really believe that stuff."

"You got your fundamentals down, all right," Dorsey said.

"Damn straight, I do," Livengood said, pausing to sip a drink and light a cigarette. "Now, I'm not saying I always know what's right and what's wrong, because that gets tricky sometimes in my business, but I grope around as best I can."

Dorsey raised his beer glass and said, "Show me any damned voter who does any better."

"They can kiss my ass," Livengood said, joining the toast. "My fat, hairy, hemorrhoidal ass."

"Mine, too," Dorsey said, before chasing the whiskey with a long swig of beer.

Frankie Livengood wasn't the only Kansan to take a lively interest in Governor Bentley's withdrawal. Some of the state's beleaguered Democrats were concluding that they were now without a prayer in the upcoming election. State party chairman Rob Chupp, making a telephone call from his antique-laden law office in Lindsborg, admitted as much to labor leader Pat McEntire, who listened at her gray steel desk in a Wyandotte County Machinists Hall.

CHAPTER TWO

"Kansans will always vote against an incumbent governor, even if it means electing a Democrat, but we don't have that advantage anymore," Chupp said. "Unless the Republicans come up with someone who's way the hell out there, we'd better find ourselves another sacrificial lamb and save any real candidates for a better run later on."

Noting that the odds against the Republicans coming up with someone way the hell out there were not prohibitive, McEntire argued for fielding a "real" candidate just in case. She admitted, however, that she was unable to think of any potential candidates who matched that description. The only Democrat she knew to be seriously considering a run for governor was Prof. Willa Kline of the Wichita State University Women's Studies Department.

"Willa Kline! Sweet mother of Jesus!" Chupp said. "When they call her a liberal, she won't even deny it. She'll probably put it in the damn ads. This is Kansas, not Massachusetts. That crazy woman is too liberal for me, and I'm too liberal for Kansas."

"Oh well," McEntire said. "She'll rev up what's left of the true believers, and she'll give the Bible-thumpers hell, too. At least until election day."

Chupp slumped back in his chair and said, "Sweet Mother of Jesus."

At the same time, budding mogul and record-setting Republican fund-raiser Chip Wentworth was in his steel-and-glass office, looking down on the traffic of Johnson County as he rode a stationary bike and barked into a cell phone. He was talking with Wichita banking executive Arvin Howard about the pressing need to elect a governor "who won't ruin the business climate in this state with a bunch of bleeding heart bullshit." In other states a listener might have assumed that Wentworth was talking about the likes of

Willa Kline, but in the context of Kansas politics Howard immediately understood that he referred to the likes of Edna Dimschmidt.

"If we don't rally the business community behind someone who understands the need for low taxes and a laissez faire economic policy, we're going to end up with some crazy right-winger in there," Wentworth said. "This state is going to get a reputation for being a loony bin of anti-abortion, anti-homosexual, anti-intellectual radicalism if we elect some polyester-wearing preacher for a governor. That's going to be hell on the economic development, I tell you. Just try getting a good Jew accountant or queer art director to move clear the hell out here and work for you when that happens."

A Wichita businessman of the old school, Howard did not ride a stationary bike during telephone conversations. He sat rigidly at his desk, holding the phone to his ear, and attempted to persuade Wentworth to help recruit a candidate who would support the goals of both the business and religious wings of the party.

"After all," he said, "they're not mutually exclusive."

"The hell they're not," Wentworth said. "We're for schools that teach kids to take their place in the work force, they're for schools that teach kids to hate fags and never use a condom. We're for a lean, mean government that paves the roads, keeps the water flowing and makes sure the banks keep lending money in Kansas, and they're waiting for the Rapture. We're for any legal business trying to make a buck, and they want to blow up every abortion clinic, titty bar and bookstore in the state. We're for open markets, and they want to build a wall around the state and set up a reservation for religious fanatics."

Howard was tempted to point out that religious conservatives such as himself also opposed unscrupulous business practices, marital infidelity and cocaine use, knowing those ideals also offended Wentworth's modern sensibilities, but he held his tongue. Instead, he tried again to argue for a centrist candidate with appeal to both factions of the party.

"No way that works, my friend," Wentworth said. "If you're not a true believer, if you aren't one of them, they'll notice it right away—because your suit is too nice, or you use the right fork or something—and there's no way you get their vote. Believe me, I know these people. I grew up with them. Johnson County is thick with them, and their spooky-looking kids, too."

"Just remember," Howard said, before hanging up, "there are a lot more poor Christians in Kansas than there are rich businessmen."

Meanwhile, Rep. Stan Patterson was making a futile attempt to convince Edna Dimschmidt that even the poorest Christians needed rich businessmen. He was a church-going man, owed his position to the support of church-going Kansans, and was as quick to cast the first stone as the next fellow, but the representative was also a prosperous insurance agent who saw no reason that God and good business should ever be in conflict.

"After all," Patterson said, in the same reassuring tone that had closed a thousand insurance deals, "the Good Book does say that 'God helps those who help themselves.' And how are our people to help themselves without jobs? The Bible also says 'be not slothful in business,' you know."

To quote the Bible to Edna Dimschmidt was to throw down a challenge. She responded with a slew of verses about filthy lucre, the love of money being the root of all evil, how money perishes with thee, and so on until the weight of Biblical authority was tilted toward her position. Then she let loose with a barrage of her favorite citations, the ones regarding the sad fate of peoples who fall into disfavor with God.

"How can you worry about economic development when the unborn babies of Kansas are slaughtered by the thousands before they can develop? How can you worry about highways when homosexuals are snatching up the precious little children who do survive the abortion mills? How can you worry about the material well-being of Kansas when its spiritual well-being is in such imminent peril?"

"Now, now," Patterson said. "I'm in complete agreement with you, of course. You know that I abhor all this sinfulness around here every bit as much as you do. I'm just saying that we need to support a candidate who will take care of both the material and the spiritual needs of the state. Besides, we're going to need the money and the votes of a few businessmen if we want to get anyone elected."

Anger was visible on Dimschmidt's face, and Whimple, who sat silently throughout the conversation, reached to touch her hand.

"You won't get anybody elected in this state without the money and the votes and the hard work of committed Christians, either," Dimschmidt said, with arms crossed and eyes fixed at Patterson's suddenly nervous face. "I've come to you because you're the recognized leader of the Christian legislators, because you're next in line to be the Speaker of the House, and because you owe all of that to Christian support. Do you really think you can count on the support of your so-called business friends? I certainly don't think so. They laugh at you behind your back, you know. I've heard them."

"Yes, Edna," Patterson said, in the same resigned tone with which he submitted to the occasional bad business deal.

"I'm for any man making an honest living, Representative Patterson, and I can assure you that Hampton Hibbert is hardly an anti-business candidate. I'm sure you know that he's been a very successful developer in many Kansas communities."

"I know that, Edna, and I know that Hampton's a good man. But I must be frank with you, Edna. A lot of his fellow business people consider Hampton a little, well, I guess you'd say overly zealous."

"In a state that slaughters its unborn babies, and condones the sins of Sodom, and seeks material things more fervently than it seeks God, a man can't be overly zealous."

"I'm just saying, Edna, that you need to tend to both the material and spiritual needs of the state. That's all."

Edna Dimschmidt stood up and smoothed her floral-patterned cotton dress. Then Ellie Whimple stood up and smoothed her own floral-patterned cotton dress.

"What you say is true," Dimschmidt said before striding out. "But I am determined that Hampton Hibbert shall become governor to emphasize the spiritual over the material. We will expect your support, or you may no longer expect ours. And may I remind you that I speak for all Kansans United for a Sin-Free Kansas?"

At that very moment, Pastor Bill Jeffries was angrily dialing the phone in his study, wondering why Representative Patterson hadn't yet returned his call. It was a poorly kept secret among the state's politically active religious conservatives that Patterson intended to run for governor if Bentley bowed out of the race, and Pastor Jeffries was annoyed that he hadn't yet been asked for his blessings. Pastor Jeffries was particularly galled by the knowledge, gleaned from a loose-lipped secretary, that Patterson was instead conferring with Edna Dimschmidt. After all, wasn't Pastor Jeffries the founder and director of Kansans for Kansas Values? And weren't its good works much greater, and its mailing list much longer, than that of Kansans United for a Sin-Free Kansas?

United States Representative Jonathan Appel learned of Governor Bentley's withdrawal by cell phone while aboard a 737 en route from Washington, D.C. to his home district, just as the plane encountered turbulence from the mountainous thunderstorm developing below. Even the smoothest flights rattled Appel's nerves, and such bumpy rides as this one were enough to make him question the political ambitions that brought him back to the district every month.

A fat woman in the next seat recognized Appel and attempted to strike up a conversation about the governor's race.

"Have you thought about running?" she asked.

Appel laughingly said he had not, trying to politely terminate the conversation so he could resume thinking about running. He'd been mulling the possibility ever since rumors of Governor Bentley's withdrawal had begun to circulate, weighing the relative prestige and power of a mere congressman in Washington, D.C., versus a governor in Topeka, Kansas. Better to be a senator, he thought to himself, but then he thought again and realized that neither of the state's Republican senators were likely to be stepping down soon. Still thinking, Appel considered that being governor might be helpful if those seats did somehow become open.

Just then the plane dropped precipitously before steadying itself to a nauseating stagger, and Representative Appel reflected on the fact that governors don't need to fly as often as congressmen. When they do fly, he mused, they get to do it in their own twin-engine Beech. Appel scratched his cheek and said, "Hmmm."

Governor Bentley's decision not to seek re-election also figured in the conversation at a cafe on the edge of a small western Kansas town called Piquant, where high school art teacher Kathy Knieble, mechanic Will Schnitzle and carpenter Harley Christianson held their daily discussions about the news of the day.

"Good riddance to the bastard," Schnitzle said. "That's what I say."

"I hate to agree with Will about anything," Knieble said, smiling at Christianson, "but I'm afraid I have to this time. Good riddance to Governor Bentley. Of course, I'm sure my reasons for saying so are very different from Will's."

Shrugging as he sipped his coffee, Christianson said, "Bentley didn't seem such a bad fellow to me. Being governor's a tough job, I'd guess, and who's to say he didn't give it his best shot."

Knieble and Schnitzle looked at one another in disbelief. Knieble then berated Governor Bentley for his niggardly budgets and knee-jerk conservatism, after which Schnitzle cursed Governor Bentley's socialistic excesses and bleeding-heart liberalism, prompting a heated argument about how, exactly, that fool had ruined the state.

Gesturing toward the window, with its scene of wheat ripening to a greenish gold beneath a brilliantly blue sky, Christianson remarked, "The state doesn't look so ruined to me."

Smiling sweetly at Christianson, Knieble suggested that he would make a fine governor. Schnitzle said that, painful as it was to agree with Knieble twice in one day, he thought so, too.

"You've been a good mayor around here," Schnitzle said. "You got that park going, kept the bills down, and you handled them state boys pretty good when we needed the highway fixed."

Christianson scoffed at the compliment.

"And you're a good man. And you fought in Vietnam," Knieble said. "That would make quite a story, and I must say that you'd cut a mighty handsome figure in the campaign ads."

Christianson looked down in embarrassment, and waved away any further flattery. Standing up, he left an overly generous tip and dismissed the conversation as crazy talk.

"Sorry, my fellow citizens, but if nominated I will not run, and if elected I will not serve. A guy would have to be crazy to get into politics in this state, and I'd like to think I'm not crazy."

Despite two more shots and two more beers, Frankie Livengood's defiance had given way to despair. He couldn't stop considering his career prospects, and no amount of alcohol could make them seem bright.

Dan Dorsey made a well-educated guess about the likely Republican candidates for governor, and as he went through the list Livengood realized that he had somehow fallen into disfavor with each one. Scanning the slates of other upcoming races in his mind, Livengood began to realize that in his twenty-five years of competitive politics he had, at one time or another, given offense to nearly every possible employer.

"Maybe I'll just move out to western Kansas and open a burger stand," Livengood said.

Dorsey tried to envision Livengood in any occupation outside politics, and failed. Although Dorsey often heard his conservative Republican friend extol the virtues of the free market, "making it sound like the goddamned Garden of Eden," he knew that Livengood did not want to work there. Private sector jobs demanded tangible results, for one thing, and Livengood's principled laziness was likely to go unappreciated there. Both men agreed that much of the harm done by government was a result of public officials being addled by a misguided work ethic and feeling compelled to do *something,* and for all his faults, Frankie Livengood was blameless in this regard.

Dorsey scoffed that Livengood loved the political life too much to quit, and that besides, there weren't any people left in western Kansas.

"Yeah, but I hate it, too," Livengood said. "And even if there aren't any people out there, they still want a good burger."

In an effort to be helpful, Dorsey suggested lobbying, saying, "There's no shame in that, lots of over-the-hill political hacks do it." Livengood rejected the suggestion with a disgusted look. "Consulting, then," Dorsey said, "you know, helping companies get around all those laws you've been passing all these years." Livengood dismissed the idea as unsporting. Dorsey then suggested that Livengood run for office himself, and both men shared a hearty laugh at the joke.

"But seriously, Dan," Livengood said, "what am I going to do?"

Dorsey and Livengood allowed the Sunflower News Service to pick up the tab, then stumbled toward the door. As they struggled to put on their coats, Dorsey asked Livengood a final question.

"Why the hell did you talk Bentley into investing the surplus, anyway? And what the hell were you thinking about with that tax cut veto?"

"It was good policy," Livengood said. "Deficits are coming, and whoever the next governor is will be glad I did it."

"A hell of a lot of good that's going to do you," Dorsey said. "C'mon, Frankie, you know better than that."

Shrugging, Livengood said, "Sometimes I get a wild hair on my ass for good policy."

As he emerged from the darkness of the tavern, Livengood was exceedingly drunk. He had taken care to have work, bar and home all within a short stagger of one another, so he was spared the anxiety of driving while intoxicated, but now he was fearful of the dark and swirling clouds that had descended on the night sky.

Knowing Livengood's phobia of Kansas weather, Dorsey patted his friend's back and said, "This, too, will pass." While glancing at a nearby lightning strike, Livengood mumbled his thanks.

"Don't worry about the rest of it, either. That shit, it too will pass," Dorsey said. "You won't starve. At the worst, you'll have to take a real job. So what the hell, just seize the day. As you Republicans like to say, show some personal initiative."

Livengood said, "It's going to be tough, Dan," then lit another cigarette.

"No doubt," Dorsey said. "But hey, '*ad astra per aspera,*' as you Kansans like to say."

After thanking Dorsey for the pep talk, Livengood leaned into the wind and stomped toward his apartment. He stopped at the end of the block to vomit, then leaned against a streetlight pole, roaring a drunken laugh as another bolt of lightning illuminated the empty street.

"*Ad astra per aspera,*" Livengood muttered as he started to weave his way home again. "*Ad astra per* fuckin' *aspera.*"

CHAPTER THREE

"The Invisible Hand"

The rest of Kansas reacted to the news of Governor Bentley's impending retirement more calmly than did Frankie Livengood.

Indeed, Governor Bentley's announcement hardly rated as "news" at all. The evening's newscasts devoted less than a minute to the story, saving more time for such features as "Are You a Sex Addict?" and "Angels—Good Friends to Have!" Bentley's bow would be played on the front pages of all the state's newspapers the next day, but in most cases below the fold, with *The Kansas City Star* running it beneath some economic news, and *The Wichita Eagle* giving it less prominence than the fourth installment of a five-part series on a handicapped child's courageous attempt to play competitive squash. Numerous small town journals would run Dorsey's account from the Sunflower News Service, typically much abridged.

According to one newspaper poll, said to be accurate within a four point margin of error, fully 76 percent of all Kansans simply "did not care" about the upcoming gubernatorial race. The pollsters did not bother to ask, but it was safe to assume the public cared even less about a poor political hack such as Frankie Livengood.

"And who can blame them? Why should anyone care what goes on here?" Livengood asked, leaning back in his office chair and addressing the question to Mark Stark. "As Whitman once wrote, 'Far from these swelling domes, topped with statues, more endless, jubilant, vital visions arise.' "

A friend of Livengood's since childhood, Stark was accustomed to the occasional outbursts of verse. He shrugged off the poetry and pressed on with his point: "I don't think you appreciate the significance of those poll numbers. More than three-fourths of this state doesn't care who runs its government. It's appalling."

"I can't believe they let you teach political science to young minds when you still don't know how to read a poll," Livengood said. "Obviously, far more than three-fourths don't care. That 76 percent figure is just the people who freely admit they don't give a damn. It's safe to assume that a similar percentage of those who say they do give a damn really don't, but don't want to make the pollster think they're stupid."

The associate professor of political science from Kansas State University was annoyed that his friend would countenance such apathy.

"Why shouldn't I?" Livengood said. "Most people figure the government doesn't have much to do with their lives, and I pray they're right."

"But it's no longer a democracy when only 5 percent of the people choose the leadership," Stark said. "It's, well, it's undemocratic. That's what it is."

"I think the word you're looking for is oligarchic," Livengood said, enjoying the opportunity to correct his academic friend. "But it's not that. The 95 percent freely choose to let the other 5 percent run things. That's democratic enough for me. I find it heartening, in fact, that 95 percent of the people in this state have something better to do. Some of them do, anyway, and who wants the rest of them meddling in the state's business?"

Even after twenty-five years of friendship, Stark still relished his arguments with Livengood. He leaned forward to make what he thought would be a winning riposte.

"But how long will your apolitical 95 percent be free to pursue these supposedly more endless and vital visions if the other 5 percent use their power to interfere? What if that 5 percent is comprised solely of people with financial interests at odds with the state's interests? What if that 5 percent chooses to impose its own vision on the rest? You may care about the other 95 percent, and I know I do, but who else? What if we're the only ones with the state's best interests at heart?"

Livengood shuddered at the thought. He shuddered again when, while strolling to lunch with Stark, he encountered Edna Dimschmidt and Ellie Whimple in the hallway. Unable to avoid eye contact, he was forced to exchange pleasantries.

"Howdy, Edna," Livengood said with a hostile politeness, and then, more genuinely, "Howdy, Ellie."

"And howdy to you, Mr. Living-good," Dimschmidt said, smiling with ferocious friendliness.

Livengood nodded with a forced nonchalance, knowing that Dimschmidt knew good and well that his name was pronounced Lie-vengood. Whimple only nodded at Livengood, then at Stark, who nodded at both women, and both pairs continued in their opposite directions.

In addition to Stark, Livengood had invited Jane Hutchinson and Mick Fixx to join him for lunch at the capitol cafeteria. He had devised a grand scheme to save himself from unemployment, and was eager to hear their reactions. Over cheeseburgers, French fries and sodas, Livengood unveiled his master plan for sustaining his career. He announced that he would find a little-known Kansan who met certain criteria, recruit this person to run for governor, run the campaign, win, and then run the ensuing administration from behind the scenes.

"It's improbable," Stark said.

"It's not right," Hutchinson said.

"I'll bet you one hundred bucks there is no way you pull this off," Fixx said.

The reactions stunned Livengood, who had expected effusive congratulations for his daring and brilliance. But knowing his listeners as well as he did, he should have been able to predict their negative reactions with near-verbatim accuracy.

Stark could have been counted on to raise the practical questions. After two decades of studying Kansas politics he knew the difficulties that all campaigns faced, so well that he instinctively doubted any of them could succeed. Indeed, at the end of every race he was mildly surprised to discover that anybody had won.

Hutchinson, a longtime environmental bureaucrat and Livengood's angelically blonde ex-wife, was predictably concerned about the ethical issues. She shared Stark's concerns about the practicality of Livengood's schemes, as always, but she still tended to worry more about his soul.

Fixx, a friend of Livengood's since their high school days who had been invited to offer an outsider's point of view, was the most easily predictable of the three. A professional jack-of-all-trades and the only one of the quartet clad in a "shit happens" T-shirt, Fixx invariably predicted the worst outcome for any Livengood scheme.

Livengood first addressed Stark's arguments. It was true that a little known candidate would by definition lack a base of support, Livengood conceded, "But I don't really need that much support to eke out a plurality in a crowded primary field, and having a base of support is only going to offend somebody else's." Fund-raising would of course be the biggest difficulty, Livengood acknowledged, "But we'll hit up all the donors who give to each candidate, get some pros on the job, and I'll get Big Jim to stake me. Then it will start rolling." Livengood could hardly deny that such a campaign faced numerous other unforeseeable difficulties, but he assured Stark that, "I'll run the perfect campaign."

The boast struck Stark as pure hubris, but it also piqued his scholarly interest. After twenty-five years of arguing about politics with Livengood, Stark could see an opportunity to test his friend's many theories against more or less real world conditions. Even the failure of such an audacious experiment would make a fine paper, Stark mused, as he silently imagined himself out on the campaign trail and away from the office, then at various symposia around the country reading his fabulously well-received "Theory and Practice of Campaigning Independently of Traditional Party Structures."

Livengood's ex-wife unsurprisingly proved harder to persuade. She insinuated that Livengood's scheme was inherently dishonest, saying that if he truly believed he was the most qualified person to be governor, well then, he should present himself to the people for their approval. She practically accused him of seeking a patsy candidate, "which would not only be a lie to the public about the true leadership of the state, but would almost certainly be a lie to the fool playing the role of governor."

Touching his fingers to his chest in an expression of excruciatingly hurt feelings, Livengood assured her that his motives were pure. Hutchinson said that she wasn't questioning his motives, but her tone of voice implied otherwise.

"I'll be honest with whoever I find. Trust me," Livengood said. "He'll be the governor, I'll be his advisor, and that will be our relationship. If he tends to follow my advice more often than not, well, I don't see the harm in that."

Hutchinson's expression remained dubious.

"Politics is all I know, Jane," Livengood persisted. "People need shoes, so they go to the guy who knows how to make shoes.

Same with food, beer, country music records, anything you need, and there's always someone out there who can do it. Well, people need a little politics, too, because that's what it takes to make the highways and the prisons and the landfills and the rest of it. And I do politics. The state needs a governor, and I know how to get one elected. It's as if the invisible hand of Adam Smith himself is nudging me along to my destiny."

It took a moment's reflection and a heavy sigh, but Hutchinson offered whatever support she was legally allowed to offer the campaign. Clearly pleased by Hutchinson's response, Livengood offered to pay her tab.

"As for you, Fixx," Livengood said, "I'll take that bet."

Wiping ketchup from his beard with the back of his hand, Fixx warned his friend that, "Sometimes that invisible hand you're talking about will ball up in a fist and punch you in the nose."

No longer concerned with any of his official duties except cashing his paycheck, Livengood began work on his plan in his office the very next day. With Stark taking extensive notes on a legal pad, Livengood outlined his theoretical criteria for the perfect Kansas gubernatorial candidate.

"First of all, he's a man," Livengood said. "I'm not saying the state won't elect a woman, and in fact it's always been ahead of the country on that, but still, better he's a man."

Stark noted the point.

"Secondly, he's a white man," Livengood said. "I'm not saying that Kansans wouldn't elect a black guy, so long as he's a bedrock conservative Christian farmer-businessman black guy with a war record, and so long as he was running against someone who's just way the hell liberal, but still, better he's a white guy."

Stark wrote "white guy" on the yellow legal pad.

"Third, he's a Christian white guy," Livengood said. "I don't mean one of those turbo-Christians, but when people ask him where he goes to church, he should have an answer."

The point was duly recorded by Stark.

"A heterosexual Christian white guy, of course," Livengood said. "He has to have a wife and at least one kid, for that matter. A dog, too, not a cat."

Smiling slightly, Stark wrote "breeder" on the pad.

"He should be at the older end of the baby boom, too," Livengood said. "That demographic likes its own, for some reason."

Looking up from his legal pad, Stark noted that the older end of the baby boom had been of draft age during the Vietnam War.

"He's absolutely got to be a vet," Livengood said. "People can't get enough of Vietnam vets. Throw a few of their dead buddies into a stump speech, and everyone who opposed or supported the war will vote for him out of guilt. Run him against someone who spent the war years in a frat house, and it'll be like the My Lai Massacre."

While scribbling "Viet vet" on the pad, Stark asked about past drug use.

"Ideally, he's never touched the stuff," Livengood said. "A candidate can survive a couple of puffs of weed these days, so long as it was a long time ago and it didn't make him cool, but it's better if he's never even tried it. Non-pot smokers are more uptight about pot-smoking than pot smokers are about non-pot smoking."

Stark asked what the candidate would look like.

"A good looking guy, but not too good looking," Livengood said. "Kansans won't elect a pretty boy. Ruggedly good looking, that's what we want."

Smiling, Stark asked if this ruggedly good looking fellow had ever had sex outside of marriage.

"Not since he got married," Livengood said. "Anyone he slept with before that had better be damned discreet, too."

Looking over the list, Stark wondered about the possibility of finding a ruggedly good looking man who had never cheated on his wife, and who had served in Vietnam but never smoked dope.

"It can be done," Livengood said. "This is Kansas."

Returning to his notes, Stark asked what sort of political experience the candidate should possess.

"Very limited," Livengood said. "He should have something on the resume, maybe mayor of a small town, just enough to keep the papers from harping on the fact that he doesn't have any experience. Not too much, though, because people hate politicians, and too much experience leaves a record. That's never good."

As he wrote down "not a politician," Stark asked what the candidate's occupation should be.

"Something manly," Livengood said. "Farmer is always a sure bet, but you can also get a good ad out of a builder, an airplane guy, someone who runs a trucking line, something like that. Whatever it is, it should be rural, because city folks romanticize rural folks and rural folks don't trust city folks."

Having finished writing down the description of the perfect candidate, Stark asked what the candidate's perfect platform would be.

"A bunch of bullshit, mostly," Livengood said. "People always say they want substantive, specific policy proposals from candidates, but they're lying. They don't know what any of that stuff even means, and if they do, they're smart enough to know that those ten-point plans aren't going to get passed, anyway. People will ask specific questions about things that specifically affect them, and we'll write all that stuff down on some index cards, but mostly they just want a general sense of a candidate's philosophy."

And what, Stark wondered, would that philosophy be?

"Mainstream Kansas conservatism, of course," Livengood said. "Lower taxes and improved services, limited government and a vague moral authoritarianism, free market economic policy and lots of eco-devo spending. We'll also stress that our guy isn't a radical right winger, of course. Our basic message will be, 'Our guy isn't nuts.' "

After writing down "our guy isn't nuts," and underlining it, Stark inquired about the issues that couldn't be dodged. How, for instance, would the candidate answer the inevitable questions about abortion?

"As vaguely as possible," Livengood said. "What you do is, you go on a bit about how terrible it is about all those unborn babies not getting born, then you blame it on the damned Supreme Court and vow to uphold the Constitution. You can be for parental consent and waiting periods and all that crap, but you don't bring it up unless you're asked. If you're talking to a pro-choice crowd, you try to let them know, as subtly as possible, that you're essentially on their side."

Thinking he had found a fatal flaw in Livengood's plan, Stark set down his pen and asked about the ferocious attacks that the pro-life activists would certainly make.

"Let 'em," Livengood said. "Let 'em pass out pamphlets in every pew in the state, and march and plant signs and sing hymns all they want, but come the primary there's only going to be so many of them."

Having studied the state's powerful anti-abortion movement for many years, and having crunched countless survey numbers about it along the road to tenure, Stark confidently asserted that, "There are more than enough of them to defeat any candidate that you might find. That's why there aren't any pro-choice candidates running in this primary."

Leaning back in his chair, Livengood smiled wickedly and said, "That's the beauty of it, you poor befuddled associate professor. The pro-lifers are so intimidating to most of the Republicans in this state that they've scared away all the other pro-choicers. Our guy gets the pro-choicers to himself, while the others split up the pro-lifers, and then we try to get a bigger chunk of the people who don't particularly care about abortion one way or the other. If it adds up to a plurality and we sneak into the general election, what are the pro-lifers going to do then? Vote for a Democrat?"

After silently dividing the percentage of pro-life Republican primary voters by the number of rumored pro-life candidates, and comparing that figure to the latest estimate of the percentage of pro-choice Republican primary voters, and adding a generous number of Republican primary voters from the "no opinion" column, Stark conceded that Livengood's scheme was at least theoretically possible.

The latest scuttlebutt held that Rep. Stan Patterson would be running with the support of Pastor Bill Jeffries' formidable Kansans for Kansas Values organization. Real estate developer Hampton Hibbert had already announced his candidacy on a stridently anti-abortion platform, and already had the support of Edna Dimschmidt and the Kansans United for a Sin-Free Kansas. The anti-abortion vote would be further splintered by Alfred "Hoss" Baker, a former Ford County Sheriff who announced his candidacy atop a horse in the middle of Gunsmoke Avenue in Dodge City, and splintered further yet by the expected candidacy of Walter "Whitey" Williams, who had long nourished a reputation as America's most outspokenly anti-abortion Insurance Commissioner. A cabal of businessmen and moderates was rumored to be backing a well-funded campaign for Rep. Jonathan Appel, and while Appel was no longer perceived by his former allies as being sufficiently committed to unborn babies, he remained indisputably anti-abortion.

"Still, you're going to have to run the perfect campaign," Stark said, scanning the numbers he had jotted across his yellow legal pad. "And you will have to find the perfect candidate."

Before leaving the office, Livengood took time to pore through the large stack of small town newspapers that were delivered to him each day. He billed the state for his subscriptions ostensibly to keep him in touch with the smaller communities, but reading such journals as *The Arkansas City Traveler* and *The Larned Tiller and Toiler* provided one of the few quiet pleasures in Livengood's hectic routine. He reveled in their raggedly written accounts of bake sales, State Fair winners and homecoming kings and queens, and he was somehow relaxed by the assorted minutia of the small town life. Sometimes he even found an epiphany, such as the one located on an inside page of *The Piquant Free Press*:

"Piquant's peripatetic local carpenter and favorite mayor, Harley Christianson, recently had quite an adventure while vacationing in Los Angeles with his wife, Christy, and son, Tyrone. While driving their rental car to a long-anticipated day at Disneyland, the family stopped at a gas station and was approached by a large man wielding a knife and demanding money. Mr. Christianson said he would comply, but as he reached for his wallet the man became impatient and grabbed Mrs. Christianson, threatening to kill her. Mr. Christianson then grabbed the robber's arm and twisted it until the knife was dropped, then wrestled the would-be robber to the ground, holding him there until Los Angeles police officers arrived to make an arrest.

" 'I was just darned lucky, I guess,' said the modest mayor, a Vietnam veteran, during an interview after Sunday services at the Piquant Lutheran Church. 'I'd have been glad to just give him the money, but he was acting awful crazy and I didn't know what he was going to do. One of the police officers told me he was messed up on drugs, which is just awful, I think. He was a skinny fellow, I'd say about 14 or so, so I'm glad no one got hurt.'

"The Los Angeles Police Department would not comment to *The Piquant Free Press* about the incident, but Mr. Christianson said he was told the suspect would be charged with assault with a deadly weapon. Mr. Christianson said he and his family enjoyed the trip to Disneyland otherwise, but added that, 'You can have just as much fun at the park we're building right here in Piquant!' "

The accompanying picture, of a white male who appeared to be in his early 50s, reminded Livengood of a face he'd seen in an old western movie. Livengood examined the photograph carefully, re-read the short item, then looked again at the photograph. He reached for a wooden file box on his desk top, flipped through to "O," then to Osborne County. Finding the listing for Kathy Knieble, a high school teacher in Piquant who had worked with Livengood on the Bentley campaign, Livengood dialed the number.

"Howdy, Kathy. It's Frankie Livengood, from the governor's office. Remember me? How the heck are you? Things are pretty good here, too, thanks. I'm calling about your mayor, Harley Christianson. That's right. You see, we're looking for someone to take over for Bentley, and after all the good things we've been hearing about this Christianson fellow, some of us thought he might make a good candidate. What's that? You were saying the same thing just the other day?"

CHAPTER FOUR

"Fanfare For a Common Man"

Harley Christianson was the seventh son of a seventh son, a distinction considered a blessing in most circumstances but a curse for the seventh son of a seventh son of a farmer. By the time the Christianson family's portion of the harsh plains of western Kansas had been divided among the Christianson brothers and various creditors, his inheritance was hardly sufficient to maintain a respectable backyard garden.

Despite his meager birthright, Harley had always considered himself blessed by God, and had lived his life in an effort to repay the debt.

An obedient son, Harley had tackled his farm chores with cheerfulness and energy, even as his brothers teased him that he'd never inherit the land he worked. He was a studious and well-behaved pupil, no matter how far removed his lessons seemed from the simple facts of his life on the prairie. From second grade on he was a faithful and gentlemanly suitor to Christy Kallenburger, despite never getting further than second base with her. He was a small but scrappy guard for Piquant High School's basketball team, an undersized but rugged linebacker and tight end for its eight-man football team, a good fielding but poor hitting third baseman for its baseball squad, and he was never known to be late for practice no matter how badly or how often his teams got whipped.

As Harley Christianson grew to be a young man he was pleased to find himself well regarded by the people of his tiny town, even if he had long since noticed that their opinions seemed to count for little in the vast world beyond Kansas.

American troops were fighting in Vietnam when Harley was graduated from high school, and after a hug from his mother and a handshake from his father he went off to join the team. He never offered any comment on the experience except to say that, "I didn't much care for it," and if not for the Army's press releases to *The Piquant Free Press*, the townspeople probably would have never learned that Harley had been promoted in the field to the rank of Sergeant, won a Bronze Star and been honorably discharged.

Upon his return from the war, Harley pursued a business degree at Fort Hays State University with help from the G.I. Bill and unceasing encouragement from his mother, who worried that Harley would be forced to move to a big city, where college degrees are necessary to distinguish oneself from white trash. Harley surprised his family and friends with his determination to stay in Piquant, explaining that the family's annual vacations, a Future Farmers of America convention and his Army stint had provided him with enough travel to conclude that, "People are just about the same everywhere, so I might as well stay put."

Harley further surprised his family and friends by earning a respectable living as a carpenter. There wasn't much of a market for carpentry in Harley's sparsely populated and self-reliant part of the world, but his skills were such that he invariably won whatever business there was. Extra money would occasionally come from the sale of the furniture Harley loved to design and build, and with careful husbandry of his earnings he was eventually prosperous enough to ask for Christy Kallenburger's hand in marriage. Many years later, after Harley's financial condition had improved sufficiently, the couple gave birth to a son.

CHAPTER FOUR

Such a life in Piquant, Kansas, proved pleasant enough for Harley Christianson. He enjoyed the slow pace and simple style of the town, and was soothed by the rugged beauty of the surrounding Smoky Hills, where the lessons he cherished most from the Piquant Lutheran Church seemed comfortingly valid. He derived satisfaction from the usefulness and excellence of his work. He loved his family, took care of them, and even on the coldest days of the Kansas winter he basked in the warmth of the love they felt for him.

Harley genuinely liked his neighbors, even the garrulous Will Schnitzle with his expletive-laden tirades against the government, and he was well-liked in return. He was honored to serve his community as president of the local Veterans of Foreign Wars chapter, as leader of the county's Rotarians, as an elder in the Piquant Lutheran Church, on a variety of committees and volunteer organizations, and for the past two years as mayor. Harley especially enjoyed being mayor, which allowed him to organize a much needed water conservation project and to personally build the park he had yearned for as a child. But he always downplayed the title with self-effacing jokes about how the other 804 people in town didn't want the job.

Harley Christianson was the rare man who did his duty without expecting the world's praise, so he was stunned to discover one day that he was being touted as a potential candidate for governor of Kansas.

He had laughed it off when Kathy Knieble first suggested it over coffee at the local cafe, but then she had called the very next day to say that a highly placed political operative in Topeka was making inquiries. A short time after that, *The Piquant Free Press* ran a story by Dan Dorsey of the Sunflower News Service naming "one Mayor Harley Christianson of the picturesquely-named town of

Piquant" on a long list of rumored candidates. When Harley ran into the editor at the town's cafe, he learned that several other papers had picked up the story as well, opening a floodgate of press speculation. Although Harley did not figure prominently in any of the other stories the editor had seen, he was mentioned in passing in papers as large and powerful as *The Kansas City Star*, *The Wichita Eagle* and *The Topeka Capital-Journal.* On a particularly slow news day, which in western Kansas means nothing is happening at all, a television crew from a station in Hays dropped by to ask Harley about all the fuss.

"I don't know what to tell you," Harley said, unintentionally looking rather gubernatorial in the suit he'd worn to be on television. "I don't have any plans to run for governor, and never said I did. I suppose I'd be willing to serve as governor if that's what everybody wanted, but I figure there's got to be somebody out there who could do a better job than me. Folks around here tell me I've been doing a pretty good job as mayor and all, but being mayor of a town this size hardly seems like enough experience for somebody to go running a whole state. I really don't know where all this talk is coming from, and to tell you the truth, it all sounds a little crazy to me."

Frankie Livengood's plan was thus far working to an unexpected degree of perfection, right down to the clear skies and calming forecast that accompanied him and Mark Stark as they drove toward Piquant with the top down on Livengood's beloved Camaro. Buoyed by the vast and subtle beauty of the countryside that rolled by, the comfortable feeling of their long friendship, and a couple of puffs on a marijuana cigarette, the pair carried on their usual arguments with a renewed enthusiasm.

CHAPTER FOUR

"So, you actually expect me to believe that this guy is really all that," Stark said.

"And more," Livengood said. "I've checked this guy out myself, and he's even better than I thought. He's a farm boy, with the 4-H and the FFA and the eight-man football and all that farm boy shit on his resume. He even went to Fort Hays State. And get this, he not only went to Vietnam, he was some sort of hero or something. Apparently he doesn't talk about it much, but we'll get him over that. And he's a carpenter by trade. A carpenter!"

"So why should a carpenter be the governor?" Stark asked.

"No reason," Livengood said. "But let someone say that's not a qualification, and we blast back that 'Oh, I suppose you wouldn't vote for Jesus, either.' A carpenter named Christianson—Jesus!"

"I see," Stark said. "And what else does our guy have in common with Our Saviour, besides his occupation?"

Merle Haggard began wailing the "Working Man's Blues" through the radio, and Livengood paused to turn up the volume before responding.

"He's squeaky-clean by all accounts, including Kathy Knieble's. Do you know Kathy? She teaches at the high school out there, helped out with the Bentley campaign, and was on the Osborne County Republican Committee before she got purged in a big putsch by the religious right. Kind of fat, but cute. Anyway, it sounds like she's been in love with this guy since kindergarten, and to hear her tell it, he's likely to be the first Lutheran ever to get canonized. Plus, Kathy said she's never heard him take a stand on abortion, so he's pro-choice by default."

"Mm-hmm," Stark said. "And has our pretty and pulchritudinous high school teacher ever consummated her forbidden love for our respected pillar of the community, in the classic small town tradition?"

"I guess you don't know Kathy," Livengood said. "She's just the type to pine away for a married man her whole life, but not at all the type to do anything about it. She's a lot younger than him, and it sounds like it's some puppy love kind of thing that's been sustained all these years by our guy being so perfect and all. Kathy's quite the authority on this guy, and she swears that he's still goofy for the wife, and she doesn't figure him for a guy who'd fool around even if he wasn't happy at home."

Livengood and Stark had arrived at the Garden of Eden at this point, so they turned into the parking lot and paid the modest fee for a tour. The Garden of Eden was an eccentric cement house and a curious collection of crudely shaped cement sculptures created by a Civil War veteran named S.P. Dinsmoor, who had built the garden while in his 80s after marrying a woman in her 20s, and the work was meant to express his idiosyncratic social, political and religious philosophies. Whenever Stark or Livengood were near Lucas, they made it a point visit the Garden of Eden.

"What makes you so sure that you'll be able to talk this Christianson guy into such an improbable scheme?" Stark said, as the pair relaxed next to the mausoleum where Dinsmoor's remains were on view in a glass coffin. "From what you tell me, he's got himself a nice little life out here in the sticks. Why should he give that up for the hassle of running for governor?"

"It just requires a shift in the usual pitch," Livengood said. "With most people, you can talk them into anything with an appeal to their ego, but I could tell on the phone that it won't work with this guy. This guy's so damned modest, he really believes he isn't qualified to be governor of Kansas. From what I could tell over the phone, the usual appeal to self-interest isn't going to work either. I think this guy really is happy with his life. It's the damnedest thing. I don't know how these people do it."

Stark had no idea, either. He paused to appreciate one of Dinsmoor's statues, this one depicting a worm being eaten by a bird, which was about to be trounced on by a cat, which was stalked by a fox, which was in the path of the arrow of an Indian, who was right in the sights of a cavalry soldier, who was being chased by a woman.

"With this guy, I have to work his sense of duty," Livengood continued. "It's a rarely used weapon in my rhetorical repertoire, but I think I remember how to use it. That's why he agreed to see me when we talked on the phone, because I told him that people around the state think he's really needed in office right away. He wouldn't have believed it, but he'd read it in all the papers."

Stark grudgingly complimented Livengood on an expert job of getting Christianson's name in all the papers.

"Oh, please, that was a cinch," Livengood said. "Dan Dorsey agreed to drop the name into one story because he thought it was a hoot, then I mentioned it to a few reporters around the rail, and after that it was entirely accurate to report that Mayor Harley Christianson of Piquant is being talked about as a potential candidate for governor."

The pair resumed their trip to the Christianson home a few moments later, turning north at the tiny town of Waldo, just a few miles from equally tiny town of Paradise. Stark was amused by the realization that they were seeking the perfect Kansas candidate by making a right turn halfway between Paradise and the Garden of Eden.

After arriving in Piquant, where Livengood was delighted to find a close resemblance to the small towns of Frank Capra movies and Norman Rockwell magazine covers, he found friendly and specific directions to the Christianson family home. Harley Christianson greeted his visitors with a friendly handshake, and apologized profusely for wasting their time.

"I really don't know what you fellows drove all the way out here for," Harley said. "I don't want to be the governor."

Livengood assured him that the drive was quite pleasant, and well worth the effort when the future of the state of Kansas was hanging in the balance. Harley and Stark both looked at him as if he was laying it on a bit thick, but Christy Christianson was still beaming about the compliment as Harley made the introductions.

As they sat down to dinner, Livengood noted with satisfaction that the Christianson home was a typical Kansas farmhouse in every respect except for the higher quality of the furniture. Starting his pitch as Mrs. Christianson passed the black-eyed peas, Livengood explained the roles he had played in two gubernatorial elections, the work he had done in the subsequent administrations, the various other jobs he had held in government, and then expressed a wish to perform the same functions for Mr. Christianson.

"This all makes sense, I guess, except for one thing," Harley said. "Why me? I'm just a simple carpenter, been mayor of a tiny little town, and that's about it."

"You're far too modest, Mr. Christianson," Livengood said, noticing the agreement on the face of Christy Christianson. "To be quite frank, sir, with my experience, credentials and good standing in the state's political community, I'll be working on somebody's campaign this year, and hopefully in his administration. It's just a matter of picking the candidate that I believe in the most, and of all the potential candidates I've seen mentioned in the press, you seem by far the most qualified to lead this state that I love so much."

As Christy and Tyrone Christianson visibly swelled with pride, Harley shook his head and said, "But you don't even know anything about me, Mr. Livengood."

CHAPTER FOUR

"That's not true, Mr. Christianson, we in the governor's office keep a close eye on the emerging leaders of our state, and we're quite familiar with your many good works here in Piquant."

"But I haven't really done that much," Harley said. "There's really not that much to be done in a little town like Piquant."

"Again, sir, you are far too modest," Livengood said. "Don't try to downplay the new park, and its lovely gazebo."

"But that's no big deal at all. Tyrone and I did most of that ourselves, in just a couple of weekends of work."

"That's precisely my point, Mr. Christianson," Livengood said. "You did it yourself. That's the kind of spirit that drew me to your candidacy, sir, and you can bet that when we get a good ad about it on television, a lot of other Kansans are going to be impressed, as well. And that's not to mention your water conservation plan, which we'll be sure to mention often and loudly throughout your campaign. It conveys a very progressive image, Mr. Christianson."

"But the conservation plan was just a matter of talking a few folks into buying some better toilets and watering their lawns every other day. It didn't even cost anything."

"Better yet. Kansans like their progressivism on the cheap," Livengood said. "Your ads will say, 'And it didn't cost Piquant a penny.' "

"Please, Mr. Livengood, stop talking about my ads," Harley said. "And stop talking about my candidacy and my campaign. I'm not running for anything."

Christy Christianson told her husband there was no harm in hearing the man out, then went into the kitchen to make coffee. Tyrone Christianson said, "Yeah, Dad, hear him out," and was told to hush up.

"I'll tell you what, Mr. Livengood, I'll tell Christy that I'm showing you boys around the shop, and we'll talk some more out there," Harley said. "There's no use getting her all revved up about this."

Once in the shop, Harley assumed a more direct tone.

"Now looky here, Mr. Livengood. I'd like to know what all this nonsense is about. You don't even know where I stand on any of the issues."

"Not precisely," Livengood said. "But I can infer from your record as mayor, and as a man, that you stand for honesty, integrity and the best interests of this state."

Harley had to admit that, yes, he did believe in all of those things. But what about the other issues?

"What other issues are there?" Livengood asked.

None came immediately to mind for Harley, who didn't often think deeply about such things. Thinking back over some recent editorials in *The Piquant Free Press,* he at last named water policy for the diminishing aquifer, reforming the juvenile justice system, the aging of the rural population and the resulting rural health care and social service problems, restrictions on corporate hog and cattle funding, and a fair formula for school funding.

"Well, OK then," Livengood said. "Where do you stand on those issues?"

"I don't have the slightest idea where I stand on those issues, Mr. Livengood," Harley said, politely, despite his exasperation. "That's my point. I don't know how to solve those problems. All I can say is that you ought to get a truckload of people who do know what they're talking about, and let them figure it out."

"But that's exactly what governors do, Mr. Christianson, and I can assure you that as your chief of staff I would able to assemble truckloads of the very brightest people in these fields, and know which ones to believe. I can assure you that none of the other candidates really know anything about these issues, either. I hate to say it, Mr. Christianson, but I'm afraid the only difference between you and them is that they're likely to wind up making their decisions based on who contributes to their campaign fund, or what benefits their own financial interests, or what pleases the activists who have backed their campaigns. I've checked you out pretty thoroughly, sir, and I don't believe you'd do that."

Harley conceded that no, he probably wouldn't do that.

When Harley excused himself to answer a phone that was ringing in the shop's office, Livengood and Stark shared their impressions.

"I have to admit," Stark said, "he seems like the real deal."

The two looked around at the furniture stored in the shop, and Livengood commented that, "I don't know much about furniture, but this stuff looks pretty damned good."

"This is outstanding work," said Stark, who knew a great deal about furniture. "Absolutely outstanding. I must say that our guy has more refined taste than I expected, too. It's a damned shame if you waste this guy on politics."

"Did you notice the amazing lack of angst?" Livengood asked. "The way he's so eerily at peace with himself and the whole damned world? I swear, this guy wouldn't get a modern novel at all. I don't know how these country folks do it, but I envy the hell out of it."

Stark hadn't been paying attention to Livengood's observation. Examining a tag hanging from an oak Morris chair, he was surprised to find a price several thousand dollars less than he had recently paid for an inferior chair at an exclusive New York City shop.

Harley returned to his guests a moment later, and resumed his arguments against being governor.

"What about abortion? Don't you want to know where I stand on the abortion issue before you put me in office, Mr. Livengood? And school prayer, and gay rights and such?"

Livengood shrugged and said, "Well, OK then, where do you stand on those issues?"

"I don't know that, either," Harley said. "I mean, abortion seems an awful thing, but I figure there's got to be a lot of situations where I'd hate to sit in judgment of some poor girl who thinks that's what she ought to do. I just do not know, Mr. Livengood. I'm a Christian man, Mr. Livengood, and I believe the Good Book when it says that 'Righteousness exalteth a nation,' but I'm not going to stand up on some podium and claim that I know what laws to sign that will make us righteous. And with all due respect, Mr. Livengood, I don't believe you're going to assemble any team of experts that's going to tell me."

Livengood asked Stark for a moment alone with Harley. Before leaving, Stark confirmed the $400 price on the Morris chair, then wrote a check for the Morris chair, and made arrangements for it to be shipped to his home in Manhattan, Kansas. Harley was clearly pleased to make the sale.

"Here's the flat-out truth, Mr. Christianson," Livengood said, after Stark had left. "I don't really know any of those answers, either. I'm just a working stiff who needs a job, and the only job I know how to do is getting candidates elected, and getting their ideas through a legislature. You should know, though, that I'm pretty damned good at it. I worked my first campaign when I was 12 years old, putting up signs and slipping pamphlets in screen doors for a nice old man in the neighborhood who was running for a state rep seat. I was a page at the statehouse at age 13, and I managed a run for a Wichita School Board post by the age of 18. I've got a political science degree from Kansas State University, and I've interned for congressmen and senators. I've worked the executive and legislative branches at the state and local level. I can raise the money, create the ads, book the air time, write speeches that won't piss anybody off, do the direct mailings, schedule your appearances at just the right places, handle the media, and attend to the billion other little details. I know this state inside and out. My file is filled with the names of every Kansas Republican who plays the tiniest role in politics, and I know every trick there is. If you decide to make this run, you won't find anyone better to run the show."

"But what if you're right about all this, and I actually wind up getting myself elected," Harley said. "What then?"

"I'm also the right guy to run that show," Livengood said.

"So why don't you just run for governor yourself?"

"Because I'm not a good enough man. I don't want to lie to you, Mr. Christianson. My ex-wife wouldn't like it. I picked you because you've got all the qualifications to win this race, whether you realize it or not. That's why I got my friend Dan Dorsey to mention you as a potential candidate in one of his stories, and it's why I created all this talk about you running. But now that I've met you face to face, I really think you've also got the qualifications to actually be the governor. Politics takes brains, and I've got that, but leadership takes character. With my brains and your character, we could do good things for this state."

After mulling that over for a moment, Harley said, "Well, Mr. Livengood, I'm still not interested in running for governor, but if I get talked into it I'll be sure and give you a call. I don't know anybody else who could help me."

"There is just one other thing," Livengood said. "You are an honest man, I will be honest with you. I'm a sinner, Mr. Christianson. I drink, I smoke, I'll take a toke or two from time to time, and I'm divorced. The ex and I get along fine, but she isn't coming back, and since she's been gone I've been known to keep some company with an occasional wild woman. Nothing to brag about, mind you, but I'd sure be embarrassed to tell everything to a fine Christian woman such as your wife. And I might as well admit that all those years in politics have entailed a compromise or two that I am not proud of, and it's earned me an enemy or two along the way. What's more, my friends tell me that I'm not always a very sensitive guy."

Harley rubbed his chin a moment, and then said, "I've never been much of drinker myself, and I've never messed with that marijuana any, and me and the wife have been pretty steady since forever, but what you do is your own business. I had a fellow working here in the shop who did all that stuff, and he was a good man for me, until he up and left."

"I'm glad to hear that, Mr. Christianson, but there's something else I've got to say. I swear by the God I still believe in that I'll always be straight with you. I'm counting on you following my advice in most cases, or I wouldn't be doing this, but if we win this thing, you're the one who will be governor. It's always going to come down to your decision, and you won't have to doubt that the information and advice that you're basing it on is the real deal. If you don't want to be governor, I can respect the hell out of that, and I'll just come up with some other way to make a living, but I've got to tell you one last thing. The very reasons you don't want to be governor are the very reasons I want you to be. I've worked for a lot of power hungry fools in my time, and if another of them has a job for me, I'll take it. But I'd rather work for you."

Harley leaned back against a counter and folded his arms, mulling Livengood's words. "I sure appreciate you coming all the way out here, Mr. Livengood, and I'm sure sorry it was all for nothing. I just don't want to be governor."

Frankie Livengood and Mark Stark settled into a corner booth at the

Piquant cafe, the former ordering a chicken fried steak and the latter a chef's salad.

"I think we've got him," Livengood said. "Once I pointed out the unlikelihood of another decent person running for governor, he started thinking about it. I could see it in his eyes. And once that wife of his gets to working on him, he'll be in for sure. She's already deciding to what to wear to the inauguration ball."

Stark agreed that Mrs. Christianson had seemed very enthusiastic about the idea.

"Kathy Knieble will keep nagging him, too, and probably a few of the locals who'd like to see a fellow Piquantian as governor," Livengood said. "After they talk him into it, he's already agreed to let me run the show."

Stark asked what Livengood had said in his absence to persuade Harley of that.

"I told him the truth," Livengood said. "I told him I was a sinner. That I was a pot-smoking, alcoholic, governmental fornicator."

"You didn't," Stark said, trying to gauge his friend's seriousness.

"I did," Livengood said. "I got to thinking about what I told Jane, and decided that all that honesty crap just might work on a guy like Harley Christianson."

Looking up, Stark noticed a thin but dangerous-looking man at the counter. The man was staring at them, in a way that made Stark flinch.

"Hey you," the man said toward them. "Are you the fellows from the government?"

That could be a tricky question in a small Kansas town, and Livengood sized this man up as someone who wouldn't like the answer. Livengood looked at Stark, whose frightened expression suggested that he didn't know what to say, either.

"I heard some fellows from the government were out here to talk to Harley Christianson about running for governor," the man said. "Are you those fellows? 'Cause if you are, that'd be the first smart thing the government's done in a long while."

Livengood still suspected it was foolhardy to reveal his affiliation with the government, but he was too curious to find out why the man thought it was a good idea for Harley Christianson to run for governor.

"Yeah, we're the guys," Livengood said. "Actually, I'm with the government—Frankie Livengood, from the governor's office—and this is Mark Stark, a friend of mine who teaches over at Kansas State."

"Huh!" the man said with disgust. "I'm Will Schnitzle, and I work for a goddamned living."

"So why would it be a good idea for Harley Christianson to run for governor?" Livengood asked, ignoring the implied insult.

Schnitzle looked as if an annoying child had just asked why the sky is blue, then said, "Because he's a good man, that's why. We haven't had one of those in the governor's office for a hell of a long time."

"That's true enough," Livengood said. "Do you like where he stands on the issues?"

"Screw the issues. He's an honest man, a good Kansan. What the hell other issues are there?"

"That's true enough, too," Livengood said. "Is Harley a friend of yours?"

"Hell yes he is," Schnitzle said. "We grew up together around here, played ball together, even went off to 'Nam in the same unit. You don't get much closer than that."

"I suppose not," Livengood said. "I understand Harley won a Bronze Star over there."

"Hell yes he did," Schnitzle said. "I was there when he won it, too, and I don't mind telling you he saved my ass."

"No shit?" Livengood said. "What happened?"

Schnitzle eyed the two strangers suspiciously, as if assessing whether or not they were worthy of a good Vietnam story, then said, "What the hell," and launched into the tale.

"Me and Harley and six other poor bastards was crossing this creek on a recon mission, you see, and we was up to our hips in this muddy water when we start taking fire from all over the goddamned place. I got me this big ol' radio strapped to my back, you see, so when I hit some deep water heading for the other bank, I start sinking like a damn ol' rock. Harley, he's up at the front yelling for everyone to get the hell out of there, but half our guys are just off the plane and don't know what the hell to do but shit their britches. I'm still over there drowning with that damned radio on my back, and suddenly Harley comes swimming down and yanking that radio off my back, then hauls my ass—which has been shot up by two gook rounds, mind you—right up behind this tree. Well, that ain't all. Then Harley goes running back right into all them bullets, dragging every sorry bastard in that platoon back behind that tree. He saved 'em all, too, except for one big old nigger boy by the name of Tyrone T. O'Riley, who was already shot to shit and then got his head blown plumb to bits just as Harley was dragging him in."

Livengood looked excitedly at Stark, already dreaming up the commercials about this incident.

"And do you know what Harley did then?" Schnitzle asked. Livengood and Stark did not know, so Schnitzle told them. "Then he goes running back into them bullets *again.* All the men are hunkered down behind that big tree, but Harley goes running into those bullets so he can haul that goddamned radio out of the creek. Damn thing's likely to get him drowned, even if one of those million bullets doesn't blast his balls off, and I'm bleeding behind that damn tree and hollering at the damned fool to get his ass back there. Jesus Christ, you don't risk your life like that for anything inanimate. You know what I'm saying?"

Livengood knew exactly what he was saying, and agreed completely.

"The son of a bitch may be stupid, but you've gotta give him credit for guts," Schnitzle said. "And that, I tell you, is what we need in a governor."

After paying the tab and leaving a generous tip, Livengood paused to thank Will Schnitzle for the story.

"We're trying to talk ol' Harley into running, you know," Livengood said. "You might want to give him a little encouragement as well."

"I'll do just that," Schnitzle said. "I'll get some of the boys down at the VFW to do the same."

"That would be mighty fine. Mighty fine," Livengood said. "And by the way, if Harley does run, and any of those reporters come around here asking about him, don't hesitate to tell them that same story you told us. If you really want to help, though, you might want to say 'African-American' instead of 'nigger.' And for God's sake, leave out that last part about the radio."

Christy Christianson had been an honor roll student, cheerleading captain, blue ribbon winner at the State Fair with her German chocolate cake, and a member of the board of the unified school district, but she and everyone else in Osborne County regarded her marriage to Harley Christianson as the greatest accomplishment in her life. She loved Harley with all her heart and soul, and didn't mind a bit that her husband was also a handsome war hero and a pillar of the community.

Being the wife of the mayor also seemed a good thing to Christy Christianson, who struggled against pride as a good Lutheran should, but who would occasionally allow herself a subtle boast at the Piquant beauty parlor. When Harley's name began to appear in all those newspapers as a potential candidate for governor, well, what woman could have resisted a comment about it to the banker's wife in the next chair?

Having someone from the governor's office drive all the way out to Piquant to talk to Harley had been so exciting to Christy she decided she needed a new hairstyle for the occasion. If Harley were to actually run, Christy decided, she would go to Wichita and have her snooty younger sister help her shop for a whole new wardrobe. And if Harley were to actually win, and she were to be the First Lady of Kansas, she would get yet another new wardrobe in Kansas City with her even snootier older sister.

"You know what, Harley?" she said, snuggling up against her husband in bed. "Maybe that Livengood fellow has the right idea. Maybe you should consider running."

"Now, you just stop," Harley said. "I don't want to be governor."

"I know you don't," Christy said, turning away and sulking persuasively. "But maybe you should stop thinking about what you want for a change. Maybe you should start think about what's best for Kansas."

CHAPTER FIVE

"Nuts and Bolts"

Harley Christianson called Frankie Livengood two days after their meeting and said that, yeah, what the heck, he'd run for governor. Frankie Livengood immediately began putting a campaign together.

The first step was to resign from Governor Bentley's administration, which Livengood did with relish.

The next step was to go get some big money.

The Livengood money trail always began at a large tract of land outside Liberal, on the spacious ranch-style home of fast food franchising mogul and longtime Kansas Republican moneyman Big Jim Morland. Livengood embarked on the journey without the company of Mark Stark, figuring that some things in life should not be seen by even the most scientifically objective observers, and that political campaign fund-raising is one of them.

Big Jim greeted Livengood with a painfully firm handshake and a solid slap on the back, then proceeded to unleash his famous brand of hospitality. A mammoth serving of barbecue, several ears of fresh-roasted and heavily buttered corn, and beer so cold that ice floated on the top were served poolside, followed by fat, pungent cigars as the two men settled into patio chairs to talk some business.

"So," Livengood said. "Who are you backing this time around in the governor's race?"

"Well now, I haven't quite decided on that yet," Big Jim said. "I thought maybe you'd have some ideas. You don't seem to come around here much without some ideas."

Big Jim, a man of about five feet, five inches and 140 pounds who had decided early in his career that the nickname Little Jim wouldn't sell a lot of hamburgers, truly liked Livengood. Shrewdness, audacity and a low regard for the intelligence of the general public were the qualities that had transformed Big Jim from the picked-on son of a Kansas dirt farmer into a multi-millionaire businessman, and he recognized Livengood as a kindred spirit. Livengood truly liked Big Jim in return, and was counting on their friendship.

"As you probably know by now, Big Jim, I'm going to be running the campaign for this Christianson fellow," Livengood said. "In fact, I might as well tell you that I'm laying the last of my political capital on this bet. Your help on this would really mean a lot to me."

"Christianson, eh? I think I've read his name in the papers a few times," Big Jim said. "He's the one who's mayor of Piss Ant, Kansas, or something, isn't he?"

Big Jim started buying into Kansas political campaigns back when he only had a few hundred thousand dollars to his name, in the days before contribution limits and other annoying campaign regulations, and by now his generosity to Republican causes had earned him gratitude and small favors from powerful officials right up to the President of the United States, but Livengood knew that his motives for dabbling in politics were far more complex than mere graft. Livengood had worked on numerous campaigns backed by Big Jim, and he was satisfied that his friend acted, at least in part, from a sincere sense of civic duty. History would ultimately judge whether Big Jim was right or wrong, but anyone who knew him personally did not doubt the honesty of his conviction that his own success was owed largely to the American free enterprise system, and that he felt obliged to repay the debt by supporting conservative candidates.

Livengood also sensed that Big Jim was a political donor because proximity to powerful people helped soothe the insecurities of an impoverished and condemned childhood. No matter how spacious Big Jim's ranch-style house, nor how long his Cadillac, nor how ostentatious his backyard barbecues, Big Jim could never shake a self-image of the skinny little runt in overalls who had mortgaged the family dirt farm to open the first Big Jim's Burger Barn. For all his bluster about pulling oneself up by the bootstraps, Big Jim retained an instinctive empathy for any underdog, and Livengood was counting on it.

"It's actually Piquant, Kansas, Big Jim," Livengood said. "But it might as well be Piss Ant. I never saw such a no-account little tank town in my life."

Convincing the average big-time political donor to make a campaign contribution is a simple matter of convincing him that the candidate is a likely winner, as Livengood well knew, but he also knew that Big Jim was not the average big-time political donor. Livengood instead spoke of the insurmountable odds facing Christianson, citing the candidate's lack of an established following, his negligible name recognition, his lack of financial backing, and all the other problems the campaign faced. By the time Livengood had concluded a compelling argument that Christianson was the darkest horse ever to enter a Kansas gubernatorial race, Big Jim was nearly hooked.

Livengood then told Big Jim about Harley Christianson, from his days getting his ass kicked at eight-man football to the park he had built with his loving son. By the time Livengood got through describing how a bullet blasted the head off a poor African-American soldier who was being rushed to safety in Christianson's arms, Big Jim was reaching for his checkbook.

"Now you're sure this guy ain't some kind of lefty?" Big Jim said. "I honor our veterans and all, but some of the Vietnam guys are kind of lefty."

"You know me, Big Jim," Livengood said. "He's a businessman, just like you."

"But he ain't one of those nut cases, is he?" Big Jim said. "I respect a good conservative businessman, but you've got to admit that some of them are nuts."

"Hell no," Livengood said. "That's going to be our slogan. 'Our guy's not a nut.' "

"And by the way, is he pro-life or pro-choice?" Big Jim asked. Livengood knew from past conversations that Big Jim didn't care if abortion was legal or not, as he was bound and determined that his only daughter would never need one, but he also knew that Big Jim would consider the political implications.

"He's reluctantly pro-choice. The only one in the primary," Livengood said, explaining his strategy of letting the rest of the field split the pro-life voice.

"And then what are they supposed to do in the general election? Vote for a Democrat?" Big Jim said, laughing delightedly. "Hot damn, Frankie, this just might work. And it'll be fun sticking it to those holier-than-thou types like Edna Dimschmidt. Shee-it, we'll even stick it to Wentworth and them richer-than-thou sumbitches, who ain't richer than me, by the way."

Big Jim wrote out a check for the maximum amount allowed by law, and Livengood placed it in his wallet. Big Jim understood that their business was not yet settled, however, as no political hack would ever drive all the way from Topeka to Liberal for a campaign contribution of the meager amount allowed by law.

Although in theory he had already donated the maximum legal amount, in practice Big Jim had numerous means of funneling more money toward the campaign. As a rich person, Big Jim had numerous rich friends who could easily be convinced to contribute. Every franchisee and manager in the entire statewide Big Jim's Burger Barn operation could be convinced even more easily to donate their special bonuses, which would be in the exact amount that could be legally donated to a Kansas gubernatorial campaign. He could also contribute as much as he liked to any political action committee of his choosing, and there was nothing to stop him from choosing one that would subsequently donate a similar amount to the Christianson campaign. If a front-running candidate staked out a unique position, Big Jim could also spend as much money as he cared to on "educational advertisements" that attacked anyone holding that position. Then, when the primary ended and the general election started, Big Jim could do it all again.

The only thing in life that Big Jim Morland liked better than finding tax loopholes was finding ways around the campaign donation limits, and he would often boast that no legislature had ever devised a campaign finance system that he could not beat. He had to admit, though, that they didn't seem to be trying very hard.

Livengood and Big Jim sketched out a plan that would quickly produce about $200,000 for the Christianson campaign, a small portion of what would be needed for the race but enough to launch a credible campaign, which in turn would generate even more contributions. The two men then shook hands, and Livengood let the handshake linger for the extra second that Kansas men use to express their most heartfelt gratitude to a friend.

"There's one thing I expect in return for this," Big Jim said.

Big Jim had never asked for anything specific in return for his political contributions, not even for a friendly degree of access to the office-holder, which of course went without saying, so Livengood was visibly surprised by the request.

"Oh, hell, don't worry. It's nothing that's going to land us on the front page of *The Wichita Eagle*," Big Jim said. "I just want you to give my girl Darla some kind of job on the campaign. Strictly volunteer stuff, mind you. Her allowance will be her salary, and believe you me, it's way more than you could afford to pay her."

Livengood vaguely remembered Big Jim's daughter as a bratty thing with science fiction braces who had once disrupted a Bentley rally with her shrill shriek, and he asked Big Jim why he would want a 12-year-old working on a political campaign.

"She hasn't been 12 for four years, Frankie. You just haven't been out to the house since you came by to hit me up for Bentley's money," Big Jim said. "She's smart, and she'll work hard. And I'll tell you what, my girl Darla can tear up those roads for you the way that only a Kansas kid with a brand new driver's license can."

"But what for?" Livengood said. "You can get her a better summer job than that."

"Well, she's all hepped up on this political stuff. She's on the debate team at the high school, she's a member of the Young Americans for Freedom, and she never misses Rush Limbaugh when she's not in school," Big Jim said. "With her summer vacation coming up, I want her to get an up-close look at how a real campaign works. All that nuts and bolts stuff."

"Well hell, Big Jim, why don't you call her in here right now and give her a look at our little plan?"

"I don't know that she needs to see them kind of nuts and bolts just yet," Big Jim said, with a laugh worthy of his nickname.

"I'm trying to keep my girl a virgin in more ways than one, you know."

Frankie Livengood usually hated meetings more than work itself, but the first gathering of his full campaign staff felt almost like a party. The meeting took place in his small apartment, everyone was an old friend, except Darla Morland, and everyone had a can of beer in hand, except for Darla Morland, and the smoky air and argumentative conversations made it virtually indistinguishable from one of Livengood's parties.

Ellen Winston, still a swell looking babe at age 51 (or, as rumor had it, age 55), and an irresistibly flirtatious force in Kansas society circles, had agreed to help with fund-raising.

Greg Page, a shaggy young man in a black leather jacket, was providing his computer skills to the campaign, creating data bases that would magically send direct mailings to all the little old ladies and assorted suckers with proven track records of voting and making small contributions to Republican political campaigns. He had agreed to the low-paying job despite his anti-capitalist principles because he liked Livengood.

Merle Lee, a gaunt man with a gray ponytail, would be doing the television commercials. Lee had launched his filmmaking career in the late sixties with a string of low-budget art films, most of them featuring a recurring image of eggs being splattered on male genitals, but since the early seventies he had made a more comfortable living doing low-budget commercials, including the popular "Toilet Man" series for a Wichita plumbing company. Livengood desired the glaringly apparent cheapness of Lee's work in his ads, believing that voters would appreciate the candidate's apparent thriftiness.

Ed Walton, a twenty-something campaign professional who was better dressed than even Ellen Winston, had been hired as the office manager. He could get the headquarters rented, the phones turned on, the computers running, the signs and pamphlets printed, the bills paid, and all the necessary fund-raising and spending reports filed. Ed Walton was the highest-paid member of the staff, Livengood notwithstanding.

Wilbur Philip, who was wearing a short-sleeved shirt and a tie that abruptly stopped a few inches above his belt line, had signed on as a policy analyst without asking about salary.

Darla Morland, a buxom blonde who possessed that wholesome sexiness unique to pampered small town Kansas girls, had so far been charged with running to the nearby convenience store for supplies. Being too young to purchase beer or cigarettes, she had proved virtually worthless at the job.

Jane Hutchinson was not there, citing the state's rules against its employees being involved in political campaigns, but she had sent much of her research and other information on environmental issues. Livengood had no intention of using any of it, but he was nonetheless pleased by her thoughtfulness.

Despite the disorganized appearance of the meeting, Livengood managed to address nearly every item of the agenda that he had written down on the top of a pizza box. By the time Merle Lee, Greg Page and Ellen Winston staggered out of the apartment at three in the morning, Livengood had developed a detailed campaign strategy and was ready to prep his candidate on their platform.

The Christianson for Governor Campaign Headquarters in downtown Topeka didn't seem like much to Frankie Livengood, just an abandoned shoe store with a pair of computers on a folding table, a state surplus desk where Darla Morland gabbed on a telephone, and a six-foot stack of yellow and blue yard signs bearing the slogan "Christianson for Governor." To Christy Christianson, who saw it for the first time when she arrived with her husband for his first campaign briefing, it seemed the most exciting place in all of Kansas.

"Look dear," she said. "All these signs have our name on them."

The space was impressive enough to thoroughly embarrass Harley Christianson, who sent his wife on a shopping spree and settled onto a metal folding chair to endure a long political discussion with Livengood. Wilbur Philip and Mark Stark arrived a few minutes later, precisely at the scheduled time.

Philip did most of the talking at first, outlining his confoundingly specific recommendations about issues ranging from rural health care to urban enterprise zones, and quoting a bewildering array of facts, figures and gibberish from the immense stack of papers he had pulled from a salesman's sample case. Livengood then translated some of the more obscure bureaucratese for Harley, who mulled the five hours of lessons for about two minutes, then remarked that, "It all sounds pretty good to me."

Philip's attempt at explaining the state's labyrinthine school funding formula finally exhausted the last of Harley's extraordinary patience.

"My head is starting to hurt," Harley said. "I think I'm getting the gist of what you boys are saying, but there's no way on God's green Earth that I'm going to remember all this little stuff. This is way worse than finals week at Fort Hays ever was."

Livengood assured Harley that he wouldn't need to remember all the little stuff.

"Most people aren't even going to want to know the gist of it," Livengood said. "If they do ask for more, we'll have it on index cards. We'll be there."

Harley was somewhat calmed by Livengood's assurances, but still nervous about being expected to know the answers to all of the state's problems.

"What about abortion? What am I going to say about that?" Harley said. "What about God and morality and such?"

At this point Philip packed his sample case, told Harley what a pleasure it was to have met him, and went on his way. Philip's bailiwick was all that could be known, and he was content to leave the rest to Frankie Livengood.

"The less said about that stuff, the better, because most people don't want to hear about it," Livengood said. "If anyone won't let you wiggle out of it, tell them what you told me back at your shop. You think it's a horrible thing, but you don't want to sit in judgment. You tell them how we support parental consent and a couple of other things, then say that you'll uphold the Constitution. If they keep pressing, just say that you don't expect to change anybody's mind on this issue, and move on. Believe me, truer words will never be spoken on any campaign trail."

Harley admitted that he had been under the impression that abortion was a big issue in politics.

"Believe me, it is," Livengood said. "Most people don't give a damn, but the ones who do—on both sides of the issue—can sink a campaign. They vote, they hector their friends into voting, they give money, plant yard signs, work phone banks, lick envelopes and generally do whatever they can to inflict hell on the other side."

"But you say it doesn't come up much on campaign trail?" Harley said.

"No, because both sides have figured out that the rest of the world is sick of hearing them, so they've figured out how to wage their little war outside the public's view," Livengood said. "Between the organizations they've joined, the petitions they've signed and the checks they've written, we pretty much know the name and address and phone number of everyone in Kansas who will vote for a candidate solely because of his pro-choice or pro-life stand. Before the primary, we'll make sure that every single one of the pro-choicers gets a nice letter and a follow-up phone call informing them of your brave stand on this issue. We'll probably have half of them addressing envelopes and making phone calls to the other half."

Harley expressed his relief that he wouldn't be talking often about abortion.

"I've got to warn you, though," Livengood said. "The other side has the names and addresses and phone numbers of all their people, too, and they're a hell-bent-for-leather bunch. And the pro-choicers around here aren't quite so revved up as these pro-lifers can get. As the only pro-choicer in this field, my friend, they are going to try and crucify you."

Harley couldn't imagine what they would do.

"Just wait'll you get a load of what they're going to mail out about you. They're going to call you everything but 'white boy.' They'll carpet every church in Kansas with pamphlets saying that you're a butcher, a Nazi, a Satanist, a liberal. Strangers are going to approach you on the street and call you a baby-killer."

Harley didn't like the sound of that.

"Aw, you get used to it," Livengood said. "If you want to run for governor, there's really no way around it. If you'd come out pro-life, our friends would be calling you racist, sexist, anti-gay, an oppressor, a Nazi, a Reaganite, stuff like that."

Harley said that he liked to think he wasn't racist or sexist, but wondered if he was supposed to be anti-gay.

"Let me put it this way," Livengood said. "You're not anti-gay, but that doesn't mean you support the gay agenda."

"What's the gay agenda?" Harley asked.

"No one knows for sure," Livengood said. "But apparently it has something to do with the National Endowment for the Arts and molesting kids."

"Well, I'm sure not supporting that," Harley said.

Mark Stark, who had remained silent since greeting Harley, couldn't suppress a laugh.

"But remember," Livengood said, shooting a cautionary glare at Stark, "that doesn't necessarily mean that you're anti-gay. As long as they're not molesting kids, and there's no government money involved, we're tolerant of homosexuals. Especially the rich ones who are registered to vote in the Republican primary."

That seemed fair enough to Harley.

"I'm curious about something," Stark said, looking up from his note-taking. "Do you have any gay friends?"

Harley considered the question a moment. He recalled a high school classmate who hadn't participated in any sports, and he remembered hearing a rumor that the boy had moved to Wichita, but said no, he couldn't be entirely sure if he'd ever even known a homosexual.

Stark smiled and said, "Yes you do. You know me."

"For real?" Harley said.

Yes, Stark said. He was a homosexual, for real.

"No fooling?" Harley said.

No, Stark said, he wouldn't fool about something like that.

"Well what do you know," Harley said. "I guess I've got me a gay friend after all."

Stark smiled back and said, "Yes, you do."

"Wait'll Kathy Knieble hears about this," Harley said. "She'll be so impressed. This is so Big City."

At that very moment, Livengood was seized by a vision of the Harley Christianson for Governor campaign's big picture message.

"There you go," Livengood said. "That's what we're running on in this race. You, Harley Christianson, and your sweet-hearted simple soul, are what we're running on."

That was all the embarrassment Harley could take in one day, and he told Livengood to stop.

"No, please," Livengood said. "If all my years in politics have taught me anything, it's that most people aren't going to take time out of a busy day and drag their weary butts into a voting booth so they can pull a lever for a ten-point plan on solid waste disposal. What gets butts into ballot boxes is a chance to vote for someone, not something. And they're going to love voting for you. When you're out there on the campaign trail, you don't have to tell them all this statistical jazz that Wilbur writes up. You just have to tell them who you are, the simple carpenter from a humble town who befriends everyone he meets, even the sinners. Add in the Vietnam stuff, stay on a fiscally conservative message, and Kansans will worship your ass."

At that, Harley put his literal foot down.

"I don't want anybody worshipping my ass, and I don't like to talk about 'Nam," he said, shaking his head in a way that seemed to settle the matter. "I didn't much care for it."

Livengood offered no further argument, and the conversation quickly returned to its previous friendly tone. After some talk of the weather, Harley thanked Livengood and Stark for their time and went to meet his wife at the Holiday Inn.

After Harley was well on his way, Livengood and Stark looked at one another and grinned.

"Remind me to call Merle Lee before we close up," Livengood said, pulling two beers out of the office refrigerator. "He needs to get his ass out to Piquant first thing tomorrow morning and get that crazy Schnitzle guy on film, with an American flag or a sunset over a wheat field or something like that in the background. And he's got to make sure that redneck doesn't say *nigger.*"

Harley Christianson officially launched his campaign on a windy day in Piquant. The flapping of a large cloth backdrop and the American, Kansas and POW-MIA flags made it impossible to hear what Harley had to say at the podium, but the assembled press corps had photocopies of the speech, and the few radio and television teams were getting a direct feed from the microphone. The assembled townspeople clapped enthusiastically despite the difficulty of hearing, and seemed not to care what Harley was saying.

Nor should they have cared. The speech was one of Frankie Livengood's masterpieces of meaninglessness.

Livengood was pleased with the turnout, which looked much larger than its actual numbers when crowded around the old-fashioned gazebo that Harley and his son had built. The press contingent was also larger than expected, and an even prouder accomplishment for Livengood.

It had been easy enough to lure Dan Dorsey, who still considered the Christianson campaign quite a hoot, as well as the always news-hungry reporters of the relatively nearby Russell and Hays radio stations and newspapers, but persuading the political correspondents of the Associated Press and the state's biggest papers to make such a long drive for a dark-horse announcement had taken all the flattery, arm-twisting and favor-trading that Livengood could muster. Ed Walton had arranged for all the phone jacks the reporters would need, plus all the Big Jim's Burger Barn burgers they could eat, in hopes that the coverage wouldn't reflect the reporters' crankiness.

A press riot nearly broke out when Livengood announced there would be no news conference, but the reporters were quickly placated by the opportunity for short individual interviews. Livengood kept a sharp eye on these discussions, and was pleased to see Harley handling himself well enough that Livengood only stepped in to answer a few questions.

The greatest accomplishment of the afternoon was the presence of a television crew from Wichita. Although Kansas' television news broadcasts rarely contained political news, Livengood had called in a long due debt from a former newspaperman who was now an assigning editor at the station. Livengood couldn't be promised more than twenty seconds on the story, which would no doubt be buried deep in the newscast, but he knew that for those few crucial seconds the viewers of the biggest television market in the state would see Harley Christianson's thick head of distinguished silver hair gently flapping in the Kansas breeze while his loving townspeople cheered on his noble quest for public service.

The newspaper coverage would undoubtedly enhance the credibility of Christianson's campaign, but Livengood knew that nothing was truly credible until it was seen on television. Livengood knew, too, that credibility was the key to raising more big money.

THE THINGS THAT ARE CAESAR'S

CHAPTER SIX

"What Did You Do in the Culture War, Daddy?"

Big Jim Morland had been right about one thing: His girl Darla could tear up the roads in a way that only a Kansas kid with a brand new driver's license can.

Frankie Livengood happily reflected on this fact as he leaned back in the front passenger seat of the large white van he had leased for the campaign (because some money was starting to roll in, and he didn't want to expose his beloved Camaro to the risks of hail season), and Darla did the driving on yet another trip down the turnpike. The extra nap time that Darla's indefatigable driving abilities could provide for Livengood over thousands of miles of campaign trail was almost worth the price of her endless chatter, and he also had to concede that she was working out well in other ways.

Darla was a hard worker, as Big Jim had promised, accepting even the most menial tasks with respectful enthusiasm, making her an ideal Girl Friday to a lazy man such as Livengood. She was already better than Livengood at dealing directly with the public, especially old people, who liked her bucolic brand of friendliness, and she had even managed to charm some of the boys from the press, who liked the way her ample butt filled up a pair of blue jeans. Livengood was almost willing to admit that she was smart, as Big Jim had also promised, and she possessed a good memory for names, faces and the other things that Livengood tended to forget.

Livengood almost even liked her. Although Livengood remained occasionally tense in her presence, probably a result of his resolve not to swear or smoke too often in front of her, sometimes he actually found her perpetual conversation pleasantly soporific. She'd talk of her family, her school, her cheerleading and other extracurricular activities, giving over-detailed accounts of what some girl said to some other girl about some boy. Or she'd talk about her family, her plans for the future, or something she'd seen on television the night before. Mostly, though, she'd talk about her boyfriend, saying much, much more than Livengood would have thought could be said about anyone who was only 17 years old. Livengood had met the boyfriend once at campaign headquarters, and decided he seemed a nice enough young man, sufficiently dickless for Big Jim's approval, and it amused Livengood to hear the poor lad described in such heroic terms. Darla glowed with an innocence Livengood could barely recall from his own Kansas boyhood, and it somehow helped him nap even with the summer sun blasting through the windshield.

Darla was certainly hepped up about politics, too, just as Big Jim had promised. It was a feeling Livengood could somewhat more readily recall, but Darla's brand of politics was strikingly different from the contrarian libertarianism that he and the other cool conservative kids had espoused back when he was an annoyingly opinionated teenager. Darla preferred an unabashedly anti-intellectual authoritarianism.

Livengood knew that Big Jim was a Baptist only to the extent that he endured a service once a week and dropped a tax-deductible check into the collection plate, but his daughter seemed to wholeheartedly embrace her most stringent Sunday school lessons as both a theological and political system. Darla Morland believed that those big city kids sold crack cocaine at their schools only because they were prevented from praying there. It was her considered opinion that the government never had any business taking custody of a child away from its parents, except in a few cases she had read about in the newspapers, and that the home schooling trend was a necessary antidote to the theory of evolution. She was sure that Satanists lurked in every day-care center and legislative committee, that certain books shouldn't be published, and that anyone who disagreed did so out of a deep-seated hatred of God.

She also thought it was too bad that Mr. Christianson wasn't doing more for the unborn babies, but that he was a nice man and that there wasn't much the evil old Supreme Court would let him do, anyway.

Darla's Baptist absoluteness was not confined to her political opinions, either. As she and Livengood sped past the Admire exit, Darla declared that she didn't think it was right for Mark Stark to be a homosexual.

"Maybe not," Livengood said, rolling the window down in order to smoke the one cigarette he had promised himself during the trip. "But what are you going to do? It wouldn't save his soul one little bit if I were to gripe at him about it all the time, and I'd wind up losing one of my favorite people to argue with. Besides, all sins being equal in the eyes of God and all, I figure that all these cigarettes I suck on cancel out his occasional—well, never you mind about Mark."

Darla also didn't think it was right that Ed Walton seemed to date so many women, or that Greg Page played guitar for a punk rock band called Satan's Butt Buddies, or that Ellen Winston had been divorced three times. She didn't come right out and say so, but Darla made it clear that she didn't think it was right for Livengood to have been divorced even the one time.

"Probably not," Livengood said. "It wasn't my idea, if that makes you feel any better about me. I would have much preferred that she stuck around and put up with all my crap for the rest of our lives. Call me old-fashioned, but that's just the way I was raised."

After a rare pause, Darla said, "Maybe you should have been a better husband."

"No doubt about that," Livengood said. He then pushed the seat into its fully reclined position, and tipped his straw fedora over his face.

Beneath the hat, Livengood smiled sadly. He couldn't muster the words to tell Darla how hard it was for a man and woman to sustain their love in a world even more wicked than high school. How could he tell her how very complicated life can be when your daddy isn't rich and there's soul-numbing work to be done? How could he begin to tell her just how true the Good Book was when it said that man is born to trouble? Never mind trying to tell her that Satan's Butt Buddies struck him as a damn funny name for a band.

As for Darla's desire to legislate Kansas into the Kingdom of God, well, there weren't enough miles of road in the state for him to tell her everything that he thought was wrong with that idea. He'd been in politics almost ten years longer than she'd been alive—he would have called her "Little Missy" at that point, had he actually said anything—and he was well-satisfied that Kansas was still at least slightly better than hell.

And why tell her anything, anyway? After squirming into a more comfortable position to feign some sleep, Livengood recalled the cocksureness of his own youthful convictions, and was pleased to realize that a few of them had survived the test of his hard times more or less intact. They hadn't made him any richer, to be sure, but they helped him to catch a few winks on the Kansas turnpike. Darla was a good girl at heart, Livengood thought as he slipped into a half-sleep, and he was hopeful that her bedrock of good character would remain after the harsh winds of life had blown away the intolerant top soil of her personality.

Besides, Livengood highly valued the friendship and money of Big Jim Morland, who was trying to keep his girl a virgin in more ways than one.

Harley Christianson arrived early at the Broadview Hotel by his usual fifteen minutes, and paced the sidewalks of downtown Wichita for three tortuous minutes before Darla delivered Livengood to the front door. While Darla went to park the van and unload two heavy and cumbersome boxes of Christianson for Governor pamphlets, Livengood sat Harley down in the lobby to soothe his nerves and remind him of their strategy for the first debate of the campaign.

The state's American Legion chapters were holding their annual convention in the hotel's "Continental Room," and Livengood assured Harley that they couldn't have chosen a better venue for Harley's debut.

"This crowd is going to love you," Livengood said, "so don't bother playing to the crowd."

Harley wondered who he should be playing to, and what exactly Livengood meant when he said "playing to."

"All the candidates from both parties are here, so that means the local TV and press are going to be here, too," Livengood explained. "They're the ones you're really talking to. Don't worry about what this crowd wants to hear, unless it's what people in general want to hear."

Harley worried aloud that it would be rude not to talk to the folks who were actually there.

"Here are some index cards Wilbur wrote up about veteran's benefits, taxes on veteran's benefits, geriatric health care and a maximum age limit on drivers' licenses," Livengood said. "That should get you through the audience's first four questions."

Harley asked what other questions might arise.

"Old people also love to talk about how the world is going to hell in a handbasket, so we're going to get a lot of 'social issues' questions here," Livengood said. "Those are the questions that count, because those are the answers that are going to be the sound bites."

Checking Harley's watch and noticing that time was running out, Livengood began to hurriedly reiterate the most important points: Be more pro-choice than the other Republican candidates, but more pro-life than either of the Democrats, assume a similarly centrist tone on everything else, and don't say anything stupid.

"And be your sweet simple self," Livengood added. "Because that's what we're selling,"

"I can remember that," Harley said. "Be myself."

"One other thing," Livengood said. "They're going to ask about the flag amendment. These guys are nuts about the flag amendment."

"I love the flag," Harley said.

"Be sure to tell them so," Livengood said.

"But do I love this flag amendment?" Harley asked.

Livengood hated the flag amendment issue, being on the unpopular side of it, and after scratching his chin a moment he asked, "Do you love freedom of speech?"

"I sure do," Harley said.

"OK, then, be sure and tell them that, too."

The ensuing debate went better than Livengood had dared to hope. The area between the extremes represented in this race, Livengood delightedly discovered, would offer much room for maneuvering.

CHAPTER SIX

Sitting on the far left of the crowded podium, by sheer coincidence, was Willa Kline, one of two Democrats seeking their party's nomination. Her two-minute opening speech was a jargon-laden jeremiad against the various forms of fascist oppression being imposed on Kansas by militaristic white men, and she seemed genuinely befuddled by the merely polite applause of her audience, which consisted almost entirely of old white men who had been shot at by actual fascists.

Also running for the Democratic nomination was Tad Jager, a cab driver from Kansas City, Kansas, who ran for the Democratic nomination for something every election year.

On the far right of the podium, also by sheer coincidence, was Hoss Baker. His opening remarks mostly concerned guns, and their usefulness in hunting, home protection and whipping up on any potential One World Government armies that might want to pick a fight with Kansas, but he also said a few words on behalf of lower taxes and unborn babies.

Seated nervously next to Baker was Whitey Williams, who spent most of his opening remarks recounting his record as Insurance Commissioner. He was slightly more passionate than Baker in his devotion to unborn babies, and more passionate yet about lower taxes, but Williams was not a compellingly passionate man.

Rep. Stan Jeffries, who spoke next, spent his first minute making clear that he cared far more than Baker or Williams about unborn babies, and spent the next minute matching their fervor for lower taxes.

Hampton Hibbert then made it clear that he was second to no one in the field in his devotion to unborn babies. Except for the split second it took to declare that he was a businessman and for lower taxes, his opening statement was an old time sermonette expressing his fierce opposition to abortion, pornography, homosexuality, and the way that Kansas was generally going to hell in a handbasket. He had the musical cadences of a television evangelist, and a blow-dried haircut and gold watch to match.

Jonathan Appel, wearing a perfectly tailored suit and a confident expression commensurate with his standing as the most powerful and recognized man on the podium, spent most of his two minutes in an effort to seem humble. The rest was spent touting a tax reduction he had co-sponsored in Congress, with a few seconds saved to say that he also was in favor of unborn babies. The small contingent of anti-abortion protesters who showed up at every political event hissed as Appel mentioned the unborn babies. Appel had never abandoned the pro-lifers on any vote, and was known in the national press—to the extent he was known at all—as an anti-abortion hard-liner, but Livengood was intrigued to note that he no longer received the pro-lifers' love.

Harley Christianson was shaking visibly as he rose to speak, and Livengood was momentarily worried that his obvious inexperience and off-the-rack suit would make him seem comically amateurish next to the smooth and congressional Appel. The Legionnaires, however, seemed to respond to Harley with an immediate good will. Reading with a natural ease from one of Livengood's better speeches, Harley offered no specific policies or any other comment on the issues, but spoke only of himself and his lifetime of devotion to God, family, community and Kansas, all explained in the humblest terms possible for a campaign speech, and all delivered with a down-home gravity that made Appel seem comically slick and congressional by comparison.

Livengood thought the rest of the debate helped convey the crucial message that Harley was, relatively speaking, not nuts.

During the question-and-answer period one Legionnaire asked the candidates where they stood on the death penalty. Kline seized the opportunity to speak out on behalf of dangerous criminals, while the Republicans seemed engaged in a contest over who could kill the most criminals in the most painful fashion. As Livengood scored it, Baker won by a nose.

"I support the death penalty, but I'd like to make it more severe," Baker said. "All these other fellows can talk all they want about how many death warrants they'd sign, but how many of them are actually willing to pull the switch? I'll do it every time, not just to save the taxpayers some money, but because that's how strongly I feel about this. And I'll tell you what, folks, I've questioned a few suspects in my time as Ford County Sheriff who'll tell you that I'm dead serious."

Harley's answer to the question, that, "There really doesn't seem to me to be a right thing to do about a murder," struck Livengood as sufficiently non-committal. A question about gay rights sent Willa Kline into such an impassioned defense of homosexuality that Livengood was surprised when she stopped short of saying that it should be mandatory. The Republicans once again became competitively indignant.

Because the other candidates had already stated their positions on the abortion issue in their opening statements, only Jager and Harley were asked about it.

"I think abortion is an awful thing," Harley said, "but there's a lot of situations where I wouldn't want to sit in judgment of some poor girl who thinks she needs one."

The statement provoked hisses from the anti-abortion crowd that had crashed the convention, but Livengood noticed it didn't seem to offend the Legionnaires, even the ones who had cheered the pro-life sentiments of the other candidates.

The debate went so well for Harley that he received the biggest applause at the conclusion, despite his insufficiently indignant response to flag-burning.

Harley Christianson started the long drive home to Piquant almost immediately after the debate, staying just long enough to shake a few hands that Livengood said needed to be shaken. Livengood lingered for over an hour, schmoozing with reporters and fawning over the most affluent-looking of the Legionnaires.

It was one o'clock in the morning when Darla drove the big white van up to Livengood's apartment building, and the day had been so long that even Darla's teenaged body was feeling tired. Darla asked if she could "use the little girl's room," and agreed to carry a couple of heavy and cumbersome boxes up to the second floor apartment. Livengood led the way for her, and was gentlemanly enough to open the door.

"Hey, Frankie," said Mick Fixx, who was sprawled on the fading rug in the middle of Livengood's living room, taking apart a window unit air conditioner. "Who's the babe?"

Livengood, showing no sign of surprise, introduced Darla.

"What's he doing here?" Darla asked Livengood.

"What the hell does it look like I'm doing?" Fixx said. "I'm fixing Frankie Livengood's air conditioner. My friend here is so goddamned smart that he can run the whole state of Kansas, but he's too stupid to fix anything that breaks down in his apartment."

Livengood apologized for Fixx's language, but admitted the truth of his statement.

"But why is he doing it at one o'clock in the morning?" Darla asked.

"Well hell, little darling, I got here before the bars closed, didn't I?" Fixx said. "Seems to me that you ought to give a working man some credit."

Darla, who did not seem to care for Mick's hirsute and unkempt appearance any more than his choice of words, excused herself curtly and went to the bathroom.

"You dog, you," Fixx said.

"Mick, please, that girl is 16 years old," Livengood said.

"Awright."

"Give me a break, Mick. I'm not quite the pervert you are."

"Keep trying, my friend," Fixx said, pulling a marijuana cigarette out of his shirt pocket and lighting it up.

A bolt of common sense flashed through Livengood's sleepiness, warning him to tell Fixx to extinguish the joint until Darla had left the apartment, but it had been a long and tiring day and this was his home, after all. Disregarding common sense, Livengood accepted Mick's offer. He instantly regretted it when Darla found him in mid-drag as she returned from the bathroom.

"Mr. Livengood!" she said. This was a bad sign, as Livengood had at long last trained her to call him by his first name. "I don't think that's right."

Livengood coughed out the hit, returned the joint to Fixx, and said, "Maybe not."

Darla, who had never seen such behavior in all her life, was not satisfied with the answer.

"Listen, Darla, I'm sorry you saw that," Livengood said. "But it's been a long day."

That wasn't satisfactory, either.

"You know that you're breaking the law," Darla said.

Fixx laughed, making it impossible for Livengood not to do so.

"Don't worry about that, Darla," Livengood said. "There's plenty more laws where that one came from. If we break them all, well, trust me, we'll make more."

Darla was further infuriated by being laughed at, and Livengood had to chase after her to make his effusive and heartfelt apologies. When Darla was placated to the point that Livengood was confident she wouldn't tell her father, he thanked her at great length for her services and suggested that she come in late for work the next day. Darla said that she wouldn't make a big deal about the incident, but added that she still didn't think it was right.

Back in the apartment, Fixx was fighting hysterics about Livengood's panicked reaction to the young girl's indignation.

"What's her problem, anyway?" Fixx asked.

"Aw hell, Mick, that girl is 16 years old," Livengood said. "You know what that's like."

"Yeah, I know what that's like," Fixx said, taking a prodigious puff from the joint before handing it to Livengood. "Sixteen's a damned fine age. Believe me, I got practical experience in these matters. A girl like that can tear a man up at that age."

CHAPTER SEVEN

"Yellow Stripes and Dead Skunks"

Frankie Livengood had successfully steered the Harley Christianson campaign toward the middle of the road, and was thus far enjoying a smooth ride.

The coverage of the American Legion debate reflected the extra hours of effort that Livengood had spent working the reporters there, with both *The Wichita Eagle* and the Associated Press stories mentioning Harley in their leads, and the three local television stations airing as many seconds of Harley as they gave to the front-running Appel and Patterson. The stories were skimpy in every case, but Livengood was satisfied that they conveyed the message that Harley wasn't a nut.

After a similar success with the Kansas City media following a debate in Johnson County, and favorable coverage from appearances in such mid-sized towns as Hutchinson, Hays, Liberal, Pittsburg, Salina and Atchison, a poll conducted by *The Kansas City Star* officially confirmed the media consensus that Harley had established himself as a legitimate candidate. Appel was leading the pack with 20 percent, Patterson was close behind at 18 percent, while Williams and Hibbert were tied with 12 percent, and Christianson was solidly in fifth place with 10 percent, with Baker lagging well behind at 2 percent. "Undecided," of course, was winning the election by a landslide.

Livengood was ecstatic to be in double digits so early in the race, and even Mark Stark had to concede that it was an impressive accomplishment for a candidate who had registered no name recognition just weeks earlier.

Looking at the numbers with an experienced eye, Livengood discerned that Patterson, Hibbert and Williams were splitting the potential plurality of religious conservatives, the key to the Christianson strategy. He also noted that Appel's support among the rest of the party was well below his level of name recognition, and seemingly soft. He also assumed that only the least ideological voters were still undecided at this point, and would thus be amenable to the Christianson message of "he's not a nut," once it was more widely exposed.

Looking at the numbers with a scholarly objectivity, Stark noticed that Appel enjoyed a two-to-one lead over Christianson.

"But that's only a ten point difference," Livengood said. "That's nothing. We've already scored ten points just from having Harley shake a few hands and charm a few reporters. Hell, Appel's been in Congress for eight years, and he's only ten points ahead."

"He obviously has a ton of money, judging by how often he's on TV already," Stark said. "Did you seen the one where he rides a horse? I hate to admit it, but I found it somewhat erotic."

"Yeah? Well, wait'll you see our ad with that Schnitzle guy telling the Vietnam story. Once a few more checks come in, we'll get it on the air and start battling Appel for that all-important couch potato vote."

Frankie Livengood's in-box began to fill with good news. There were messages from the political action committees that routinely donated to any candidate with any chance of winning, from other potential contributors seeking a bit of personalized flattery before they wrote their checks, along with the names of reporters from across the state, and people wanting to volunteer or sell their services to the campaign. There were even messages from the occasional curiosity-seeker from outside the state.

Even the most perfunctory fund-raising was tiresome to Livengood, so he decided take a break one afternoon by returning a call to Rebecca Reynolds of the New York City-based Coalition for Women's Reproductive Rights, who, according to Darla's neatly written message, was offering assistance of some kind to the campaign. Livengood knew well that keeping to the middle of a Kansas campaign trail meant steering clear of eastern feminists, but he thought it might be some fun to brush her off.

"Is this Mizz Rebecca Reynolds?" Livengood said, when the call at long last went through. "Well, howdy. This is Frankie Livengood from the Harley Christianson for Governor campaign out here in Kansas. How's every little thing in New York City?"

Like many urban Kansans, Livengood enjoyed acting rural for the benefit of easterners.

"Very well, thank you," Reynolds said, with an accentless voice that disappointed Livengood. "And thank you so much for returning my call. I had called you because I was interested to read a report on the Internet that said your candidate is running as a Republican on a pro-choice platform. Is that report correct?"

"More or less," Livengood said. "We're more pro-choice than the other guys, but maybe less so than you would prefer. That's what we're aiming for, at least. We're still just a wee bit pro-life when it comes to parental consent and a few other things."

"I see," Reynolds said. "But would it be fair to say that your candidate is pro-choice at least to the extent that he would not support any policies that exceed the parameters of Roe v. Wade, as defined by court decisions? In other words, does he support the basic right of a woman to control her reproductive fate?"

"Yeah, sure. Why not?"

"In that case, Mr. Livengood, the Coalition for Women's Reproductive Rights is prepared to offer its assistance to your campaign."

"I don't know that you really want to do that, Mizz Reynolds. Abortion politics can be a tricky business here in Kansas. It's not something any sane person would want to get mixed up in."

"Am I to assume, then, that the scope of women's reproductive rights in Kansas will be determined by insane people?"

"Most likely," Livengood said.

Reynolds saw that as all the more reason for the Coalition for Women's Reproductive Rights to enter the fray, and urged Livengood to accept a $1,000 check that a contributor had earmarked for pro-choice Republican candidates running in traditionally conservative states.

"I'm sure not accustomed to turning down money, Mizz Reynolds," Livengood said. "But I'm afraid that amount won't be worth the trouble that it's bound to cause when a name like Coalition for Women's Reproductive Rights, with an address like New York City, pops up on our disclosure statements. Me, I love everybody, but I've got to tell you, a lot of my fellow Kansans—even some of the ones who don't mind the occasional abortion or two—they don't like out-of-staters or feminists meddling in the local politics. Kansas is just funny that way. You don't know what it's like out here."

In that case, Reynolds said, she wondered if Frankie Livengood and the Harley Christianson for Governor Campaign might do the Coalition for Women's Reproductive Rights a small favor. Livengood, still playing the part of the rural Kansan, said he would be pleased as punch to oblige.

"I'd like to come to Kansas and observe your campaign," Reynolds said.

"What for?" Livengood said.

"Because Kansas, according to my research, is a hotbed of religious conservatism. If I can see first-hand how a pro-choice candidate can win there, or why he doesn't, the lessons should serve me well in friendlier districts. You're quite right about one thing, Mr. Livengood. Kansas is indeed a funny place, and I really don't know what it's like out there. Frankly, I have no idea. But if I'm going to do my job well, I need to know."

"Sort of a 'know thine enemy' kind of deal, you might say."

"You might very well say that, Mr. Livengood."

Livengood sensed that he had carried a private joke too far, once again, and now he didn't quite know how to brush off Rebecca Reynolds and her Coalition for Women's Reproductive Rights. Then, while stalling for time, he decided that maybe he hadn't yet had all the fun this situation might afford.

"Yeah, sure. Why not?" Livengood said. "Come on out to Kansas and take a look-see. Hell, I'll even send my girl Darla out to pick you up at the airport."

Hampton Hibbert was a man who relished his many earthly enemies, secure in the Good Book's assurance that the friendship of the world is the enmity of God.

Such faith had sustained Hampton Hibbert through the series of hostile schoolyards he encountered as a child, when his father had roamed the plains states searching for work in the oil fields that blossomed there. The piety that his mother had imbued in him through nightly Bible studies at a series of storefront and Quonset hut churches did not prevent his perpetual unpopularity, but it did offer some consolation for the loneliness, and he noted with pleasure that the world could be even crueler to his faithless classmates.

As a young man freshly graduated from an unaccredited Arkansas Bible college, Hibbert happily discovered that the Biblical values of hard work, thrift and sobriety offered even more tangible compensations in a free-market economy. The roughs and rounders that he worked with on various construction crews may have laughed at Hibbert as they drank and whored away their wages, but that only sweetened his satisfaction when he started to sign their paychecks. The Good Book had promised Hibbert that a man diligent in business shall stand before kings, not mean men, and although Kansas provided a disappointing lack of kings to stand before, he was content to stand among its multi-millionaires by the time he reached the age of 30.

Marriage to a dowdy but obedient woman followed Hibbert's first million, and the birth of a daughter followed the second. Settled at last in the gargantuan home he built for his family near his wife's hometown of Haysville, Hibbert looked upon his works and called them good.

Still, Hibbert continued to be haunted by an unshakable sense that God's purpose for him had not yet been fulfilled. No matter how many gated subdivisions he built on the sites of old neighborhoods, no matter how many strip malls and Wal-Marts he sent into competition with the small town corner stores, and no matter how many new mega-churches he erected, Hibbert felt that he wasn't doing enough for America. Every time he turned on the television or glanced at a newspaper, he saw additional evidence that the country was on a dangerous drift away from traditional values, and it anguished Hibbert's heart.

Then, one life-changing night at the Four Square Church of the Rock and the Ark in Haysville, Hibbert heard the call to battle against the modern world. To most of the congregation it was Edna Dimschmidt's usual stump speech, delivered with her usual zeal, but for Hibbert it was a clarion blast of the same rich pitch that Joshua had sounded at Jericho. Dimschmidt had specified that "only the most righteous among ye" would lead the battle she so loudly proclaimed, and after a long and deliberative look around the congregation, Hibbert knew she must have been talking about him.

A long conversation followed over tuna fish casserole at the Hibbert home. While Mrs. Hibbert and Ellie Whimple sat in near-total silence at the table, Hibbert and Dimschmidt spoke rapidly, sharing the delighted agreement and reciprocal flattery of newfound soulmates. Dimschmidt and Ellie left the Hibberts' home at 11:00 p.m. with a donation that most charities would find stingy, but which the Kansas United for a Sin-Free Kansas considered miraculous, and a partnership was forged.

Hibbert and Dimschmidt became frequent companions, although always in the silently jealous company of Ellie, Mrs. Hibbert and other Kansans United for a Sin-Free Kansas. Together they waged public relations assaults on abortion clinics, gay bars, motion picture theaters, bookstores and other offensive businesses throughout the state, using tactics that ranged from picket lines to swamping local officials with letters. Many Kansans, including a conspicuously large number of the ones who lived in the houses and shopped at the stores and worshipped in the churches that Hibbert built, came to join them. A newsletter and web site funded by Hibbert kept the growing number of Kansans United for a Sin-Free Kansas informed of which candidates the organization deemed least sinful, and it did not go unnoticed in the corridors of power that many of those candidates won.

Eventually, Hibbert announced his candidacy for the office of governor of the great state of Kansas. Edna Dimschmidt stood proudly at his side, while Mrs. Hibbert and Ellie hovered just behind.

"If they want to call me a radical Christian, let 'em. I'll take that as a compliment," Hibbert said, to the roaring approval of the one thousand or so Kansans United for a Sin-Free Kansas. After delighting the crowd further with some rhetorical smiting of homosexuals, pornographers and the press, Hibbert thundered that moderation in the face of such sin would itself be sinful.

"The only things you'll ever find in the middle of the road are yellow stripes and dead skunks!" Hibbert roared. Though an old joke, it got a huge laugh from the Kansans United for a Sin-Free Kansas.

Consultants sent by several national religious conservative organizations urged Hibbert to strike a more moderate tone, and backed up their advice with lots of survey figures and focus group comments, but none could dissuade Hibbert from delivering his message with the fervor he truly felt.

When the first newspaper poll showed that he had won 12 percent of the vote, Hibbert considered himself vindicated. Hibbert had spoken God's truth, and God had delivered unto him an army of supporters. Surely, Hibbert fervently believed, their numbers would grow with the truth.

Then came the phone call from Dan Dorsey of the Sunflower News Service, who had somehow discovered the result of one particular sin that Hibbert had committed sixteen years earlier. Dorsey asked for Hibbert's comment, explaining that the story would shortly be sent out over the wire for the next morning's papers, and after much stammering Hibbert said he would call right back. Hibbert immediately called Edna Dimschmidt.

After reading accounts of Hampton Hibbert's illegitimate child in two-dozen Kansas newspapers, Livengood pulled a bottle of bourbon from his lower desk drawer, poured a small glassful and took a long swig. He then took a calculator from the upper drawer and attempted to quantify just how badly he was screwed.

If Hibbert's twelve points were to go entirely to Patterson, a scenario Livengood considered probable, Patterson would be at 30 percent, a nearly insurmountable number in a six-way race. If Hibbert's twelve points were split evenly between Appel and Patterson, which Livengood considered overly optimistic, then Appel's twenty-six points would become tough to beat. Livengood speculated that Whitey Williams or Hoss Baker might pick up a substantial portion of the Hibbert block, but their recent campaign performances gave him little hope.

Mark Stark, who dropped by with his legal pads to observe the latest twist in the campaign, checked Livengood's figures and found them reasonable. Trying to be hopeful, he suggested that Hibbert might not be forced out of the race. After all, Stark argued, this is the modern world.

"No, this is Kansas," Livengood said. "The only people who have illegitimate kids are poor white trash, no-account colored folks and Hollywood movie stars, none of which are a significant voting bloc here. We're screwed. This bastard's bastard has reduced me to hoping that Edna Dimschmidt truly can work miracles."

Meanwhile, Hampton Hibbert's moral crisis had created a difficult political dilemma for Jonathan Appel. Arvin Howard, who directed Appel's efforts in south-central Kansas, urged that the campaign make an aggressive appeal to the voters who would no doubt be abandoning Hibbert's candidacy. He suggested a television spot touting Appel's solid voting record on moral issues, and noted that it could be aired cheaply during the Sunday morning religious shows. In his most diplomatic tone, Howard added that it wouldn't hurt to do a little shoe-leather campaigning on those issues as well.

"You don't have to stand in front of the clinics and sing 'Oh What a Mighty God' with them again," Howard said. "Just get out to the meetings, attend some services, and talk with the folks."

Howard resented the annoyed look on Appel's face. Despite his success, Howard still considered himself one of those church-going west-siders who had fueled Appel's upset victory in that long-ago first race, long before the congressman began to consider himself above such rabble.

"I could still charm them up," Appel told Howard, after some consideration. "At least I don't have any bastard kids out there."

The voice of Chip Wentworth blared through the telephone speakerphone, urging Appel not to do it.

"You'd be going in the entirely wrong direction," Wentworth shouted, his slightly winded voice indicating to Howard that he was riding that damn stationary bike again. "Patterson and Williams and that Baker guy are all going to ratchet up the holy-roller rhetoric to get all those Hibbert votes, and they're going to wind up scaring all the normal people into our camp. All we have to do is let them knock each other out, and keep on issue with social moderation and economic conservatism."

Appel remarked that the Christianson guy seemed to be making inroads into the normal people vote.

"Forget Christianson," Wentworth said. "You're a member of the United States House of Representatives. He's a simple carpenter, for Christ's sakes. Who the hell do you think people are going to follow?"

Howard winced at the comment, then winced again when he noticed Appel shaking his head.

By that point, Rep. Stan Patterson and Pastor Bill Jeffries were putting the final touches on their new campaign strategy, having begun work on the plan long before Jeffries called the tip in to Dan Dorsey.

Talking the boy's mother into a public disclosure had not been easy, but Pastor Jeffries had finally persuaded her by pointing out that the truth would not only set her free, it might very well increase the scandalously low child support that Hampton Hibbert had been paying. The boy, a sullen youth named Billy Wiggins, who had one of those absurd haircuts that the young people favor these days, had proved a harder sell, refusing to cooperate until he had negotiated a satisfactory financial settlement of his own.

Whitey Williams, whose previous campaign slogan was "A Competent Man for Kansas," was hastily seeking a more explicitly religious message. A short time later he was in a television studio filming a new commercial about abortion, with the director pleading for just a little bit more passion.

Two days after the story about his illegitimate son had appeared in every Kansas newspaper, Hampton Hibbert and Edna Dimschmidt strode together onto the pulpit of the Four Square Church of the Rock and the Ark. Hibbert nodded to acknowledge the presence of three-thousand screaming Kansans United for a Sin-Free Kansas, and then stared into the cluster of television cameras.

"Yes, I, too, have sinned," he said, "and today I want you to meet the result of that sin."

Onto the stage strode Billy Wiggens, wearing a churchly three-piece suit and a haircut very much like his father's. Father and son embraced, and the crowd went wild.

"I want you to know that this beautiful young boy, this fine young Christian man, could have been aborted," Hibbert said. "His mother will tell you, with tears in her eyes and shame in her heart, that at one point she wanted to do just that. And the Supreme Court of the United States of America had ruled that she would have been within her constitutional rights to do so."

The people booed at such a ferocious volume that Hibbert raised his palms to quiet them, lest the television cameras not be able to record his words.

"But I implored this child's mother to not commit this foul act, and with the help of the Lord I was able to dissuade her," Hibbert continued. "Through our prayers together, and our study of the Bible, she even came to love the child that was growing within her womb, and she promised that she would give him a fine Christian upbringing on her own."

The crowd cheered again, albeit less loudly.

"Tragically, my sin was compounded by the fact that I was a married man. My holy commitment to my wife, and the daughter she had borne me, would prevent me from fully assuming the role of father to this child. Such is the nature of sin, my friends, that it begets other sin. Any sin keeps us from leading a fully righteous life, my brothers and sisters."

Except for an occasional "amen," the crowd was perilously quiet.

"But the precious blood of The Lamb allows me to stand before you today as a forgiven man, with my son at my side, asking for your support as I continue my campaign for governor."

Father and son then embraced, and the crowd roared. When young Billy shouted, "Thank you, Daddy, for letting me live," the shouts shook the very foundations of the Foursquare Church of the Rock and the Ark, overpowering the public address system that Hibbert's tithing had bought.

Even Frankie Livengood, who had driven down the turnpike to witness whatever miracle Edna Dimschmidt might work, was on his feet shouting, "Praise the Lord!"

Outbidding Jeffries and Patterson for the boy's cooperation had been almost physically painful for such a frugal man as Hibbert, but it proved well worth the price. The next poll released by *The Kansas City Star* showed that Hibbert had actually moved up a few points.

Appel was still in the lead but stuck at 20 percent, with Hibbert and Patterson now tied at 18 percent, while Williams had faded to 9 percent and Baker had slipped out of the poll entirely. Christianson had also moved up since his campaign had begun airing a new ad about his Vietnam service, and was now at 14 percent, but to Frankie Livengood the most interesting aspect of the story was Hibbert's apparent survival.

Hibbert was quoted as saying that, "I'm still in this race because of the faith and the loyalty of those who support me, not because of their numbers. Not only will we stay on the campaign trail, we'll stay on the right side of it, and this campaign will continue its holy mission of bringing righteousness to Kansas."

Looking up from his copy of *The Kansas City Star* with a smile, Livengood reached into his lower drawer for a celebratory swig from the bottle of bourbon. Not only would the Hibbert campaign continue its holy mission of bringing righteousness to Kansas, it would also continue to split the pro-life vote until primary day.

Despite the good news, Livengood was slightly unsettled to see a Kansas candidate survive an out-of-wedlock birth scandal. It marked the end of yet another iron-clad rule that he once could have counted on, and it troubled his Kansas conscience that the poor white trash and the Hollywood movie stars had seemingly nudged the state another step closer to legitimizing illegitimacy.

Still, looking at the picture of Billy Wiggens and his brand new haircut on the front page of *The Kansas City Star*, Livengood raised his glass and said, "You magnificent bastard, you."

CHAPTER EIGHT

"Thou Shalt Neither Vex a Stranger, Nor Oppress Her"

By the time she had traveled the seventy miles or so from the Kansas City airport to the Christianson campaign office in downtown Topeka, Rebecca Reynolds of the Women's Coalition for Reproductive Rights had already had enough of Kansas. Between *The Kansas City Star*'s account of the previous day's Hampton Hibbert rally, Darla Morland's extensive commentary on the same matter, and the 102 degree heat, she had reached a preliminary conclusion that the scope of women's reproductive rights in Kansas would most likely be determined by insane people.

Reynolds turned out to be a tall, slender, slightly buck-toothed woman, in her mid- to late-30s by Frankie Livengood's estimation, with a wised-up and distinctively big city look about her. Livengood had a fondness for wised-up women and a weakness for the big city look, and Darla noticed that he was less gruff than usual as he was introduced to Reynolds in his office. Reynolds greeted Livengood cordially but warily, as if approaching the shaman of some remote, primitive and potentially hostile tribe of Republicans.

Idle chit-chat ensued, with Reynolds asking a series of questions about Kansas that one might ask when preparing a third-grade geography report, and Livengood struggling vainly to make the answers interesting. Her questions about the gubernatorial race gradually became more specific, his answers increasingly vague. Giving up on the possibility of a friendlier conversation, much less anything more, Livengood explained that he would be out of the office for the next three days while traveling to several towns across the state, apologizing profusely for being forced to do so.

Taken aback when Reynolds asked if she could accompany him, Livengood said, "You might prefer to stay here in Topeka for a few days, instead. I'm heading deep, deep into Kansas. It might be a good idea for you to get acclimated before you go there."

Stiffening her spine with feminist indignation and an anthropological derring-do, Reynolds said that she was quite ready to explore the state, and had come all this way for precisely that reason. Livengood shrugged his shoulders and said, "Well, you asked for it."

The forecasts had indicated hot and clear, but Livengood scanned the morning skies nervously before deciding to drive his beloved Camaro. He drove to the downtown Ramada Inn to pick up Reynolds, persuaded her to let him leave the top down, then headed south on Highway 75.

The conversation was polite but perfunctory, with Reynolds talking about herself only to the extent one would on a resume. She had grown up in Connecticut, the only daughter of two professors, and had attended private schools before enrolling at Columbia University, where she was graduated with a bachelor's degree in sociology. She began her career at a women's shelter, worked a series of jobs with non-profit organizations, and had been in her current position for two years.

Livengood, who had attended second-rate public schools, enrolled at Kansas State University only by virtue of the state's open admissions policy, been a career-long hack, and was defensive about it, spoke little of himself.

Eventually the conversation gave way to silence and relief. As Livengood wordlessly relished the beauty of the lushly green countryside that rolled by, he found himself wondering how the familiar scenery might seem upon first viewing to someone more used to the congested and gray streets of New York. He asked Reynolds what she thought.

"What's with all the signs?" Reynolds said. "All these religious signs."

Livengood hadn't noticed any signs.

"They're all over the place," Reynolds said. "Here's another one coming up, 'Jesus died for your sins.' I've seen 'Jesus Saves,' 'Righteousness exalteth a nation,' 'What's the cost of an abortion? One human life,' 'Choose life,' 'John 3:16,' and a faded, falling-apart sign that said something about 'parity,' whatever that means. Not to mention all the crosses on the hillsides, or the welcome signs for churches outside every single town we've been through."

"Oh, those," Livengood said. "People put those up."

Reynolds rolled her eyes, and expressed sarcastic relief that Jesus wasn't doing it Himself.

"No, no. I mean that it's just regular people, farmers and church groups and such, putting up signs," Livengood said. "They've got some land, they've got some wood and paint, so they put up a sign."

Reynolds announced, after some thought, that it made her uneasy. At that, Livengood exhaled with great exasperation, then wondered aloud what it is about folks from Back East.

"Some guy sticks a cross in a jar of piss and you write him a grant, but some farmer sticks a cross in his own hill and you want to sue him for creating a hostile environment for the heathens. I swear, Back East is a bunch of vampires, a bunch of black-clad, pale-complected soul-stealers who recoil at the sight of a cross."

Reynolds said that Livengood didn't know anything about Back East.

"I lived in New York City for a year, working for an advocacy group," Livengood said, happily adding to her annoyance when he said that it advocated school vouchers. She was further annoyed to hear that he'd also spent a year in Washington, D.C., working for Congressman Appel.

Despite her extensive travels throughout Europe, Reynolds had never been more than a hundred miles west of New York or a hundred miles east of San Francisco. Finding herself at the disadvantage of knowing less about Kansas than Livengood knew about New York City, and feeling defensive about it, Reynolds slumped in her seat and looked out the window at yet another sign, this one boasting that "One Kansas Farmer Feeds 87 People—and You!"

She glumly protested that at least people Back East aren't so aggressive about pushing their beliefs in other people's faces.

"You could have fooled me," Livengood said, snorting derisively. "Between the TV networks, Madison Avenue and the pointy-headed 'intelligentsia,' it seems to me that the biggest business you've got Back East is aggressively pushing your beliefs in other people's faces. Lord Almighty, Back East has a billion signs for every fool idea from non-alcoholic beer to Broadway musicals to socialism, and you don't even notice that anymore. Someone puts up a sign inviting you to Sunday services, and Jesus, that you notice."

Livengood was beginning to enjoy the rant, but he suspected that Reynolds was taking it personally. She was looking sullenly out the window, her arms folded beneath her pert breasts, and he felt compelled to apologized.

"I didn't mean you. You seem all right to me," Livengood said. "We're touchy, we Kansans. Most of us figure it's a pretty good life out here, but it's never on TV, except as a sheep-screwing joke or baptism shtick or yet another *Wizard of Oz* gag, and everywhere else is always faster, cooler, better. Every now and then *The New York Times* or PBS will send a reporter out to Kansas, and they always make it sound like a damn anthropological expedition to some remote, primitive and potentially hostile savages, except without the reverential awe they'd have for some bone-wearing jungle tribe. So, anyway, we get touchy, and I'm sorry."

Reynolds glumly accepted the apology, and quietly looked out the window. Several minutes later she remarked that the landscape was prettier than she had expected.

Livengood stopped at a law office in Ottawa, where he was to meet with the Franklin County Christianson for Governor Committee, which consisted of a lawyer, a banker, a librarian, and a farmer. Joining the meeting at Livengood's invitation, Reynolds was struck by the simplicity and unembarrassed cheapness of the office, the group's inordinate interest in the recent weather, and the seeming complexity of their political discussion. Although she knew nothing of water policy, school funding, railroad regulations or the other issues they discussed, the group's questions certainly sounded intelligent, and Livengood's answers sounded reasonable and authoritative.

Reynolds was disappointed that the subject of abortion did not arise until the end of the meeting, when the farmer asked what had brought her all the way out there from New York City.

"We don't like to talk about that," said the librarian, whose smile could put a friendly end to any discussion.

"Talk about that can get pretty ugly pretty fast around here," said the lawyer.

"Ain't no use trying to change a rooster's cock-a-doodle-do," said the farmer.

"But it sure has been nice to meet you," said the librarian, who seemed to have urgent business back at the library.

After a similar meeting in Osawatomie, Livengood headed straight to a local drive-in and bought a double chili cheeseburger, a large order of fries and paper plateful of fried okra. Reynolds scanned the hand-painted plywood menu for something remotely vegetarian, found nothing but the fried okra, and Livengood wound up taking her to the local grocery store, where she was able to purchase the ingredients for a rudimentary salad. They ate at a picnic table near the John Brown Museum.

"I'm a great admirer of John Brown," Livengood said, between large bites of the double chili cheeseburger.

Reynolds, who of course knew that Brown was a prominent abolitionist, nodded in agreement.

"He killed a bunch of people near here, you know," Livengood said. "He used a saber, sliced up a whole family."

Reynolds set down her fork, looked around for any lingering evidence of the massacre, and admitted that she didn't know that.

Livengood delighted in telling his state's history, and gave a brief course about "Bleeding Kansas." He told of the idealistic New Englanders who had sacrificed their comfortable lives to come to Kansas, their brutal battles with pro-slavery settlers and the border ruffians, his own lingering prejudice against Missourians, and Kansas' eventual entry into the Union as a solidly Republican and Free Soil state.

Reynolds liked the story, hearing it as a tale of people from Back East bringing enlightenment to the benighted prairie.

"You could call the abolitionists idealistic intellectuals, or you could call them a bunch of zealous Bible-thumpers," Livengood said. "In any case, you have to admit that we Republicans were right about that issue."

Reynolds reluctantly conceded that one issue.

Livengood waved his Styrofoam cup of soda to the memory of John Brown, "whose body lies a molderin' in the grave," and Reynolds reluctantly joined the toast with her bottle of water.

As they drove on toward Wichita, Reynolds spoke more freely about herself.

She said that she had gone to church as a very young girl, but could only remember a few Episcopal chants and a vague sense of awe, as she had stopped going shortly after her father left her mother. She mentioned that her mother was prone to depression and her father was prone to women embarrassingly close to her age, embarrassing Livengood with her frankness about such personal information. She spoke at greater length than Livengood would have preferred about her failed marriage and many other relationships with men, and offered less detail than he desired about a couple of lesbian flings, all in a tone that struck Livengood as disconcertingly nonchalant.

During a stop at a bar in the alleged town of Matfield Green, Reynolds spoke more passionately about her career, which seemed to provide the sense of awe she had known as a 6-year-old Episcopalian. She nostalgically recalled her days working at a shelter for battered women, openly boasting of the abusive men she had stared down, and explained how it fueled her passion to serve womankind.

Armed with a master's degree from New York City College, and alarmed by the rising tide of anti-abortion sentiment that she had been reading about, Reynolds joined the Coalition for Women's Reproductive Rights. Rising quickly through its ranks to the position of assistant director, Reynolds enjoyed a wide degree of freedom to do anything she deemed appropriate for the cause of women's reproductive rights, so long as it was within the organization's budget.

As they resumed the drive to Wichita, Livengood interrupted Reynolds' monologue to ask why she had come to Kansas.

"I'd never had anybody turn down money before," Reynolds said. "I thought I had better come out and see what kind of place this is."

Livengood drove along Highway 54 to the eastern edge of Wichita, where the farmland gave way to airplane factories, car lots and shopping malls. To Livengood it seemed the ugliest stretch of road in the world, but to Reynolds it was long-awaited evidence of civilization. After meandering through some older and more elegant neighborhoods of the city on his way to downtown, Livengood parked in a garage next to a large steel-and-glass box of a building. Reynolds remarked that it almost seemed like a real city.

"This is the big, bad city as far all the rest of the Kansans are concerned," Livengood said. "They think it's nothing but a bunch of black gangsters toting guns, Jew bankers foreclosing on honest farm folk, homosexual artists scrawling sacrilegious paintings, and rich yuppies looking down on people who work for a living. All of which is true to some extent, I suppose. Keep in mind, though, that it's closer in size to Matfield Green than it is to New York."

Livengood said he wanted to say "howdy" to his friend Arvin Howard in the steel-and-glass box building, and asked Reynolds if she'd mind staying in the lobby while he did. She stared at the Alexander Calder mobile hanging from the ceiling, studied the clothes worn by the women passing along the sidewalk, and was surprised by how quickly Livengood returned.

The two walked from the bank building to a nearby cluster of aged warehouses that had been transformed into a reasonable facsimile of an urban nightclub district, where Livengood planned to eat, drink and kill some time. Along the way, Livengood pointed out the Eaton Hotel, explaining that temperance radical Carry Nation had once attacked its bar with an ax, destroying a nude painting of Cleopatra in the process.

During dinner at a semi-swank restaurant, Reynolds enjoyed the first palatable vegetarian dish she had found in Kansas. She asked who Carry Nation was, and why she would attack a bar with an ax and destroy a nude painting.

"Carry Nation was a big, mean Kansas woman," Livengood said. "That's a good thing, too, I guess, because she had one of those abusive husbands you were talking about earlier. She blamed it on the booze he was always drinking, because they didn't know about patriarchy back then, so she figured she had God's permission to go around smashing up bars. That would have been bad enough, but she got a whole temperance movement going in the state, and next thing you know there's Prohibition."

Reynolds asked what became of Carry Nation.

"I don't know. She died, I guess," Livengood said. "You can't say she died off completely, though. It's still hard to get a drink in a lot of Kansas counties, and you've still got a bunch of big, mean Kansas women roaming the plains with God's permission for all kinds of craziness. Just wait until you meet Edna Dimschmidt."

As it turned out, Rebecca Reynolds would meet Edna Dimschmidt later that evening. The confrontation would come shortly after the evening's debate at a Catholic church in the sprawling subdivisions of west Wichita.

Prior to the debate, Livengood introduced Reynolds to Harley Christianson, who had been pacing nervously outside the building while awaiting their arrival. She was struck by the candidate's modesty and courtly charm, while Harley was just plumb pleased to meet anyone from New York City.

Reynolds listened with particular interest as Livengood warned Harley that abortion and various moral issues were likely to be raised often in the debate.

"People in Wichita can get a lot more revved up about things like abortion, homosexuality and pornography than folks do back in Piquant," Livengood said. "They actually have all that stuff here. A lot of the hard-core pro-lifers are here tonight to cheer Hampton, and Patterson's people are likely to get a little raucous, too, so don't get flustered. Just stick to your usual statements, and don't let them goad you into saying anything else."

Reynolds suggested that it wouldn't hurt to offer a more impassioned defense of abortion rights.

"No offense, ma'am, but I can't really get very passionate about abortion rights," Harley said. "I'm not going to say you can't have any, and I don't recommend you using any of them, either, but I'm not going to get all fired up about it one way or the other."

Reynolds, looking around the room at the wide variety of anti-abortion T-shirts among the crowd, decided she would settle for that.

The first portion of the debate was devoted to local concerns such as trains, which apparently came through town so often that it disrupted automobile traffic, and water, which was said to taste funny in the city.

As Livengood had predicted, the debate soon turned to abortion. He was amused to see the appalled expression on Reynolds' face as the candidates tried to top one another with ever greater concern for unborn babies, and he couldn't help chuckling at her reaction to a question about partial-birth abortion, with each candidate offering a grislier description of the procedure.

More frightening to Reynolds was the audience, which hooted and hollered as if at a professional wrestling match.

Harley made a quick exit after the debate, and Livengood seemed eager to do the same, but Reynolds insisted on gawking at the protestors for a few more minutes. When Livengood spotted two women in floral pattern dresses approaching, he grabbed Reynolds by the arm and attempted to pull her away, but she was too strong.

"Hello, Mr. Living-good," the taller woman said, smiling contemptuously.

"Howdy," Livengood said, trying to think of some way to mispronounce "Dimschmidt." After nodding to Ellie Whimple, he said, "What brings you here tonight?"

"God's good grace," Dimschmidt said.

"I came in a Camaro, myself, and I've got to be leaving in it now," Livengood said. After a jab from Reynolds' elbow, Livengood said, "This is Rebecca Reynolds. She's, uh, a friend of mine."

"I'm with the Women's Coalition for Reproductive Rights," Reynolds said, meeting Edna Dimschmidt's stare unflinchingly. "I'm flattered that Frankie considers me a friend, but I'm actually here to observe the campaign. My organization is very concerned about anti-choice candidates such as your Mr. Hibbert."

"You should be concerned," Dimschmidt said. "I imagine that women such as yourself will find it very uncomfortable when candidates such as Mr. Hibbert assume their rightful places in the halls of power across this nation, and the murder of unborn children is no longer one of your legal choices. A nation that allows that has broken its covenant with God, and cannot stand."

Reynolds' steely gaze would not admit it, but she regretted having provoked this confrontation. There was something about Edna Dimschmidt's eyes that frightened her, in a way that countless abusive husbands had not.

Livengood already knew better than to argue with Edna Dimschmidt, but he felt an obligation as Reynolds' host to step in.

"I saw where your man Hampton got himself a new covenant with his illegitimate son, too," Livengood said. "That was quite a beautiful bit of politics you pulled off there, I must say. You're really getting good at this business, Edna. I don't know anyone else who could have made fathering an illegitimate child seem so noble."

Dimschmidt looked at Livengood with a burning contempt; Reynolds with a new fascination. Livengood smiled with infuriating friendliness, and Dimschmidt responded in a cruelly kind tone.

"None of us are perfect, Frankie. Not even yourself. Hampton committed a horrible sin, as he fully confessed, but he chose the only moral course of action that the situation permitted. I think that is noble."

"I loved the part where the kid yelled, 'Thank you Daddy, for letting me live,' " Livengood said.

"Every birth is the result of a blessing from the Lord," Dimschmidt replied. "Perhaps if your own birth had depended on the intervention of a life-loving Christian, your cynical wisecracks wouldn't come so easily."

Reynolds, ready to re-join the fight, said that, "Perhaps you wouldn't be so certain of God's plan for other women if you had ever faced an unwanted pregnancy yourself."

Dimschmidt's stern expression warned Reynolds not to make any assumptions about what she had faced in life, and Reynolds was once again quiet. Dimschmidt was exulting in her triumph when Livengood spoke again.

"I'm afraid your omniscience isn't working at full strength tonight, Edna. As a matter of fact, my own birth did depend on the life-loving Christians of Kansas and their old pre-Roe abortion laws. My mother was a hooker, you know, and there's really no telling who my father was, but they say she did a thriving trade with the soldiers up at Fort Riley. Dear old Ma would often tell me, while she was shuttling me from one perverted relative's dump to another's, that she would have aborted me in a second if she'd had the chance."

Dimschmidt looked at Livengood with contempt, Ellie regarded him with sympathy, and Reynolds gazed with awe.

"No pity, Edna, please," Livengood said. "I get just enough kicks from time to time to concede that it's a blessing to me that she didn't abort me, but what about everybody else? In the good old days you want to bring us back to, they'd go to extraordinary lengths to keep the blessed circumstances of my birth from ever happening. Used to be, that's what good God-fearing women like yourself busied themselves with. Admit it, Edna, whenever you look at me you can see the reason why. You're not really going to tell me, are you, Edna, that it's a blessing on the Earth to have a mean old bastard like me running around?"

Dimschmidt was momentarily speechless, except to mutter that of course she loved Frankie Livengood, but he didn't stick around to exult in his triumph. He grabbed the now-compliant Reynolds by the arm, said, "I love you, too, Edna," then disappeared through the nearest fire exit.

Frankie Livengood and Rebecca Reynolds beat a hasty retreat to a small tavern across the street from Wichita State University, in the heart of the Wichita ghetto.

Several of the patrons greeted Livengood by name, and despite the thick cigarette smoke, Reynolds felt at ease for the first time since arriving in Kansas. Faded psychedelia and left-wing cartoons covered the unfinished walls, stickers bearing such slogans as "Save the Stupid, Close the Churches" were plastered about, and something about the fashionably disheveled appearance of the customers was reassuringly familiar to her.

In the corner, a tattoo-covered hillbilly trio was playing guitar, banjo and a one-string bass fashioned from an old Ford gas tank, singing a song that rhymed "double-wide" with "mail order bride," while an obviously gay couple dressed in cowboy clothing chatted giddily at the bar. Reynolds realized she couldn't escape the state's bucolic atmosphere even in its most bohemian bar, but at least it seemed to offer some refuge from the likes of Edna Dimschmidt.

"Where did that woman come from, anyway?" Reynolds asked Livengood, as they sat at the bar and sipped beers.

"She came from Kansas, just like me," Livengood said. "I warned you, we get into some hellacious arguments out here."

After a long pause, Reynolds thanked Livengood for intervening in her argument.

"No problem," Livengood said. "Arguing with lunatics is just part of my job. In fact, it's most of my job."

After another long pause, Reynolds asked if Livengood was any more committed to women's reproductive rights than his candidate.

"Not really," Livengood said. "Don't get me wrong, now. I'm not looking to oppress anybody or anything, but it's not an issue that's ever affected me in a personal way, if you know what I mean. Knock on wood."

Livengood rapped his knuckles on the bar.

"I hope that knocking on wood isn't your only form of birth control," Reynolds said. She ordered another beer, and wondered aloud how any thinking person could not be more adamant about women's reproductive rights.

"There are too many damned issues, for one thing," Livengood said. "This is a semi-arid, landlocked state, you might have noticed, and even in the middle of a crisis pregnancy, you're still going to need a glass of water. All but five of the counties in this state are continuing to decline in population, you know, and it's not because of abortion. For another thing, as much as Edna pisses me off, she makes too much sense to me."

Reynolds snorted, almost spitting out the beer she was drinking.

"Calm down, calm down," Livengood said. "I'm not saying she's right. I'm just saying that she makes enough sense to give me pause. And I'm not saying that you're wrong, either, because you make plenty of sense to me, too. I'm like Harley, I don't know for sure which side is right, so I don't presume to tell anybody else what to do. That makes me pro-choice by default, and that'll just have to be good enough for you."

That wasn't good enough for Reynolds, who ordered another beer.

"It doesn't have anything to do with the way you were born, does it?" Reynolds asked.

"What the hell do you know about the way I was born?" Livengood asked, in a way that seemed to preclude any discussion. "I was born a sinner, just like you and everybody else."

Reynolds drank her beer in silence while Livengood offered a toast to all the unborn sinner babies.

"Did I hear you talking about unborn babies?" asked the bartender, a heavyset man with the words "Scroat Belly" emblazoned on his T-shirt.

"Indeed you did," Livengood said. "Marv, meet Ms. Rebecca Reynolds, who has come all the way to Kansas from New York City on behalf of the Women's Coalition for Reproductive Rights to do battle with the likes of Edna Dimschmidt."

"It sure is a pleasure to meet you," Marv said, offering a handshake. "Give 'em hell."

Reynolds happily shook his hand, and said she was pleased to at last meet a true supporter of abortion rights in Kansas.

"It's not that I'm all that pro-choice," Marv said. "I just can't stand those pro-lifers. They drive me nuts, with their chanting and singing and praying and all. I used to tend bar at a little place next to the clinic over on Central, back during the Summer of Mercy protests."

Livengood remembered that bar fondly, right down to a Roger Miller record that was on the jukebox, and Reynolds interrupted him to ask Marv about the protests.

"It was the damnedest thing I ever saw," Marv said. "Some big pro-life outfit came into town with the idea of closing all the clinics down, and after they hit all the political churches in town they had thousands of protestors running all over the place, waving signs and crawling on the streets and singing their stupid songs. It killed the bar, of course. Who wants to run a gauntlet of dead fetus pictures just to get a beer? If it weren't for all the press and TV guys who came to town, there wouldn't have been any damn business in there. But do these pro-life crusaders care about a neighborhood bar? Hell no. They were saving the unborn babies. Anything they did, they were justified because they were saving those unborn babies. Break the law, push people around, drive a poor guy crazy singing 'Oh What a Mighty God' all the time. They don't give a damn, because they're saving the unborn babies. You know what I say to that?"

Reynolds did not know, but was eager to learn.

"I say, fuck the unborn babies."

Livengood laughed heartily, and suggested to Reynolds that the Women's Coalition for Reproductive Rights might have found itself a new slogan. Reynolds ignored the remark, and asked Marv what he thought had happened to the clinic blockade movement.

"They passed some new laws," Marv said. "All these Christians here in town don't mind taking an air-conditioned bus ride to the city jail for a two-hour stay, if that's what it takes to save their precious unborn babies, but when it means a long stretch up in Leavenworth, well, suddenly all those unborn babies are on their own."

Reynolds did laugh at that, and had Marv pour her another beer.

"Don't get too cocky about those laws," Livengood cautioned. "A couple of hours in city jail may not be that big of a deal to my buddy Marv, but I can assure you that it's a major life event to the sort of lawn-mowing, credit card-carrying, baby-having middle class white people who signed up for the blockades. I was down here for the Summer of Mercy myself, and it put the political fear of God into me."

Reynolds asked Livengood what he was doing at the Summer of Mercy.

"I was working for Appel at the time, and I came back here to handle the press," Livengood said. "That's when I first met Ellie, that mute little mouse who was with Edna tonight. She was sitting in front of the clinic, crying her eyes out, and I stopped to see if she was OK, and she told me that babies were being murdered on the other side of the wall and that she couldn't stop it. I didn't know what to tell her."

Reynolds admitted she didn't know, either.

"On the whole, the protests were making me more pro-choice by the minute, and my boss was getting more pro-life by the minute," Livengood said. "I wound up going on TV and doing one of my rants, and that was the end of my career in Washington."

Reynolds said she admired his courage.

"I lost a perfectly good wife somewhere in there, too," Livengood said.

"She should have been proud," Reynolds said.

"I suppose she was, for a while," Livengood said. "But my less heroic attributes always come to the fore during periods of unemployment. I can't blame her. What the hell, all part of life's rich pageant, I guess."

Reynolds said she liked the band and didn't want to talk any more politics. Livengood happily agreed, and watched Reynolds start on another beer.

"Besides, I'm starting to kind of like you," Reynolds said. "For now, I will accept your half-hearted support of my right to live as I please."

"Here's to it," Livengood said.

Reynolds arrived at the Broadview Hotel in a drunken enough state that Livengood felt obliged to help her to her room. As Livengood jostled with the key, she said again that she kind of liked him.

"You're OK by me, too," Livengood said. "I liked the way you took on Edna. It's been a fun day."

"It was sweet of you to say what you did to Edna," Reynolds said, leaning against Livengood. "Such a country gentleman, you are. I thought it was really sexy the way you talked about your mother."

Livengood sighed with relief as the door opened. Reynolds fell across the bed, and suggested that Livengood join her there to continue their discussion.

"I have a strict rule against discussing politics in bed," Livengood said.

Reynolds said they didn't have to talk about politics, or talk at all.

"I have another strict rule about not getting into bed with women on a first date, especially when it wasn't even a date," Livengood said. "Especially when they've been drinking as much as you have."

Reynolds asked Livengood if he found her attractive.

"I think you're beautiful," Livengood said. "Ask me again when you're sober, and you'll find out."

With a poutiness that Livengood didn't expect from a woman who had confronted Edna Dimschmidt, Reynolds said that Livengood was too much a damned country gentleman. He bade her good night and went to his room.

Livengood slept well that night, as befits a man who has worked a long hard day and declined to take advantage of a woman's inebriated condition. He lusted for Rebecca Reynolds in his heart, however, and sleep did not come until he had committed the sin of Onan.

CHAPTER NINE

"The Things That Are God's"

With a violet and pink sunrise reflecting in the rearview mirror, Frankie Livengood and Rebecca Reynolds sped through the multiplying new developments of west Wichita toward the vast emptiness of western Kansas.

"When we get there, you'll probably be wondering where all the people are," Livengood said, between deep gulps from a large Styrofoam cup of black coffee. He waved the cup at the endless rows of newly built homes with backyard swing sets and satellite dishes. "That's where they all are. A lot of the small towns have just about emptied out over the past three generations or so, and much of the great Kansas dirt farmer diaspora wound up right here, or in places that look exactly like it."

Reynolds remarked how many places she had seen that looked just like it, and not only in Kansas. She asked what people could possibly be doing in such places.

"They came in search of jobs, a piece of land to call their own. You know, the usual," Livengood said. "All they brought with them were a few old faded photographs, some rusty guns and the lessons they learned in the old country church. Then they try to live the same settled and simple small town life that their parents and grandparents lived, only right here in the middle of what is more or less urban modernity, and that's pretty much how you wind up with scenes like the one we had at the debate last night."

With a harrumph, Reynolds said that much of the audience looked a bit too pasty to have been working hard on the farm recently.

"Most of them grew up in cities or suburbs," Livengood said, "but they were raised by people who lived in the towns and country. Or they were raised by people who were raised by people who lived in the towns and country. You don't get the country out of people in so few generations. The most vocal are always the third-generation, just like any immigrant group."

After a dissatisfied swig from her own cup of coffee—she was appalled to discover that coffee regular meant black coffee in Kansas—Reynolds said, "I would think their time could be better spent debating policies to revitalize the rural economy, so they can go back."

With a shrug, Livengood pointed out that the Harley Christianson for Governor campaign had proposed a plan to improve the state's rural health care. "These poor bastards have been paying up to half of every dollar they ever made into a system that promised to take care of them," Livengood said. "Even though it wasn't my dumb idea, we do need to keep that promise. Let 'em die off with some dignity, you know."

That didn't strike Reynolds as very visionary.

"So, what am I supposed to do?" Livengood said. "What's causing the de-population of the plains is bigger than the state government, you know. It's even bigger than the almighty feds. It's market forces, the most powerful forces in the universe, next to God. In some parts of the universe, market forces may actually be more powerful than God."

Looking at the vast fields growing emptier as they left the city behind, Reynolds asked if Kansas was one of those parts of the universe.

"I'd like to think it isn't God that emptied the prairies," Livengood said. "Some bright guys at the ag colleges and the big agribusiness companies came up with ways to get more and more wheat and meat out of fewer and fewer people, and that was that. So, all the good country people have to move to the outskirts of some dirty old big city and start acting like an uglier version of the people on TV. It's a shame, but there you have it."

Being from New York City, Reynolds wondered why the people didn't at least protest about it.

"Most of the kids would just as soon get an air-conditioned job and hang out at the mall, anyway, and most of the old folks are too damned tired to argue about it after a lifetime on tractors in the Kansas sun," Livengood said. "Besides, even if Kansans were to throw a protest, do you see any network TV cameras around to broadcast it?"

Looking out the window at a barn that dotted the landscape, Reynolds said she could see what he meant. Still, she wondered why there wasn't some sort of revolution afoot.

"These folks are too stubbornly individualistic for revolutions, and too smart to think that they're going to come up with anything better," Livengood said. "Kansas is a state of true belief, and we believe in progress and all that. Your average Kansan believes in himself, too, and his ability to survive any changes that come along without some government program. He believes in that more than he believes in a guy like me, and I think that's wise."

Rebecca agreed that, yes, that might be wise.

Livengood stopped at the World's Largest Hand Dug Well in Greensburg, where he insisted with a straight face to the flummoxed guide that he had dug a bigger well in his backyard, and then he showed Reynolds the hard tack biscuit that had been embossed in a

Civil War veteran's grave at the town cemetery. He introduced her to a philosophical old farmer who had transformed a field outside of Mullinville into a garden of steel sculpture political statements, and he took her to an ice cream parlor in downtown Garden City, where a group of giggling young Vietnamese women were the only visible evidence that it wasn't the 1950s. Mostly, they drove through miles and miles of empty road until Livengood's meeting in Holcomb.

At the Holcomb meeting, the talk was of pigs and cows. Reynolds had been stunned by the endless herds of cattle they had encountered in southwest Kansas, as well as the overpowering stench of their waste, but she was even more surprised to hear Frankie Livengood assure the small gathering of Christianson supporters that his candidate would agree to various regulations on the cattle and hog operations. The supporters, which conspicuously included people as young as 30 or so, seemed greatly pleased by his assurances.

"It's good politics," Livengood explained, sensing Reynolds' amazement that Harley was such an environmental candidate. "People are very split on the big cattle issue out here. Big cattle and hogs are good for the economy, bad for everything else. There's probably more people in the pro-cattle category—I haven't checked the polls lately—but they're going to split their votes among all the other candidates, anyway. Besides, folks are pro-life as all get-out out here in the west, and this is the only issue we've got for them, except for Harley being a western Kansan himself."

Reynolds asked if Harley, being a western Kansan, had any thoughts on the matter other than politics.

"Harley's pretty well sold on this idea," Livengood said. "Jane, my ex-wife—she's quite the environmental nut—worked him pretty hard about it."

CHAPTER NINE

Reynolds wondered if Livengood had any thoughts on the matter, aside from politics. Although Livengood seemed to spend most of his time in Johnson County, Topeka and Wichita, Reynolds had noticed that he seemed happiest among the emptiness and the slowness of this region. She wondered if that might be why he was willing to put aside his beloved free market principles for this improbable place.

"Naw. It's just that the older I get, the more pragmatic I get," Livengood said. "These crazy sons of bitches who actually live out here, they can come up with whatever arrangement they like for their little out-of-the-way chunk of the world, as far as I'm concerned. If they need the damned government to play a role, fine, just so long as they don't start a range war."

The only topic that the handful of Christianson supporters in Oakley wanted to talk about was water, and what would happen when the Great Lake-sized aquifer beneath them had all been sucked up. The meeting was short, due to everyone's willingness to admit their lack of ideas, but Livengood spent another hour swapping dirty jokes with a pair of old men. The sun was still shining brightly when Livengood finally drove out of town, so Reynolds was surprised to discover that it was already 8:30 at night.

Livengood apologized for the lateness of the hour as they sped west on Highway 40, and asked Reynolds if she would mind spending the night at his father's home near Weskan.

"What do you mean, your father?" Reynolds said. "I thought you didn't know where your father was."

"Of course I do," Livengood said. "He's been over by Weskan for years."

"I thought your father was some anonymous drunken sailor or something," Reynolds said. "I thought your mother was a hooker."

"What are you talking about? My father's probably never been within five-hundred miles of an ocean in his life, and I can assure you that he's never been any closer than that to a bottle of booze," Livengood said. "As for my mother being a hooker, well, all I'm going to say about my mother is that the woman was a saint. A damned saint. Where did you get such crazy ideas?"

"From you, damn it," Reynolds said. "You told me that yourself, at the debate, just last night."

"Oh, yeah. I told Edna that," Livengood said, beginning to remember. "I was just making a point."

"You lied to Edna Dimschmidt?"

"It wasn't a lie, it was a rhetorical device," Livengood said. "There are plenty of people out there who did have whore moms who got knocked up by drunken sailors, you know. So whatever my point was, it was still valid. It's just not as effective to say it happened to someone else."

Knowing that she would never have made a drunken pass at the son of a tee-totaling father and a sainted mother, Reynolds was angry.

"Don't take offense," Livengood said. "But I find that, as a general rule, women in particular tend to respond better to an argument when it's presented in a personal anecdote."

Just when Reynolds thought she couldn't get any angrier, Livengood drove up a long gravel drive to a small clapboard house, where a man, looking very much like an older and fitter version of Livengood himself, stood waving. Next to the house was a small clapboard church, with a sign proclaiming "Church of Jesus Christ the Saviour, Franklin Livengood, Sr., Pastor."

The two Franklin Livengoods embraced with requisite embarrassment, then shook hands. Livengood introduced his father to

Reynolds, identifying her as both a friend and a worker for the Women's Coalition for Reproductive Rights in New York City.

"New York City?" the pastor said to her, with the amazed cadence that Kansans always seemed to use when speaking those words. Shaking her hand enthusiastically, he added that, "You're a long, long way from home, young woman. We'll have to break out the best hospitality we have for you."

There was very little vegetarian fare and no alcohol among the best hospitality that Pastor Livengood had to offer, but he proved both an excellent cook and an accommodating host, and his friendliness and unassuming manner quickly overcame Reynolds' instinctive uneasiness with ministers. She even found herself laughing at some of the jokes that the two Livengoods shared over the dinner table.

After some talk of the campaign in the pastor's sparsely furnished living room, Livengood excused himself to take a walk. He did not feel comfortable smoking in front of his father, and his father appreciated that.

"He's a good man, my Frankie," the pastor said.

"Yes. I believe he is," Reynolds said. "I've only known him the past two days, but they've been long days."

The pastor asked once again if he could provide anything for Reynolds, perhaps some more ice for her tea, and she gratefully declined. Not knowing how else to fill the momentary silence that followed, Reynolds asked the pastor's opinion of Harley Christianson.

"Mr. Christianson is also a good man," the pastor said, "and in some ways that Frankie is not. I met Mr. Christianson at a Knights of Columbus meeting, and he seems a committed Christian."

"Is that important?" Reynolds asked, slightly more curiously than accusatorily.

"It's important that public officials be of strong character, certainly, because the temptations of office are great," the pastor said. "In my experience, the sort of commitment that Mr. Christianson seems to have can forge a very honorable character. Good people seem to come from many faiths. I'm wary of granting power to a man who doesn't believe I have God-given rights, but I suppose good people can serve government without faith at all."

The answer seemed fair enough to Reynolds, and ample permission to probe the pastor's political beliefs more thoroughly. She asked if the pastor was generally in agreement with his son on the issues of the day.

"I suppose so," the pastor said. "I must confess that I don't follow the issues of the day very closely, just what I read in the rather skimpy newspapers they publish in this part of the world. I try to concern myself mostly with the things that are God's. The things that are Caesar's, I trust to Frankie."

Reynolds, having assumed that most Kansas clergymen were avid about the issues of the day, showed surprise.

"That's a reference to the Gospels of Matthew, Mark and Luke," the pastor said, assuming that most Ivy League graduates aren't familiar with the Bible. "It tells of how the Pharisees tried to trick Jesus into their political struggle with the Romans. They asked if they should pay taxes, and He pointed out that the coins they were expected to pay had Caesar's name and face. 'Render unto Caesar the things that are Caesar's, and unto God the things that are God's,' He told them. I often use those very words to ward off political discussions, myself, and it usually works."

It didn't work with Reynolds, who found that she was enjoying the conversation too much to stop at such a hint. She asked if the pastor regarded the scripture as a divine endorsement of a separation of church and state.

"Not in the sense that you may mean," the pastor said. "These days, people believe in separation of church and state because they think the latter is so terribly important that it shouldn't be tainted by the silly superstitions of the former. I believe that any man or woman's personal relationship with God is of such paramount importance that the silly superstitions of government shouldn't be allowed to interfere with it."

Reynolds congratulated the pastor on being so moderate, and he laughed.

"Next you'll be accusing me of being liberal, and I'll wind up losing another church," the pastor said. "I can assure you that mine is a very extreme, and extremely traditional theology. I preach the virgin birth of Christ, His sinless life, His sacrifice on the cross, His resurrection and its promise of salvation—all the things that put that skeptical look on your face. I'm proud to preach it all."

Embarrassed by the skeptical look on her face, Reynolds apologized.

"I noticed that you didn't flinch at the mention of the Women's Coalition for Reproductive Rights," Reynolds said, leaning toward the pastor. "Frankly, some of the Christians I've met have not been so friendly."

"It's a new and not at all improved theology that requires one to be rude to a guest," the pastor said. "Besides, I have no quarrel with your work. As I understand it, you're not interested in forcing anyone to have an abortion."

Surprised, Reynolds asked if Pastor Livengood considered abortion a sin.

"Indeed I do," the pastor said. "You may find this laughably unfashionable, but I also consider homosexuality a sin, as well as pre-marital sex and pornography and drugs and divorce and a host of other things that you are legally entitled to do. I'll preach against them from the pulpit as long as I can, and many times I've sat up all night trying to help someone resist the temptation to exercise these rights, but I don't charge the government with the responsibility of eliminating sin, and I won't forcibly interfere with your right to choose these things."

"Why not?" Reynolds asked. "If these things are bad—if you have it on divine authority that they are—why should I be able to choose them? Wouldn't you be doing me a favor by preventing me from choosing these sins?"

"Not at all," the pastor said. "It wouldn't save your soul one little bit."

This line of argument had never come up in any of Reynolds' symposia, where souls rarely figured in the discussion, and the pastor noticed that skeptical look on her face again.

"There's room to think about the soul on the plains, Miss Reynolds, and time, too," the pastor said. "That's why we have so many Christians here, I think, and so many ax murderers. One often finds himself alone with his soul out here, and it can be very disquieting."

After just two days on the prairie, alone with her soul and Frankie Livengood, Reynolds could nod knowingly.

"I do believe we have a soul. And I believe that the role of the church is to save as many of them as we can," the pastor said. "But one saves his or her soul by an act of his or her free will. One cannot impose salvation on another. That idea has been tried, and the results did not do credit to Jesus Christ."

"What about the unborn babies?" Reynolds asked, stunned by the quickness with which she had picked up the local lingo. "I mean, what about the argument that a fetus has a soul, so abortion should be illegal?"

The pastor looked out at the endless blackness beyond his front window, slid a few comfortable inches into his chair, and shrugged his shoulders.

"That's a difficult issue for me," the pastor said.

After a long pause, during which she also examined the darkness beyond the window, Reynolds said she could well understand.

"I believe in the inerrancy of the Bible, Miss Reynolds, but not the inerrancy of my understanding of it," the pastor said. "I minister to the aging farmers and farm wives that we have out here, and abortion, homosexuality and all the other hot political issues don't come up much. Here, it's mostly the same old problems people have had since the beginning of time. Living in poverty with dignity, aging without bitterness, facing death with faith, finding God in loneliness. There's nothing the government can do about these things, nothing that modern society can do. It takes a preacher and a church and plenty of hard work."

Reynolds surprised herself by complimenting the pastor on a life well lived.

"It's been gratifying for me," the pastor said. "I know how hard it was for Frankie, though. We moved all over the state of Kansas when he was a boy, from small town to big city to yet another small town, and he never knew any financial security. And him without a mother."

It took several seconds of hemming and hawing to find the words, but there was no way that Reynolds wasn't going to ask about Mrs. Livengood. The pastor smiled faintly before he spoke.

"She was a wonderful woman," he said. "Kind, loving, very intelligent, and so very beautiful. I always imagined myself with a kind, loving and intelligent woman, but even in my boyish dreams I never allowed myself to wish for such a beautiful woman. She passed away shortly after Frankie was born."

An intense quietness pervaded the room, and both Reynolds and the pastor examined the darkness beyond the window. After several moments, Reynolds offered her sympathies.

"Thank you," the pastor said. "The doctors had warned her that the pregnancy would be difficult. They warned her of the risk."

Having carefully considered the wording of her question, Reynolds asked if Kansas law at the time would have allowed Mrs. Livengood to terminate the pregnancy.

"I don't know," the pastor said, his expression indicating that he was considering the question for the first time. "I remember the doctor implying that he was willing to perform an abortion, but I really don't know if that was because of the law, or because he thought it was kinder to put it that way. In any case, Sarah insisted on carrying the pregnancy to term. She was adamant."

Many years of talking about abortion had not provided Reynolds with anything to say. The pastor smiled again to ease her discomfort.

"I have Frankie," the pastor said. "I'm very proud of him, of the man that he is and the work that he does. If you'll forgive me a bit of professional pride, it does somehow seem a step down from God's work, but there's no denying that Caesar's work needs to be done, too."

Reynolds smiled, and the pastor smiled back.

"I've always loved him with all my heart, and I think he knows that," the pastor said. "I hope it does him some good. He's a good man, my Frankie, but his soul is troubled. He's always seemed to feel, well, as the book of Isaiah puts it, a 'transgressor from the womb.' "

Somehow, the ensuing silence did not seem awkward to Reynolds. She leaned forward and squeezed the pastor's hand. He smiled again.

"It's OK," the pastor said. "It was her choice."

Reynolds and the pastor had moved on to more comfortably trivial topics by the time Livengood returned, bearing cola and a fresh bag of ice from the town's sole convenience store. He was struck by the apparent friendship that had occurred between his father and Reynolds, and he was worried.

"Fathers always have a knack of revealing the most embarrassing information about their sons, especially to women," Livengood said to Reynolds, after his father had gone to bed. "What did he tell you?"

"He told me that you have a troubled soul."

"Oh, that," Livengood said. "Thank God he didn't mention that I used to wet the bed."

Livengood draped a sheet over the couch, while Reynolds whispered a salacious joke about soothing his soul. She retired to a small guest room containing nothing but a bed, nightstand and picture of Jesus. She slept soundly, in spite of the quiet and stillness of the prairie night.

The drive back to Topeka would take up much of the next day, and Livengood was eager to visit both Mount Sunflower and the Garden of Eden, so he and Reynolds left his father's home as early as coffee could make possible. The morning was still tolerably warm, so Reynolds allowed Livengood to put the car's top down before they headed north on the county road.

Ancient country music poured from the car's radio, while Livengood warbled along in his lowest voice and tapped the steering wheel as he drove. Reynolds tried to imagine Livengood in New York City, and asked how he fared there.

"On the whole, I liked it fine," Livengood said. "I was young, I was making decent money for someone so young, and there was plenty to do. I was overwhelmed, to tell you the truth, by how much there was to do in that city. Altogether too much for a nice young Kansas Christian to do, if you know what I mean."

Reynolds knew exactly what he meant. She asked why he left.

"It's hard to say," Livengood said. "A lot of reasons, I guess. For one thing, for all you hear about the cuisine, I could never find a decent chicken fried steak. And for all you hear about the culture, I could never find a bar with Bob Wills on the jukebox."

Having lived more or less happily without chicken fried steaks and Bob Wills music, Reynolds didn't know what he meant. She asked Livengood to be serious.

"Seriously," he said, "there was a lot I didn't like about it. Some of it was just different from what I'm used to, I admit, but some of it, well, God help anyone who does get used to it. Listen, I was raised better than to put down someone's home, but with all due respect, there was too much trash on the streets. Too many windows broken out. Too much graffiti. Too many panhandlers and hookers and scary-looking kids running around. Too much noise. Too much government. The whole damn city, when you get right down to it, was too damn much for this Kansas boy."

Reynolds looked forward at the long straight road that bisected the wide brown prairie, found it to be too damn little, and said, "So, you came back here?"

"I got to talking about it one night with Wilbur Philip," Livengood said. "He was with the same group—in fact, he got me the job—and we spent half the night talking about how you would even start on a job like that city. I can still remember what Wilbur wound up saying. He told me, 'Frankie, the best thing you can do is get back to Kansas, and make sure it doesn't get this fucked up.' "

Reynolds suggested that perhaps Livengood and Wilbur just couldn't hack it.

"Wilbur could. He still lives there, and just came back for this job," Livengood said. "As for me, you may be right. Maybe I just couldn't hack the big city, and came back home because the rents are cheap, the dress code is lax, the competition is second-rate and the living is easy. But what the hell. Folks here need politics, too, and I'm happy to do it for them. It would be a hell of a country if everybody tried to the run the federal government, that's for damn sure."

A sign pointed toward Mt. Sunflower, and Livengood followed its directions along a dirt road. Searching in vain for a mountain among the gentle hills of grass, Reynolds asked, "What the hell is a Mt. Sunflower?" Livengood explained that Kansas, beginning just west of Wichita, sloped imperceptibly upwards toward the west at a rate of about eight feet per mile. Mt. Sunflower, being the highest slope on the border with Colorado, was therefore the highest point in the state. After a few more miles of increasingly rough road, the Camaro pulled up to a steel sunflower sculpture that marked the spot.

Livengood got out of the car and stretched his arms, heaving a satisfied sigh and seeming to exult in the place. Reynolds got out of the car with her arms folded, and anxiously scanned the horizon for a sign of human habitation, finding nothing but grass and sky. She asked why Livengood chose to be second-rate and live easily here, of all places.

"Choose? Who chooses?" Livengood said. "God made me for this place. He made this place for me."

Livengood stretched his arm and pointed toward the rising sun, then traced the hazy line of the horizon with his index finger, spinning slowly round and back to where he'd started from.

"Just look at this," Livengood said. "Land, air and a great lake of water below us. You can do whatever you want here."

Taking her own look around, Reynolds concluded that there was nothing at all to do here.

"Why do you need something to do, when you can do whatever you want? It's a newer garden of creation, with ample space for great deeds or small pleasures," Livengood said, spinning around again for another look at the miles and miles of prairie. Stopping, he declared it a tabula rasa.

Taking another look around for herself, seeing no other people for miles and miles, Reynolds realized that she could, indeed, do anything in this place.

So, she walked behind Livengood and put her arms around him. She kissed his ear, unbuckled his belt, then spun him around forcefully and pressed her wet mouth against his startled face. Livengood responded quickly, and removed her clothing with the same urgent dispatch with which she removed his. Livengood pulled an Army surplus blanket from the trunk of the car and threw it across the grass, then was pulled down onto it by Reynolds. A short time later, as a pair of disinterested Herefords looked on, Livengood and Reynolds both reached what he would later jokingly call "the highest point in Kansas."

Two and a half hours later, Livengood and Reynolds were still naked in the back seat of the Camaro, holding one another and sharing unexpectedly tender words. As Reynolds began to clothe herself, Livengood leaned over the front seat and began twisting the radio knob in search of a weather forecast.

"What is with you and the weather?" Reynolds asked. "All of you Kansans seem to have an unusual fondness for it as a topic of conversation, but you're downright weird about it."

"That's because the weather hasn't tried to kill you yet," Livengood said. "The heat's tried to kill me, the cold's tried to kill me, and so has flooding and drought and snow and hail and ice and more lightning than you've ever seen in your life. I've taken a direct hit from an F-4 tornado, and I don't mind telling you that it put the fear of God in me."

Reynolds laughed and cracked an obligatory *Wizard of Oz* joke. She stopped laughing when Livengood tuned in an announcement that eastern Colorado and western Kansas were under a tornado watch. Livengood got out of the car and looked intently toward the west, then declared that, "I don't like the look of those clouds."

Reynolds looked and saw an immense tower of eerily dark cloud, lit occasionally by eruptions of lightning, looming on the horizon. The radio announced a tornado warning for Colorado's Kit Carson County, which Livengood said was just a few hundred yards to the west, and they both hurriedly dressed.

Livengood slammed the accelerator on the Camaro and sent dirt flying as he sped down the road, with Reynolds checking a map for the town where the radio said a tornado had been spotted, silently calculating how long it would take to arrive. As he sped eastbound on Highway 40, Livengood continued to watch the storm building angrily in his rearview mirror.

The clouds chased them all the way to Topeka, forcing Livengood to the cancel his planned stop at the Garden of Eden.

CHAPTER TEN

"The Character Question"

Frankie Livengood was on a roll. The weather was as hot and dry as Livengood liked it, he was regularly having sex with a tall, slender, slightly bucktoothed woman who had that big city look, and the poll numbers showed his candidate moving into position for an upset that would make him a legend of Kansas politics.

Then came the phone call from Dan Dorsey of the Sunflower News Service. He was calling to ask if Livengood was aware that Will Schnitzle, star of the Christianson campaign's television commercials, was the Supreme Commandant General of something called The First Regimental Kansas Free Citizen Militia Brigade.

After an uncharacteristic amount of hemming and hawing and stammering, Livengood admitted that no, he was not aware of that fact. Dorsey then asked if Christianson was aware of Schnitzle's involvement with a militia, and Livengood further hemmed and hawed before admitting that he did not know. Livengood asked when Dorsey intended to run the story.

"We're sending it out tonight," Dorsey said. "As a matter of fact, I'm coming up on deadline right now."

Livengood asked if there was any possibility that the story might wait another day.

"I'd love to cut you some slack, Frankie, but I can't," Dorsey said. "I've heard that both *The Star* and *The Eagle* are prowling around in Piquant, and I can't let my papers get scooped."

"Can you give me an hour?" Livengood asked.

Something in the sound of Livengood's voice caused Dorsey to reluctantly agree, but he emphasized, "One hour, Frankie," before hanging up. Livengood immediately phoned Christianson, who was just sitting down to a plate of franks and beans in Piquant.

"Were you aware that Will Schnitzle is the Supreme Commandant General of something called The First Regimental Kansas Free Citizen Militia Brigade?" Livengood said, trying not to sound panicked and doing a poor job of it.

"No, I wasn't," Christianson said, with a calm that suggested he didn't understand the significance of the question.

"Oh, well, thank God for that," Livengood said.

"How come?" Christianson said.

"Because Dan Dorsey's about to break a story that Will's some kind of militia nut," Livengood said. "At least we'll be able to say you didn't know it."

With a laugh that suggested he still didn't understand the significance of the situation, Christianson said, "Oh, I knew he was some kind of militia nut, all right. I just didn't know what he called himself, or what he called that bunch of idiots he runs around with."

There was a brief pause while Livengood banged his head against his desk, then Livengood said, "Awright, awright, don't panic. You had heard that Will was involved in some kind of group—right?—but you had no direct knowledge of it."

"But of course I did," Christianson said, sounding not at all panicked, but slightly eager to get back to his franks and beans. "Hell, I drove Will out to their crazy-ass shooting sessions a couple of times, when his pickup was on the blink."

Christianson could hear the sound of Livengood's head banging against the desk a few more times, then Livengood's voice saying, "OK, OK, you may have had direct knowledge of Will exercising his constitutional rights to bear arms and assemble peaceably and all that crap, but at least we can say that you had no knowledge of any intention on Will's part to undermine the government—right? We can say that, can't we?"

"Well now, I wouldn't exactly say that," Christianson said. "Heck, Will was all the time talkin' about overthrowin' the government and killin' all the traitors and such. I mean, he'd go on and on about it, to where you couldn't get him to shut up. From what he told me, that was what all that running around in the fields and shooting at things was all about, getting ready for the big revolution and such."

After a couple more bangs of his head against the desk, Livengood said, "This is bad, Harley. Very bad. We're trying to convince a sizeable plurality of voters in this state, mostly middle-class urban white collar types, that you're a very reasonable guy. Now, I happen to know that you're a reasonable type of guy, but how the hell would I know that if I didn't know you, and all I did know was that the star of the television commercial you've been running every night on the six o'clock news for the past two months is Supreme Nutcase of the First Kansas Loony Brigade?"

Harley allowed that Livengood posed an interesting question, but asked to be excused from the discussion because his franks and beans were getting cold.

"But Harley," Livengood said, pleadingly, "what the hell am I going to tell Dorsey? He's sending this story out to all of his papers in less than an hour."

"Tell him it ain't no biggie," Harley said. "Honestly, Frankie, Will and his buddies are just a bunch of big old boys who still like to run around in the fields and shoot things up. It strikes me as damned silly, but what's it hurt? Will's an old buddy of mine and all, but he don't know his ass from an inner tube with wrinkles painted on it, and I just don't fret much that he's going to overthrow the government of the United States of America."

Livengood's head hurt too much for any more banging of it against the desk, but he did give his forehead a stinging slap before saying, "This is very bad, Harley. Very bad. We're going to need a better story for this."

"You're good at that story stuff, Frankie, but I don't want you telling Mr. Dorsey any lies about me not knowing any of this," Harley said. "I know you'll handle it fine. Now if you don't mind, Christy's whipped up some franks and beans that are starting to get cold. Call me back after supper, and we'll chat some more about this if you want."

Livengood gave his head one final bang against the desk, then called Dorsey.

"Your story is going to kill us, old friend," Livengood said.

"Most likely," Dorsey said. "You're going to need a damn good quote in this story. You got it?"

"I got jack shit," Livengood said.

"You don't want that in the story, do you?"

"I don't want you to run the story."

"You know I can't do that, Frankie. Listen, I'm not happy about having Appel for governor, and Harley seems like a good guy, and you know I love you, but I can't do that."

"Yeah, yeah, I know. I still love you, too, you fat bastard, but you've got to do me one favor. Don't say we declined to comment. Say that we were unavailable for comment."

"Aw, Frankie, don't ask that," Dorsey said. "You're talking to me right now. You're available. You've never asked to me print anything untrue before. So please, don't ask me now."

"I'm available, sure," Livengood said. "But I'm not available for *comment*, do you see? I've got nothing to say right now, so even though you're talking to me, I'm not available to *comment.* Can't you give me just this one tiny line? When we come up with our response, you get it first, I swear. We'll give up a night of TV so you can have it first. Please? You always said I was like the son you never had."

"I've never said any such thing, and you know damn good and well I've got a son," Dorsey said. "But what the hell. Dan Jr.'s an ungrateful little bastard, and at least I know you'll kiss my butt for this. As far as I'm concerned, you were unavailable for comment. But you'd damned well better call me tomorrow, well before deadline, with your side of this shit, for your sake as well as mine."

Despite Livengood's deep-seated fear of flying, he was on a chartered plane to Piquant early the next morning. After a jarring landing on the rugged stretch of field that served as the county airport, and an unexpectedly complicated negotiation for the aging white van that was the local rental car fleet, Livengood drove hurriedly to the Christianson farmhouse. He arrived in time for breakfast, and spoke excitedly over a plate filled with pancakes, eggs and link sausage.

"Any association with a militia group is going to kill us," Livengood said. "We've got to dis-associate ourselves. That's all there is to it."

"But Frankie, I'm not a member of that bunch of idiots," Harley said, sipping his coffee with a nonchalance that suggested he still didn't understand the significance of Dorsey's story. "I never was associated with them at all."

"But their Supreme Commandant General is the star of your television campaign," Livengood said. "That's associated as all get-out."

"Well, hell, Frankie, that was your idea," Harley said. "I tried to talk you out of putting that story on TV."

Livengood paused to swallow a mouthful of pancakes, noticing despite the distractions that they really were quite delicious, then said, "If you wanted to talk me out of it, you only needed to mention that Schnitzle is a militia nut. Why didn't you tell me?"

"It hardly seemed worth mentioning," Harley said. "Like I keep saying, they're just a bunch of old kids running around the woods shooting things. Come pheasant season, the fields will be full of them."

"Damn it, Harley, we're not going to win any votes in Kansas by comparing militia nuts to pheasant hunters. We've got to dis-associate ourselves from Schnitzle and these guys with some strong statements."

Harley was enjoying his breakfast, and shrugged as he chewed. After a large swallow he said, "Well, yeah, sure. I'm not in favor of Will Schnitzle overthrowing the government, and I don't mind saying so. Just point the cameras at me, and I'll say it."

"That's not good enough, Harley. You've got to say that you weren't aware of Schnitzle's anti-government intentions until this story, and that you'll no longer have anything to do with him. You've got to denounce this guy like crazy, and say that the only reason you ever had anything to do with him was on account of you saving his life while being a war hero."

Harley shook his head and bit into a forkful of sausage. After some leisurely mastication, he told Livengood, "No way. First off, it isn't true that I didn't know what he was hoping to do, and I'm not going to start lying to folks at this late date in my life just to be governor. Secondly, Will's been a buddy of mine since we were kids, and I'm not going to turn my back on him just to be governor. People deserve an explanation for all this, sure enough, and I don't mind telling them that Will's a sort of nutty guy who's harmless enough and with a good heart, but that's it. I'm going to own up to giving an old friend a ride to the field where he likes to run around and shoot things, and if the people of Kansas figure that that disqualifies me from being governor, well then, that's just fine by me. Maybe I never did want to be governor too bad in the first place."

Something about Harley's expression made clear that further efforts to change his mind would be pointless, so Livengood ate his breakfast. Halfway through the pancakes he had resigned himself to losing the election, but by the time he swallowed the last bite of sausage he had regained some hope that Harley's honesty may prove the best policy after all.

"That's some mighty fine cooking, Mrs. Christianson," Livengood said, provoking a smile from her worried face. "I'll tell you what we're going to do, Harley. You get on the phone with Dan Dorsey, talk to him real plain like you've done with me, then take Mrs. Christianson and Tyrone out on a long drive where the TV reporters can't get to you. I'll be unavailable myself for the rest of the day, too, because I promised Dorsey he'd get our side of the story before everyone else. The TV people will kill us on the evening news tonight, but what the hell. You get up tomorrow morning and talk with everyone again, real plain again, and we'll see how it goes. If the people of Kansas figure this disqualifies you from being governor, I reckon that's fine with me, too. Maybe I never wanted to be the governor's chief of staff all that much, anyway."

The plane ride back to Topeka would have terrified the most foolhardy of daredevils, much less a sensible acrophobic such as Frankie Livengood. After taking off in an aging single-engine plane from a landing strip pocked with prairie dog holes, Livengood experienced a profound sense of terror when the plane encountered the huge black clouds of a storm system that had unexpectedly developed over Topeka.

"Hmmm," said the pilot, turning to Livengood. "Just how important is it for you to be in Topeka?"

"Pretty damned important," Livengood said, just as the cloud lit up with a blinding flash of lightning. "But not really. I mean, we could turn around and get the hell out of here if you want."

"Hmmm," said the pilot. "By the time we get this puppy turned around, that storm'll probably have caught up to us. We may be just as well off trying to land it. What do you say?"

Livengood had no confidence whatsoever in his own opinions regarding aviation, and little more confidence in any pilot who would ask him about such matters, but he instructed the pilot to make a decision. The pilot, who had a discomfortingly young face behind his mirrored sunglasses, said, "We're heading down, then. Hang on tight."

Livengood buckled his seat belt and tightly gripped the leather strap dangling beside the door. The plane began to bounce up and down, then the winds began to push it from side to side. The noonday sky had turned black, and the darkness was interrupted by frequent flashes of lightning bolts that seemed to shoot right at the plane. Livengood used the split seconds of illumination to study the face of his pilot.

Surely, Livengood figured, the pilot wouldn't be able to maintain such a carefree attitude if the danger were as severe as Livengood assumed.

"Pretty bad storm, huh?" Livengood asked.

"I seen worse," the pilot said.

Another gust of wind pushed the plane from an eastward to a northward direction, and then the plane dropped a distance that seemed about a hundred yards.

"I'll tell you what," Livengood said. "This seems like a pretty bad storm to me."

"I seen worse," the pilot said. "Plenty of times."

Sirens were blaring when the plane finally landed at the Topeka airport, and the frantic voice from the control tower screamed over the radio that Livengood and the pilot were to take underground shelter in the airport as soon as possible. Livengood had become so jittery from the flight that he was unable to unlatch his seat belt or open his door, but the pilot calmly helped Livengood extricate himself from the seat belt, then leaned over and pulled the latch on the passenger door.

"Some storm, huh?" the pilot said.

"I'd say so," Livengood said.

"Worst I ever seen," the pilot said.

The pilot let loose with a hearty "wooh," and shook his head as he ran through a few post-flight routines, commenting in a low tone that he felt lucky to have survived such a storm in such a flimsy plane.

"I thought you'd seen worse," Livengood said. "I thought you'd seen worse lots of times."

"Hell no," the pilot said. "And I hope to never see one like that ever again. Not from the air, at any rate."

Before Livengood began a full gallop toward the airport's underground shelter, he paused to thank the pilot for his complete lack of candor.

The entire staff of the Christianson for Governor campaign, along with Mark Stark, Rebecca Reynolds and Jane Hutchinson, gathered the next morning at the headquarters to watch the noonday television news broadcasts, which were dominated by coverage of Harley Christianson's media conference regarding Will Schnitzle and

The First Regimental Kansas Free Citizens Brigade. It marked the first time that Livengood's ex-wife and current paramour had met, and Livengood was so preoccupied with the campaign that he didn't notice their conspicuous discomfort.

Dan Dorsey's exclusive interview with Christianson had run in the morning editions of most of the Sunflower News Service's client papers, and Livengood was pleased with the tone of the article. Christianson was given a fair chance to state his side of the story, and had done well. Livengood held firmly to a hope that Christianson would be as persuasive in addressing the much larger audience of television viewers.

The news conference took place in the yard of Christianson's farmhouse. Realizing that Christianson's only hope was complete honesty, Livengood had stayed in Topeka.

All three Topeka stations led their broadcasts with up to three full minutes of the news conference, one of the rare occasions during the campaign when a political story was given such prominent play on television, and Livengood was relieved that Christianson's own words filled most of the time. Christianson's performance was, as even Mark Stark and Rebecca Reynolds agreed, an inspiring bit of heartfelt hokum.

"Now, I'm not going to stand up here and denounce my old friend Will Schnitzle, any more than any of you would denounce any of your old friends," Christianson said. "But I'm sure as heck going to disagree with some of his ideas, just as I'm sure all of you would disagree with some of your friends' ideas."

Livengood would have preferred to have the statement broadcast in its entirety, but he was grateful that such rustic sound bites were included on each of the stations. He didn't even mind when Christianson explained that the Schnitzle ads had run because "some smart folks back in Topeka talked me into it. I would have just as soon skipped all that Vietnam War business in the first place. I didn't much care for it over there, to tell you the truth." The televised image of handsome Harley Christianson, standing in front of the honest Kansas farmhouse, combined with his plain-spoken appeals to friendship and patriotism, proved so persuasive that even the reporters were offering kind comments. One of the news anchors, during his supposedly unrehearsed conversation with the reporter at the conference, said that, "It looks like this story may have blown over."

The rest of the staff was jubilant, but Livengood remained nervous. His mood lightened with a couple of bottles of beer, which Ed Walton had kept on hand for emergencies, and Livengood reflected between sips that Walton was well worth the big bucks he was being paid. Livengood eventually joined in the party that had spontaneously erupted at the headquarters.

"It looks like this story may have blown over," Darla said.

"I think we're in the clear on this one," Walton said.

"That should be the end of that," Ellen Winston said.

"We sure as hell dodged a bullet this time," Philip said.

Even Mark Stark was swept up in the good feeling, going so far as to hug Darla Morland and offer a toast.

"To Harley Christianson, and his innovative strategy of loyalty to his friends and loyalty to the truth," Stark said. "May it carry him to victory, from Strawberry Hill to Mount Sunflower!"

Everyone in the room raised a bottle to the toast—a bottle of Diet Coke, in Darla's case—and chanted, "Victory! From Strawberry Hill to Mount Sunflower!"

Jane Hutchinson, whose two bottles of beer had exceeded her annual limit for alcohol consumption, winked knowingly at Livengood as she raised her glass, and said, "And here's to Mount Sunflower! Do you remember the highest point in Kansas?"

Livengood smiled knowingly in return, but only for the brief second it took until he noticed Rebecca Reynold's glare.

Reynolds was aggressively quiet at dinner that evening, and Livengood resigned himself to the likelihood that there would be no desserts of any sort.

"Is there anything wrong?" Livengood asked, figuring that the evening was shot, anyway.

"No," Reynolds said, with a sharpness that belied the answer.

"I thought there might be something wrong," Livengood said.

"Why should there be anything wrong?" Reynolds asked.

"I don't know," Livengood said, with complete honesty.

"You fucked her at Mount Sunflower, didn't you?" Reynolds said.

"Who?" Livengood said.

"What do you mean, *who*?" Reynolds said. "Just how many women have you fucked on that goddamned hill?"

Livengood, who was admittedly quite stupid about these kinds of things, had to contemplate the answer a moment, realizing full well that Reynolds had heard his ex-wife's joke and correctly inferred its meaning. He marveled at how women pick up on such things.

Reynolds' apparent jealousy stunned Livengood, who had expected her to be modernly insouciant about such matters as ex-wives and past sex acts, and sophisticatedly non-committal about their relationship. That was the appeal of that big city look, after all.

Livengood certainly never expected that anyone would develop true romantic feelings for him, and he was rendered speechless by the creeping realization that Reynolds seemed to be doing just that. Further complicating a situation already well beyond Livengood's ken, he was experiencing unsettling feelings of his own.

"Jesus, Frankie," Reynolds said. "You even used the same damn joke."

The time was not yet nine o'clock, so Livengood called Harley Christianson for yet another conversation about the militia scandal.

"I think it went pretty good," Harley said. "That's what all the folks around here are telling me, at any rate."

"Yeah, it went well," Livengood said. "I don't think we lost much, but I'm still afraid that we lost some."

"Ah, what the hell," Harley said. "I told the truth. What else could I do?"

Livengood was still struggling for an answer to that question, and admitted that he hadn't yet thought of one.

"The truth is powerful medicine, Harley, sure enough," Livengood said. "But I'm telling, you, it's no panacea. It's no vaccine against a malicious rumor, and it can't cure people of what they want to believe."

"So I'll ask you again," Harley said. "What else could I do?"

Livengood still didn't have answer for that question, except to tell Harley that, "We need Appel to do something stupid. A million attack ads on him aren't going to make the public forget that you blew up that federal building down in OKC trying to overthrow the government with some militia brigade. We're just going to have to count on Appel doing something very, very stupid."

Congressman Jonathan Appel had coasted to re-election in his last two races for the United States House of Representatives, and was outspokenly annoyed about the necessity of actual campaigning in his bid for governor of Kansas. He complained about it frequently to Willie Schlag, the pimple-faced son-of-a-contributor who drove Appel to the far-flung events he was required to attend.

"Goddamn this state is big," Appel said, as their van barreled along Highway 54 toward a senior citizens' center in Pratt. "What the hell is all this land *for*, anyway?"

Willie Schlag didn't know the answer to Appel's question, but he did know that he wasn't expected to express an opinion in any case.

"Goddamn," Appel said, furiously twisting the knob on the radio and finding only country music, farm reports and right-wing rants. "Can't even get any smooth jazz out here in the middle of all this damn flat land. What the hell is it all for, anyway?"

Jonathan Appel had been raised on the harsh ground of western Kansas by a stern father and a sterner mother who had attempted to teach him austerity, humility and hard work, but eight years in Congress had undone all of their efforts. He had become accustomed to luxury, deference from others, and especially ease of transportation, so much so that he was no longer fit for long rides in a bumpy van under Kansas' searing summer sun. By the time Schlag pulled into the parking lot of the senior citizens' center, Appel was in a profoundly sour mood.

"About goddamn time," Appel said. "Park this sumbitch right here in front, and let's find a Coke machine."

Appel was already out of the van and checking his hair in the rearview mirror when Schlag noticed that they had parked in a space reserved for handicapped drivers. Schlag stepped out of the van, mustered his courage to speak, and informed Appel of the violation.

"Fuck the handicapped," Appel said. "Goddamned cripples. What the hell are *they* for?"

"But it's illegal, sir," Schlag said, slipping into a pubescent falsetto for the final word.

"Damn it, boy, don't you tell me what's illegal," Appel said. "I'm a Congressman. I make the damned law. Now let's get in there and kiss some geezer ass."

Meanwhile, Benny Barbosa, who had been checking the color focus of his video camera against the glaring white of Appel's van, began capturing the Congressman's arrival on tape. Barbosa had been assigned by his Wichita television station to shoot some footage for a profile of Appel, and wasn't expected to bring back anything but standard stump speech fare, so he was particularly delighted by what he saw unfolding through his viewfinder.

"Check it out, Chad," Barbosa said to his reporter, who was looking in the rearview mirror of their sport utility vehicle and straightening his silk tie.

"Check what out?" said Chad Skyler.

"Appel's parked in a handicapped space," Barbosa said.

"So what?" Skyler said.

"What do you mean, 'So what?' " Benny said. "It's fucking illegal. We just caught a Congressman breaking the law, on tape, and you're asking, 'So what?' What the hell kind of reporter are you, anyway? This dog shit assignment of yours has just turned into the lead story of the newscast, of the whole campaign for that matter, and you're asking me, 'So what?' Where the hell do they get you guys, anyway?"

Skyler was so much better dressed than the slovenly Barbosa that he would not dignify the question with an answer. He did, however, ask if Barbosa was sure about parking in a handicapped space being illegal.

"Of course it is, dumbshit," Barbosa said.

"Well, maybe Appel doesn't know that," Skyler said.

"Of course he does, dumbshit," Barbosa said.

"Well, maybe he didn't know it was a handicapped space," Skyler said.

"Of course he did, dumbshit," Barbosa said. "I taped the kid pointing at the sign, and Appel telling him to park there anyway."

"We don't know what he said."

"Well then, get a damned lip reader."

"Yeah, right," Skyler said. "That'll work."

"Listen, dumbshit," Barbosa said. "I'm not driving all the way out here and back for stock footage when we've got the biggest story of the campaign right here on tape. You're going to confront him about this, or I'll do it myself and take all the credit for a change, instead of none."

As reluctant as Skyler was to confront a real Congressman, he was even less willing to let a cameraman take all the credit for a big story. After quizzing Barbosa further about handicapped spaces, he charged toward the Congressman, brandishing a microphone. Catching the Congressman at the door, he asked, "Why, sir, did you violate the law, and the rights of our differently-abled citizens, by parking in this clearly marked handicapped space?"

Barbosa was grinning behind his camera as Appel stammered away in an obvious attempt to stall for time. Barbosa felt almost omnipotent at that moment, armed with a weapon so powerful that he could not only make a Congressman seem a pathetic fool, he could even make Chad Skyler seem a crusading reporter.

"Handicapped space?" Appel said, doing a creditable job of looking perplexed. "Whatever do you mean?"

"That is your van, sir," Skyler said, pointing toward the vehicle with an indignant flourish worthy of a Shakespearean tragedy. "And that sign, sir, clearly marks the space as reserved for our differently-abled citizens. Have you no shame, sir?"

Appel looked at the van with dismay, then toward Schlag with paternal disappointment.

"Good heavens, son," Appel said. "You've parked in a handicapped space. Move that van immediately, dear boy, and please be more careful in the future."

For the first time in his young life, Willie Schlag felt the white heat of a television camera's light in his face, and combined with the unjust wrath of a United States Congressman it was too much for a teenaged son-of-a-contributor to bear.

"B-b-but sir," Schlag blurted out. "You told me to park there."

"Of course not, son," Appel said, smiling as he patted the lad on the shoulder. "I wouldn't tell you to park in a handicapped space, now would I?"

"B-b-but you did, sir," Schlag said, slipping again into his adenoidal falsetto. "I mean, I pointed the sign out and everything. Then you said, 'F—' "

Appel quickly interrupted Schlag and resumed his reassurances to the camera. Schlag sulked away toward the van, leaving Appel to improvise a few more comments for Skyler, who was already making a mental list of the larger market stations where he would send tapes of this story.

The Harley Christianson for Governor Headquarters was a happy place in the aftermath of that evening's newscasts. Skyler's station had provided all of its affiliates in the state with the story of Appel's illegal parking, dubbed "Handicapped Parking-gate," and hours later Livengood was still delightedly replaying a videotape.

"Check it out," Livengood said to Mark Stark, running the conversation between Appel and Schlag in slow motion. "Here's the kid pointing to the sign, and you can see he's telling Appel about it.

Now watch Appel's lips—you can see every word. 'Fa … uck … the … han … di … capped.' It's clear as day."

Stark had to admit this was good news.

"Good news my ass," Livengood said. "This is the best news since Jesus brought salvation to a fallen mankind. Appel has not only insulted every handicapped person in the state, but every law-abiding bastard who ever had to walk an extra block to the mall because of the damn cripples. Plus, he's lying his ass off and blaming some pimple-faced kid. People hate that, you know. And I'll tell you, that potty mouth of his ain't going to win him any votes around here, either. Hell, what he did is way worse than Harley blowing up that federal building down in OKC."

Stark had to admit that Livengood had a point.

"We'll make damn sure that people get the point, too," Livengood said. "We're already working up an ad with this footage. Merle's got this lip-reader to translate the conversation with the kid, and the best part is that she reads lips because she's deaf, so she's practically handicapped herself. When she says, 'At this point Congressman Appel used an obscene term to disparage our handicapped citizens,' sounding all weird like she does, it's real effective. Big Jim's starting up a group called Differently-Abled Citizens for Parking Justice to pay for a series of 'educational' ads, and we're going to saturate the airwaves with it starting this week. Appel's ass is cooked, if you ask me."

Stark wrote the prediction down in his notes.

CHAPTER ELEVEN

"The Smoke-free Room"

Frankie Livengood often felt nostalgic for an earlier, more robust era of Kansas politics. As he sat in the lobby of Chip Wentworth's Johnson County office, he had a particular longing for the days of the smoke-filled room.

The chrome-and-steel couch where Livengood sat afforded a fourteenth-floor view of the vast expanse of shopping malls, fast food joints and freeways that made up the affluent Kansas City suburbs, and it seemed to Livengood a most inappropriate setting for a deal that was likely to determine the next governor of a state such as Kansas. More disappointing yet, a severely blond receptionist was eyeing Livengood's anachronistically disheveled form, and she clearly intended to enforce the posted rules and deprive him of a celebratory puff on a cigarette during his moment of triumph.

Chip Wentworth had invited Livengood to the meeting on the same day that *The Kansas City Star* had published a poll indicating that Jonathan Appel was hemorrhaging support in the wake of his handicapped parking scandal, with eight of the ten points that Appel had lost winding up in Harley Christianson's total. The invitation had been extended with Wentworth's usual coyness, but it didn't take a seasoned political hack such as Livengood to figure out that Wentworth was looking for a safe place to swim after abandoning Appel's sinking ship.

Although Livengood held a mild dislike for Wentworth, and was pleased to see him on the desperate side of a negotiation for a change, he planned to be generous. Wentworth could move a large amount of money to a campaign, held considerable sway among the informal network of moderate conservatives in the party apparatus, and was especially influential in populous Johnson County, where Christianson had been weak since the very first poll. Livengood remained patient during the fifteen minutes he was made to wait, and readied himself to be friendly toward Wentworth.

Livengood was still waiting when Arvin Howard arrived at the reception desk and was pointed to the couch by the severe blond receptionist. Howard plopped onto the couch and shook Livengood's hand without smiling.

"So how're things in Wichita?" Livengood asked. "How's Appel doing down there?"

Howard smiled even less, and asked what the meeting was to be about.

"I dunno," Livengood said. "You're the one he's been working with on this campaign, but I'm guessing that he's decided to maybe work with me."

"So why did he drag my ass all the way up the turnpike? Can't he jump ship without me?"

"Maybe he's figuring on talking you into doing the same. It wouldn't be a bad idea, you know. I don't think you're going to get Appel elected at this point, so you might as well join up with the next administration on the ground floor. I'd sure as hell love to have you."

"Thanks, Frankie, but I think I'll wait to see what Wentworth's got up his silk sleeve."

The severely blond receptionist escorted the men in to see Wentworth, who offered them his famously firm handshake.

"Thanks for coming all the way up here, gentlemen," Wentworth said, leaning back in his chair and revealing a pair of perspiration-free armpits as he clasped his manicured hands behind his head. "I thought it would be a good time for us to get together and talk some politics."

"That's my favorite subject," Livengood said. "Especially these days, now that my guy has got the lead in all the polls, and his only challenge for the moderate voters seems to be dropping out of sight."

Wentworth smiled slightly, nodded without commitment and said, "Maybe. Then again, maybe not. We just might have a few tricks left on behalf of our guy, right Arvin?"

Howard shrugged. Livengood, who fancied himself the sort who figuratively eats arrogant young hot-shots like Chip Wentworth for breakfast, sneered.

"What tricks?" Livengood said. "Your guy's dead, and you damn well know it."

"Don't be so sure about that," Wentworth said. "Your guy's on record against the flag burning amendment. Don't ask me how I know, but I do happen to know that a group called Flag-Loving Kansans for the Flag is about to provide the soft money for a series of television ads educating the public about your guy's very un-American stance on this issue."

"Unless your ads include actual footage of my guy saying 'fuck the flag,' I'm not scared," Livengood said. "My guy still got his ass shot at in Vietnam for the flag, and we've got people besides militia nuts to talk about it. That trumps your guy's National Guard service and co-sponsorship of some flag burning amendment any day."

Wentworth looked at Howard for help, and realized none would be forthcoming.

"Still, I think you're celebrating a bit prematurely," Wentworth told Livengood. "Your current totals won't hold up if Hibbert and Patterson swing a deal for unity in the religious wing."

"That would require Edna Dimschmidt and Pastor Jeffries making peace, and that's not going to happen until they die and go to heaven," Livengood said.

"Perhaps some key people in Appel's campaign might swing a deal with Patterson," Wentworth said. "He could moderate his image with the right help, and start picking up some of those votes that Appel seems to be losing."

"Not with two weeks to go before the primary, not after all these months that Patterson's been trying to thump Bibles louder than Hibbert," Livengood said. "You're a bright guy, so you know there's nothing you can do to get Appel elected at this point."

After a hearty laugh, Wentworth said, "I like you Frankie. I like your style. I'm not so crazy about the haircut or that suit you're wearing, but I like the way you talk. I'm starting to like your candidate's chances of winning, too, and I'd like to get in. You know what I can do for you, so I guess it's just a matter of hammering out what you can do for me."

"Well, now, let me think," Livengood said. "If I were the chief of staff in a Christianson administration, I guess I could choose not to cut any of the money you're already getting out of the eco-devo funds, or any of the state contracts you've already got. Other than invitations to the inaugural ball and an occasional meeting with us, that's about it."

"That's not bad," Wentworth said. "At least you're not being vindictive. That's another thing I've always liked about you, Frankie. You're a pragmatist."

"Pragmatically speaking," Livengood said, "I'm afraid you're not going to be much help to me outside this district."

"That's why I asked Arvin up here," Wentworth said. "Arvin, I thought you'd like to join us on this new partnership."

Howard, who had been staring at the traffic outside the office window, turned and looked at Wentworth angrily. Several seconds later, he said, "Screw you."

At that, Howard stood up and strode out of the office. Livengood hastily said his good-byes to Wentworth as he followed, finally catching up to Howard at the elevator. "Don't be offended, please, Frankie," Howard said. "I can't support your candidate, but I respect you for sticking with him. I expect my friends to have that kind of loyalty."

"Chip's an asshole, Arvin, but he's an asshole with a point," Livengood said. "Your man's going down, and there's nothing you can do to save him. Now, you know I'm not going to hurt you when we get in office, if we get in office, but it sure would be nice to have your help in getting there. My guy's a good guy, Arvin, I swear. He's not so far off from where you stand, either. So why not join up?"

The elevator began its descent, and Howard stared at the numbers over the door as they counted down toward "L." As they passed the second floor, Howard at last spoke.

"Your guy is pro-choice, Frankie. I'm adopted, you know, and maybe I wouldn't even be here if my birth mother could have chosen a legal abortion."

Livengood fought against an instinct to argue, to point out that Arvin's birth mother could have chosen an illegal abortion almost as easily, but he knew from hard-earned experience that such arguments rarely changed a person's mind. Instead, Livengood told Howard that, "This election isn't going to change the abortion laws much."

The two argued the point until they reached Howard's Cadillac, and as he unlocked the door, Howard told Livengood, "I know that it's probably not going to change it. But still, I can't help you."

"Come on, Arvin," Livengood said. "Abortion isn't the only issue in this state, and you're with my guy on almost every other one."

"I know that, too, Frankie. I try not to make a big deal about it, and I don't go around blowing up abortion clinics, but I don't support pro-choice candidates. I may try to help you beat an even more pro-choice Democrat in the general, but I just can't help you beat a more pro-life Republican in this primary. It's nothing personal, and I hope you know that, but I just can't help you on this."

Livengood shrugged and said, "I understand. I just hope you know that it's nothing personal when we kick your guy's butt clear across Kansas."

"That's all right," Howard said, laughing. "Appel's a jerk, anyway. But what the heck, he's a pro-life jerk and the one I signed up with, so I guess I'll go down with his ship."

Livengood gave Howard a friendly punch on the shoulder and said, "You're all right by me, Arvin. It sucks having Wentworth for an ally instead of you."

"You're all right yourself, Frankie, for a baby killer," Howard said, smiling as he started up the car. As he pulled out of the parking spot, he lowered his window and urged Livengood to drop by the next time he was in Wichita and have a beer. Livengood noticed the "We Vote Pro-Life" bumper sticker on the Cadillac, and a disappointed smile crossed his face. Livengood lit a cigarette and started stocking up on nicotine before returning to Wentworth's office.

More campaign chores kept Livengood busy until eleven o'clock in the evening, when he arrived at his apartment to find Mick Fixx half-assedly repairing a leaky kitchen faucet.

CHAPTER ELEVEN

"Your damn phone's been ringing all night," Fixx said, handing Livengood a half-smoked marijuana cigarette. "Mostly political people, from the sound of the messages they've been leaving, but some bitch named Rebecca called twice and sounded pretty desperate to hear from you. What's the deal with her?"

"I don't know what the hell the deal is with that woman," Livengood said. "I guess I'd better call her and find out."

"Are you fucking her?"

"Yeah, I'm fucking her, you gushy romantic fool, you. We got a little carried away up on Mount Sunflower while I was campaigning out west, and it sort of carried on until about a week ago or so."

"You must really like her, then," Fixx said. "You've always had this weird thing about not fucking a woman unless you really like her. I don't know what happened a week ago or so, but from the sound of the messages she left, she's ready to resume getting carried away again. Do you want my advice?"

"Just give me that joint," Livengood said. "Your advice, I don't need."

"My advice is to agree to whatever the hell she wants, short of marriage, and start fucking her again," Fixx said. "Fucking with somebody you really like would be a good thing in your otherwise shitty life. Just don't let her find out that you also fucked Jane up there on Mount Sunflower. She's probably already plenty pissed off about you being in love with your ex-wife and all, and I'd hate to see you fuck up some good fucking again. Don't be a dumbshit, Frankie."

Livengood was annoyed at Fixx's obscenity, and further annoyed at his acuity. He went to his bedroom and called Reynolds, who sounded sleepy when she answered.

"Sorry about the hour," Livengood said. "It's been a long day. I've had to make a lot of deals."

Reynolds assured him that she was still awake, and appreciated the call.

"I've got some news I've been eager to share with you," Reynolds said. "It looks like I'm going to be staying in Kansas for quite a while."

"Why? Because of me?"

"Don't be ridiculous," Reynolds said. "The Coalition is going to pay me to work on the Kline campaign, then as a lobbyist."

Livengood felt relief that he wasn't responsible for any change in Reynolds' life, but he was also disappointed that she considered the idea ridiculous.

"Congratulations," he said.

"Thanks," she said. "I won't be here forever, but it will be for quite a while. So, anyway, I got to thinking that I could sure use your company while I am here."

Livengood stretched out on the bed and stared at the ceiling, as if expecting to find the correct reply written there. Not finding it, he improvised badly, expressing concern that he might fall in love with her.

"I'm not at all worried about that," Reynolds said, laughing for the first time in weeks. "Not with your pathological attachments. I just want someone to be with in this godforsaken state of yours, and so far you're the only one I can talk to. If we fall in love forever and ever, then what the hell."

Glancing at the alarm clock next to his bed, Livengood was reminded of what a long day it had been. Too tired to stall for time to think, he asked Reynolds if she would care to spend the next night with him.

"I'll be looking forward to it," Reynolds said, before hanging up.

Fixx was amused by the downcast expression Livengood wore when returning to the kitchen, and he roared a great hearty laugh before saying, "So, you're going to start fucking her again, or what?"

"She's coming by tomorrow night," Livengood said. "But what the hell. Life is all about compromise, my friend. It's all about compromise."

"The hell it is," said Fixx, who had another idea of what life was all about.

Twenty-five thousand Christianson for Governor yard signs sprouted on the lawns of Johnson County within three days of Livengood's conversation with Chip Wentworth, and a sudden surge of campaign contributions from previously pro-Appel moderates paid for a saturation ad campaign on the area's infamously expensive airwaves. The next round of polls provided further evidence that Christianson had gained a large number of voters in the county, and with one week to go before the primary he was now leading the race by a comfortable five points.

Livengood's only remaining fear, which he nourished lovingly, was that the other candidates would join together in attacking the new front-runner during the final series of televised debates scheduled for each region of the state. Livengood frequently pointed out to Mark Stark that the only sensible thing for Patterson and Hibbert to do was gang up on Christianson, and Stark frequently replied that neither Patterson nor Hibbert were likely to do the sensible thing.

Stark's assessment proved correct. None of the final debates featured any mention of militias, or any other subject embarrassing to Christianson, even when the questions seemed to be nudging the other candidates in that direction. Instead, the other candidates contented themselves with attacks on one another.

Representative Patterson was bold enough to make oblique reference to Whitey Williams' divorce and re-marriage, saying, "I don't think that the people of this state would want a governor who's had one wife too many."

Williams responded by saying that, "It's better to have had one wife too many than to have had one wife too few," causing the crowd to gasp.

"I have forthrightly and frankly confessed my sin of fathering an illegitimate son, and begged forgiveness from God and Kansas," Hibbert said, "but with God Almighty as my witness, at least I have never parked in a handicapped space, or wished a vile sex act upon our differently-abled citizens."

Appel, who had endured such verbal slaps throughout each debate, and was beginning to look as if he had suffered a similar number of actual slaps, urged that the voters "consider the important issues."

Each of the debates included several minutes of discussion about the subjects that Appel seemed to regard as "important issues," and Livengood was pleased to notice that Christianson was now handling these questions as well, if not better, than any of his rivals. Wilbur Philip acknowledged that Christianson's knowledge now exceeded the content of his index cards, and that the candidate had actually contributed several good ideas to his platform. Even Stark was complimentary about Christianson's ability, highly unusual among politicians, to answer follow-up questions without falling back on the standard repertoire of cliches.

"Gentlemen, I think we kicked some ass," Livengood said, over a round of beers after the final debate.

"Hear, hear!" Philip said, raising a bottle to Christianson's performance.

"To Harley Christianson, the greatest orator to hit the prairie since William Jennings Bryan!" Stark said.

Christianson had predictably declined an invitation to the party, and the three men laughed freely at the joke.

"He did all right," Livengood said. "At least he didn't take any big hits. At least he didn't have to talk about Will Schnitzle and the First Regimental Kansas Free Citizens Militia Brigade."

"Nobody was going to bring that up, because it would give Harley a chance to talk about how he served with Schnitzle in the politically magical land of Vietnam," Philip said.

"No, I think it was just too damned tempting to get a few last kicks in on Appel's dying carcass," Stark said.

"No, that's not it, either," Livengood said. "Patterson and Hibbert are just following the plays that Jeffries and Dimschmidt send in, and those two aren't even trying to stop us anymore. They already know that they're not going win this race, and at this point they're just trying to win the biggest number of religious right votes, so they can claim to be the leaders of the wing and hold their noses up the highest during prayer meetings."

"So what are you saying?" Stark asked. "That they hate each other even worse than they hate a bunch of infidels like us?"

"Of course," Livengood said. "After all, we're going to hell. Edna and the pastor are going to have to spend eternity with each other up in heaven, and they're already jockeying for position at the Lord's great table. They could cut a deal to beat back the infidels if they wanted to, but I was watching them backstage at the debate tonight, and I'm telling you, they don't want to. No doubt about it, friends, we're going to hell via the governor's mansion."

"You seem awfully cocky about that," Stark said.

Feeling very cocky, Livengood even ventured a prediction of the final score.

"Baker's going to get the usual 5 percent from the lunatic fringe, Williams will barely do better with 8, Appel's going to limp in around 10, Patterson will finish with 22, Hibbert claims the religious title with 25 percent, and my guy wins the day with 30 percent. You can write that down."

Livengood leaned back and blew a line of smoke in the shape of a three, and placed a perfect smoke ring just to the side of it. The boys were mightily impressed, and all felt very much like old-time political pros as they drank and cussed and complimented one another on the great days that awaited the state of Kansas.

CHAPTER TWELVE

"Grand Old Party Animals"

Sophisticated exit-polling techniques had long ago taken the suspense out of election day, and that was one change that even a steadfast Luddite such as Frankie Livengood could endorse. Armed with substantial data indicating that Harley Christianson would win the Republican nomination for governor, Livengood arrived at the election night campaign party in an unusually calm mood.

In keeping with his longstanding election day tradition, Livengood had slept well into the afternoon before rising to a leisurely breakfast of toaster pastries, black coffee and marijuana. He then strolled the two blocks from his apartment to the elementary school cafeteria where he voted, an act he had reveled in at every opportunity since his 18th birthday. The steel gray voting booths with retracting curtains had long since been replaced by a small box of buttons and electronically displayed ballots, but even this affront to Livengood's old-fashioned sensibilities couldn't deprive him of the joy he felt when voting for a candidate of his own creation.

Livengood then drove to the Harley Christianson for Governor Headquarters, where he found Darla Morland waving a large Christianson for Governor sign at passing motorists and chanting, "Hey, hey, ho, ho, Mr. Christianson is on the go." Livengood congratulated Darla on her hard-working spirit and bade her to continue. As he entered the headquarters, Livengood found Walton, Philip, Page and even Stark smiling broadly over the newer poll data that was spread over his desk.

Only after his own examination of the data did Livengood join in the smiling. There was much information to consider, because the sudden infusion of Wentworth's money had allowed Livengood to indulge in his passion for polling, and it all confirmed that Christianson would finish with a winning plurality in the race. Another batch of fresher numbers then appeared on Greg Page's computer screen, bolstering the conclusions of the previous figures, and another round of smiling, back-slapping and hand-shaking commenced.

Livengood's only remaining duties of the primary campaign were to call Christianson and plan his appearance before the television cameras, then begin negotiations for the support of the losing candidates, and then celebrate with as much vigor as his jaded mind and aging body would allow. He decided to deal with the most pleasant duty first, and phoned Christianson.

"Congratulations, Mr. Republican Party Nominee for Governor of the Great State of Kansas," Livengood said. "We've had exit pollsters at eighty precincts since the polls opened, and they're all telling me that you're a lock."

Christianson excused himself to inform the missus, and a moment later Livengood could hear an ecstatic shriek over the line.

"She's just plumb tickled to death to hear that," Christianson said when he returned the phone. "Me, I'm a mite nervous about it."

"This is the first time in months that I haven't been nervous," Livengood said. "We've got a lock. All you've got to do is drive out here to Topeka with Christy and Tyrone, give a short speech I've already got written up, and answer a few questions for the TV and newspaper folks. There's going to be a hell of a party afterwards, but you can skip it if you want and head right up to your room. I've booked the Governor's Suite for you at the Ramada. Tomorrow morning's the unity breakfast, and I'll have that scoped out for you by then. After that you get a few weeks off, and the general's going to be a piece of cake."

"Then what?" Christianson said. "That's what I'm nervous about."

"What? Government work?" Livengood said. "That's the last thing I'm nervous about."

"So what's in this speech I'm supposed to read?"

"The usual," Livengood said. "You talk about how great all your opponents are, what an honor it is to kick their asses, the whole humble bit. You thank your wife, your kid, all the little people who've worked so hard, maybe your second grade teacher or something. Then you say that now isn't the time for a big policy speech, because it isn't, and then you get the hell off the stage. Then you find yourself surrounded by a bunch of crazy reporters, and you make up the answers as you go along."

"Sounds good to me, I suppose," Christianson said. "If you don't mind, when I get to the part where I thank all the people who have worked so hard, I'd like to give a special mention to you."

"That's not a good idea, Harley. Trust me. You do not want to mention me in your speech."

"No, really, Frankie. I sure as heck wouldn't be standing up there as the Republican nominee for governor of this state if it weren't for you."

"Maybe so, Harley. But that's precisely what we don't want anyone to know."

"If you say so, Frankie," Harley said. "Well, thanks anyway."

After hanging up, Livengood noticed that Jane Hutchinson was standing in the doorway, smiling at her ex-husband.

"Congratulations, Frankie," she said. "The boys have been showing me the exit polls. It looks like you pulled it off. You may not want the rest of the state to know it, but I know it."

Livengood hadn't seen a similar smile on Hutchinson's face since their courtship, and he leaned back in his chair with a joyous cockiness that he hadn't exhibited since approximately the same era.

"And you said it couldn't be done," Livengood said, waving his hand flamboyantly.

"No I didn't," Jane said. "Mark said it couldn't be done, and Mick even bet you a hundred dollars that it couldn't, but I never doubted your abilities. I knew you could do it."

"Yeah, that's right," Livengood said. "You were the one who was arguing that I shouldn't do it."

"Now you remember."

"Oh well," Livengood said. "At least you had complete confidence in my ability to do the wrong thing, no matter how daunting the odds."

"Don't start, Frankie. I just came by to congratulate you. I don't know anybody else who could have done it, and you deserve acknowledgement for that."

"Thank you," Livengood said.

"What's next?" Hutchinson asked.

"Well, first we win the general, then in another four years we do it again."

"What do you do in between?" Hutchinson asked.

"I dunno," Livengood said. "Govern, I guess."

"You've put a perfectly nice man in charge of a perfectly nice state," Hutchinson said. "I hope you'll be able to come up with some good use for this."

"For you, babe, I'll do something great with it. I promise."

Hutchinson laughed slightly, leaned over to kiss Livengood lightly on the forehead, and said she was needed back at the Department of Health and Environment.

"Are you coming to the party?" Livengood asked. "It's going to be an epic. Lots of liquor and drugs and conservative political talk. Satan's Butt Buddies are playing after we get rid of the damned TV cameras and the older volunteers."

"I think I'll be turning in early tonight," Hutchinson said. "Besides, I hear you've got yourself a big city girlfriend, and I don't want to interfere."

His victorious mood thoroughly diminished as Hutchinson walked out the door, Livengood stormed outside to demand that Darla cease her annoying chatter. He remained sullen until fresher and even more promising exit poll numbers flashed across Greg Page's computer screen.

When the polls closed and the party started, the starkly utilitarian storefront campaign headquarters was transformed into a festival of red-white-and-blue bunting, blaring television sets and beer-swilling Republicans. Livengood was eager to join the celebration with alcoholic abandon, but good form required him to wait until the election results were conclusive before meeting his counterparts in the other campaigns, so he stayed responsibly sober while anxiously waiting for a news organization—any news organization—to call the race.

The roar and swirl of the party was almost intoxicating enough. Mick Fixx was regaling Big Jim Morland with off-color jokes, and Big Jim rewarded him with raucous laughter and shouts of, "You're all right." Chip Wentworth and Ellen Winston shared sips of something expensive from his silver flask, and flirted with the easy cool of the affluent and oft-married. Greg Page, in his black leather jacket, and Ed Walton, in his blue sport coat, shared recollections of rock 'n' roll concerts from long ago. Cathy Knieble batted her eyes futilely at Mark Stark. Wilbur Philip argued health care issues with an elderly woman volunteer whose name Livengood couldn't quite remember. A ton of people that Livengood did not know were also in attendance, and from the way they were hitting the barbecue, Livengood expected they would weigh another collective ton before the party was over.

Rebecca Reynolds entered in a black dress that Livengood would never forget, and gave him the first public kiss of their relationship.

"I have to get over to Willa's party soon," Reynolds said. "But I wanted to drop by first and congratulate you. The word is all over town that Christianson is the Republican nominee."

"Our party's going to last longer than Willa's party," Livengood said. "Will you come back?"

"Count on it," Reynolds said, giving him another, longer kiss.

All in all, it seemed a good enough party to Frankie Livengood, even if he did have to stay sober.

The Patterson for Governor party was a much more subdued affair, a condition due in part to the preponderance of teetotalers among the supporters, and in part to the realization that they would lose this election. Pastor Jeffries was nonetheless cordial as he greeted Livengood and escorted him to an office at the back of the headquarters.

"I guess you heard that the AP has called the race," Livengood said. "There's always a chance that the late returns will change the percentages, of course, but right now it seems that Mr. Christianson will be the nominee."

"It would seem so, indeed," Pastor Jeffries said, a pastoral smile settling on his face. "You're to be congratulated."

"And may I congratulate you on a well-run race, as well, and on the enthusiasm and hard work of your many supporters," Livengood said. "If the numbers hold up and Mr. Christianson does win, we'd certainly be fortunate to have some of that on our side, Pastor Jeffries. And of course, we'd be fortunate to have the benefit of your considerable expertise and influence."

"I certainly intend to support the Republican nominee in the general election, Frankie, although I'm afraid that now I must be getting back to my spiritual work and won't be able to offer much in the way of 'political expertise and influence,' " the Pastor said. He shifted his smile slightly to warn Livengood that he was in no mood for blandishments. "As for our supporters, well, naturally I cannot say what they will choose to do with their votes. I suppose that some will support Mr. Christianson as a superior alternative to Ms. Kline, while others will decide that neither candidate offers a godly use of their franchise."

"I'll tell you what," Livengood said, in a tone that promised an end to blandishments. "So long as you're not talking your people into sitting out the race, that's about all I can ask of you. However, if you were to help us identify which supporters might support us as a superior alternative to Ms. Kline, then a Christianson administration would be in debt to you."

"It would indeed be nice to have the government in debt to us, for a change," Jeffries said, with a chuckle that wasn't at all pastoral. "I can't help but wonder, just how large is this debt?"

"What do you want?" Livengood asked.

"It would be nice to have the administration's support for a bill that Representative Patterson intends to introduce regarding various issues of great importance to the Christian community," Jeffries said.

"I can't endorse a specific proposal until I see its details, of course," Livengood said. "But for you, I like the concept."

Pastor Jeffries shook Livengood's hand and wished him a good evening.

The Appel for Governor party seemed a remarkably swinging affair to Livengood, considering the meager seven percentage points that the candidate had won. A Dixieland band, clad in straw hats and red-striped vests, was making a game attempt at smooth jazz, while men in blue suits and women in black gowns were doing an upper-middle class version of dancing. The candidate himself was loudly and unabashedly drunk.

"Goddamn, Frankie, you guys kicked my ass," Appel said, his arm slung around Livengood's shoulder.

"Sorry about that, Congressman," Livengood said. "It's just politics."

"Easy for you to say, you smart bastard," the Congressman blared. "Do you have any idea what it's like to be facing unemployment?"

"Who, me?" Livengood said, recalling the time Appel had fired him, while slinging his arm around the Congressman's shoulder. "You've just got to show some of that old-fashioned American enterprise that you're always preaching. *Ad astra per aspera* and all that."

"You didn't leave the winner's party to tell me that shit, did you, Frankie?" the Congressman said. "I'll bet you're here because you want my lousy 8 percent."

"Please, Congressman," Livengood said, a wounded expression on his face. "I came here to congratulate you on a race well run, and to wish you good luck in your future endeavors, and to see what we can do to assist you in those endeavors. Of course, the 8 percent would be nice."

"What the hell can I do for you? You've got me unemployed."

"You can endorse us in your usual eloquent way, naturally, and I was thinking maybe you could share your mailing lists and fund-raising contacts. Anything you can do to help us identify your supporters."

"Well, they ain't the cripples, that's for damned sure," Appel said, laughing loudly and slapping Livengood on the back just a bit harder than was necessary to convey friendship.

The Hibbert for Governor party was no party at all. As Livengood entered, he mused that hanging out with the Apostles in the days between the crucifixion and the resurrection would have yielded more laughs, and he shuddered at the sight of Edna Dimschmidt's dour countenance as she approached him.

"Hello, Frankie," Dimschmidt said. "What brings you here?"

"Howdy, Edna. I thought we needed to talk about the general election, get ready for the unity breakfast tomorrow morning."

"We'll be counting on your support, of course," she said.

"Maybe you haven't heard, Edna, but the way the AP is calling the race, we'll be counting on your support."

"The AP is reporting its projection. All of the votes haven't been counted yet."

"Yeah, Edna, that's true. But we've both been around a long time, and I don't think either one of us can remember the last time their projection on a race like this was wrong. So far, their projections agree exactly with our exit-polling."

"All of the votes haven't been counted yet," Dimschmidt said, "I still have faith."

"So let's talk hypothetically," Livengood said, summoning his final reserves of patience. "In the event that the projections are correct, what are your people going to do?"

Dimschmidt stared contemptuously at Livengood and said, "Mr. Hibbert's supporters are free to act as they please."

"True enough, Edna, but it seems they're often pleased to do whatever you tell them to do. What advice do you expect to give them?"

"I expect for Hampton Hibbert to win this race," Dimschmidt said. "If the Lord wills it that Hampton does not win, I cannot say what I will do. I do not expect that I will do anything to help Mr. Christianson become governor of this state, but then again, neither do I expect that I will do anything to help the likes of Willa Kline."

"That's good enough for me, Edna."

"It will have to be. Now, if you will excuse me, I'd like to re-join my party. We were about to offer a prayer of thanks to the Lord, and ask that He watch over Kansas in its hour of darkness."

Livengood decided that Hoss Baker and Whitey Williams could be dealt with over the phone, and handled the calls despite the party noise seeping through his office door. Baker was deafeningly enthusiastic in his support for the Christianson campaign, and clearly eager to do whatever he could to defeat the socialistic threat of Willa Kline, and Livengood assured him that some appropriate job would be found for "ol' Hoss." Williams offered his congratulations and a promise to vote for Christianson, but explained that his new job with a Kansas City insurance firm would not allow him to engage in political activities.

The only chore that remained for Livengood was guiding Harley through his victory speech and his first press grilling as the

Republican nominee, but it soon became apparent that Harley no longer needed such assistance.

Harley had arrived looking gubernatorial, in the most nicely fitted suit that he had ever worn, with Christy Christianson looking the part of First Lady in a businesslike skirt and jacket. After offering a congratulatory round of handshakes to the campaign staff, he took Livengood aside and explained that he had written his own speech.

"I stuck to the same basic format you described, and I kept it short just like you wanted," Harley said. "But I wanted to kind of personalize it a bit. It's a long drive over here from Piquant, and it gave me time to think of a couple of things I wanted the folks to know."

Livengood asked if he could read the speech, but Harley pointed to his head and said, "It's all up here."

"Go for it," Livengood said, reluctantly. "Just don't go wishing any vile sex acts on our differently-abled citizens or anything."

A huge roar erupted from the crowd when the Christianson family took to the podium set up at the rear of the headquarters. Harley gave an embarrassed wave to the crowd, hugged his wife, and tapped the microphone to test if it was working.

"Thanks for coming, everyone," Harley said, eliciting an unexpectedly loud response from the crowd. "They tell me I've won the Republican nomination for governor of Kansas, and I've got to tell you that it feels a bit overwhelming. You see, I've been proud to be a Kansan all my life, and it seems like I've been a Republican for just as long, so having all the Republican folks in this state honor me this way, when they had such a good bunch of candidates to choose from, is truly more than I ever dreamed of having happen. I really mean that, too, because I never did dream of this. I just wanted to be a good carpenter, be a good husband to this beautiful lady here and a good father to this nice boy, and maybe help out the people in my hometown however I could. Now that I might actually become the governor of this great state, well, I find that I really don't know what to say. There's a bunch of smart folks helping me out here, and I think we've come up with some good ideas about things we might do if we wind up winning this race, but I guess now really isn't the time to go into all that. If anybody's still up out there and watching this on TV, I guess I just want y'all to know that I'd sure be honored if I won the next race against Ms. Kline, and that I'd do the best I could to do something great for this state. Kansas has been pretty good for me, so I reckon it deserves something great from me. That's about all, I guess."

The crowd was momentarily silent as it came to the realization that the speech actually was over, then burst into the loudest applause of the evening. Reporters swarmed around Christianson as he stepped off the podium, and Livengood was pleasantly surprised with the answers his guy provided.

After the departure of the Christiansons, Darla Morland and the reporters, the party grew rowdier. Big Jim and Mick Fixx, by now the best of friends, were shouting hearty "yee-haws" at passersby. Cathy Knieble and Mark Stark laughingly danced disco steps. Chip Wentworth and Ellen Winston had slipped into a broom closet together. Wilbur Philip enjoyed his first good drunk in fifteen years, and seemed to be enjoying the conversation of the equally inebriated Ed Walton for the first time ever. Scores of people that Livengood barely recognized slapped him on the back and praised him by name, then joined in the swirling revelry.

By the time Satan's Butt Buddies launched into a double-time rendition of its newest song, "Bomb the Poor," even Frankie Livengood was feeling young.

"I guess it is rather impressive, what you've pulled off," said Rebecca Reynolds, who had dropped by after the conclusion of the Kline for Governor party. "I must admit, I never would have thought that a Republican bash would be so much wilder than a Democrat's. How do you do it?"

"The first thing you do, you win the damned race," Livengood said. "That's the tricky part, you know, although I'm sure you'd be hog-tied and dipped in dog shit before you'd compliment me on that."

Reynolds laughed and complimented Livengood on his colorful country colloquialisms, but offered no kind words about his political skills. Instead, she smiled and said, "Willa and I are going to beat your boy."

"It's very kind of you to enliven the party with jokes," Livengood said, "but please, let's not talk any more politics tonight. After the unity breakfast tomorrow morning, I'm taking a week off from the whole damned subject."

"Then let's dance," Reynolds said.

Livengood declined to dance, explaining that years of religious training had left him unable to do so, but he surprised both himself and Reynolds by embracing her and kissing her forcefully. Big Jim and Mick Fixx responded with their heartiest "yee-haw" of the evening, and both Livengood and Reynolds acknowledged their cheers with a bow.

"Would Willa Kline mind if you spent the night with me?" Livengood asked.

"Of course not," Reynolds said. "We're all about choice at the Kline for Governor campaign."

Rebecca Reynolds was a talented and intense sex partner, and her expert ministrations later provided an apt conclusion to Livengood's day of triumph. Still, even as Livengood succumbed to the effects of a long and physically strenuous day, success and sexual satisfaction, his mind was troubled by the question of what he would do next. As sleep slowly overtook him, Livengood's troubled thoughts segued into a dream.

In the dream, Livengood was led by Jane Hutchinson and the ghost of his mother to a flat and empty land where a long, dark river flowed, where both women and a vague sense informed him that something great would soon be required of him. He tossed and turned in protest throughout the night.

CHAPTER THIRTEEN

"The Great Debate"

Frankie Livengood was well aware that life is full of rude awakenings, but it struck him as especially unkind when the voice of an irksome radio talk show host jolted him from his slumber. Livengood slammed the "snooze" button on his clock radio, and ten minutes later the radio host's voice again demanded that Livengood get out of bed.

Reynolds rolled over to find out why Livengood was getting up so uncharacteristically early.

"Goddamn unity breakfast," Livengood said, as he scoured the floor for clothes. "It's an old Kansas Republican tradition. It goes back even further than me."

"Can't you guys try having a unity brunch?" Reynolds asked, wiping her eyes and squinting them into focus.

"Not in Kansas," Livengood said. "The farm vote's still important out here, and the farmers like to see you up early. Brunch would be way the hell too decadent, like driving a foreign car. I swear, Rebecca, you've got a lot to learn about Kansas politics."

"What the hell is a unity breakfast, anyway?"

"All the GOP candidates meet up at some diner and get their picture taken together as they ingest enough cholesterol to kill a cow," Livengood said. "Then all the reporters run back to their offices and write up stories saying that the Republicans are unified. If anyone doesn't show up, they're sending a signal that they don't support the nominee, and the reporters all run back to their offices and write that the party isn't unified."

"Will all the candidates be there?"

"They damn well better be," Livengood said. "I did all the obligatory ass-kissing last night, and they all assured me they'd be there. Appel probably doesn't remember it, but someone will remind him."

"So the party's unified?"

"For breakfast, anyway," Livengood said. "At least, I don't expect any trouble from anyone. Even mean ol' Edna said that she and Hampton wouldn't make trouble, and that's about as unified as you can expect any political party to be."

"Then maybe I should get to work," Reynolds said. "It sounds like you guys are going to be tough to beat."

"Go back to sleep. That's what you ought to do," Livengood said. "There's no point knocking yourself out trying to win this damn thing, believe you me. I'll be back inside of two hours, and you can use your wiles to pry a few more political secrets out of me, if you want."

Reynolds's drowsiness was greater than her annoyance, so she rolled back over for another two hours of sleep.

The next day's Kansas newspapers would feature a photo of the smiling faces of Sheriff Hoss Baker, Insurance Commissioner Whitey Williams, Hampton Hibbert, Rep. Stan Patterson, Congressman Jonathan Appel and nominee-elect Harley Christianson, all gathered around plates heaping with pancakes and sausage. Livengood thought that Appel appeared a tad hung-over, and Baker just a bit maniacal, but otherwise he was satisfied that the coverage of the first day of the general election race would be helpful to Christianson's campaign.

CHAPTER THIRTEEN

No amount of coffee could make Livengood eloquent at such an early hour, but he managed to make passable chit-chat with the other hacks, formulate a few coherent quotes for the newspaper reporters, and even scavenge a few resources from the wrecked campaign organizations of the other candidates. With great relief, Livengood noticed that Edna Dimschmidt had chosen not to accompany Hampton Hibbert.

Rebecca Reynolds was getting out of bed just as Livengood was crawling back into it, and he watched with his usual sadness as she dressed.

"Aw, baby," Livengood said. "Come on back to bed."

"Sorry," she said. "I have to get to work."

"Aw, baby," Livengood said. "It's the day after election day. Except for a handful of poor dumb bastards who have to go to the unity breakfast, nobody in Kansas works on the day after election day."

"Hearing you talk about Republican unity made me realize how much we have to do," she said.

Livengood looked at her with a mix of disappointment and incredulousness.

"You don't really think you're going to win this, do you?" Livengood asked. "There's no way you're going to win it, and there's nothing you can do to change that, certainly not right now. You might as well get back in bed for some of my hot Republican lovin'."

Something about the way Reynolds rested her fist on her hip told Livengood that she did not enjoy his joke.

"So what are you saying?" she demanded to know. "That I'm not good enough to beat you?"

"Sheesh," Livengood said. "It's not like that at all. I'm not saying that you can't do it because you're not smart enough, or hard-working enough, or anything like that. I'm just saying that you can't do it because it can't be done."

"And why the hell not?"

"Because Willa's a liberal Democrat. A very liberal Democrat. Kansas is a conservative Republican state. You can do the math yourself. Things might be different if this game were being played back in your old New York neighborhood, but you're not in New York City anymore."

Reynolds sat on the side of the bed, thought for a moment before turning toward Livengood, and said, "Well, I have to try, damn it."

"Of course you do, Rebecca, and I understand that. You're committed to your beliefs, and you're willing to fight for them, and I respect that," Livengood said. Patting the bed, he added, "But come on. There's no use knocking yourself out."

Reynolds stood angrily and resumed dressing.

"We'll find out what's possible," Reynolds said. "Willa and I are going to take our ideas to the people of the state, and make them listen."

Livengood, knowing Kline's ideas and those of the average Kansan, warned her against that strategy.

"We'll out-work you, too," Reynolds said. "You'll probably spend the rest of this day in bed, even without me in it, and your announced intentions for the next two weeks are to drink, smoke and watch baseball as much as possible."

"That's because I know what I'm doing. Unlike you," Livengood said. "Everybody in this state takes two weeks off from politics after the election, and any noise you make in that period will only be resented. Trust me."

Reynolds did not look as if she trusted him.

"I'm just trying to be helpful," Livengood said. "I don't want you to be hurt when we kick your ass clear across the state and back. I don't want to run up the score on you, but that's what's going to happen."

At that point, Reynolds left with a slam of the door.

The only baseball game that Livengood could find that afternoon was the one being played by some 10-year-olds at a park near his apartment, but he found it a pleasant enough atmosphere for soaking up the late summer sunshine, smoking cigarettes and sneaking drinks of whiskey from a small flask. The game's conclusion provided some entertainment value, as well, with the fat kids overcoming a seven-run deficit by scoring eight runs in the bottom of the ninth inning on ten consecutive walks.

Reynolds was true to her vow to get Willa Kline's ideas before the public. Kline passionately argued for gifted programs in urban schools while at a meeting of the Cattleman's Association, and during the question-and-answer session she confirmed a rancher's suspicion that she was a vegetarian. A rare television camera followed Kline to an elementary school assembly, where she gave a speech on the benefits of ethnic diversity, complete with visual aids, and angrily berated a third-grader who snickered at the tribal costumes of a certain indigenous New Guinea tribe. At the officer's club at McConnell Air Force Base, Kline offered a lengthy explanation of her belief that war is not healthy for children and other living things. Kline spoke about abortion nearly everywhere she went, and with such enthusiasm that Livengood told Reynolds he was tempted to run out and get one for himself.

After a respectfully apolitical couple of weeks, Livengood returned Harley Christianson to the campaign trail. Christianson rode on the back of a '64 Mustang in the Carnival Days parade in Kinsley, a '54 Bel Aire in the Rooks County Free Fair, a '27 Model T at the Buster Keaton Film Festival in Iola, and a Darryl Starbird concept car at the Old Settlers Day parade in Mulvane. He ate kolache in Wilson, Swedish meatballs in Lindsborg, spaghetti in Pittsburg, soul food in Nicodemus, borscht in Moscow and bratwurst in Hillsboro. While at a Knights of Columbus meeting in the Strawberry Hill district of Kansas City, he even ate a Croatian concoction he couldn't quite pronounce. He told jokes to the old folks at the Satanta Senior Center, spun humorous anecdotes of his college days to the Fort Hays State University Young Republicans, spoke of his undying respect for slain law enforcement officers at the Kansas Fraternal Order of Police Convention, and during his visit to the Cattleman's Association he waxed eloquently about the wonders of red meat.

Harley had begun to take a lively interest and active role in the weekly staff meetings devoted to policy positions, and was increasingly eager to share his newfound enthusiasm for the issues, but Livengood was able to dissuade him.

Some discussion of the issues was unavoidable during the traditional State Fair debate, but even there, Livengood urged Harley to let Kline do most of the talking.

"Remember, this woman has a self-righteous streak longer than Edna Dimschmidt's, and she has the very same effect of firing up all the faithful and pissing off all the infidels," Livengood said, just before Harley took the stage. "Fortunately for us, there usually aren't a lot of left-wing ideologues wandering around the Kansas State Fairgrounds. Mostly we've got a bunch of regular rural folk out there, so all you need to do is remind them that you're regular rural folk, too, and give the shortest version of our answers that you can get away with."

As the debate commenced, Livengood met Reynolds on the tiered seats beneath the canvas tents, offering her a bite of his Pronto Pup.

"What on Earth is a Pronto Pup?" she asked.

"It's like a corn dog, only at the State Fair," Livengood said. "At the State Fair, we call 'em Pronto Pups. Are you sure you don't want a bite?"

Looking disdainfully at the mustard-soaked item in Livengood's hand, Reynolds declined.

"I could get you a pork burger, if you'd prefer," Livengood said. "I'm afraid that the advent of a falafel stand at the Kansas State Fair still awaits the reign of Willa Kline."

The State Fair debates always took on the flavor of a sporting contest, and it quickly became apparent which candidate the audience regarded as the home team. Harley was greeted with a loud and warm response after his introduction, with added applause for the mention of his boyhood on a farm and his service in Vietnam, while Kline was met with distinctly polite-sounding applause, and even had a few boos mixed in when women's studies and the Democratic Party were mentioned during her introduction. Looking around at the preponderance of flannel-clad and overalled farmers in the audience, all cheering Harley's vague opening remarks as they would a touchdown run, Reynolds wondered aloud what Kline could do to sway such a crowd.

"Nothing I can think of, and I think of that kind of stuff for a living," Livengood said. "The best you can hope for is that Willa doesn't get this bunch any more riled up than it already is."

The cool reception seemed to stun Kline, who clearly had expected that such a plainly proletarian crowd would better appreciate her benevolent concern for them. Kline fancied herself a latter-day version of the famed prairie populist "Sockless" Jerry Simpson, albeit with a better vocabulary and nice socks, but she sang from the populist songbook with her usual political tone-deafness. Reynolds and a few others in the audience might have heard Kline's highly specific proposals, but the rest heard only the general message that Kline identified with the working man—despite his racism, sexism, homophobia and bad taste—mainly for his ennobling oppression at the hands of evil Republicans.

Having spent much of his life in conversations with the sort of people in attendance at the State Fair, Livengood was well aware that most were Republicans themselves, and that to the extent they considered themselves oppressed, they believed it was at the hands of highfalutin pointy-heads such as Kline. She even spoke of harvesting winter wheat during wintertime, and was visibly annoyed by the resulting laughter.

All Harley had to do was be himself, Livengood thought to himself, and he was pleased to note how well his candidate was starting to play that role.

The performance so pleased Livengood that he celebrated with a cigarette, a large root beer and another mustard-soaked Pronto Pup. Reynolds again declined an offer of a bite, this time more curtly.

Willa Kline at last encountered a friendly audience when she ventured to an anti-globalization rally at the University of Kansas, where several dozen young men and women cheered ever more loudly as Kline's rhetoric grew ever more radical. By the time Kline declared that her campaign for governor of Kansas was nothing less than an assault on white supremacist, heterosexualist patriarchy itself, Frankie Livengood half-expected the young audience to spontaneously begin slam dancing.

Livengood had made the twenty-minute drive from Topeka to assess Kline's campaigning, and he was visibly amused by the results. Rebecca Reynolds, who sat with him in the back of the university's Lied Center, was so pleased with the proceedings that she did not notice.

"This is where the groundswell begins," Reynolds said. "It always starts with the students."

"Some groundswell," Livengood said, leaning back with his feet atop the seat in front of him. "There's a hundred times as many students watching the Jayhawks get their asses kicked down at the football stadium."

"The ones at the football stadium are too apathetic to make a difference. Change always begins with the radical front."

"The only thing radical about these kids is their haircuts and their tattoos, and that doesn't even shock Mom and Pop anymore, so they have to support a Democrat," Livengood said. "The only thing they're going to change is themselves, when they start getting more and more conservative with every student loan bill they have to pay. By the time they make a dent in the principal, my guy Harley won't be right-wing enough for them."

A pink-haired sophomore with a barbed-wire tattoo on her biceps strode to the microphone during a question-and-answer period and demanded that all progressive students support Kline because she was a woman, prompting cheers. A few questions later, a conspicuously clean cut young man in a crew neck sweater suggested that casting a vote based on a candidate's sex might actually be, well, sexist, but he was shouted down by a student of indeterminate sex who had earlier taken to the microphone to demand free speech.

Later, over coffee in a swank bistro on Massachusetts Street, Reynolds spoke rapidly of how well the evening had gone.

"Oh, please," Livengood said. "You're just lucky there weren't any media there tonight."

"I wish there had been," Reynolds said. "I would love for the rest of the state to see the kind of enthusiasm we inspire in young people. But alas, the revolution will not be televised."

Livengood had grown increasingly fond of Reynolds, but his political instincts were stronger than his romantic impulses, and after a moment's hesitation he made his next move.

"Are you sure about that?" Livengood said, with a doubting tone precisely pitched to provoke Reynolds' pride. "Then why not televise your revolution against Harley Christianson and all other forms of patriarchy? We're committed to another debate, and the site hasn't been scheduled yet. If you and Willa want, we could have it here, on your home field."

Reynolds regarded Livengood with suspicion, and demanded to know why he should make such a generous offer.

"This race is getting boring," Livengood said. "I want to give you two gals a sporting chance against my guy."

"It's good to know that chivalry isn't dead. At least not in Kansas," Reynolds said. "I don't mind exploiting it. The final debate is going to be here, and I'm holding you to that."

Ben Hart, the president of the University of Kansas' Young Republicans Club, called Frankie Livengood to offer his group's assistance with the debate. Livengood gratefully accepted, saying that he would be especially appreciative of any help Hart could offer in the way of keeping Young Republicans away from the event.

"Well, gee," the young man said, sounding perplexed. "I was thinking more along the lines of helping you get out a crowd. You know, to show the TV viewers that Mr. Christianson has a lot of support out there."

"People already know by now that Harley has a lot of support out there," Livengood said. "We need to make them think that Willa does, too, or they won't bother to get off their fat butts and waddle down to the polls. We want to make them think that an invasion of pink-haired, tattooed, anti-American neo-hippies is imminent, and that only a Christianson victory can repel the onslaught."

After a moment's silence, the young man said he wasn't quite sure about that. He had been looking forward to a free and open debate, and an honest discussion of the issues.

"You're a good Republican, right?" Livengood asked.

"Yes, sir," the young man said.

"You believe in conservative causes?"

"Very much so, sir."

"What's your major?"

"Poli sci."

"You wouldn't be thinking of pursuing some sort of career in politics, would you?"

"Yes, as a matter of fact."

"Well, then," Livengood said. "Help me out on this, and you'll be off to a hell of a start. There will always be plenty of free and open debate—believe me, kid, you'll get a bellyful of it—but this may be your last chance to help knock off an honest-to-God, out-and-out liberal. It's something you'll be able to tell your grandkids about, like bagging the last California condor."

After a moment's consideration, the young man mumbled his agreement and asked Livengood for further instructions.

Livengood was delighted by the fashionably extreme appearance of the audience at the final candidates' debate of the gubernatorial race.

Due to a small number of handbills which the Kline campaign had distributed around campus calling for concerned students to voice their opposition to Harley Christianson, and to a larger number of handbills which the Christianson campaign had distributed in local bohemian haunts calling for the same thing, the audience was almost entirely in support of Kline. Only a handful of carefully selected Young Republicans attended.

Ben Hart was seated near the stage, on the aisle where a microphone was placed, dressed in a collegiate slacks-and-jacket ensemble and armed with an index card Livengood had provided. He had been instructed to wait until the audience had worked itself up to a certain level of frenzy, and as he looked around at the two hundred or so other students, he couldn't help but wonder just how frenzied such people might become.

Backstage, Livengood was frantically offering a few words of last-minute advice to Harley Christianson.

"With any luck, it's going to get pretty ugly out there," Livengood said. "You're going to get heckled, you're going to get called all sorts of nasty things, and if things go according to plan, they'll probably even try to shout you down. Are you ready?"

"I reckon so," Harley said, still unsure of this particular political tactic. "I just need to keep my cool, be polite to Willa and don't say anything stupid."

"Exactly," Livengood said. "Just try to come across all reasonable-like."

Livengood had worried that questions about property tax appraisals, local option budgets and utilities regulations would not enthuse a college-aged audience, so he was delighted when Christianson's proposal to gradually reduce automobile taxes was met with chants of "racist, sexist, anti-gay, Christianson is in the way." When the forum was opened to questions from the audience, a young woman with purple hair and a vampiric complexion seized the microphone to denounce the handful of modest abortion restrictions that Christianson had endorsed, prompting rowdy cheers of "Stay out of my uterus" as Harley tried to answer. A conspicuously effeminate young man asked the next question, having something to do with a revolutionary movement in Peru, and when Harley frankly responded that he didn't know what the young man was talking about, chants of "Yankee go home" echoed through the hall.

Things were going well enough that Livengood signaled Ben Hart to ask a question, and the young man nervously approached the microphone. Following a lengthy discourse by a ponytailed young man about cultural imperialism, and the brief responses of both candidates, Hart sputtered out his question.

"This is for Ms. Kline," Hart said, trying to sound extemporaneous. "I've read a paper that you published two years ago in the feminist journal, *Womyn's Struggle*, and I'd like you to expound on your statement there, that 'fellatio is the ultimate symbolic form of carnivorism, which in turn is a particularly oppressive means of imposing the patriarchal will on society.' I must say, this strikes me as an inappropriate attitude for anyone who aspires to be governor of a state in which so many fine people earn their living in the cattle industry."

Although the last beleaguered campus liberals of Kansas weren't up to a full-scale riot, they came as close as their courage would allow. A campus police officer separated Ben Hart from the large and heavily tattooed woman who began beating him and scratching his face, while other officers rushed in to quell the ensuing melee. Kline's efforts to quiet the crowd were futile, and the broadcast's final credits scrolled across a scene of Harley

Christianson looking anachronistically reasonable-like amid the ruckus.

Livengood happily envisioned the panicked reactions of thousands of blue-nosed, blue-haired, cable-free Public Broadcasting System viewers as they watched the spectacle unfold. Rebecca Reynolds was so pleased by Kline's runaway victory in the debate that she felt generous toward Livengood, and concluded the evening by resuming their sexual relations.

After that, enough money rolled into the campaign for Frankie Livengood to splurge on the wholly unnecessary luxury of massive exit-polling. By the time he awoke at 11:45 a.m. on election day, Livengood was already assured, with the highest degree of scientific certitude that modern polling methods could provide, that Harley Christianson would be the next governor of Kansas.

Livengood was awakened by a phone call from Greg Page about the polling results, interrupting his recurring dream about the land of the long, dark river. An unexpected sense of worry haunted Livengood, even as he savored the victory with his ritual coffee, pastries and marijuana, but he was feeling almost jaunty by the time he strolled into his neighborhood polling place to add his vote to Christianson's total. Buoyed by his participation in democracy, as well as the other stimulants, Livengood arrived at the Harley Christianson for Governor Headquarters with a strut that his colleagues hadn't seen for many years.

"Congratulations," Greg Page said, looking up from his computer screen. "The numbers are down slightly from this morning, confirming my suspicion that Kline voters tend to sleep later than Christianson voters, but they're still in the major butt-kicking range, and they figure to hold up all day."

Livengood looked over Page's shoulder at the numbers and smiled.

"We could be looking at a record," Page said. "Harley's winning out west by margins that Stalin would have envied, and he's got substantial majorities in every county but Wyandotte and Douglas, and even there he's doing well. I'm doing a search for any bigger landslides in state electoral history, just in case you want to mention that in the victory speech."

After patting Page on the back and praising his efforts throughout the campaign, Livengood adjourned to his office and called Harley Christianson.

"Congrats, Governor," Livengood said. "The exit polling says you're the big winner."

"So I hear," Harley said. "Greg told me when I called in this morning."

Livengood was disappointed that Harley had heard the news elsewhere, but he knew that was the price for sleeping so long past dawn. Besides, Livengood figured, even Harley must have foreseen this victory.

"Pretty exciting, huh?" Livengood said.

"Tyrone's been running around the house shouting ever since I went down to vote this morning and all the TV and newspaper folks were there," Harley said. "And Christy's downright bonkers about it. Goodness, Frankie, you can't imagine how excited she is."

Livengood claimed to have some idea of how excited Mrs. Christianson must be.

"As for me, well, I'm a little nervous about the whole thing," Harley said.

"Nothing to be nervous about," Livengood said. "Just get into town before seven or so, because they're going to call this race early and we don't want to keep the media folks waiting around. About

7:30 or so, you give another victory speech, a lot like the one after the primary. The reporters will want to ask you about the race, but you just chalk it up to hard work and the little people and all that humble stuff. No one's likely to ask about policy stuff, but if they do, you can say you're saving all the big pronouncements for the State of the State speech."

"That's the part I'm a little nervous about," Harley said. "Have you figured out what we do next?"

"Oh yeah, that," Livengood said. "I'm a little nervous about that myself, but don't you worry. I'm working on it."

"I know you are, Frankie, and I appreciate that," Harley said. "And I want you to know how much I appreciate all the hard work you've already put in. Not every man gets to make his wife as proud as I seem to have done, and I know it would have never happened without you."

"It's been an honor," Livengood said. "And a blast."

"I'm just hoping that Christy'll be every bit as proud of me in four years," Harley said. "And that goes for the whole state of Kansas, too. I'm proud of this state, Frankie, and I want it to be proud of me."

Livengood had no words of reassurance, except to reiterate that he was working on it, but he did urge Harley to include the line about being proud of the state in his victory speech.

The Harley Christianson for Governor campaign's victory party at the Ramada Inn was a subdued affair. The enormity of the victory had created a sense of anti-climax among the participants, many of whom were further quieted by the realization of the responsibilities their victory would bring. The presence of so many reporters also kept the revelry within the bounds of propriety and the law.

CHAPTER THIRTEEN

The party at the Willa Kline for Governor Headquarters was far livelier, as Livengood was surprised to discover when he arrived around 10:00 p.m.

"Well, look who's here," Reynolds said, interrupting her conversation with Kline. "If it isn't the Kansas Kingmaker himself, our own Frankie Livengood."

"Hey, Rebecca," Livengood said, surprising her with his humble tone. "Howdy, Willa. Congratulations on a well-run race."

Kline shook Livengood's hand and made a self-deprecating joke about the race. Livengood laughed, and urged that Kline call him if the Women's Studies Department at Wichita State University ever needed help from the governor's office.

"You must be happy," Reynolds said.

"I guess so," Livengood said. "Not half as much as Harley's wife, but I guess it's just not in my nature to be that happy, thank God. I hope you're not mad at me."

"Just a little," Reynolds said. "You promised me that you wouldn't run up the score on us."

Livengood shrugged apologetically.

"Aw, what the hell," Reynolds said, as she started a long swallow from her glass of bourbon and Coke.

"Yeah," Livengood said. "What the hell."

"All day long I've been thinking, over and over again, about what we could have done differently," Reynolds said. "But you know what? I don't think there's anything we could have done. I just don't think you can get a Democrat as liberal as Willa Kline elected in a conservative Republican state like this."

Livengood pretended to ponder her theory for a moment, then told Reynolds that she just might be right.

CHAPTER FOURTEEN

"What Frankie Livengood Did Next"

Governor-elect Harley Christianson had promised the people a smooth transition of power, so Frankie Livengood made his best effort not to be caught gloating around his soon-to-be-unemployed former colleagues in the administration of Gov. Chuck Bentley. The task proved especially difficult during a meeting shortly after the election with the outgoing governor himself.

"Well, Frankie boy," Governor Bentley said, leaning back in his gubernatorial leather chair and swirling the ice in a scotch on the rocks. "It looks like you're going to outlast me around here after all. I reckon that congratulations are in order."

"Thank you," Livengood said, squirming in his seat as he struggled to keep his no-gloating pledge. "Sir."

"No shit, son," the governor said. "That was one hell of a job you did for your guy. One hell of a job."

"Well, thanks again," Livengood said, wishing desperately for just one tiny gloat. "Of course, I had me a hell of a candidate this time around."

Bentley laughed, as if the barb had missed its target, then chuckled, as if he appreciated the effort.

"Yes, indeedy," the governor said. "You had yourself a hell of a candidate this time around. Mayor of Piquant, Kansas. Makes furniture. Saved a militia nut in the war. Come to think of it, I guess he must have had himself one hell of a campaign manager."

"Maybe so," Livengood said. "Maybe so."

"On the other hand," Bentley said, "it's been my experience that in this state, the tricky part is getting yourself re-elected. It's also been my experience, unfortunately, that you're not such hot shit at that part, Frankie boy."

Livengood had assured Harley that he would not gloat, but he'd given no assurances about putting up with petty insults from lame duck governors. He crossed his legs and slid back in his chair, then squinted one eye and wryly raised his lip to the side of his face, all of which warned Bentley that Livengood was about to talk back.

"So why didn't you run again, Governor?" Livengood asked. "I have to admit, I've been so busy the last few months that I really can't remember what went wrong."

Bentley laughed as if genuinely amused.

"What didn't go wrong?" Bentley said, still laughing. "I'll admit that my crazy-ass ex-wife didn't help matters much, but sooner or later you'll remember that what mostly went wrong was you and your goddamn advice. 'Invest the surplus,' you said. 'Veto the tax cut,' you said. 'People will appreciate what you're saving them on down the road,' you said."

"It was good policy," Livengood said.

"Good policy my ass," the governor said. "It's good goddamn policy because the savings turn up in the next term, which turns out to have somebody else's ass sitting in this chair. The best policy is to get re-elected, and worry about the deficits then."

"Aw well, what the hell," Livengood said. "I thought you didn't want to be governor anymore, anyway. You've got a nice life to get back to, which is more than I could ever say."

"Damn right I got a good life to get back to. Better than this shit," Bentley said. "But I'll tell you something, son. I didn't build me that good life by having people tell me they didn't want me on the job, or by getting beat at anything. Maybe I didn't want to be governor anymore, but I don't like it that I couldn't have been even if I did want to."

"I'll keep that in mind for the next four years," Livengood said, meeting Bentley's stare unflinchingly. "With a little bit of luck, I'll be keeping it in mind for the next eight years."

"You're going to need a lot more than luck, boy," Bentley said, starting to smile again. "You don't like losing any more than I do, and you damn well know it, so you just try to remember my advice. Getting re-elected is always the best policy."

"I'll keep that in mind," Livengood said. "That might come in handy."

Frankie Livengood handled the rest of his transition chores across the street from the statehouse, in a small room in the Docking Office Building, the better to avoid encounters with the likes of Gov. Chuck Bentley.

The first order of business was selecting a staff for the new administration, a task that Harley Christianson had happily ceded to Livengood, who went about it just as happily. Livengood had long pipe-dreamed about choosing his own co-workers, and he reveled in the opportunity to toss out the resumes of several of his least favorite people.

Finding suitable candidates, however, proved more difficult than rejecting the unsuitable. After engaging Ed Walton as office manager, finding a position for Greg Page to use his technological and research skills in whatever manner he wanted, begging Wilbur Philip to accept the duties of budget director, and creating an educational advisor spot for Cathy Knieble, Livengood realized he had already hired nearly every friend he had, or at least the ones who could be recommended in good conscience to Harley Christianson.

During a brief lunch, Livengood offered Jane Hutchinson any job she wanted in the new administration.

"I do appreciate the offer," Hutchinson said. "I just don't think I'd be qualified for a policy-making job."

"Since when do you have to be qualified for a policy-making job?" Livengood said. "Where would I be if I'd ever had that attitude?"

Hutchinson thanked him again for the offer, but said she didn't see any chance of accomplishing her goals in the Christianson administration.

"And why not?" Livengood said.

"Because you want to get re-elected, and any politico as smart as you knows that fixing what's wrong with this state's environment is not going to achieve that objective."

Livengood was pained by her reasoning, but relieved by her answer.

When the staff had been assembled, Livengood turned to the task of preparing a budget proposal. Harley was eager to involve himself in this process, and he did so despite Livengood's increasingly unsubtle suggestions that the job was best left to professionals. With the same steady workaholism that he had applied when learning carpentry, Harley pored through reams of reports and stacks of statistics, and peppered Livengood, Philip and anyone else nearby with questions about the bizarre vocabulary and arcane bookkeeping gambits contained therein.

Even more annoyingly, Harley soon began to have his own ideas about how much should be allotted to each of the state's programs. At first Harley's suggested figures were stingy, just as Livengood had expected from a private sector sort taking his first serious look at the incomprehensibly huge amounts of government spending. A short time later Harley's proposals tended toward the profligate, just as Livengood had expected from someone being subjected for the first time to the sales pitches of advocacy groups.

"Please, Harley, you've got to stop going to these hearings," Livengood said, after the governor-elect had returned from an afternoon of tearful testimony by several mothers of children with special needs.

"Gee, Frankie," the next governor of Kansas said, obviously disappointed that his chief of staff did not share his enthusiasm for helping the specially needy children. "I thought they made a pretty good case."

"Of course they did," Livengood said. "They all do. That's why you've got to stop going to these hearings."

Harley tried to restate the case for fully funding their proposals, but without the heart-rending presence of the specially needy children he was unable to duplicate the rhetorical effectiveness of the hearings. Still, Harley argued as best he could on behalf of the mothers, who were hard-working members of the middle class, admirable in their love of family, blameless for the special needs of their children of God, and otherwise quite unlike Harley's idea of the kind of people who hit up the government for money.

"And you should have seen those kids," Harley said. "I swear, Frankie, it would have broken your heart."

Livengood waved his hand, as if trying to shoo away any misunderstanding about what he was about to say, then spoke in his most empathetic voice.

"I have seen those kids, Harley, and it did break my heart," Livengood said. "I'm not so cold that it doesn't affect me. Not yet, anyway. But I've also seen the sickly old people that you're scheduled to meet with on Wednesday, and I know that they'll break your heart, too. So will the veterans on Thursday, and so will the folks who will be here on Friday trying to save their small-town school. They all make a good case. They'll all break your heart. But what really breaks your heart is realizing that you can't help all of them, because what's left over in this damn budget after the federal mandates are met and the entitlements are paid for is just chump change compared to what people need. So please, Harley, stop going to these damn hearings."

Harley repeated that Livengood should have seen those children. Livengood put his hand to his chin, trying to think of an argument more persuasive than cute, specially needy kids.

"You keep looking at these things on a case by case basis, and you'll wind up as liberal as Willa Kline," Livengood said. "If you're going to be true to the conservative philosophy that people voted for, you have to look at this on a macro level. You have to look at the big picture."

Harley thought it over from the taxpayer's point of view, and admitted that Livengood had a point. Still, there was something so compellingly sad about those specially needy children and their loving mothers. Harley stared sadly at the stacks of papers on his desk, as if trying to discern the big picture within them, but only seeing the human suffering each statistic represented. His glum expression overwhelmed Livengood's fiscal conservatism.

"If it'll make you feel any better, I'll get Wilbur to look into what we can do for these kids," Livengood said. "But really, Harley, you have to realize the limits to our power here. Otherwise we'll just wind up getting replaced, and probably by people who aren't as sensitive about retarded kids as you and me."

After a moment's contemplation, Harley told Livengood that it was harder than he expected being the governor.

"Aw, you'll get used to it," Livengood said. "There's bound to be hearings coming up with some regular Joes who really, really need a tax break for their cute kids, and you can sit in on those."

The budget proposal was finished early on a Friday afternoon, and Livengood looked upon his work and called it good. Harley still didn't like the sum that had been set aside for the specially needy children, but he was nonetheless shocked at the size of the overall budget. Various other voices registered complaints with Livengood, ranging from the usual business associations and advocacy groups, griping about their pet projects, to Jane Hutchinson, grousing about the lack of environmental spending, to Rebecca Reynolds, who made an utterly unrealistic demand for abortion subsidies to poor women.

Livengood knew that such wailing would continue for the next four years, and for another four after that if he was lucky, so he took off early on that Friday and attended a basketball game between the Washburn University Ichabods and the Pittsburg State University Gorillas.

Despite Mrs. Christianson's meticulously laid plans for an elegant evening, the inaugural ball turned out to be a relatively raucous affair.

Mick Fixx resumed his friendship with Big Jim Morland in the time it took to swig two shots of bourbon, and the pair were soon loudly doing a sort of harmonizing along with the band's rendition of "Roly Poly." Ellen Winston, whose scandalous reputation almost obliged her to make some sort of scene on such occasions, danced in a flamboyantly suggestive manner with a few of the married campaign contributors. Greg Page kept disappearing from the proceedings for several minutes at a time, often in the company of

Livengood, returning each time with ever redder eyes. Merle Lee tried unsuccessfully to flirt with a succession of women, seeming to gain determination with each rejection. Wilbur Philip indulged in alcohol, which was unusual for him, and engaged in uncharacteristically frank discussions about his personal life with several co-workers, who were surprised to discover that he had one. Dan Dorsey, who stood out in his brown suit among the black tuxedoes, drank as much as he could while still keeping legible notes.

Reynolds attended in a revealing gown purchased during a recent trip to New York City, and with Hutchinson having declined an invitation to the ball, Livengood displayed his new relationship conspicuously. When the introductions were exchanged with Pastor Jeffries and his wife, who apparently was named "Mrs. Pastor Jeffries," Livengood defiantly mentioned Reynolds' occupation. Although Mrs. Pastor Jeffries was unsmiling and silent, Pastor Jeffries politely explained that he could not support her in her political endeavors, but wished her happiness in the rest of her life.

Pastor Jeffries was equally friendly in his dealings with the aggressively inebriated Chip Wentworth, who tried to engage him in a theological discussion. Arvin Howard, whose mere presence at the ball greatly pleased Livengood, further gratified his host by breaking up the debate before Wentworth's blasphemies were overheard by Darla Morland and her equally sensitive boyfriend.

Mark Stark spent most of the evening on the arm of Mrs. Christianson, who thought his indefatigable dancing ability and far-ranging conversational skills made him the perfect ball escort. She was also delighted to hear Stark announce that he had arranged for Harley's large inventory of hand-made furniture to be sold in a very fashionable New York store. The news of Stark's deal had made Mrs. Christianson giddy with anticipation of riches beyond Kansas.

CHAPTER FOURTEEN

Livengood, having already arranged transportation back to his apartment for himself and Reynolds, allowed himself to become fully drunk. Just as he reached that long-awaited state, Governor Christianson requested a moment of his time.

Livengood followed Harley into the bitter cold outside the concrete convention hall, and asked what could be so important as to interrupt such a festive occasion.

"I still don't know what we should be doing," Harley said. "I keep running that inauguration speech over in my mind, and it just didn't say anything. I'm not saying you didn't do a good job with it, but it was just a bunch of platitudes about good government."

"That's what made it such a good speech," Livengood said. "What we're aiming for here is good government, and that's the government which governs least. The specifics can wait until the State of the State speech."

"But I keep running that State of the State speech over in my mind, and there's nothing in there, either," Harley said, his head down and his hands jammed in his pockets as he paced in the icy wind. "I mean, there's nothing big in there. Didn't God put me here to do something big?"

On the purely intellectual level where he preferred to dwell, Livengood believed that political power derived from the people, not God, and that history proved it was dangerous to proceed on any other assumption. In his heart he believed that God worked in mysterious ways, but even there he was skeptical that God would resort to such mysterious means as Big Jim's hamburger money, Merle Lee's television ads and Livengood's political tactics. Intellectually and instinctively, he knew better than to wade into such matters with Harley.

"Let's just not make God any promises we can't keep," Livengood said. "I think that if we can just keep Kansas a relatively sane place for the next four years, then God ought to be plenty pleased with that."

Harley, seeming not to notice the cold, stared at the stars. After a few seconds that trudged along as if sloshing through the snow, Harley turned to Livengood and asked if they could pray together.

"Jeez, Harley, I don't know," Livengood said. "I'm a little uncomfortable about dragging God into this political stuff, and besides, I'm a little drunk."

"Please, Frankie. We're going to need His help."

Livengood had to agree that a little bit of divine intervention might prove useful in the upcoming years, but he explained that he didn't feel right about asking for it. Harley asked why not.

"Like I say, I'm a little drunk," Livengood said. "Besides, it's been my habit to keep my prayers private. I was always taught that prayer should contain a fair degree of confession, and I really don't think you want to hear any of that."

"Please," Harley said, squeezing Livengood's arm with a strength that conveyed his need. "Please join me in this prayer."

Livengood reluctantly agreed, even after seeing that Harley intended for the prayer to be offered on their knees. Slowly dropping his rented pants onto the snow-covered grass, Livengood lowered his head and clasped his hands as Harley began to pray.

"Dear Lord in Heaven," Harley said, in a respectful but familiar tone. "We seek Your guidance on this beautiful night on Your wonderful Kansas prairie. We come to You as sinners, as weak men who stray too often from Your path of righteousness, but we come to You with humility and a sincere desire for Your wisdom. You have granted us a position of power among men, and we offer You our thanks for this honor, and petition Your blessings as we seek to uphold its awesome responsibilities. We ask Your forgiveness for the sins we have committed, so that we may go with the Holy Ghost as we seek to serve Your people in the way You would desire. We ask that You grant us wisdom, strength, compassion. In Christ's name we pray. Amen."

Livengood opened his eyes to see Harley smiling toward the stars, and he muttered an ashamed, "Amen."

Livengood recounted the incident to Rebecca Reynolds, who rolled her eyes and offered him another drink.

"It was bad enough when I had all these damn voters to deal with," Livengood said. "Now I've got God on my back."

Reynolds laughed, kissed Livengood on the cheek and attempted to joke him out of his suddenly contemplative mood. He kissed her on the lips, and she kissed him back lasciviously. They adjourned to an empty coatroom.

Several minutes later, Darla Morland entered the coatroom in search of her mink stole, shrieking when she discovered the activity within. Livengood yanked his head from between Reynolds' legs and gave chase, apologizing to Darla to an extent that would keep her from reporting the incident to her father. The sound of Reynolds' throaty laughter could be heard in the background.

The next two years passed without further incident, or at least without any incidents that led to damning headlines. The economy of Kansas stumbled along at the same unsatisfactory pace as the rest of the country, the government of Kansas delivered on its promises of roads, prisons and the occasional social program with as much efficiency as anyone might reasonably expect, and there was a happily boring lack of scandal associated with the Christianson administration.

A slew of abortion bills were proposed in the legislature, but each was stillborn in committee, so Reynolds had only personal quarrels with Livengood. Wentworth, Big Jim and the various other big contributors were satisfied to be free of any governmental hassles, and made no further demands on the administration. Even such a diligent pressman as Dan Dorsey failed to find newsworthy faults in the administration, and most of the Kansas media weren't even bothering to look.

Only Harley seemed dissatisfied with his two years of service in the governor's office, but somehow Livengood was able to restrain Harley's desire to do something big, arguing with all his rhetorical might that the administration was thus far proving worthy of God's blessing.

"When you get to heaven, you can tell Him that you didn't screw anything up," Livengood said. "Believe me, He'll be impressed. He doesn't get to hear that from ex-governors very often."

Harley shook his head and stared out the window, as if the answer he was seeking might magically appear on the drugstore billboard across the street. He asked Livengood about the results of the recent legislative elections.

"So the religious right picked up a few more seats," Livengood said. "That doesn't mean anything about you. They still don't have enough votes to push their agenda through, so what the hell."

Harley reiterated that he wanted to do something for Kansas. He mentioned God again.

"I think you're set with God, Harley," Livengood said. "It's the rest of us you ought to be worried about, and so far we all seem to love you."

Livengood bopped out of the governor's office with characteristic cockiness, but the glowering visage of John Brown startled him into a more humble gait. Although he'd seen the mural thousands of times, Livengood had never noticed just how reproving was the look on John Brown's face.

CHAPTER FIFTEEN

"Edna Dimschmidt and the Terrible Swift Sword"

The inauguration of the heathen Harley Christianson caused a crisis of faith for Edna Dimschmidt, leading her down a perilous new path on her spiritual journey.

That journey had begun shortly after the Second World War, when Edna Herschenshorn was born into a church-going family in the town of Clompsville. Edna's father had won war hero status by charging a German machine-gun nest during the Battle of the Bulge, and was rewarded with a job tapping the massive natural gas fields of southwestern Kansas. Her mother, a silently obeisant daughter of the Dust Bowl, was satisfied to make a home on her husband's modest wages.

Young Edna liked to help her mother bake pies, to run along the dirt roads that led out of their town, and to play with her dolls and imagine that she lived a life more like the ones she saw once a week at the local theater. Best of all, she liked the services at the small white church she attended with her father and mother on Sunday mornings, and with her mother on Sunday and Wednesday evenings. The services were the only time in Edna's life when she sang, or heard talk of ideas even bigger than Kansas childhood, or was free to feel without limitation. The services also offered the soul-comforting assurance that she would have the last laugh on those richer and more glamorous city slickers in the movies, who seemed to taunt her with their distance and indifference.

Such consolations became increasingly important to Edna after she lost her father. Charging a German machine-gun post was one thing, but living with young Edna and her mother atop a massive field of natural gas was another thing, so one sunny day he packed up a few things and deserted. One rumor had him moving to Wichita for work in an aircraft factory, another had him moving to Amarillo with a Mennonite woman gone bad.

Amateur psychoanalysts across the state of Kansas would later speculate that her father's departure had created "abandonment issues" for Edna. Sometimes when she told her life story to spellbound audiences at protest rallies, she would admit as much, and in as many words, but at the time a more pressing concern was her fall from the graces of the lower-middle class to the perdition of the lower-lower class. Edna's mother had never aspired to learn any ability other than making a home to the satisfaction of a man, and her desultory search for unskilled labor led young Edna through a series of cheap apartments in a succession of ever drearier towns.

The only constant in Edna's life was the church. She clung ever more fiercely to the comforting knowledge that someday she would inherit a mansion in the sky, while those who were more fortunate than herself on Earth would not. At the age of 13 she was born again in the chlorinated water of a concrete baptismal tank, swearing to herself and her mother that she would never stray from the one true way of the Lord.

It didn't take, though, and by the age of 15 Edna had strayed so far as to sass her mother on a regular basis, smoke cigarettes, and stay out until well past midnight with boys who listened to rock 'n' roll music and wore greasy hair and black leather jackets. By the age of 16 she was having sex with a few of the more complimentary boys, and she did so with the same degree of fervor she had previously devoted to religion. Later, at the height of her political notoriety, some of those former boyfriends would brag to their disbelieving friends that she had been the best piece of ass they'd ever had.

After a brief confinement in a Wichita home for wayward girls, young Edna attained the age of discretion and began a life of independent destitution in the city. By now the boys she ran with were wearing naturally greasy hair and fringed leather jackets, and she followed one to the fringes of what passed for a hippie scene at Wichita State University, where she partook of many pleasures of the flesh and dabbled in radical politics. By the mid-seventies, young Edna had become addicted to various drugs, engaged in sexual relations that were suspiciously pragmatic if not outright prostitution, and was poorer than her mother had ever been.

A job installing detonation caps at a munitions factory in Parsons led Edna back to the small town life, which in turn led inevitably back to a church. At the first service she attended, complete with songs and big ideas and those old familiar feelings, Edna answered the preacher's call and re-dedicated her life to Jesus Christ and God's one true way.

This time, it took. Edna foreswore drugs, alcohol, fornication and leftist ideology, never to look back except in regret and shame. She attended every service held at her church, read the Bible every day, and strove to live by the concepts they taught. Although no longer sure of her own salvation, she once again savored the certain damnation of a world that had so badly mistreated her.

She was soon able to obtain a higher-paying job back in Wichita, with a lesser chance of accidental explosion, and was once again in the comforting bosom of the middle class. She occasionally dated, but only with suitably pious and upwardly mobile men.

One such man was Barney Dimschmidt, and after participating in Edna's first minor sexual transgression since her re-conversion, he asked for her very expert hand in marriage. Despite Barney's sexual awkwardness, and in part because of the admirable lack of experience that it belied, Edna accepted. One chaste year later, Barney and Edna were married and living in a split-level home in Goddard.

The marriage was mostly silent and incessantly dull, but Mrs. Edna Dimschmidt found it altogether preferable to her loud and interesting past. Two years went by in splendid monotony. Except for her failure to become pregnant, and the continued existence of people with even more money and status than herself, she had nothing to complain about in her nightly prayers.

Then, on a calm and sunny spring day in the suburbs, Edna Dimschmidt experienced a sharp stomach pain and discovered a stream of blood trickling down her thigh. A day later Edna and her husband met with a doctor in his office at a west Wichita mini-mall, and were told that she had miscarried a three-week-old embryo. The doctor further explained that the same condition which had caused the miscarriage would likely prevent Edna from ever becoming pregnant again.

Barney Dimschmidt took the news well, with relief for his wife's safety, but she wept openly. He had never seen her do that, not even at her mother's funeral.

The incident did not shake Edna Dimschmidt's faith, but rather strengthened it. Resigned that she would never honor God with another life, she doubled her resolve to honor Him with the one life that He had given her.

Barney Dimschmidt was religious, but not to the same extent as his wife, whose fervency began to strain his patience. Edna began to spend so much time at church services that it interfered with his work and weekend recreations. Her increasing outspokenness, about an ever-widening range of subjects, became even more problematic.

Sex soon became a chore that Edna performed perfunctorily, and Barney started to resent the passion and inventiveness that his wife had seemingly expended on a succession of thugs and hippie freaks in the wilder days she now spoke of so shamefully.

Sometimes, usually when one of the shapelier saleswomen or secretaries would pass by his desk at the real estate office, Barney Dimschmidt longed for wilder days of his own. One day a 23-year-old saleswoman recognized that longing in his leer, and returned a look that expressed similar desires of her own. An affair ensued, followed six months later by Barney's demand for a divorce.

Edna Dimschmidt would never admit to the sense of relief she felt, preferring to play the role of heroic victim. No longer constrained by the burdens of wifely obedience, she was now free to fulfill her preferred obligations on a full-time basis. Because of Barney's affair she received generous alimony payments, as well as a scriptural loophole for a sin-free divorce, even if the scriptures in question did refer only to a woman's adultery.

Dimschmidt seized the opportunity to assert herself into a more prominent leadership role in her church's struggle against the vices of the modern world.

Dimschmidt's church already had leaders, however, and on scriptural grounds they were convinced that women should keep silent in the church. On practical grounds, they were particularly opposed to women so potentially troublesome as Edna Dimschmidt. With scriptural grounds of her own, Dimschmidt took her struggle to the protest rallies that were becoming increasingly popular among Kansas' politicized Christians.

Of all the vices of the modern world, Dimschmidt's favorite to struggle against was abortion. Dimschmidt knew in her brain, and could feel in her barren womb, that abortion was murder, plain and simple. Backed in this view by the Bible and the scientifically irrefutable videotapes she had seen at various meetings, Dimschmidt felt justified to use any means to prevent abortion, making it an especially appealing cause. Saving the unborn babies proved more fun than mere housewifery, and more in keeping with her heroic self-image.

For the most part, Edna was content to patrol the sidewalks outside Wichita's abortion clinics, shouting accusations of baby-killing and genocide at the varied young women who attempted to gain entrance. Armed with her "AKCs," which was the abortion protest lingo for picket signs proclaiming that "Abortion Kills Children," she was on the sidewalk nearly every minute that she could spare from her part-time job at a southside convenience store. Other protestors began to appear, and Edna reveled in their respect and willingness to follow her orders. The reporters who dropped by from time to time began to count on her for inflammatory quotes, furthering her reputation as a leader of the state's burgeoning anti-abortion movement.

When the big protests broke out, with thousands of latecomers joining the struggle on the sidewalks at the behest of high-profile organizers from far out of town, Dimschmidt suddenly found herself out of the limelight. She resented the arrogant out-of-towners and their dilettante baby-savers, and vowed that they would not usurp her rightful place in the history books that were sure to be written when abortion was vanquished.

Eventually the out-of-towners went back out of town, just as Dimschmidt had known they would, and only she and a few stalwarts remained on the sidewalks to continue the struggle. Of these, the most loyal to Dimschmidt was Ellie Whimple.

Ellie Whimple grew up in the Catholic faith and never encountered any compelling reason to doubt it, even when her parents died in a gruesome car accident when she was only 13 years old. Being orphaned seemed to strengthen Ellie's deep-seated faith, and exacerbate her passionate yearning to be told what do, and when the out-of-town protestors came to her church, seeking recruits, she gratefully followed them to the sidewalks of Wichita.

Before she was allowed to commit any acts of civil disobedience, Ellie attended a course of workshops where she viewed several scientifically irrefutable videotapes. She became utterly convinced that babies were being killed within the walls of the abortion clinic where she was to march, to the extent that when she arrived at the clinic gates for the first time she fell into a fetal position and began crying uncontrollably. Paralyzed by the idea that she was powerless to stop the slaughter going on just a few feet away, Ellie could not even unfurl herself as the police hauled her off to a city bus and on to jail each day of the summer.

Even by the surreal standards of the big protests, Ellie Whimple was quite a sight. Most of the other protesters began to avoid her, and before long even the huggiest among them had stopped trying to interrupt her inconsolable grief. A man that she later came to know as Frankie Livengood tried to offer his assistance on one hot and raucous day, but he was so uncomfortable and awkward in the attempt that she begged him to go away and leave her alone. Only Edna Dimschmidt fully shared her pain, and hugged her, and took her home for food and sleep, and promised to help her save the unborn babies by any means necessary. Only Edna Dimschmidt cared enough to tell Ellie what to do.

As much as Ellie hated to abandon her daily ritual on the sidewalks outside the clinic, she followed without question when Dimschmidt decided to concentrate on saving babies through the political process with her newly formed Kansans United for a Sin-Free

Kansas. Dimschmidt had concluded that most of the so-called baby-savers in Kansas would not follow her to prison, but a worthwhile number of them might follow her to the polls.

Kansans United for a Sin-Free Kansas was one of many anti-abortion organizations active in the state, but it quickly distinguished itself as the most radical. Nearly all of the other groups refused to endorse violence as a means of stopping abortion, no matter how tepid their condemnations of that method, but Kansans United for a Sin-Free Kansas was unequivocal in stating that abortion could ethically be prevented by the same wide range of means allowed to stop any other murder. Most of the other groups disavowed any agenda beyond saving unborn babies, but Kansans United for a Sin-Free Kansas was unabashed in proclaiming that banning abortion would merely be a first step toward the legal prohibition of many unsavory things.

Dimschmidt soon recruited a small but efficient army of supporters who were willing to perform a variety of tedious and time-consuming chores, and compiled a much larger list of people with similar views if less commitment. Politicians were now courting her approval, and the press frequently sought her colorful quotes.

With a significant bloc of legislators, three State Board of Education members, and commissioners of twenty-eight counties in her debt, Dimschmidt began to think about what a boon it would be to God if the governor of Kansas were also within her sphere of political influence. When Dimschmidt met Hampton Hibbert after delivering a standard stump speech at a church in Haysville, the idea began to consume her.

Persuading Hampton to run proved simple, and persuading him to grant her complete control of the campaign was only slightly more difficult. Dimschmidt then shaped him into a legitimate contender with a savvy that surprised even herself. She had the

Kansans United for a Sin-Free Kansas working at peak efficiency, shrewdly manipulated her numerous press contacts, and directed campaign appearances with the flair of a Broadway impresario. What little money she was able to raise in church basements and mass mailings was productively spent on television and radio advertisements, and she impressed even her adversaries with her talent for these media.

Pastor Jeffries and his protégé, Rep. Stan Patterson, whom Dimschmidt regarded as accommodationists to the vices of the modern world, were forced to acknowledge her influence when they unsuccessfully attempted to negotiate her out of the race. Even Frankie Livengood, whom Dimschmidt regarded as the very personification of the vices of the modern world, had been forced to acknowledge that she handled the Hibbert sex scandal well. Dimschmidt was convinced that these enemies would, in the words of a cherished verse from the Book of Psalms, "lick the dust."

Then came the election, and Edna Dimschmidt was plunged into a deep melancholy.

If Dimschmidt could not recruit a mere plurality of the Kansas Republican Party to join her struggle against the vices of the modern world, what chance did she have of persuading a majority of voters in a country that included such places as New York and California? Feeling betrayed by her countrymen, Dimschmidt began to suspect that democratic processes would not be useful in her quest.

She continued to preach, and with ever more fervor, to the extent that even the most outspoken of Kansas' preachers soon became nervous about her beliefs. The abortion protest movement was waning, too, so Dimschmidt and Ellie reluctantly returned to full-time jobs at a south Wichita grocery store. Dimschmidt assured Ellie that she had not abandoned her struggle against the vices of the modern world, but she temporarily reduced it to attendance at the occasional seminar about the impending one world government and monthly visits to gun shows.

Ellie did not share Dimschmidt's newfound passion for guns and the rhetoric of violent revolution, nor did she feel quite right about the way Edna would read the paper every morning and always find another reason to despise Gov. Harley Christianson. As far as Ellie could tell, the governor didn't seem to be doing much about anything; but in a world where sin ran rampant and babies were being slaughtered, and the rightful leaders were relegated to working the register at a southside grocery store, such inaction was amply evil for Dimschmidt. When a slate of legislative candidates backed by Pastor Jeffries was elected two years into Harley's first term, Dimschmidt was determined to rectify the rule of evil men in Kansas.

Despite her unvoiced misgivings, Ellie assisted Dimschmidt in her constant search for any piece of available information about Christianson, even going along on a long drive to Piquant for more research. A slightly familiar man at the counter watched inscrutably as Dimschmidt and Ellie prayed over their chicken fried steaks at the town's diner.

"What brings you ladies to a town like this?" the man asked, just a moment after hearing Dimschmidt say, "Amen."

While Ellie looked silently at her plate, Dimschmidt looked at the man with an intimidating expression.

"What are you gals called?" the man said, obviously unintimidated. "Where you from?"

"I'm Edna Dimschmidt, and this is my friend Ellie Whimple. We're from Wichita, we're here on business, and if you don't mind, we're trying to eat."

"What kind of business are you gals in?"

"We serve the Lord," Dimschmidt said, without looking at the man at all.

"Ha," the man said. "I'm Will Schnitzle, and I work for a goddamn living."

Will Schnitzle liked to think of himself as the most fucked-over man in America, and the few people who had ever bothered to listen to him had to agree that he made a strong case for the claim.

Born poor and ugly to the meanest man and wife in northwest Kansas, Schnitzle grew up on the family dirt farm with a lack of almost everything except ass-kickings. His father beat him on a regular basis, right up to the very minute of his fatal heart attack, and then all of the neighbor boys save Harley Christianson pitched in with typical small town helpfulness to beat him even more. As a teenager Schnitzle joined the Piquant High School sports teams, making ass-kickings an extra-curricular activity.

Then Schnitzle found himself waist deep in some damn Vietnamese swamp, with bullets flying every which way and bombs blasting every few feet and all manner of death and destruction suddenly springing up from bushes and trees and tiny children. Nobody even bothered to give him a reasonable explanation for that ass-kicking.

Will Schnitzle had been dead broke and without prospects when he left for Vietnam, and he returned to find himself even poorer. America had gone crazy in his absence, in ways that diminished his modest store of self-worth.

Having served his country in battle did not seem to warrant the same respect that America had accorded the crusty and conceited World War II veterans of his town, or even the somewhat younger men who had gone to Korea, and what little fanfare the town did muster was mostly for the benefit of Harley Christianson and his couple of decorations.

Being white was no longer as prestigious as before, either. A war on poverty had been declared back on the home front, but it seemed to Schnitzle that its biggest battles were being fought far away from him. No one was holding protests or being interviewed on the evening news for the sake of the poor people of towns like Piquant, and no anti-defamation league was demanding that smart-ass comedians stop telling jokes about them. A few well-dressed black men in New York City tried to assure him that he still enjoyed many unfair privileges as a white man, but Schnitzle, watching their fuzzy images on the aging American-made television in his northwest Kansas trailer park, was unconvinced.

Schnitzle was rarely out of a job, for there's always work for a man who can take an ass-kicking, but the money he earned and the small profit he derived from the family's miniscule farm was barely sufficient even for his modest needs. When the price of farmland began to rise dizzyingly in the seventies, a man from the United States Department of Agriculture urged Schnitzle to borrow against that value and buy even more.

At his mother's urging, he took a wife, who bore him a son.

When the land boom ended, the man from the Department of Agriculture recommended bankruptcy. In a land where longhaired hippie freaks could make a killing singing folk songs against God, Schnitzle discovered that a hard-working white man couldn't make a living growing wheat. Except for the love of his wife and son, Schnitzle's only consolation was that so many of his neighbors were also losing their farms.

Schnitzle's violence toward his wife had grown more frequent and severe as his financial situation worsened, and she eventually divorced him. He was ordered to pay an unrealistic amount of alimony and was denied any contact with his son, except under his wife's supervision at her far-away new home. As far as Schnitzle was concerned, the government had taken away the love of his wife and son.

Determined to learn the cause of his problems, Schnitzle commenced an intensive study of the many theories available at the gun shows he attended. Schnitzle was not surprised to discover that a nefarious cabal of Jews, bankers, Eastern business magnates and communist saboteurs was responsible for his difficulties, but he was startled to find out that English common law, his status as a free-born white man under the Fourteenth Amendment, his Kansas citizenship under the Tenth Amendment, and the power that grew out of the barrel of the Second Amendment all offered him possible solutions. Schnitzle was particularly impressed with a treatise that explained how all of his debts were invalid by virtue of the illegality of America's currency system, although he was suspicious that the man who sold it to him insisted on being paid in cash.

There was a massive military establishment backing the counterfeit government, so Schnitzle decided that he should get an army of his own. He found a handful of other dispossessed farmers who shared his concerns that the impending one world government might attempt to impose its will on Piquant, and they began training for a defensive effort in the fields outside of town. The group was dubbed The First Regimental Kansas Free Citizen Militia Brigade, and Schnitzle, by virtue of his military experience, was dubbed Supreme Commandant General. The post was far more fun than the work he had found as a mechanic, and far more in keeping with his heroic self-image.

The First Regimental Kansas Free Citizen Militia eventually grew to twenty-three troops, and Schnitzle became ever more confident of his ability to whip any one world governments that might come around, despite the joshing that he was subjected to by some of the townspeople. His long-battered ego got yet another boost when boyhood friend Harley Christianson ran for governor, and the strange city boy who ran the campaign signed him to star in the television commercials.

Then came the dreaded media, who discovered Schnitzle's militia activities and deviously tried to use them to disparage Christianson's candidacy. The attention scared off all but a handful of Schnitzle's troops, to a point they were no longer an effective military deterrent. Worse yet, Harley Christianson himself had betrayed Schnitzle by refusing to endorse the constitutional legitimacy and patriotic necessity of the First Regimental Kansas Free Citizens Militia Brigade. In fact, Harley's cowardly attempts to distance himself from the group had encouraged the ridicule Schnitzle was forced to endure from his fellow citizens.

Schnitzle's resentment festered with every day that Harley Christianson spent in the splendor of the so-called Kansas government. The longstanding hatred that Schnitzle now felt for the government—the faceless institution that had deserted him to a boyhood of poverty and deprivation, sent him to an unsung war, conned him into bankruptcy, and ripped his son away from his home—now wore the face of the only person he actually knew who possessed some of its power.

When the two ladies from Wichita asked him at the local cafe if he knew Gov. Harley Christianson, Schnitzle looked them straight in the eyes and said, "Hell yes, I know that bastard."

The ensuing conversation between Dimschmidt and Schnitzle lasted until the cafe closed, and then continued over strong coffee at Schnitzle's trailer home. Dimschmidt and Ellie left to check in at a nearby motel around 2:00 a.m., but rejoined Schnitzle a few hours later for more talk of Gov. Harley Christianson and everything else that was wrong in the world. Letters, phone calls and an exchange of visits extended the conversation for several more months.

Dimschmidt did not share Schnitzle's racist beliefs, but neither was she personally offended by them, and on almost every other subject she found that they were in complete agreement. She was also impressed with his willingness to defy authority, and with the hardened physique that made his claims seem plausible.

Schnitzle was equally taken with Dimschmidt. He liked her ideas, admired her ability to quote scripture and theologically justify his ambitions, and for reasons he couldn't name he suspected that she would be good in bed.

Ellie Whimple did not like Schnitzle at all, and she worried that his growing closeness with Dimschmidt would ultimately be harmful to somebody. Nonetheless, she voiced no objection when Dimschmidt announced that what was left of Kansans United for a Sin-Free Kansas would move to Piquant to merge with what was left of the First Regimental Kansas Free Citizens Militia Brigade.

CHAPTER SIXTEEN

"The Long, Dark River"

The sky looked endlessly blue to Frankie Livengood as he leaned back in his leather chair and gazed contentedly through his office window, happy with the calm that had descended on the capitol after the legislative session, blissfully ignorant of the storm that was gathering in southwest Kansas.

The massive black clouds developed rapidly over Ford County, but in spite of high winds on the ground they moved slowly, pouring torrential rains along the Arkansas River. The cowboys of the Beef-Tek Industries ranch east of Dodge City nervously eyed the clouds for tornadic swirls as they scrambled to bring in equipment and calm their 100,000 head of cattle. One flash in a bombardment of lightning, and its immediate clap of thunder, so frightened the animals that they charged against the gate and made a crashing escape onto the open plains. Several of the men made chase on horse and truck, and two vaqueros who had been repairing a section of the waste lagoon near the river were summoned to help.

No tornado swooped down from the clouds, but that was about the best that the cowboys could say of the storm. Lightning disabled the electrical and telephone systems, straight-line winds in excess of eighty miles an hour wobbled everything that was meant to stand up straight, and flash flooding climbed up the river banks and washed away everything in its path. The un-mended portion of the waste lagoon didn't stand a chance, and two weeks' worth of feces from 100,000 head of cattle was rushed downstream toward the Wichita River Festival.

A large percentage of Wichita's 300,000 or so people were gathered along the Arkansas River banks in downtown Wichita for the city's week-long festival, with its water skiing exhibitions, canoe races and bathtub regattas, and many of them were angered by the arrival of massive amounts of fecal matter. They were not placated by the arrival of Frankie Livengood, who joined with experts from the Kansas Department of Health and Environment in a diligent effort to lessen the political damage. The festival went on, with all participants duly warned of the health risks involved in taking to the river, but despite Livengood's public relations efforts there was a flash of public outrage, and much was made of it by the local newspaper and television stations.

Within a few months the river had returned to its usual high level of fecal contamination, and the public and media had returned to their usual low levels of concern about it.

That was not the end of the matter for Frankie Livengood, however. Gov. Harley Christianson, who had been in Wichita as a personal guest of festival mascot Admiral Windwagon Smith, continued to take a lively interest in the incident, and the river's perpetual problem with various forms of pollution. Worse yet, he began to get ideas.

"I've been thinking," the governor said one day, after summoning Livengood to his office. "It's about that river pollution thing."

"Now, sir," Livengood said, hoping to stop the conversation before it could take root. "I really don't think anyone could have expected us to do anything about that. There was a storm—this is Kansas. There was a gigantic feedlot—this is Kansas. Shit happens, as they say. We're supposed to check up on every pile of cow manure in the state?"

"Yeah, I think we are," Harley said. "There's supposed to be some kind of regulations about these things, and we're supposed to enforce them."

"Aw, come on, sir. There's a jillion of these damned regulations, maybe two jillion. We can't be expected to enforce them all. Believe me, nobody wants us to. It would take more bureaucrats than anyone would ever want to have around, and half those regulations are just plain nonsense anyway. I know, because I was in on most of them."

"But surely you have to agree, Frankie, with the regulations that say you can't dump the dung from a hundred thousand head of cattle into a river that people are trying to race bathtubs on. That one seems pretty commonsensical to me."

"I'll tell you what, sir. I'll get in touch with all the inspectors and field agents and whatnot down in Ford County, and I'll personally kick their asses for not knowing that a flash flood was coming while a waste lagoon was being repaired. Will that make you feel any better?"

"No, no, no," the governor said, waving his hands and grimacing. "That wouldn't make me feel one bit better. Just write those boys a note or something, and see if they need any help down there. I've been looking into this, and the fact is that most of the rivers and creeks in this state are too polluted to swim in or fish out of at any given time. The only thing that's going to make me feel any better is if we clean up those rivers and streams, and that's exactly what I aim to do. Frankie, we're going to clean up this damn mess."

Livengood exhaled deeply, steeling himself for the task of talking Harley out of another idea.

"That sounds very expensive, sir," Livengood said. "And if you don't mind my saying so, it sounds liberal. I don't see any political advantage to it at all."

"Is that why you got into this business? To gain political advantage?"

"No sir, that's not why I got into this business," Livengood said. "But I have found that it's the only way to stay in this business. And I might add that I've stayed in it long enough to know that cleaning up rivers and streams is not a practical goal for this administration."

"Why not?"

Livengood couldn't believe that he had to explain such things to a governor, but he proceeded to do so nonetheless.

"First of all, the beef people and the big corporate farms would slaughter us. Their manure and chemicals are in the water, you know, along with some help from a few other well-lobbied industries, and these people are not without their resources. They've got money out the ass, they've got a whole bunch of legislators whose constituents depend on those industries for jobs, and the state government itself relies heavily on its share of their corporate profits. And you know what? They're not bullshitting you when they say that any possible solution you come up with to your problem will endanger those profits. Plus, their TV ads are better than ours, and they've got lawyers like you wouldn't believe."

"Well then, Frankie, we'll just have to sit down with these folks and work something out," Harley said.

"Good luck. I've been dealing with these guys ever since I was a young punk, and I don't remember them ever asking what they could do to help out with the state's environment."

"Well then, Frankie, we'll just have to go to the people with this."

"That's the bigger problem, sir. There's no upside here, because the people aren't going to like this idea any better than big beef and big agribusiness folks. What you're proposing would be very, very expensive, and a big chunk of that money would have to come from taxpayers who believe they're already paying too much. People may bitch and moan a lot about wanting the rivers cleaned up, but when it comes right down to it, clean rivers are not high on the list of things they would choose to spend their money on. We've done polling on this, and people would rather buy a new bass boat to go float on dirty water than stand on the shore and admire the clean stuff. Besides, even if you were able to get tough regulations on runoff and enforce them efficiently, they'd just pack up their operations and head off to Oklahoma or Texas or some other place where people don't mind driving past a dirty river on their way to a job. Hell, for that matter, they'll probably get a bunch of new tax abatements when they do. When you run off a multi-billion dollar business or two, you make it tough on the Kansas way of life. You've got a lot of jobless and pissed off Kansans, and the ripple effect is going to be felt in the voting booths as far east as Johnson County."

Harley Christianson leaned back in his chair and scratched his chin, which Livengood understood to mean that he was about to say something final.

"Did you ever swim in a Kansas river, Frankie?"

"No, sir. I wouldn't want to do that."

"I haven't done it in years, because I can't. It dawned on me during the River Festival what a shame that is. When I was a kid we used to go down to swim in the Saline River all the time. Did a lot of fishing there, too. You do much fishing when you were a kid?"

Livengood, an avid indoorsman, admitted he did not.

"We used to do a lot of fishing down there on the Saline River," Harley said, looking as if he were wondering how long it had been. "You know, it seems to me that it used to be an important part of the Kansas way of life, too. That, and swimming in the river without catching dysentery."

Livengood did not want to lose the cushiest job of his life because of mere nostalgia, but he could see from the wistful look in Harley's eyes that the governor would not be easily dissuaded.

"Perhaps you're right, sir," Livengood said. "It sounds like an excellent initiative for your second term."

"But I might not have a second term," Harley said. "There's no telling what the Lord has in store for us."

"If you pursue this aggressively in the next session, I can tell you exactly what the Lord will have in store for us. You'll be back in Piquant, I'll be in the unemployment line, and we'll both be reading in the papers about how the new governor is lobbying the feds for laxer runoff regulations. It doesn't take a prophet to see that coming, sir."

"I want those rivers cleaned up, Frankie."

"And so do I, sir. It's just that I think we'd be better off trying to do it in another session. We're lucky that all of Pastor Jeffries' people didn't make any trouble for us last time around, but that's because they're still a few votes shy of getting some of their crazier ideas passed. If you get them lined up with a few of the beef and agribusiness legislators, all hell could break loose down on the floor next time around. I really do not want that to happen, sir."

"Why should Pastor Jeffries' people object to cleaning up the rivers?" the governor asked. "It seems to me they'd want to have a state where they can go swimming and fishing in the rivers."

Livengood exhaled again, slightly exasperated at having to explain such things to a governor.

"Some of them think that Jesus is going to be here any minute and set things right on his own, and that it's a show of bad faith to try and fix anything for a long haul. Some others think that environmentalism is some kind of pagan earth worship cult, and that any attention you pay to the nature spirits is going to make God jealous. The rest may think it's a sin that the rivers are so filthy, but since no one's having a good time with it, they just don't much care."

"That doesn't make any sense," Harley said. "Haven't these people ever heard of stewardship? In my church they taught me that 'the Lord God took the man and put him into the Garden of Eden to cultivate and *to keep it*.' "

"If only they had all gone to your church, sir," Livengood said. "The thing you have to remember is, it doesn't have to make sense. This is what these people believe, and that's all that matters."

"Damn it, Frankie, we've got rivers of bullshit running through this state," Harley said. "You know I don't like to use that kind of language, Frankie, but that's exactly what it is and there's no use saying 'fecal contamination' or 'runoff pollution' or any other polite way of putting it. Doesn't it bother you to have a literal river of bullshit running through Kansas?"

"Maybe I've just become too accustomed to the figurative one, sir, but no, it doesn't bother me," Livengood said. "It seems almost appropriate to me."

Harley stood, walked around the desk and patted Livengood on the shoulder.

"I've let you call most of the shots around here, Frankie, and I have to admit that you've done a good job of keeping things under control. I'll give you that. Nothing's gone terribly wrong so far."

"Thank you, sir," Livengood said, visibly uncomfortable with the governor's gesture. "But I don't think you fully appreciate the magnitude of that achievement. If you did, I'm sure you wouldn't put it at such risk."

"I'm sorry," Harley said. "I have to do this."

Livengood couldn't think of any reason why Harley had to do anything, and said so.

"I've been praying on this," Harley said. "Ever since you got me elected to this office I've been praying about it, and it's led me to the conclusion that this is what I'm supposed to do. I'm not going to tell you that God spoke to me or anything quite so dramatic as that, and I really can't explain it to you at all, but that's what I believe. Like you say, it doesn't have to make any sense."

Harley leaned against his desk just in front of Livengood, and smiled at him with a look that signaled the end of debate on the matter. Frankie Livengood shrugged, said, "What the hell," and promised to immediately begin the Herculean task of cleaning up the rivers of bullshit.

Livengood's first step toward saving the rivers of Kansas was to fly to Washington, D.C., and see if he could get the feds to do it.

Rebecca Reynolds accompanied Livengood, and her companionship proved the only enjoyable aspect of the weeklong trip. None of Livengood's numerous contacts in the various bureaucracies showed any interest in taking Livengood's task off his hands, especially when they understood that part of the bargain was the official opposition of the governor, and his few remaining friends on the staffs of the congressional delegation thought he was playing another of his practical jokes.

Still, Livengood enjoyed being in Washington again, and Reynolds was giddy to be back in a real city. After two years on the prairie she was exhilarated by the hotels, shops, restaurants, museums, and merely by the millions of people and their overwhelming sounds and smells and strange appearances. She also enjoyed at last having the advantage of being more knowledgeable about and comfortable in their environment, and the subtle change it brought about in their relationship. The sensations of the city had a powerfully aphrodisiac effect on Reynolds, so Livengood had no serious complaints with his new role and considered himself well compensated for the trip's lack of professional success.

At a famously fancy restaurant on the Potomac, they dined on fresh seafood, a rare delicacy for Kansans, and followed it with a hand-in-hand stroll along the riverbank. Pausing at a spot with a scenic view of the Washington Monument reflecting in the glistening water, they kissed and smiled.

"I love you," Reynolds said.

The statement startled Livengood. Reynolds had often spoken of strong feelings, a special bond, a certain affection, but never had used the word "love" to describe her emotions. Unsure of the proper response, Livengood hugged her in a blatant stall for time.

"Do you love me?" she asked.

Groping for an answer, Livengood rapidly inventoried his feelings. He acknowledged to himself the enjoyment he derived from their conversations, and how rare that was. He thought of her endearing melancholy, and how she almost seemed to understand his own. He remembered the aching loneliness of the years that had preceded her, and admitted that if Reynolds had not alleviated it, she had at least shared it. Plus, the sex was great.

At the end of the list, Livengood still didn't know if he loved Reynolds, or even if he would ever dare to love a woman again.

"I love you, too," Livengood said.

Almost immediately upon his return to Topeka, Livengood convened a meeting of everyone on the administrative staff who would be involved in a major initiative to clean up Kansas' rivers and streams. He explained that the governor was determined to make the project a crowning achievement of his administration, and that it must therefore be as well researched and carefully conceived as possible.

"If it takes two years, so be it," Livengood said. "I want this puppy perfect when we unveil it."

Wilbur Philip pointed out that in two years they would be in the next term, and asked if Livengood had considered that Harley might not be in office.

"The important thing," Livengood said, "is that we do a good job on this."

Philip pointed out that the solutions to the runoff pollution problem were already known. "It's just that they're very expensive and will meet with opposition from the beef and agribusiness industries."

Livengood said he was hopeful that such bright minds as he had assembled in the meeting would be able to find an original solution, one less costly and more agreeable to the hard-working and tax-paying people of the state's cattle and farming industries.

"I don't know, Frankie," Philip said. "It might take us more than a couple of years to do that."

"Whatever it takes," Livengood said. "The important thing is that the press doesn't get hold of this before we're ready."

Livengood was just minutes away from making his usual early exit from the office the next Friday when a call came from Dan Dorsey of the Sunflower News Service, asking for information about the governor's new environmental crusade.

"Sorry. Don't know anything about it," Livengood said. "No environmental crusades going on around here. Who the hell's giving you this stuff?"

"Harley did. We had a long interview about it this afternoon."

"Damn it," Livengood said.

"You know, I thought you might say that," Dorsey said, chuckling. "Yeah, Harley went on about it at great length. He got to reminiscing about the ol' swimming hole down on the Saline River, the God-given fishing rights of Kansans, the streams flowing from the Garden of Eden and man's dominion over nature, all that shit. Very touching. Great quotes."

"Did he say what we were going to do about it?"

"He said that you and your people were working on it. He said you were going to have the big master plan all ready to go at the start of the session. That's why I'm calling you. I was hoping you could tell me the master plan."

"Well, Dan, I think I'd best not comment on that right now," Livengood said. "We're still putting the finishing touches on this bad baby, and until we do, we'd rather keep it under wraps."

"You don't have the slightest idea what you're going to do, do you, Frankie?"

"I think I'd best not comment on that right now."

An avalanche of angry mail and cranky phone calls followed the publication of Dorsey's interview with Gov. Harley Christianson, and Frankie Livengood was beginning to get that old familiar feeling of being hated by a majority of his fellow citizens. It was a particular pleasure, therefore, to see the approval and affection apparent on the face of Jane Hutchinson when she unexpectedly dropped by his office.

"I love you, Frankie Livengood," Jane said, greeting him with a hug.

"I'm damned glad to hear you say that. On a day like today I'd be damned glad to hear anybody say that, but it's especially nice coming from you. I mean, considering that you divorced my ass."

"Let's not talk about that," Hutchinson said. "Let's talk about the rivers. I'm so proud of you for doing this."

"Yeah, well," Livengood said, wondering what to say. "What can I say?"

"You can say why you decided to do this, for one thing," Hutchinson said. "I talked about how important this is for all those years we were married, and you'd only say how politically risky it would be. You used to make me so mad."

"Yes, I guess it is risky," Livengood said. "I admitted as much to Harley when I proposed this idea, but we got to talking about the importance of clean water and all that shit, and he agreed with me that it was worth the risk. For the sake of the children."

"Harley's a good man," Hutchinson said. "I just knew he was from the first time you told me about him."

"He's the best," Livengood said.

"You're the best," Jane said. "Harley's a sweetheart, but I know who really runs things around here. When I read the story, I knew you must have come up with this idea, and I was so proud of you. I think you've really grown."

"I'm a growing boy, no doubt about it," Livengood said. "Of course, it's not just for the sake of the children, you know. I knew how important this was to you. I wanted to please you, and I wanted you to know just how much I've grown."

Jane smiled and said, "I believe you."

"I wanted you to know that I'm willing to put principle ahead of politics, just like you used to nag me about all the time,"

Livengood said. "I was kind of hoping that you might, you know, sort of see me in a whole new light or something."

"Let's not talk about that," Hutchinson said, still smiling. "Let's talk about the rivers."

Livengood was sullen at dinner that evening, and Reynolds attributed his emotional distance to the controversy that had resulted from the governor's interview. In an effort to cheer him up, she said, "I love you," and after an anxious moment or two he said the same thing. The exchange did not cheer up Livengood, so Reynolds finished dinner in silence and worriedly drove home to Lawrence.

Big beef and big agribusiness began their counter-offensive before Livengood could even begin to formulate a battle plan. Rancher, businessman and ex-Governor Chuck Bentley, who was commissioned by a consortium of industry leaders to direct the lobbying campaign against Christianson's clean river ambitions, fired the first volley during a meeting in Livengood's office.

"It's so good to see you again, Frankie boy," Bentley said, shaking his former aide's hand with painful firmness. "Now, what's all this bullshit I'm hearing about the rivers here in Kansas?"

"Well, sir," Livengood said, trying to sound polite and not intimidated. "It would seem that the governor is intent on cleaning them up. That would be the current governor, of course."

"I guess it would be," Bentley said, laughing big. "None of the past ones would be so damn stupid."

"So what's so stupid about clean rivers?"

"It's not that we're against clean rivers, of course," Bentley said.

"Of course not," Livengood said.

"It's just that we don't want to clean them up by any means which would negatively impact the beef and farming industries which are so vital to this state's economy, if you know what I mean."

"I guess we shouldn't have any problems, then, because Governor Christianson and I share that preference," Livengood said. "You just tell me how the hell to do that, and we'll write it up in a bill and get it passed together. How about it?"

"I'll tell you what, Frankie. My colleagues and me, we were thinking that the current regulations are working just fine. Beef prices are still way too low, but other than that, we really don't have much problem with the status quo. We'd prefer something a bit more laissez faire on the regulatory end, but what the hell. Let's just work out something symbolic, and we all go home happy at the end of the next session. We might even cough up a nice big campaign contribution to help you and your guy get back for the next session."

"If it were up to me, Governor Bentley, I'd take that deal in a heartbeat," Livengood said. "Unfortunately for everyone concerned, it ain't up to me. Harley's in charge here, and he's hell-bent on getting those damned rivers cleaned up for real."

"Don't go sticking my hand up a horse's ass and telling me it's pussy," Bentley said. "Everyone knows who's in charge here, and it ain't some yahoo carpenter from Piquant, Kansas. This is exactly the kind of cockamamie scheme a punk like you would pull."

"The hell it is," Livengood said. "Believe me, I've learned my lesson. I just want to get my guy re-elected, and I don't need you to tell me that this isn't going to help. This is Harley's idea from the get-go, and like I say, he's hell-bent about it. He's been praying about it or something."

"Praying about it? Jesus Christ," Bentley said. "What the hell kind of nut case are you working for?"

"Harley's a good guy. He's just got a thing about rivers, that's all."

"All right then. I guess we'll just have to slaughter y'all."

"Aw, come on," Livengood said.

"Sorry, Frankie boy. If you guys try to pass one more fucking regulation, if you try to make my people spend one damned dime more on their operations, if you make us liable for one more lawsuit or send one more goddamn inspector out, we are going to make you want to spend the rest of your miserable lives at the bottom of one of those precious rivers."

"I appreciate your candor, sir."

"In that case, fuck you," Bentley said. "I don't just mean that we're going to spend a shitload of money on any old asshole who wants to run against your guy, I mean that we're going to screw up your next eighteen months so bad that Willa Kline could kick your asses in a rematch. Except that you won't get a chance to run against the crazy bitch again, because you're going to get beat in the primary. There's two kinds of Republicans in this state, son, and that's money Republicans and God Republicans. The money Republicans are already mad at you for just thinking about spending all those bucks, and by the time we get through advertising on this, all the God Republicans are going to think you're a bunch of earth-worshipping pagans who don't think Jesus is coming."

Livengood started to say, "You wouldn't," but he knew they would. "Come on," he said, instead. "We don't even know yet what the hell we're going to do. Maybe it won't be so bad."

"You say that your guy's hell-bent on cleaning up those rivers for good?"

"I won't lie about that," Livengood said.

"Then I won't lie to you, either," Bentley said. "Nobody's come up with any way to do that without making more regulations, costing us more money, making us liable for more lawsuits or making us put up with more hassles over what's already on the books. And I don't think that you or anybody you've got working for you is smart enough to do it. So, you can either talk your guy out of this, or you can get ready for the fight of your life."

"It was good to see you again, Governor," Livengood said, extending his hand warily for a parting handshake. "And thanks again for the candor."

"It's my pleasure, Frankie boy," Bentley said, noting with satisfaction the sweat on the younger man's palms. "I'm sure I'll be seeing you again real soon."

Frankie Livengood gave a bleak report to Governor Christianson about their progress in cleaning up the rivers. He explained that the only tentative proposals that the staff could offer were politically untenable, and that they faced an influential and well-financed opposition. He asked the governor to reiterate why the hell they were doing this.

"I've been praying on it," Harley said. "It's hard to explain."

"Please try, sir," Livengood said. "You've put me in a hell of a spot here, and I need to know how I got here if I'm ever going to get us out."

Harley looked about the office, as if the answer were to be found somewhere in the ornately framed works of art or the richly oaken furniture. After several false starts, he at last said, "I never figured on being in an office like this, Frankie, and sometimes I'm still trying to figure out just what in tarnation I'm doing here. I asked God about running for this office the first night you came out to see me about running, and I asked Him again when you got me elected.

I asked Him again, with you by my side, during the inaugural ball. Do you remember that?"

Livengood said he hadn't forgotten.

"Maybe it doesn't make any sense to a smart fellow like you, Frankie, but I'm just an old country boy who needs to pray on these things. Most of the time it sets my mind right so I can come up with an answer by myself, but sometimes—don't think I'm nuts or nothing—sometimes I'd swear that God just sends me down an answer. Do you think I'm nuts?"

Livengood said that he didn't think Harley was nuts.

"I'm not saying that God says actual words to me, like in the movies. I'm just saying He gives me an answer. Sometimes He sends it through Christy, or one of my friends, or sometimes I find it in the Bible. Sometimes, I swear, He just puts it in my brain where I can find it. Do you know what I'm trying to say?"

Livengood said he could understand, sort of.

"This time, though, it's a little different," Harley said. "At first, He didn't send me any kind of answer, so I just figured that I'd do whatever you thought was best, because you seemed to know what you were doing. You didn't screw anything up, and just like you said, He seemed satisfied with that."

Livengood said that he certainly hoped so.

"Well, I kept praying on it. I kept praying we wouldn't screw anything up, but I couldn't shake this feeling that we were supposed to be doing something more, so I prayed on that, too."

Livengood nodded.

"Well, a few months ago I started getting these dreams, about a river," Harley said. "I didn't dream that God was talking to me or anything like that, but I figured that He sent the dream."

"I wouldn't read too much into that, sir," Livengood said. "Maybe it was just some Freudian thing. A river can be very sexual."

"Maybe so, Frankie. Maybe so. But I don't think so."

Livengood asked what occurred in the dream. Harley looked around embarrassedly, as if someone might have slipped in unnoticed to eavesdrop.

"It's hard to explain, because it's not so much what happens as it is the way I feel," Harley said. "I'm in this place I've never been before, and I'm there with Christy and my momma, who died over twenty years ago, and there's this long, dark river running by. Like I was saying, nothing much really happens in this dream, but I have this powerful feeling that I'm supposed to be doing something. At first I didn't know what it was I was supposed to be doing, and Christy and my momma would never say anything, they'd just look at me like I'm supposed to be doing something. So, I got to praying on it. The dream kept coming back, and the feelings started getting more specific, until I realized that I was supposed to do something about the river. The next time I had that same dream, I noticed why the river was so dark. It was so dark because of all this cow dung that was floating along in it."

Livengood thought about it for several moments, a hand over his mouth.

"That must have been the River Festival incident, sir," Livengood said, hopefully. "Anyone would have had that dream."

"That's the weird thing about it," Harley said, as if revealing the surprise ending to a campfire horror story. "I was having this dream two weeks before that happened."

Figuring Harley for the superstitious sort, and being thoroughly spooked himself, Livengood decided it would be best not to reveal that he had long been haunted by the very same dream.

"I wouldn't worry about it, sir," Livengood said. "Those dreams, they're only in your head."

CHAPTER SEVENTEEN

"Riders on the Storm"

The third legislative session of Gov. Harley Christianson's first term was hell on such a lazy man as Frankie Livengood.

Every session had been too much work for Livengood's tastes, but he couldn't recall any of the previous twenty-five being quite so tiring. In addition to all the usual difficulties, he was shepherding Governor Christianson's plan for the rivers through the legislative process, encountering well-funded and formidably organized opposition at each step. Meanwhile, his usually placid personal life was strewn with womanly complications, from Rebecca Reynolds' unexpected domestic desires to Jane Hutchinson's new-found respect to Darla Morland's arrival at Washburn University with instructions from Big Jim Morland for Livengood to find her a job. That's not to mention the weather that had rolled down from the Arctic Circle on opening day and blanketed the capital city with snow, which Livengood mentioned often and in the most profane terms he knew.

Then, the riders started showing up. Riders always showed up in bills, typically having little to do with the ostensible purpose of the bill itself, but Livengood had never seen so many, or so many with so much ambition. Rebecca Reynolds reported, in a self-righteous and panicked tone, that she had found attempts to restrict abortion rights hidden in everything from the highway bill to a proclamation declaring the polka the official state dance. Cathy Knieble started finding a wide range of educational reforms, from creationism to the disestablishment of the public school system, popping up in tax bills and boxing match regulations. Mark Stark undertook a search for riders affecting homosexuals, and discovered several hidden away in such innocuous places as the Park Services appropriations and a proposal for stricter admissions standards to regents universities. Wilbur Philip was horrified to find that his precious budget proposal had been pockmarked with dozens of similar riders.

It seemed to Livengood that the riders exceeded even the vast frontiers of the legislative rules about germaneness, and he said so to Rep. Stan Patterson during a brief hallway conversation. Patterson, newly installed as the Speaker of the House, appeared to enjoy telling Livengood that he disagreed, and would use the powers of his post to ensure the riders were given due consideration.

The riders started to gather unexpected momentum. Reynolds spoke anxiously of several legislative allies who were no longer returning her calls, and inquired coyly about the likelihood of a veto if the restrictions were passed. Knieble wrote a memo warning Livengood that several of the more controversial educational reforms seemed headed to the floor, and that several vetoes would almost certainly be needed to prevent the wrath of the educational establishment from raining down on the governor. Mark Stark meticulously composed several notes about measures he considered harmful to the gay community, and asked for Livengood's reassurance that the governor would not allow them to pass into law without the two-thirds supermajority needed to override a veto.

Sifting through the large pile of documents atop his desk, Livengood noted without surprise that the riders had originated with legislators associated with Pastor Jeffries and the Kansans for Kansas Values, but he was struck by the observation that the newly converted supporters were mostly legislators associated with Chip

Wentworth and his network of money-minded moderates. Recalling that Wentworth's extensive business holdings in the state included a large share of Beef-Tek and several other agribusiness concerns, he concluded that an unholy alliance of God Republicans and money Republicans had ganged up on him.

Explaining the situation to Christianson during a long meeting at the gubernatorial mansion, Livengood urged an unconditional surrender.

"We can't give up the river bill," Governor Christianson said, settling uncomfortably into a leather chair and waving his hand in a gesture of finality. "I've kept praying on it, and we're not giving up the river bill."

"But sir," Livengood said, leaning forward across the governor's desk and clasping his hands in a supplicating fashion. "It's not going to pass. It's not going to come close to passing. It's not even going to get a vote in subcommittee, and if it did it would lose. Even if it did make it through there, it doesn't stand a chance of getting a vote in committee, and if it did it would lose. Even if it somehow passed through the committee, it would get slaughtered on the floor of the House. Even if it somehow got through the House it would be beaten badly in the Senate. Even if the million-to-one odds came through, and it somehow passed in both houses, it would be so watered down with amendments and loopholes and lack of funding that it wouldn't make a single Kansas river one bit cleaner. It's just a whole lot of paper that's never going to be law, and we're not giving anything up if we let it go."

"We have to try," Harley said.

"I'm trying my ass off, sir," Livengood said, pleadingly. "I'm working these idiots day and night. I'm wining them and dining them and offering them deals for every kind of hometown pork they can think of. I've got every environmental group in the state, region and country leaning on their members to work the legislature, as if that would do any good. I've cashed in every favor I ever did for the newsboys to get them to do sob stories about dead fish and fecal-contaminated swimming holes. I've tried every trick I know, and I'm telling you, this bill ain't gonna pass."

After politely listening to Harley's advice about noses to grindstones and the old college try, Livengood warned him of the potential political ramifications of his quixotic effort. He explained about some of the legislation likely to be passed if Harley didn't back down, and about the controversies that were certain to ensue.

"I'm still the governor," Harley said, as if reminding himself of the fact. "I can veto the bad ideas."

"And then they win everything," Livengood said. "They'll paint you as a baby-killing homo-lover who tried to wreck the Kansas economy for a pagan earth-worship ritual, and you'd better not doubt that they can do it, too, when they get through airing all the ads that big money can buy. People are going to believe it, too, and you'll never make it through the primary. On the other hand, if you don't veto half this stuff, people are going to think you're some kind of fag-bashing woman-hater who tried to wreck the Kansas economy. Either way, you'll be out of office, and you'll never have another chance to clean up the rivers."

Harley crossed his arms and looked toward the floor. After a few moments of thought he looked up and told Livengood, "I've been praying hard on this. You work out anything you can about the rest of this nonsense, and do it any way you want to, but don't give up the river bill."

Frankie Livengood scheduled a meeting with Chip Wentworth at an expensive Overland Park restaurant known for its wide selection of wines. After a brief exchange of friendliness while they swigged their first drink, the two men talked politics.

"Since when are you so hot on unborn babies and prayer in school?" Livengood asked. "And since when are you so down on fags? What the hell does that have to do with the price of stocks on Wall Street?"

"It's not about any unborn babies," Wentworth said, smiling his approval on the conversation's newly frank tone. "And I have lots of faggot friends, so don't try to make it out like I'm some kind of homophobic rube."

"I hear that," Livengood said. "It's about your God-given right to dump immense amounts of your bullshit in the rivers, isn't it?"

"That bill would be an economic disaster for this state, and you know it," Chip said. "The only reason you're beating the bushes so hard for it is because that yokel governor of yours would fire your ass if you didn't."

Livengood waved for another drink of his own, and did not deny Wentworth's statement.

"I really would hate to see you lose that job," Wentworth continued. "I always liked you, Frankie. I'm still a Kansan, too, so I hate to think what might happen to our beloved state if your bumpkin of a governor were left to his own devices. On the other hand, I don't want to let you pass a bill that's going to drive a vital industry away from this state."

Livengood suggested they find a way to make them both happy.

"Oh, please," Chip said. "What could possibly make us both happy? You've got a lot of smart people in those government offices, and have they come up with any ideas that would clean up the rivers without costs to industry? We've got a whole lot of smart people working for us on the same thing, believe it or not, and they haven't come up with anything that would make us both happy. Until they do, I'm afraid we're going to have to settle for what makes me happy."

Livengood took a bite of his T-bone and chewed long enough to collect his thoughts.

"But that still doesn't explain why your guys are signing on to all of these damn riders," Livengood said. "You don't need that. You know damn good and well that the river bill isn't going to pass. It doesn't have a prayer. You don't need to be doing any favors for a bunch of votes that you're going to get anyway."

"It's not going to pass this year," Wentworth said. "That's true enough. But what about next year? The way your governor talked about it in the State of the State, and the way he's been preaching for it all over the state, it seems quite clear to me that he'll be right back on this next year, and the year after that, and the next two years after that. Unless he's back in Piquant making chairs, of course, which would be preferable to fighting this damned thing for another four years. I may not like these crazy riders that Pastor Jeffries has come up with, but I'm willing to let your governor veto them and take the heat. It'll make it that much easier to get us a new governor."

"What if that new governor is Pastor Jeffries himself?"

"Pastor Jeffries has always proved willing to negotiate with the business interests in this state," Wentworth said. "Unfortunately, it would seem that I'm no longer able to say the same thing for you or your guy."

"You know me, Chip. You know I've always been willing to negotiate with the business interests in this state. I've always believed that if guys like you want to work a little harder and be a little smarter than the rest of us, and you can cut enough mutually beneficial deals to get a little richer than the rest of us, well then, hell, that's a lifestyle decision, too. That deserves the government's protection just as much as being a fag or aborting an unborn baby. That's what makes me a Republican, damn it, and I'm no more apologetic about it than you are. All I'm asking is that you let this river bill of Harley's die a natural death, and don't let Jeffries gum up the works with a bunch of other ideas that are just as bad for business. Honestly, Chip, I'm surprised you let that guy sucker you into a deal like this for a bill that's already dead."

Wentworth chewed his prime rib thoughtfully, and offered Livengood an apologetic smile.

"It's not like that," Wentworth said. "I'm not going to sit here and listen to you say that Pastor Jeffries suckered me into this deal. The fact is, he forced me into it, fair and square. He got me and Bentley into one of his come-to-Jesus meetings, and told us that if we didn't go along with this fag and creationism and abortion crap, he'd see to it that the damn river bill did pass. You've already got all those damned Democrats lined up for this thing, along with that suicidal son of a bitch Republican that you snookered into sponsoring it, and Jeffries is telling us that he'll throw in every Bible-thumper in the House and Senate. He could do it, too, now that he's undisputed Protestant Pope of Kansas. The way we do the math, that's enough votes to make this thing close. Uncomfortably close. I don't like the way Jeffries is trying to clean up everybody's mind in this state, but better that than to have your guy trying to clean up the rivers."

"Well then," Livengood said. "Maybe I can get you out of your deal with Jeffries, and we can swing a little deal of our own. Me and my people don't push so hard on this river bill, you and your people let those riders drop, and Pastor Jeffries and his people can go back to saving souls one at a time."

"Maybe," Wentworth said. "The problem is, if we play it that way, your guy's got a decent shot at getting re-elected, and I don't think that stubborn son-of-a-bitch is going to let you get away with this for another four years."

After simultaneously signaling for more drinks, Livengood and Wentworth resumed eating beef and talking turkey.

At lunch the next day, Jane Hutchinson continued to get new ideas for strengthening the river bill, and she was delighted with the way Livengood continued to say, "Yeah, sure, why not."

Flush with the hope that waste lagoons would someday be required to withstand twelve-inch rains throughout Kansas, Hutchinson gave Livengood a hug and kiss when he dropped her off at her office. When he returned a tighter hug and a wetter kiss she allowed it, but only for a second before saying, "I'd better get going."

The negotiations were no more conclusive when Livengood met with Pastor Jeffries for a long stroll around the capitol grounds.

"Since when are your guys so dead set against clean rivers?" Livengood asked, smiling hard enough to make it seem a friendly question.

"Oh, Frankie, please," Pastor Jeffries said. "It's not that we're against clean rivers. Not at all. How could you say such a thing? It's just that we're also for a healthy economy and good jobs in Kansas, and this bill of yours would seriously threaten that. And I think you know that it would, Frankie."

Livengood shrugged, smiled hard again and said, "Maybe, maybe not. But I know that's not really why you're doing this."

"It's not the paganism of the bill that bothers me," Pastor Jeffries said. "Like most Kansas Christians, we believe in stewardship of nature. It's just that we truly are worried about the negative economic effect on the families of this state."

"Some of those riders that you're introducing might have a negative economic effect on the state, as well," Livengood said. "And if they were so very much within the mainstream of Kansas Christians, you wouldn't need to be hiding them in appropriations bills and swinging deals with Wentworth and the moderates to get them passed."

"Perhaps I wouldn't have to be swinging deals with Wentworth and the moderates if the current administration were more amenable to policies that bolster Christian civilization," Pastor Jeffries said. "And perhaps the next administration will be willing to deal with us on matters of importance to the state's spiritual health."

"So who says we can't deal?" Livengood said. "Harley's a good Christian man, and it's not like I worship the devil or anything. We're for spiritual health as much as the next guy. If you were to help us out with this river bill, you'd be surprised at how many of these riders you could get into law, and without sneaking them into official state bolo tie proclamations. Of course, we can't give you all of them, but we could give you enough of them to make it worth your while."

"I can't do that," the pastor said. "We can't give up on any of them, because we can't give up on what's right."

"What would you be giving up?" Livengood said. "You know you can't get half this stuff passed even with Wentworth's help, and you don't have anywhere near enough votes to override a veto on the other half. There's a bunch of this stuff that won't stand up for ten seconds of constitutional scrutiny, anyway. You'd just be giving up a whole bunch of paper that never stands a chance of becoming a law."

"Then have the governor veto it, by all means," Pastor Jeffries said, smiling even bigger than before. "It will make it all the easier to get rid of Harley Christianson in the primary. Then we can get an even better deal, and pass the things that we really want."

"Why are you so eager to get rid of Harley?" Livengood asked. "I mean, we're open for business."

"He'll only go so far with us," Pastor Jeffries said. "Our aim is to eliminate abortion in this state, or at least go all the way to the Supreme Court in the attempt, and Governor Christianson has indicated that he will be an impediment to that. I get the impression of a very stubborn man from your governor, and I do not doubt that he would remain steadfast in his opposition to that goal for another four years. I also believe that he would be an obstacle to our efforts to turn back the gay agenda, to make our schools hospitable to Christianity, and to once again make Kansas' government reflective of the values of its people."

"We're not anti-gay, but we don't support the gay agenda," Livengood said. "If the schools are making Christian kids uncomfortable somehow, we'll be glad to help you correct that. For three years now our administration hasn't done anything, much less anything wrong, and I can't think of anything more dear to the hearts of average Kansans than that. I don't see why we can't do business."

"What about abortion?" the pastor asked, showing genuine interest in the possibility of a deal for the first time in the conversation. "Your governor ran on a pro-choice platform, as I recall."

"We're not all that pro-choice," Livengood said. "The Supreme Court has declared a basic right to abortion, and we don't go any further than that. There's a lot of things they've allowed about abortion that Kansas hasn't tried yet, you know, and there could be some room to deal on that. The governor's main concern is the river bill, and what do you guys care if we clean up the rivers?"

Pastor Jeffries breathed deeply, savoring the icy cold air, pondering the situation. He did not trust Livengood, but he trusted Chip Wentworth less, and experience had taught him that it was always good to have a back-up deal in the works. He shook hands heartily, promised to talk again soon, and asked that God bless Frankie Livengood.

After an already difficult day of negotiations, Livengood came home to find Reynolds in his bed, alluringly nude and asking if he loved her.

Livengood sat on the edge of the bed, loosened his tie, and while removing his shoes said that, yeah, he loved her. Reynolds rubbed his shoulders sympathetically, then ran her hands down his tired body, hoping to provoke a more emphatic response to her question.

As frustrating and fatiguing as the session had been for Livengood, it was proving a most exhilarating experience for Reynolds. No longer confined to the ivory towers of her effete eastern intellectual circles, she was directly engaged on the front lines of the battle for women's rights, perhaps even on the verge of actual practical results, and it had a salutary effect on her libido.

A short time later, as Livengood smoked a post-coital cigarette, Reynolds returned to the question of whether he loved her or not.

"Why wouldn't I?" Livengood said. "I'm sorry, it's just that I've had so much talk of relationships today. It's hard for me to make decisions about personal matters."

Reynolds said she wasn't asking him to marry her.

"That's good, because now's not the time for commitments," Livengood said. "Now's the time for making compromises and cutting deals and surviving the session."

As the session dragged on, the riders began to gallop through various subcommittees and committees toward the House and Senate floors.

They even made their way into the headlines of Kansas newspapers, where they were noticed even by such determinedly uninformed citizens as Mick Fixx, who provided Livengood with a veritable cornucopia of opinions about money-grubbing businessmen, Bible-thumping Christians and tree-hugging environmentalists. His frequent presence in the apartment also meant that Livengood had to constantly check the ashtrays and other areas for evidence of marijuana smoking, lest they be discovered by Darla Morland, who often dropped by with copies of brand new riders as one of her intern duties.

At a businessmen's bookstore on a seedy block of downtown Kansas City, just down the street from the civic center that was hosting the annual convention of Kansas and Missouri ministers, Pastor Jeffries came across a most interesting magazine article.

Pastor Jeffries had perused the sports magazines for a full fifteen minutes before he was alone at the back of the store, and then sidled his way to the end of the wall where the pornography was located. He was ready to reassure anyone who might find him there that he examined such material merely for the sake of better understanding some of his more morally challenged parishioners, but he preferred not to have to make such explanations.

Riffling through the homosexual titles, but only because that was an abomination that he needed to understand in order to help a few of his young parishioners avoid its mortal consequences, he chose one featuring a particularly handsome model on its cover.

The magazine turned out not to be pornographic, except for a few fashion advertisements, but Jeffries' disappointment was allayed when he noticed a picture of Gov. Harley Christianson on one of the pages. The mug shot accompanied an article headlined "Gorgeous Furniture From a Gay-Friendly Governor," which reported that Christianson-made furniture had become the latest rage among well-heeled New York homosexuals. Several New York art critics were quoted about the high quality and innovative design of Christianson's work, and a Kansas State University assistant professor named Mark Stark was quoted about the Governor's lack of political initiatives against homosexuals.

Copies of the article, with no explanation for its discovery, were soon posted to every household on the Kansans for Kansas Values mailing list. Press reports about Christianson's popularity with the gay community quickly appeared in most Kansas newspapers, followed by segments on each television station in the state. Less than twenty-four hours later, jokes about the same subject were being told at various water coolers and lunch counters in every county.

Two members of the Alpha Kappa Sigma fraternity at Kansas State University heard the jokes, deduced their meaning and decided that they didn't like having a governor who made furniture for New York City homosexuals. When they learned that the very same teacher who had failed them in an introductory political science class was apparently a New York City homosexual himself, they confronted Mark Stark about it late one night in a secluded part of the campus.

"Are you some kind of faggot?" the bigger of the two asked.

"Yeah," the smaller one said. "Are you some kind of faggot?"

Stark looked about for any other people, and upon finding none he told the young men that he was busy and must be going.

"Where you going?" the bigger one asked. "Some kind of faggot thing?"

"Yeah," the smaller one said. "Some kind of faggot thing?"

Stark began to walk away, but the younger men blocked his path. He chose another direction, and they blocked it as well. After making a final look around for help, Stark breathed deeply, held up his palms in a calming gesture, and began to tell the boys that they had made a mistake. In mid-sentence he punched the larger of the young men square in the nose, kicked the stupefied smaller young man in the groin, and ran toward the nearest street light with all the vigor of the non-smoking, five-mile-a-day man that he was.

Still shaking with rage and fear when he arrived at his home, Stark immediately picked up the phone and dialed Frankie Livengood.

"I just met up with a couple of goddamn Kansans for goddamn Kansas Values," Stark said. "They were wanting to beat me up for being a faggot, and for having the audacity to sell some of Harley's furniture to some other faggots."

After a stunned moment, Livengood asked how badly Stark was hurt.

"Hell, they didn't hurt me," Stark said, sounding insulted. "I punched one in the nose, kicked the other one in the nuts and got the hell out of Dodge."

"Good work," Livengood said.

"But they sure as hell pissed me off."

"I can't blame you. I mean, this is pissing me off, too."

"That's not why I called."

"So why did you call?"

"I'm calling as a goddamn constituent of your governor," Stark said. "I'm calling to let you know that when I haul these sons of bitches into the dean's office for disciplinary action, I don't want to get fired under the provisions of some goddamn law that your governor didn't have the guts to veto."

Livengood sighed and looked at the phone, wishing he could reach through it to pat his friend on the shoulder.

"You know that Harley doesn't want you to get fired, and neither do I," Livengood said. "I'm doing the best I can over here."

The silence lasted long enough for Livengood to light a cigarette and take several long drags. When Stark's voice reappeared, it sounded apologetic.

"I didn't mean to take this out on you guys," Stark said. "I'm just worried. That's all. I'd heard rumors about you and Jeffries and a deal for the river bill, but I guess I should have known better."

"I wish you'd give me a little more credit," Livengood said. "Harley, too."

"You've been a good friend," Stark said. "Harley, too. I trust you both."

This time it was Stark who waited through a long silence, and when Livengood spoke again he sounded unsure.

"Just promise me that you'll take care of yourself," Livengood said. "I mean, we're doing the best we can over here, but there's a lot of nut cases in this state, and in the end it's really all up to them."

Livengood was already suffering a bad day at the office when he encountered the terrifying sight of Edna Dimschmidt, Ellie Whimple and Will Schnitzle walking past the John Brown mural.

"Hey Edna," Livengood said, warily, when his eyes met with the trio. "Hey, Ellie. Hey, Will. What brings you folks to the capitol?"

With considerable wariness of her own, Dimschmidt told Livengood that she and Schnitzle were about to convene a Common Law Court in the old Supreme Court Chamber of the statehouse. She said that permission to do so had been duly granted by the proper authorities, and when Livengood responded with a skeptical expression, she produced a piece of paper that indicated the First Regimental Kansas Free Citizens Militia Brigade and the Divinely Chartered Commonwealth of Kansans for a Sin-Free Kansas had indeed been authorized to occupy the old Supreme Court Chamber, under the provisions of an act allowing any Kansas group to use said room for educational purposes. She concluded her answer with a huffy, "Ha."

"So what kind of educational purposes will your Common Law Court serve?" Livengood asked, examining the document carefully.

"We're going to teach everybody here a thing or two," Schnitzle said, sneering at Livengood. "You'll learn plenty."

Frankie Livengood celebrated quitting time with a shot from the bottle of whiskey he kept in his lower desk drawer. He was trying to convince himself that his situation was unlikely to get any worse when Darla Morland knocked at the door. After hastily hiding the bottle and glass, he bade her to come in.

"Is everything OK?" she asked. "You look terrible."

"Nothing is OK, and that's why I look terrible," Livengood said. "But never mind about that. What can I do for you?"

Darla asked if she could sit down, Livengood waved his permission, and she gently lowered herself onto the chair in front of his desk. She made several failed attempts at talking, but mostly she looked down at the floor. It was the first time Livengood could ever remember when Darla Morland did not know what to say.

CHAPTER SEVENTEEN

"Just spit it out," Livengood said. "Whatever it is, I can take it. I'm an old pro at this stuff."

"That's why I wanted to talk to you," Darla said. "Because, you know, you've sort of been around. I always knew you were a nice guy, and you've always been very kind to me, but you've, you know, done stuff."

Livengood raised his eyebrows and held his palms up to admit that, yes, he had done stuff.

"Most of my friends, most of the people I talk to about things, they haven't done that stuff," Darla said. "So, I thought maybe you could help me with something."

Livengood didn't know what she was talking about, but he was beginning to understand that it was something of a personal nature. Although reluctant to involve himself in such matters, he did like Darla and felt a certain obligation to her, and given the frightened look on her face he couldn't find any satisfactory way of ending the conversation.

"Of course I'd like to help," Livengood said. "I mean, I have done stuff, but I'm a nice guy. I always thought you were an all right kid."

After a long, hard look at the floor, Darla raised her head and said, "I'm pregnant."

Livengood pulled the bottle and glass from his drawer, and helped himself to a long swig of whiskey, saying, "Damn, damn."

Darla was looking at the floor again, and Livengood moved to the front of his desk to pat her on her shivering knee and assure her that it was OK.

"I mean, it's not really OK, of course," Livengood said. "I just mean that it's OK with me. Not that it's OK with me, I don't mean that, I just mean that I'm not going to give you any shit about it or anything. These things happen. I didn't figure on it happening to you, but these things happen."

Darla was not cheered by Livengood's statements. He leaned against the desk, took another swig of whiskey, and tried to think of something more helpful to say.

"Damn," Livengood said. "Damn."

Darla began to cry. Livengood, who was admittedly quite stupid about crying women, did remember to offer her a tissue.

"There, there," Livengood said. Then, "Damn."

After what seemed eons of crying, Darla began to tell Livengood about the terrible dilemma that her pregnancy posed. When she said she couldn't even bring herself to face her father with the news, Livengood also wondered how Big Jim Morland was going to take this.

"What about your boyfriend?" Livengood asked. "I never got to know Bart very well, but he didn't strike me as the type to abandon a girl in a situation like this."

"His name is Brett, and he's not the father," Darla said. "Brett would never have to deal with a situation like this. It happened when I was delivering some papers to your apartment, and Mick was fixing a crack on your bedroom walls. He said I have such beautiful eyes."

Livengood no longer had to wonder how Big Jim Morland was going to take this. He poured himself another shot, and drank deeply. Fixx was just the sly sort, Livengood reflected, to compliment such a buxom and callipygian woman on her rather average eyes.

"Mick Fixx already has two kids he's not taking care of," Livengood said. "He's not bad with household repairs, and he's all right as a friend, but he's no father."

Darla started crying again. Livengood reached for another tissue and said, "There, there."

"What am I going to do?" Darla asked, pleadingly. "You've done stuff. What do I do?"

Livengood did not have an answer, nor did he find one in the next shot of whiskey he swallowed.

"I don't know," Livengood said.

"How do I raise this child?"

"I don't know."

"I can't just give him up, can I?"

"I really don't know."

"Do I get an abortion?"

"I really, really don't know about that," Livengood said.

Darla started crying again, and Livengood pulled up a chair beside her to hold her hand. Except for an occasional "there, there," or an "I don't know," or a "damn," Livengood sat silently with her as she cried for another two hours.

When there was nothing to do but go to sleep, Livengood walked with Darla to the nice new car that Big Jim Morland had bought her. Before driving away, she asked Livengood again what she should do. He had no answer for her, and admitted as much.

Home at last, Livengood took a long drag on the remains of a marijuana cigarette that Mick Fixx had left in an ashtray in the kitchen. He then crawled into bed, determined not to think about anything. As he slowly and fitfully fell into a deep sleep, he began to dream once again of the long, dark river, and the hard words of his mother and a woman he had once loved, and the inescapable sense that something great was expected of him. He awoke unrested.

CHAPTER EIGHTEEN

"What the Law Could Not Do"

Another dissatisfying day of lawmaking had crawled far into the night, and at long last Frankie Livengood was able to shut the door of the governor's office, wave goodnight to John Brown's angry visage, and go home. He sloshed through several inches of gray half-melted snow toward his car, scavenged his pockets for keys, then looked up to see the blank faces of Will Schnitzle, Edna Dimschmidt and Ellie Whimple. They were a disconcerting sight, especially in the dark with no one around.

"Howdy, Will. Hey, Edna. Howyadoin', Ellie?" Livengood said, anxiously fumbling for the car key. "What's shakin'?"

"You're under arrest," Dimschmidt said.

"Under the authority of the Common Law Court of the Divinely Chartered Commonwealth of Kansans United for a Sin-Free Kansas, we are taking you into the custody of the First Regimental Kansas Free Citizens Militia Brigade," said Supreme Commandant General Schnitzle.

"Can we do this later?" Livengood said, rolling his eyes. "It's been a long day, one hassle after another, and I'll tell you, I've had enough."

Only Ellie showed any sympathy, and Livengood did not hold out any hope that she would take charge of the situation. Dimschmidt and Schnitzle glowered at him. Schnitzle said, "This is no bullshit, you're under arrest."

"Me? Why me?" Livengood asked. "Hell, I'm just the chief of staff. Why don't you arrest Harley?"

"Harley's got a security detail," Schnitzle said, "and you don't." He reached into his coat, produced a pistol and pointed it toward Livengood.

"For crying out loud," Livengood said. "Put that gun away. Am I going to have to call a cop?"

Schnitzle cocked the gun, and Livengood, suddenly remembering that both Dimschmidt and Schnitzle were both more or less insane, said, "OK, OK, OK. You make your point. I'm under arrest. Just uncock the pistol. That's all I need right now, is to get shot."

"Get in the van," Schnitzle said, the gun still cocked.

Dimschmidt began walking toward a large brown van, and Livengood followed with Schnitzle holding the gun to his back. Livengood entered the van through a side door, and followed Schnitzle's instructions to lie face down on the cold steel floor with his hands behind his back. While Dimschmidt handcuffed Livengood's hands behind his back, Ellie gently placed a strip of tape across his mouth, interrupting his pleas to loosen the handcuffs, which were tightly pinching his wrists. "Sorry," Ellie said.

"Shut up," Schnitzle said, sliding into the driver's seat and slamming his foot onto the accelerator, sliding the van out of the icy parking lot and into the night.

After a bumpy ride along a circuitous route that Livengood estimated to be six or seven miles, during which the seriousness of the situation began to gradually dawn on him, the van came to a skidding halt under a street light. The door opened, Schnitzle grabbed Livengood's ankles and dragged him to the edge of the van, then tossed him onto his feet. The four of them stood before a shopping mall storefront, where a small wooden sign above the door read, "Women's Health Services, Inc." While Schnitzle pried open the cover of a small metal box on the side of the building and snipped a specific pair of wires, Dimschmidt proceeded to pick the door lock with an efficiency that astonished Livengood.

"It's OK," Ellie told Livengood. "We have permission from the Court."

Livengood was led inside and handcuffed, this time not so tightly, to a pipe running across the front room. Dimschmidt, Schnitzle and Ellie then hurriedly unloaded a series of boxes from the van and placed them in a back office. After a period of fifteen minutes or so, during which Livengood could hear snatches of excited conversation between Dimschmidt and Schnitzle regarding detonators and response times, the trio emerged from the room and attached a series of wires along the doors and windows. Dimschmidt walked to a telephone, punched three numbers and smiled happily at Livengood as she waited for an answer.

"Hello? This is the acting governor of the Divinely Chartered Commonwealth of Kansans United for a Sin-Free Kansas," Dimschmidt said. "I hereby inform you that officers of the First Regimental Kansas Free Citizens Militia Brigade and I have seized Women's Health Services, Inc., a business operating in violation of the Biblical laws of this land at 10281 West Sanger Road. We intend to destroy this property by explosion, and have already placed a large amount of dynamite in the building in order to do so. We have also taken into custody one Frankie Livengood."

Livengood was pleased that she at last pronounced his name correctly, but chilled by the seriousness of her tone. She sounded as serious as any abortion clinic bomber he'd ever read about.

"He is an agent of the conspiracy that is unconstitutionally acting as the government of Kansas," Dimschmidt continued, "and we intend to try him on a variety of capital charges. Should he be found guilty, he will be duly executed in the blast that will destroy this building. Do not attempt to interfere. If you do, we will detonate the large amount of explosives that we have placed in several surrounding buildings. Any attempt to enter the building will also detonate the explosives. You will provide us with transportation and safe passage from this site when our work is completed, and if you do not, we will destroy the entire mall. Thank you very much. Jesus loves you, goodbye."

About ten minutes later, the room was awash in the flashing blue lights of a dozen police cars. A voice blared through a bullhorn to the bombers to come out with their hands up, but they remained kneeled behind a large desk, praying. At the conclusion of their prayer, Schnitzle responded through a bullhorn of his own that they had business to attend to, and would not be out until it was settled. Waving a gun over his head before rising from behind the desk, he pointed the barrel at Livengood's head as he unlocked the handcuffs.

"You're coming with us to the back office," Schnitzle said. "It's Judgment Day."

Livengood was handcuffed yet again, this time to a metal chair in the middle of the room. Dimschmidt and Schnitzle sat imperiously behind a desk, while Ellie gently but painfully removed the tape from Livengood's mouth.

"Don't you think this is starting to get a bit out of hand?" Livengood asked. "I mean, really."

"Shut up," Schnitzle said, pointing the gun at Livengood's head persuasively.

"You're here to face the following charges," Dimschmidt said. "You are charged as an accomplice to the murders of countless unborn Kansans, as an accomplice to the extortion of many millions of dollars from Kansans on behalf of an unconstitutional government that ignored the will of the people, and as an accomplice to that same unconstitutional conspiracy to thwart the will of God for his people. How do you plead to these charges?"

Hoping to buy time for the police officers who were surely moving into position for a rescue, Livengood demanded answers to several questions about the court's jurisdiction, such as where the hell it got one in the first place. At great length Schnitzle explained the English Common Law tradition, the Interstate Commerce Clause of the Constitution, the rabbinical court traditions of the ancient Hebrews, the Dimschmidtian theory of God's covenant with His Church, and the true meaning of the Fourteenth Amendment to the Constitution as ascertained by a short wave radio talk show host in northern Michigan.

"So you basically just declared yourselves in charge?" Livengood said. "You didn't like what the government was doing, so you made yourselves the government?"

"Shut up," Supreme Commandant General Will Schnitzle said, pointing at Livengood with the barrel of the gun from which his judicial authority actually derived.

"How do you plead?" Dimschmidt demanded.

"Not so fast. Sheesh," Livengood said. "You know, our counterfeit courts would at least give a guy some time to think about this stuff, maybe even consult with a lawyer. They've also got a Ninth Amendment, by the way, which prohibits cruel and unusual punishment. I don't know if you'd consider death by explosion to be especially cruel, but you've got to admit that it's a damned sight unusual."

"Shut up," Schnitzle shouted.

"What is your plea?" Dimschmidt shouted.

"All right already. I'll cop to the sloth and gluttony raps. What can you offer me on the other five deadly sins so I can go home?"

Schnitzle rose up angrily from his seat and walked around the desk toward Livengood. He once again cocked the gun, and held it against Livengood's temple, grinning with power. Ellie reached for Schnitzle's arm, but a grim-faced Dimschmidt pulled her back and said, "No."

For the first time, it fully dawned on Livengood that Dimschmidt and Schnitzle were both crazy, and not just crazy in the loose and non-clinical sense that he had used when he spoke of them in the past. They were crazy in the sense that they could kill someone, or any number of people, and without regard to the thickening circle of police officers that were surrounding the building. Although some instinct continued to fight against the realization, Livengood at last understood that he might soon die.

"I submit to this honorable court a plea of not guilty on all charges," Livengood said, in measured tones. "I humbly ask this court to hear my case."

Livengood could hear the slight rumble of police sharpshooters setting up positions around the building while Dimschmidt and Schnitzle deliberated whether time would permit a defense. After a few anxious minutes, Livengood was told that he would be allowed to speak.

"First of all, when I signed up for government work, I thought it was the legitimate government. I didn't know about all that Commerce Clause stuff. I guess we do extort tax dollars, but that's the only way we can get people to pay them," Livengood said, speaking slowly to stall for more time. "As for this stuff about me ignoring the will of the people, well, I don't know where the hell you got that idea. I've been a slave to the will of the people my whole career. So is everybody I work with. We do polls, focus groups, voting trend analysis and any kind of high-dollar research you can think of, all in a constant effort to figure out what the hell the will of the people is.

When we think we've figured it out, we'll give it to them, no matter how stupid it is. Once the people realize how stupid it is, we'll do something else. Then, if we get a couple of angry phone calls or letters about it, or somebody rounds up a couple of friends for a rally against it, we'll do something else besides that. We're suckers for the will of the people, that's what we are."

"Ha," Schnitzle said. "The people of this state are angry."

"Of course they're angry," Livengood said. "They're always angry, and they always will be angry. You know, Will, if you do wind up shooting me, I hope you do get to be the government. I could die happy knowing that you're going to spend the rest of your days sitting in an office listening to whiny constituents. You just try to pave their roads and run schools for their kids and do the million other things they want out of government. And you just try doing it without spending any more than the cheapskate amount they're willing to pay. I'm telling you, you're going to find out it's a hell of a lot less fun than running around in the woods playing army with your buddies."

Schnitzle waved the gun again, and Livengood was quick to add that his remarks were meant with all due respect to the Court.

"You may have your phony election results," Schnitzle said. "But it's the special interest fat cats who conspire with you to bankroll your campaigns who really run things."

"Some conspiracies," Livengood said. "So I got a bunch of Big Jim's hamburger money, and I'm disinclined to regulate hamburgers as a result. Big deal. Those donations are all on record. Anything we might do on behalf of Big Jim or any other fat cat will also be on record. Anyone who gives a damn can find out about it and vote against us. As it turns out, they don't give a damn. If they ever do, then I find another sugar daddy or I find another job. If the fat cats get what they want, that doesn't mean it's not the will of the damn people. Hell, Big Jim got to be a fat cat by serving the people's will for hamburgers. I don't want to believe it any more than you do, but we really do live in an actual democracy. You may think you've got mean ol' Caesar himself sitting here in front of you, but in this state and this country, the people are Caesar. You're not going to get rid of them."

Schnitzle proceeded to recite everything that had gone wrong in his own life, with a particular emphasis on the government's indisputable role in his misery, and dared Livengood to explain how such injustices could possibly occur in a real democracy.

"Because a democracy means that the people are in charge," Livengood said. "Just take a look around at these people. These people whose will you so admire. Just look at the bullshit they buy, the fads they embrace, the weird ideas they believe, the way they fuck up their lives. Isn't everything that goes wrong in this country sufficiently explained by the fact that these people are in charge? Why do you go look for hidden conspiracies to explain this mess?"

Schnitzle sneered at Livengood's disrespect for the people.

"You're the one who's saying that everything's gone so wrong," Livengood said. "The way I figure it, we're muddling along pretty good here. We're doing a damn sight better than anyplace that isn't a democracy, as far as I can tell. So we haven't made things perfect. What has? Do you do your job so well that it solves people's marital problems? I don't know what the hell you've been doing for a job lately, Edna, but have you done it so well that everybody you deal with is happy with their life? Why should you expect that I can do my job any better? We're just here to pave the roads, keep the schools supplied with chalk and swing sets, and help out the occasional poor person. Trust me, that's plenty tricky enough. If your new government aspires to anything bigger than that, well, good luck."

"Our government will aspire to create a righteous nation, for a righteous nation doth exalteth the Lord," Dimschmidt said. "Which brings us to the next charge, thwarting the will of the Lord."

"I don't know what the will of the Lord is," Livengood said. "I thought it was the will of the Lord that we should 'pray for kings and all who are in authority, in order that we may lead a tranquil and quiet life in all godliness and dignity.' That's all I ever wanted. My whole career in government has been devoted to keeping Kansas in such a state that people could lead a tranquil, quiet, godly and dignified life. If they don't want to live that way, well, you're the ones who are so fired up about the will of the people, not me."

"Great wickedness is rife in this state," Dimschmidt said, staring hatefully at Livengood. "You have done nothing to stop it. Those who commit the sins of Sodom and Gomorrah seek protection from your government. Gambling and drunkenness are countenanced by the state. Prayer has been banished from your schools. The contract of marriage is no longer enforced. Such wickedness will surely incur the wrath of God."

"I'm telling you, you've got the wrong guy. I've never tried to grant those who commit the sins of Sodom and Gomorrah any more protection than those who don't. I'm sure not trying to force anybody into any sodomy. The gambling and drunkenness that you're referring to, hell, that came about by popular vote on referenda that I worked against. I didn't banish prayer from the schools, either, and I even did my fair share of praying back in my own student days. As for enforcing the marriage contract, well, hell, how am I supposed to keep somebody's wife with him? I couldn't even keep my own wife from walking out on me."

"These are the laws of God," Dimschmidt shouted.

"Then let Him enforce them," Frankie Livengood said. "My job is helping an elected governor implement the laws of Kansas. I figure that if I can do that, it'll be just that much easier for people to follow God's laws on their own. Or not, if they don't want to. Whatever they choose to do in regard to God's law, God will take care of them in his own way. The stuff He's left up to us, like the roads and the utility regulations and all that crap, I'll tend to that to the best of my ability, and according to the will of the idiot people."

"Those people have souls," Edna said.

"I know they've got souls," Livengood said. "I wish them and their souls the best."

"Those souls are in peril," Dimschmidt said.

"I don't doubt it a bit," Livengood said.

"And yet your government stands by while those souls perish," Dimschmidt said. "The people must act so that the nation perish not. If your government will not lead them to salvation, we claim a divine charter to do so on God's behalf."

"Good luck," Livengood said. "I'm a Christian, too, damn it, but I thought only Jesus could save your soul. I didn't know I was supposed to get another law passed. I thought that 'For what the law could not do, weak as it was through the flesh, God did, sending His own Son in the likeness of sinful flesh and as an offering for sin, He condemned sin in the flesh.' You seem to think that you can pass a law that could do even what God cannot, to force people to into their own salvation. It's blasphemy, if you ask me."

Edna Dimschmidt was not about to sit there and be accused of blasphemy, and have scripture quoted to her, by the son of a whore and drunken sailor.

"Enough of your devilish manipulations of the Word of God," Dimschmidt said. "You have allowed the murder of unborn babies."

Livengood was momentarily silent in face of the accusation. He looked to Ellie, who had leaned forward to hear his response, and gave her an apologetic look.

"Maybe so," Livengood said. "I just don't know."

"I do," Dimschmidt said. "I know with every fiber of my being that abortion is murder."

"Of course you do," Livengood said. "Everything you know, you know with every fiber of your being. There's not a doubt in your mind about anything. Not a chance that any argument, any evidence, any benefit to the rest of the world will shake your certainty about what you believe. It's always God's will with you, but it's always God's will as revealed to Edna Dimschmidt, and any other idea is a sin that you think you're entitled to fight by any means you choose. That's why I never liked you, Edna. There's no 'Come let us reason together' in your Bible, no way to cut a deal. How the hell am I supposed to keep things tranquil and quiet so folks can lead a godly and dignified life when there are people like you running around?"

"Enough," Dimschmidt shouted. "Enough of your mocking and blasphemies. Thousands of unborn babies are slaughtered on Kansas soil, and you have done nothing to save them."

Shaking with anger, Dimschmidt declared that the defense must rest. A judgment on Livengood would be rendered, she said, after a short conference with Schnitzle in another room. Ellie was charged with guarding the prisoner.

Ellie Whimple stared at Frankie Livengood apologetically. He managed to smile at her.

After a long period of silence, Livengood asked, "Don't you think this has gone far enough?"

"It's just beginning. This is just the first abortion mill that we'll stop from killing unborn babies. I'm sorry they might kill you, Frankie, but they'll be saving more than one unborn baby in the process. There will be more life this way, so that's good."

"This isn't an abortion mill," Livengood said. "If this were a real abortion clinic, your Supreme Commandant General would have had to contend with a real security system. They just counsel people here. There won't be any unborn babies saved here."

"Do they counsel people to have abortions?" Ellie asked.

"They tell women what their options are," Livengood said.

"Maybe we'll stop them from counseling a woman about her abortion option," Ellie said.

"They'll just do it someplace else," Livengood said.

"I suppose," Ellie said.

"The only thing that Edna and Will are going to do is kill me, and you'll be down one life. Maybe we'll all get blown up, and we're down four lives. What with all these cops and reporters and people hanging around outside, we might be down more than four lives."

"I suppose," Ellie said.

"So come on," Livengood said. "Unlock these handcuffs, and let me get out of here. Please?"

Ellie unlocked the handcuffs, a remorseful expression on her face, and told Livengood that he could exit through the front door, because the wires there were not attached to the explosives. Livengood told Ellie that they needed to leave, and right away.

"I can't leave," Ellie said. "I have to stay. We're going to save some unborn babies sooner or later."

"You're just going to get yourself killed," Livengood said.

"Well, I still can't leave," Ellie said.

"Damn it, Ellie. You don't have a choice."

Years of street protests and a Spartan existence had hardened Ellie's boyish frame, while a long career behind a desk and a host of unhealthy recreations had left Livengood a dissipated man, but his advantage in mere bulk was such that he managed to throw her over his shoulder and make a lumbering dash toward safety. He smashed his shoulder painfully against the doorframe as he exited the office, bouncing him in the other direction so that he pounded Ellie's head against the door with a resounding thwack and an ear-splitting shriek, but by some miracle neither Edna Dimschmidt nor Will Schnitzle came running to her rescue.

The Acting Governor of the Divinely Chartered Commonwealth of Kansans United for a Sin-Free Kansas and the Supreme Commandant General of its First Regimental Kansas Free Citizens Militia Brigade had not taken long to render a verdict. They had entered the deliberation room already agreeing that Livengood was guilty on all charges, and it pleased them to note how closely their judgment resembled their pre-judgment.

In keeping with the rules of their Common Law Court, which had been purchased in pamphlet form at a patriot's convention in the Springfield, Missouri, Holiday Inn, the two wrote down their decisions on small pieces of paper, folding them two times. When they each opened the other's paper, their eyes met in shared delight. The next step in the procedure was to write down their sentencing recommendations, and when they both opened the papers to read "death penalty," their gaze became hypnotic.

Somewhere in the back of Dimschmidt's mind she remained conscious of the need for a quick dispatch of justice, if they were to make their planned escape, but those thoughts were barely discernable against the unexpected passion she now felt.

Schnitzle had never expected to get out of the building alive, but went along with Dimschmidt's suicidal scheme for a lack of anything better to do. Now, looking at the angular lines of Dimschmidt's face and the firm yet supple shape of her body, he decided to face death with an exuberance that he had never before experienced in his long life as the most fucked-over man in America.

There was something about the hardened muscles and leathery complexion of Schnitzle, too. It was that, or the aphrodisiacal effects of her divinely appointed power of life and death, or maybe just the inevitable consequence of more than ten years of celibacy. For whatever reason, Dimschmidt did not resist when Schnitzle began to undress her. Moments later, their screams of passion made it impossible to hear Ellie's screams of pain and distress.

With another crash of his shoulder and another whack of Ellie Whimple's head on the frame of the outer door, Livengood emerged from the storefront and rushed toward the police. Mistaking the man with a screaming woman on his shoulder for a kidnapper, and the screaming woman for a kidnapping victim, the police snatched Ellie away and wrapped her in a blanket while they pummeled Livengood with nightsticks, kicking and punching him repeatedly.

Inside the office of the director of Women's Health Services, Inc., Dimschmidt and Schnitzle were nearing a physical climax of their passion. They thrashed about wildly on the director's desktop, then fell off and rolled together across the floor. They stopped against the wall, where they continued their uninterrupted coupling. Dimschmidt kicked her feet as a powerful and long-forgotten sensation began to ripple through her body, toppling a small table on which Schnitzle had earlier placed one of the bombs.

The crash triggered the device, which in turn triggered a series of bombs that had been placed throughout the building. Dimschmidt and Schnitzle were, in the words of a lead that Dan Dorsey wrote but did not dare to publish, blown to Kingdom Come.

Frankie Livengood was rushed to a hospital to recover from the wounds from the police beating and the small piece of burning debris that had landed on his back during the explosion. After telling a small army of detectives everything he could remember about the night's events, he fell into a drug-induced sleep.

He awoke groggily, ate a few tiny bites of the breakfast that was delivered to his lap, then greeted a steady stream of visitors. Rebecca Reynolds arrived early, frantic with concern about Livengood, and he had just managed to calm her nerves and send her back to work when Jane Hutchinson appeared, also in need of comfort and reassurance. Darla Morland brought a floral arrangement, ignored Livengood's comment that he would have preferred cigarettes, and in the ensuing conversation revealed that she had not yet reached a decision about her own health issues. Mark Stark came bearing apologies for his outburst over the telephone, and in complete agreement about Livengood's assessment of the number of nut cases in Kansas. Dan Dorsey stayed for twenty minutes, even after Livengood declined to grant an interview. Mick Fixx called from Livengood's apartment, offering to stock it with any supplies that Livengood might need during his recovery. Harley Christianson, accompanied by a much larger than usual contingent of Highway Patrol escorts, offered his best wishes for a speedy recovery and insisted that Livengood spend at least another day of rest at home.

Livengood accepted the offer, although he knew that his apartment would offer no refuge from the stress of the legislative session. Predictably, his phone rang all through the day with calls from legislators, lobbyists, the governor's staff and various other people with problems that required his immediate attention. He also made several calls of his own to check on the status of various riders and the river bill, and found that neither situation had improved noticeably in his absence from the capitol.

Still, Livengood felt a small amount of satisfaction in being alive after such a close encounter with death. He took stock of his life during a lull in the phone calls, and was surprised by the conclusion that it might be worth living.

Then the phone rang, and the snarling voice of Big Jim Morland shattered his illusions.

"God damn you Frankie Livengood," Big Jim shrieked. "I didn't send my daughter to work for you so she could get knocked up by one of your bum friends—"

Livengood set down the phone, rubbed his eyes and breathed deeply. He picked up the phone again.

"—low down piece of shit, you," Big Jim was saying. "Smoking dope in front of her, fucking in a goddamn coatroom, swilling booze and cussing. No wonder she gets these ideas. Introducing her to a bunch of Satan-worshipping punk rockers, college faggots and New York City feminists. Jesus Christ, no wonder she's out fornicating like a whore."

And so it went for several minutes. Livengood listened to every word, and offered no defense. He tried to squeeze an apology into Big Jim's tirade, but didn't get a chance before the call ended with a slam.

Livengood hung up his phone and returned to the couch. After staring at the ceiling for two straight hours, ignoring the constant ringing of the phone, he arose and began ironing his clothes for the next day's work.

He was not a happy man, but at least Livengood now knew what he was supposed to do.

CHAPTER NINETEEN

"Frankie Livengood's Call to Glory"

Frankie Livengood strode past the John Brown mural and into his office, his glaring eyes no less intimidating than those of the great abolitionist himself. Two quickly ingested cups of coffee were the first order of business, followed by Livengood's habitual haphazard review of the various memos, reports, documents and newspaper clippings that somehow appeared on his desk each morning. He then went outside to smoke a cigarette, as was his wont, and returned to his office for his usual third cup of coffee.

After a series of phone calls were placed to various women's organizations, high school assemblies and collegiate political clubs, Livengood called Gov. Harley Christianson on a cell phone number. Christianson was speaking on behalf of rivers at a school assembly in Atwood, and Livengood told him that he needed to continue his drive for public support by appearing at several more engagements that had just been arranged.

"You're really getting them to put the pressure on up here," Livengood said, eyeing the three lonely letters in the stack he had designated for positive messages about the river bill. "Even if you don't get back before the end of the session, you've got to stay out there and keep rallying the people."

Having persuaded Harley to accept a schedule that would keep him away from the capitol until the session had adjourned, Livengood asked a secretary to arrange a meeting with Pastor Jeffries and a later conference with former Gov. Chuck Bentley and

Chip Wentworth. He then shut his office door to call Rebecca Reynolds.

"Can you meet me for lunch?" Livengood asked. "We have to talk."

Reynolds met Livengood at his apartment, where they sat at a counter by the kitchen and ate the microwaved remains of the prior evening's pizza.

"You've been asking lately about the future of our relationship," Livengood said.

Reynolds laid her slice down, then placed her chin on the palm of her hand, looking at him curiously. Livengood usually wasn't the one to broach the subject of their relationship.

"I don't think you should plan on there being one," Livengood said. "A future, I mean, for our relationship."

Rebecca slowly picked up the slice, took a crooked bite, and chewed on it at great length.

"Why not?" she said.

"It's all so damned complicated," Livengood said. "I guess it's just because I can't go where you're going, and you sure as hell don't want to go where I'm going."

"You said you loved me."

It was Livengood's turn to chew at great length.

"I do love you," Livengood said. "It's just that I don't love you the way I would if my career wasn't so out of control, if it weren't always out of control, if the rest of my life wasn't just as bad, if I weren't such an asshole. I don't love you the way I would if I wasn't such an asshole. I should love you that way, because you're the smartest and the toughest woman I ever knew, and you make me laugh, and you soothe me, but I can't."

"I always knew about all of those things," Reynolds said. "I still don't see why our situation needs to change so suddenly. This has been mutually beneficial. Hasn't it?"

"It has," Livengood said. "But it won't turn out to be beneficial for you, not if you stay here for me."

"You're not the reason I've stayed here, and I'm not going to pack up and move back home if you stop seeing me."

"You're here for now," Livengood said. "But it won't be forever. You're only here because your fight is here, and I'm only in this fight because I'm here."

Reynolds shrugged, admitting that she knew that, too.

"How do you think that fight is going, by the way?" Reynolds asked. "I keep trying to count the votes on these riders, and it's too close for my comfort."

"I don't know," Livengood said. "Your estimate is probably better than mine, because I'm trying to follow all of these riders, and they keep coming faster than I can count."

Reynolds asked if she could count on Livengood to help win vetoes if the bills passed, regardless of their personal relationship.

"I'm doing the best I can," Livengood said. "I don't know what the hell is going to happen."

The sadness on Reynolds face was painful to Livengood, and he tried not to look. When he assured her that he wanted to do what was best for her, she snapped that self-sacrifice did not become him.

The door slammed, and Livengood nudged the last of his slice across the plate. "Damn it," he mumbled. "I'm doing the best I fucking can."

Livengood's meeting with Pastor Jeffries took the form of another long walk around the capitol, which the pastor insisted on despite the cold temperatures and bitter wind. The pastor explained that the walk was for the sake of exercise, but Livengood assumed it was meant to emphasize the pastor's advantaged position in their negotiations.

"You seem to be doing quite well this session," Livengood said, buttoning the top of his coat and pulling his hat down against the wind. "From what I can tell, several of your reforms seem to continue gaining support from some of the most unexpected people."

"The Lord certainly seems to have blessed our efforts," the pastor said, striding along at a brisk pace. "I shall continue to pray that Governor Christianson might see the light, and not interfere with those efforts."

"You never know," Livengood said.

The pastor stopped suddenly, and smiled at Livengood. "I thought I did know," he said. "I had always thought, based on some of the extremely liberal positions Governor Christianson took in the campaign, that he would not support our agenda."

Livengood, who was becoming numb from the cold, noticed that the pastor wasn't even shivering.

"To be frank with you, Pastor, I don't think he's exactly rooting for it to get passed. We also don't expect that all of it will. We're optimistic, in fact, that some of the more, shall we say, controversial aspects of your agenda most likely won't pass. What does pass, though, will pose a difficult question for the administration. After all, I can well imagine what a shrewd political operative such as yourself might do in the next election with a veto of, say, your abortion restrictions."

The pastor chuckled his agreement with Livengood as he continued their walk.

"On the other hand," Livengood said. "I'd hate to think what could happen in a general election if Harley were to sign on to everything you guys have got cooking. The rest of the electorate isn't quite so committed to Kansas values as the Republican primary votership."

The pastor walked silently for several steps, then said, "Of course, if the governor were to sign on to enough of what we've got cooking, we could offer him a substantial amount of help in a general election."

"We could certainly use it," Livengood said. "The governor's single-minded pursuit of the river bill has put us in such bad stead with the money-changers in the party, it's getting hard for me to see where else the help could come from."

The pastor, now especially pleased with his advantaged position in negotiations, picked up the pace.

"I suppose I could offer some help with the river bill, but I'm not sure how much," the pastor said. "Several of the senators and House members that I get along with best have their own objections to that legislation. In fact, I'm afraid it would take a miracle, one that you're not capable of, to raise that bill from the dead."

"That's the way I figure it, too. But I've got to make it close. Harley cares about nothing else, and I'd like to keep my job."

"I could help, I suppose," the pastor said. "I mean, since it's not going to pass. But, as the Good Book says, to whom much is given, much is expected in return."

"I don't know how much I can help with that," Livengood said. "Here's your problem, Pastor. Those riders of yours are only as good as the bills that they're riding on. Right now, I'm figuring on shooting down most of those bills on their own merits, and you've got to admit that you're riding on the backs of a lot of bills that a good conservative usually would be dead set against. Do you really want to pass all those appropriations just to get some of these riders through?"

The pastor's pace slowed, and he stopped to consider the question.

"We can always move them around," Pastor Jeffries said. "The Speaker of the House, the President of the Senate and most of the committee chairs are friendly to the cause."

"I don't know," Livengood said, leading the walk at a quicker step. "It's going to take some expert maneuvering to get everything you want without a whole lot of what you don't want. Frankly, Pastor Jeffries, I'm surprised you weren't more bold."

The pastor hastened to catch up, and asked exactly what Livengood meant by his remark.

"I mean, with you having the business people in such an inferior negotiating position and all," Livengood said. "If I had been in your shoes, I would have lumped everything into one big package, one gigantic omnibus morality act, and gotten it passed in one fell swoop. That's how I would have played it."

"Hmm," the pastor said, now shivering slightly. "That would almost certainly provoke a veto, wouldn't it?"

"It depends," Livengood said. "I mean, we wouldn't want everything in there."

"Of course not," the pastor said, laughing slightly. "Even we wouldn't want *everything* in there. Some of our membership is very adamant about some of those things, but they don't necessarily enjoy broad support."

"That's no problem," Livengood said. "Just put half the stuff you don't really want in the House bill, the other half in the Senate version, and we'll yank it all out in conference committee, when the two chambers work out their differences on the final bill. You go back to your people and say 'Hey? What could I do? They pulled it out in conference committee.' "

"Can we really swing that?"

"No sweat," Livengood said. "When you get to the end of the session, and it's two in the morning when those conferences finally end, well, half the time nobody's even read a third of what they're voting for. I'll be in there for the governor, and you'd be surprised what I've swung in conference committees. Hell, if your people still don't like what gets left out, feel free to blame it on Harley. We could use that in a general election to get our moderate image back."

The pastor nodded, visibly impressed.

"So what do you have to have?" Livengood asked.

"Abortion restrictions, certainly. And we're committed to making our schools safe from homosexual recruitment. Something about alcohol and pornography will be necessary. We might be willing to scale back the plan to disestablish the schools, though. Who needs to be taking on the teachers' unions?"

"Of course not," Livengood said. "What you've got would make for a very interesting piece of legislation, though, you have to admit."

"Would Governor Christianson veto it?"

"Perhaps he could be persuaded not to," Livengood said.

"You seem to have a great deal of influence with the governor," the pastor said. "Indeed, it has been my observation that you have a very great deal of influence on the governor."

"You're a very astute man, Pastor Jeffries."

"And as you say, Frankie, you want to keep your job."

Livengood nodded his agreement.

"On the other hand," the pastor said, eyeing Livengood suspiciously, "Governor Christianson has always struck me as a more steadfast sort of fellow than that. I don't respect his convictions, of course, but I must say that I've always rather respected the courage he's shown for them. I've always thought him a rather ethical fellow, in fact. In a terribly misguided way, of course."

"The governor is a very ethical man," Livengood said. "That's why he needed me to get him elected, and that's why he's going to need me if he has any hope of getting re-elected. That's also why you're dealing with me, while the governor is out rhetorically tilting at windmills. He's steadfast like you wouldn't believe, sure enough, but fortunately for you he's steadfast mainly about this river bill. You help me keep the vote on that close enough, deal with me some on your proposals, and I can assure you he won't interfere."

They were heading back to the capitol now, and the pastor was proceeding at a pace that admitted he was cold.

"One last thing," Livengood said, as they thawed by a furnace vent in the west wing hallway. "Just make sure your bill comes up before the river bill. If you've got any deals cooking with Wentworth and Bentley, you'll want to hold them to it before your end comes up. Forgive my language, Pastor, but those guys will screw you over without a moment's guilt about it."

The pastor smiled condescendingly, and said that of course he had already considered that possibility. Although he hated to think such things of another human being, much less a fellow Republican, Jeffries had already arrived at the same plan.

Three days later the talk of the capitol was House Bill 58299, dubbed "The Omnibus Morality Act" by its principal sponsor, House Speaker Stan Patterson. The furor even spread beyond the capitol, onto the front pages of every newspaper in the state, then onto the nightly newscasts of every television station, and was even the subject of an alarmed report on National Public Radio. Numerous groups rallied in support of the measure, with one rally sponsored by Kansans for Kansas Values out-drawing the previous evening's heavy metal concert at the Kansas Coliseum in Wichita. A smaller number of groups scrambled to mobilize a grass-roots opposition movement, making frantic phone calls for help to advocacy groups and media experts from New York City and Washington, D.C.

The bill was also the first topic of conversation in the meeting Frankie Livengood attended with Gov. Chuck Bentley and Chip Wentworth.

"Jesus, Frankie," Wentworth said. "What's Harley going to do with this bastard of a bill if it gets passed? Between the abortion stuff and the homo stuff and the porn and the gambling and the liquor laws and whatever else they've put into it today, there's something in there for almost everybody to hate. Hell, I'll bet there won't be fifteen or so Kansans who aren't in constant violation of at least one provision of this thing, and that sure doesn't include you or me."

Livengood drank his rum and Coke, and shrugged. "Maybe so. But you can look at it another way, too. Almost everybody hates somebody who will be in violation of this bill, and that gives it a lot of popular appeal. I'll try to talk Harley into a veto, but it would be a hell of a lot better for him if it failed on the floor and he didn't have to."

Governor Bentley sneered at Livengood and blurted a derisive, "Huh."

"Right now, Governor Christianson doesn't seem to give much of a damn about the Omnibus," Livengood said. "All he really cares about is his precious river bill."

"I can't believe that guy," Wentworth said. "This morality crap is the biggest story in the state, and Harley's still out talking to high school assemblies about a bill that's dead and buried inside the business section."

"The damn river bill is all I care about," Bentley said. "If this morality crap makes it easier to get rid of Christianson and his damn clean-up-the-rivers crusade, that's fine by me. I'm way past the age of caring about abortions, I'm no homo, and I'm stocked up on all the porn and liquor I'll ever need. All I care about is whether your tree-hugging son of a bitch of a governor is going to drive me out of businesses with taxes and regulations and users fees."

"I'd be happy to talk about that," Livengood said. "And I think you'll be happy to hear what I have to say."

Wentworth and Bentley both leaned forward to listen.

"Chip's right about everything," Livengood said. "The morality bill is the big story out there, and it's the biggest obstacle to another four years of gainful employment in the high style to which I have become accustomed. The river bill is as dead as ever, nobody gives a damn, and I'm willing to jettison it."

"Huh," Bentley blurted, leaning back and sneering again.

"Chuck's right," Wentworth said, slumping back in disappointment. "Harley will never go for it. The guy's beating a dead horse here, but I've got to give him credit for being stubborn. Your Harley's one steadfast motherfucker."

"He's an idiot," Bentley said. "From what I hear, he's the kind of fool who'd run into machine-gun fire for a damn radio."

"You're right again, Chip," Livengood said. "Harley never would go for it. He's way the hell too steadfast for a smart play like that. Fortunately for us, Chuck's right, too. Harley's also an idiot. So we can jettison the river bill without him even knowing it."

Wentworth and Bentley leaned forward again.

"Have you guys actually read this river bill?" Livengood asked.

Both men shook their heads.

"I have," Livengood said. "The son of a bitch is seven inches thick. It took a whole team of bureaucrats to write it, and it takes a whole team of bureaucrats to read it. Most of it is standards and regulations and goals and lofty ideas, but the meat of it is in two or three sections that appropriate money and levy fines. That kind of thing can be simply stated, so it's small. It's so small you wouldn't even notice if it were missing. If you catch my drift."

The men's expressions indicated they caught his drift.

"You put in just a couple of word changes here and there, which my sponsor could easily be persuaded to accept, and a smart consultant could get you around the rest of the bill without much of a problem at all," Livengood said. "Being a policy wonk of long standing, and having been intimately involved in the writing of this legislation, down to the minutest detail, I might very well make an excellent candidate for such valuable consulting work myself. If you catch my drift."

Again, they caught his drift.

"This sounds like another of your bullshit schemes," Bentley said. "Why should we accept even a de-fanged river bill? We're perfectly happy with the onerous regulations the state already has on the books."

"I'm handing you a public relations bonanza," Livengood said. "You guys can run commercials that say you worked hand in hand with government to pass the strictest standards and goals in the country, and you'd be telling the truth."

Wentworth looked to be more impressed than Bentley with Livengood's line of argument.

"This is another of your goddamn schemes," Bentley said. "Unless we get rid of him here and now, your crazy-ass governor will just be back next session to put the teeth back in. This is just your way of doing it."

"What the hell are you so afraid of?" Livengood asked. "The governor is going to get his river bill passed, and as far as he's concerned he's cleaning up the rivers. If some tree-hugger outfit brings our minor revisions to his attention and he tries to put it back, the legislature is just going to tell him that they've already passed a river bill and don't want to mess with it anymore. You'll find it much easier to beat back the environmentalists when you've already got a river bill."

Wentworth, who had been scribbling names and numbers on a napkin, told Livengood that, "Even if you make the bill so that we can live with it, I still don't think you can round up the votes to get this turkey passed. You're starting from just Democrats, and it's too far to go."

"Not if we get your new-found religious friends on board," Livengood said. "After we beat his Omnibus Bill, Patterson will be so pissed that he'll probably have his guys vote for the river bill just to get back at you."

"Well," Bentley said. He was still sneering at Livengood, but his look no longer conveyed skepticism. "Now that does sound like one of your goddamn schemes."

Livengood noticed that Wentworth now seemed skeptical.

"I don't know about this," Wentworth said. "It just doesn't seem the kind of thing you'd do, Frankie, screwing over Harley like that. I've always admired the way you do business, but I can't believe you'd screw a governor."

"Huh," Bentley snorted. "That's exactly the kind of thing this son of a bitch would do. Shee-it, this son of a bitch here'll have you assuming the position on a full-time basis, no matter who you are."

One drink later, the men came to an agreement.

Frankie Livengood went home and called his ex-wife.

"You've got to join the staff, Jane, and take over this river bill project," Livengood said. "You've got to."

"We've talked about this," she said. "Why do we always have to have the same arguments?"

"This is no argument," Livengood said. "You've got to do it."

"Why, Frankie? Why do I have to do it?"

"Two reasons," Livengood said. "One is that we'll have rivers of bullshit running through this state for the rest of our lives if you don't. The other is that you'd be a damn hypocrite for the rest of your life if you don't."

"This is just another reason that I don't want to do it. It is not good for our relationship."

"I've been thinking about that, and I've decided we don't need a relationship, anyway," Livengood said. "You dumped my ass for no good reason except me being an asshole, so who needs a friend like that? Now it's your turn to enter the fray, and see how holy you are in there, or admit that you aren't one damn bit more noble than I am."

"Frankie, please."

"No, Jane. It's my turn to lecture you for a change. Harley needs you. Your state needs you. Goddamn nature needs you."

"This is your job, Frankie, not mine."

"This is my job, but that's all," Livengood said. "What the hell do I care about a river? This is your cause. At least, you always said it was."

"Why are you so angry? We'd been getting along so well. I was starting to respect you again, and for the first time in a long time."

"It was all an illusion, babe," Livengood said. "I'm the same as ever."

After a long silence, Livengood said good-bye and hung up.

The final day of the session began much like any other for Frankie Livengood, except for the excitable crowd of pro-morality demonstrators that he wended through on his way to the office. Once safely inside, he did the two cups of coffee, the quick scan of the desk and the trip outside for a quick smoke.

He met briefly with Bentley and Wentworth, who gave their approval to the version of the river bill that Livengood had swiftly moved through committee. Being distrustful of people in general, and Livengood in particular, Bentley had hired a team of crack lawyers to examine the document before giving final approval, and with considerable satisfaction he told Livengood that his services probably would not be needed for the beef industry to avoid any difficulties with the bill. Bentley said that the Senate version of the bill was preferable to the one from the House, and Livengood assured him that he would personally attend the conference committee's negotiations to assure the best possible river bill.

Pastor Jeffries dropped in on Livengood an hour later to gloat about the growing momentum for the Omnibus Morality Act. After a complete poll of both houses of the legislature, Jeffries said, he had counted enough votes for a comfortable, if not veto-proof, victory. With a flourish, he withdrew from his pocket a list of the "yeas" and "nays" he had collected. Livengood examined the document carefully, silently subtracting from the list the moderate and pro-business legislators who would soon be freed from the deal that Jeffries had cut. He handed the list back with a congratulatory smile, trying to conceal the nervousness he felt after counting a winning tally for the bill even after the subtractions were made.

A few minutes later, Rebecca Reynolds found Livengood at his usual smoking spot, despite his effort to hide behind a column. She jabbed fingers at his chest as she launched into a tirade about the Omnibus Morality Act.

"The way I count it, it's going to win big," Reynolds said. "I thought I could at least count on a few of your money-grubbing capitalist exploiters to help me out on this, but they're still signed on for some damn reason. What the hell is wrong with this state of yours? You people are all insane."

"It's not going to win big," Livengood said. "It's going to be close, but I'm working on it. You need to be working on it, too, not standing here punching a hole in my chest."

"You need to be working on that hick governor of yours," Reynolds said. "The only thing that's going to stop this thing is a veto, and I don't care if it does piss off your precious primary voters. They're all a bunch of wackos, anyway."

With that, Reynolds stomped back into the capitol.

Livengood smoked another cigarette, dropped its butt to the ground and crushed it with his foot, then closed his eyes and bowed his head to pray a prayer for forgiveness. He then proceeded directly to the floor of the House of Representatives, where he scanned the room for the legislators whose names he had culled from Pastor Jeffries' list of pro-morality voters.

Twenty-five years of experience went into Frankie Livengood's efforts to work those legislators. He used every method of persuasion he had ever learned, called in every favor he was owed, offered every bit of pork he could think of. He made every threat he could get away with, and warned several legislators who had once been associated with Edna Dimschmidt that he might be inclined to mention them in the interviews he was planning to give about her terrorist activities.

For the most part, he used the oldest and most reliable strategy ever devised against the political power of Christianity.

A Catholic legislator from western Sedgwick County was informed by Livengood that the anti-gambling provisions of the bill would be used by certain anti-Catholic legislators to eliminate the bingo nights that provided essential funds for several Catholic works. A Baptist legislator from Rooks County was warned by Livengood that the support for parochial schools contained in the bill was just the beginning of its nefarious hidden Catholic conspiracies. An Assemblies of God legislator from Miami County was told by Livengood that certain Baptist legislators intended to write the prayer that would be forced on children under the Prayer in School provisions of the bill. A Seventh Day Adventist legislator from Wyandotte County was horrified to learn from Livengood that a group of Methodist legislators had ensured that the creationism bill would not include the Great Flood Theory so dear to his church's heart. A lifetime of listening to sectarian squabbles enabled Livengood to pry several legislators away from Pastor Jeffries' carefully cultivated coalition, and he was almost disappointed to discover how easy it was.

Livengood took a seat next to Pastor Jeffries in the House gallery to watch the voting on the Omnibus Morality Bill. He noticed that the pastor showed disappointment when several of his Kansans for Kansas Values lit up red lights on the large display board to indicate a "nay" vote. When red light after red light started appearing next to the names of the moderate legislators included on his list of guaranteed "yeas," Jeffries seethed. By the time the final tally showed the bill losing by a margin of eighteen votes, Pastor Jeffries's face was tightly drawn and crimson red with anger.

"What happened?" Livengood asked, doing his best to feign shock. "I thought you had everybody lined up."

The pastor crossed his arms and continued to stare at the display board.

"I can understand why a few of your people would get cold feet at the last minute, but why did your entire bloc of moderates run out on you?" Livengood asked. "I had assumed you'd cut some sort of deal with Wentworth and Bentley and those guys."

The pastor, still staring at the display board, did not deny it.

"You did? Didn't you?" Livengood said. "I knew it. A smart guy like you. You probably told them that you'd go for the river bill if they didn't do the right thing on your bill. That would have been the smart play. For the sake of morality, I mean."

The pastor kept right on staring.

"That's just like those guys. Believe me, you can't trust them," Livengood said. "What a couple of Judases."

The pastor at last looked at Livengood, and thanked him for his sympathy.

"We may not always agree on everything, Pastor, but at least I know you're a man of your word," Livengood said. "If you ask me, you ought to just turn around and show Wentworth and Bentley and the rest of those guys what a man of your word you are. If you said you'd throw your support behind the river bill if they didn't do the right thing for the morality bill, then by golly, you ought to do just that. Harley's still not going to get that thing passed, but you can still swing enough votes to make it close enough to put the fear of God in them."

Three hours later, after a meeting between Jeffries and several of the legislators, Livengood was told that the Kansans for Kansas Values were no longer in favor of rivers of fecal matter.

At midnight, the river bill at last went to the floor of the House for a vote. Frankie Livengood once again sat next to Pastor Jeffries in the House gallery to watch the final score tally for the long, hard-fought game. The pastor smiled smugly at Livengood when the first of his allies lit up a green light in favor of the bill, then showed surprise when a veritable Christmas tree of green lights began flashing next to the names of even the most business-minded and beef-allied moderates. When a substantial number of the Democratic minority and a handful of the maverick progressive Republicans pitched in with their own green lights, the bill had won.

"What happened?" the pastor asked. "I didn't think you had the votes lined up."

"Praise God," Livengood said, patting Pastor Jeffries on the back. "His loyal servants have brought a great victory for the Christianson administration."

"What in tarnation is going on?" the pastor asked. "I'm sorry, but I don't believe for one second that God Almighty has personally intervened here just to help out Frankie Livengood. My guess is that Wentworth and Bentley and those guys have screwed you, too."

Frankie Livengood looked convincingly shocked.

"Do you think so?" Livengood asked. "I'd better check this out."

At one o'clock in the morning, Livengood found Pastor Jeffries in the Senate gallery, waiting for the upper chamber's vote on the river bill.

"You were right, of course," Livengood said. "I took a close look at that bill, and sure enough, Wentworth and Bentley and those guys have screwed me. Somehow they yanked out all the enforcement and money provisions of the bill in committee, and all we've passed is a bunch of meaningless bureaucratic nonsense. I can't believe my sponsor let this happen, but I guess that when Wentworth and Bentley and those guys are throwing their filthy lucre around, you can't trust anybody."

The pastor seemed to take considerable consolation in telling Livengood that he had told him so. With a degree of sympathy worthy of his profession, Pastor Jeffries asked if there was anything he could do to help.

"Maybe there is," Livengood said. "And you'd be proving yourself a man of your word in the process."

The pastor showed interest.

"Look, the House river bill and the Senate river bill have a couple of minor differences, so they're going to have to go into conference on this thing," Livengood said. "All you've got to do is have Patterson and your Senate people pick the right guys for that committee. Then we put enough teeth back into this baby to take a big ol' bite out of Wentworth's and Bentley's butts, we write up a report that doesn't really let anyone in on what's going on, and then at three in the morning we run it past a bunch of sleep-deprived legislators and onto the governor's desk before the lawyers get a close look at it."

The pastor seemed dubious.

"Come on," Livengood said. "I'm handing you a public relations miracle here. You get a chance to show all those liberals that you're not just a bunch of power-mad religious fanatics, and you prove your clout to the business wing in the process. If anything goes wrong, you just blame it on the governor."

Only six members of the Kansas legislature had shown enthusiasm for the river bill in its original incarnation, and Livengood struggled to disguise his happiness when they were all announced as members of the conference committee. Bentley, who was still manning the lobby, reluctantly accepted Livengood's assurances that the members were picked to enhance the bill's credibility with the environmental lobbyists who were still hovering about.

The negotiations went all too smoothly for Livengood, who was hoping to drag the meeting far enough into the morning to ensure that all of the bill's opponents would be too drowsy to recognize the significance of the changes. The wording of the conference committee's report proved difficult, however, with several of the members insisting on a more plainly spoken account of their work, and it was nearly four o'clock in the morning before Livengood had persuaded them to accept a technically accurate but impenetrably legalistic statement.

Most of the House and Senate had to be nudged awake at their desks when the amended version of the bill went up for a vote, and except for two senators who had been shaken awake by Governor Bentley, all voted just has they had done in the earlier roll calls. Except for the formality of the signature of Gov. Harley Christianson, the river bill was now a law.

Frankie Livengood returned to his office, slumped onto his leather chair and spun around, drinking in the elegance of the wood-paneled walls and marble trimmings. He chuckled to himself as he loaded a cardboard box with the few personal items he had used to decorate the space.

He emerged from the governor's office and stopped for a long look at the John Brown mural outside the door. A janitor sweeping nearby was startled when the man in the frayed brown suit let loose with a sad laugh and began singing, "John Brown's body lies a-molderin' in the grave … "

Frankie Livengood drove to the gate of the governor's mansion, where he was waved past the gate by a guard whose name he could not remember, then drove to the front door. Harley Christianson answered the door in a bathrobe and a pair of pajamas, and said how surprised he was to see Livengood at such an early hour of the morning.

CHAPTER NINETEEN

The two men walked to the kitchen, where Livengood sat down at a counter while Harley prepared coffee. The governor poured two cups, and said how proud he was of the work Livengood had done on the river bill.

"I'm sure glad to hear that," Livengood said. "I'm afraid that the preparation of that particular omelet required the breaking of an extraordinary number of eggs."

Harley sipped his coffee, and smiled at Livengood without a trace of concern.

"Whatever you did, it worked," Harley said. "I never would have believed it. I thought that bill was dead from the get-go. I thought I was on another suicide mission trying to get that thing through. Just goes to show, I guess, what can happen when you're committed to the right."

Livengood took a long draw of his own coffee, and smiled back.

"I'm not kidding, Harley. I had to break a hell of a lot of eggs," Livengood said. "You're going to have to fire me."

"The hell I will," Harley said, laughing. "What would I do without you?"

"You'll get along fine," Livengood said. "Just ask Wilbur about the policy stuff, because he knows it inside and out, and he'll always be straight with you. Don't let anyone know about it, but go to Mark Stark for anything you need to know about the politics stuff, because he wrote a book on everything I know, and he's also got a few good ideas of his own. For the administrative stuff, I think you should promote Kathy Knieble to chief of staff, because she seems to know what she's doing and she's ferociously loyal to you. You're also going to need someone to keep the wolves away from this damn river bill for the next four years, and I recommend that you do whatever you have to do to get my ex-wife on board for that. She really believes in all this jazz, and she's a good woman."

"That's all well and good," Harley said. "But I'm not firing you."

"Damn it, you have to," Livengood said. "I came up with the only possible way to get your stupid river bill passed and kill that stupid Omnibus Morality Act, and I've pulled it off right down to the last step, which is you firing me."

Livengood slammed his fist against the counter to stop Harley's chuckling, and explained everything he had done in the previous days.

"Don't you see? I'm no damn good to you anymore," Livengood said. "I've completely screwed the most prominent leaders of both wings of my party, and I'll never be able to deal with them again."

"There was never anything to worry about with that Omnibus thing," Harley said. "You know I would have vetoed that. I'm perfectly willing to work with these folks on making Kansas more moral and all, but I'm not going to let them bully anybody."

"If you'd been forced to veto that thing, you never would have had a chance to get re-elected," Livengood said. "It's going to be tough enough as it is, but at least now you've got an outside chance. If you don't fire me, though, Wentworth and Jeffries are both going to take it personally, and you don't stand a snowball's chance in hell of getting back into office."

Harley still seemed unconcerned.

"I know you don't care about being governor, but now you have to do it," Livengood said. "If you aren't around to veto the inevitable effort to repeal this river bill, the rivers of bullshit will continue to flow through Kansas for the rest of your life."

Harley smiled on one side of his face and dismissed Livengood's proposal with a wave of his hand.

"And you've got to give Big Jim Morland a call and tell him that you fired me," Livengood said. "You're going to need his help and a whole lot of his money if you're going to have a chance, and that's another thing that won't happen with me around."

"Sorry, Frankie," Harley said. "I'm just not going to fire you."

"Well, then," Livengood said, rising slowly and putting his hands on his hips. "I quit."

With that, Livengood gave Harley a lingering handshake and walked out of the mansion. Livengood started his Camaro, pointed it westward and drove.

CHAPTER TWENTY

"Kansas Pastoral"

A long stream of billowing dust followed Dan Dorsey's Buick as he sped down a Wallace County dirt road. He was the only thing moving on the western Kansas prairie for as far as his eye could see.

Dorsey stopped in the middle of the road near a windmill, the first sign of human habitation he had encountered for miles, save the barbed wire fence and telephone lines and the road itself. After wiping the sweat from his forehead, he re-checked the directions he had scribbled on a crumpled piece of paper from a reporter's notebook. He squinted toward the horizon, a thin unbroken line between the brown earth and the washed-out blue of the late August sky, then put the car in gear and continued south.

Five and a half miles later, Dorsey could see two small buildings, one a limestone house of traditional prairie design, the other a strange combination of pioneer hovel and space-age diner. Dorsey slowed to read a billboard by the road, which said "Livengood Buffalo Burgers" atop a cartoon rendering of Frankie Livengood, with a balloon caption coming out of his mouth to say, "Mmm, that's livin' good!" After pulling into the dusty parking lot of the hovel-diner, Dorsey walked through the screen door and found Livengood sitting alone on the counter, reading a newspaper.

"Holy shit," Livengood said. "Look at this. What could have possibly dragged your tired old ass all the way out here? We don't get many big city newspaper reporters around here, you know."

The two men shook hands, slapped one another on the shoulder, and inquired how the hell the other had been.

"I was on my way to the Rockies, and figured it would be worth an extra few hundred miles to see what's become of you," Dorsey said. "I'm heading out to Grand Junction, to my retirement home. Sunflower News got bought out, you know, and they pushed me out. They figured they'd be better off with some young punk that doesn't know a damn thing about Kansas politics."

Livengood offered his condolences.

"The bitch of it is, they're probably right," Dorsey said. "These kids today, they work hard, they don't smoke, and they're an obsequious bunch of bastards. Who can compete with that? Anyway, I heard this improbable rumor that you were flipping burgers out in western Kansas. Since it was about you, I figured it was improbable enough that it might be true, so I had to see for myself."

"So look around, and see for yourself," Livengood said. "If you want to eyewitness me flipping burgers, I'll be glad to cook one up for you. Since you've come so far, just to see me, I'll even give you a discount."

Livengood placed two thick buffalo burger patties on an aged but well-scrubbed grill, dropped a metal basket full of potato slices into a gurgling vat of oil, then took two long-necked bottles of beer from a cooler and handed one to Dorsey.

"So," Dorsey said, drumming his fingers on the counter top. "What the hell are you doing out here?"

"I'm not sure," Livengood said, leaning against the counter and resting his chin on the palm of his hand. "After I quit on Harley, I felt like going for a drive. I wound up out here, somehow, so I dropped in for a burger. There was this long-haired guy behind the counter, and we got to talking about what a bitch it is to work for a living. He offered to swap the whole business for my car. That included the house, the grill, the beer signs, everything, so I figured what the hell and took the deal."

"I see," Dorsey said. "And how's the free market treating you out here?"

"Not so bad," Livengood said. "Enough folks wander through for me to eke out a living, given that everything's paid for and there's food around. I won't be taking any trips to New York City on what I'm making, but what do I want to go to New York City for, anyway?"

Dorsey noted that Livengood seemed to be getting by, and added that a man ought to be satisfied with that.

"The worst part is the damn taxes and the regulations and all that rigmarole," Livengood said. "I'm flipping burgers for a living, and my tax statement is thirty pages long. It's ridiculous. I'm in the middle of nowhere, but I've got more inspectors showing up than you'd need to run a large city. You know all that bullshit I used to talk about—over-regulation and high taxes? Well, it turns out that it was all true."

Dorsey wondered about the rest of Livengood's life, noting that it seemed rather dull in the middle of nowhere.

"Wonderfully dull," Livengood said, raising his arms in praise. "Exquisitely, sublimely, divinely dull. As dull as I always imagined Heaven itself to be."

"I can understand that," Dorsey said. "Things were getting a bit too exciting for you back in Topeka. Especially there at the end."

Livengood nodded as he flipped the burgers.

"You did the only thing you could do," Dorsey said. "It was the most impressive piece of bullshit I ever saw in my life, and for whatever it's worth, I think you did the right thing."

Livengood laughed, spitting a bit of foam from the beer he was trying to drink.

"I sure as hell hope so," Livengood said. "Let's see, I sowed dissension in the church invisible to screw a preacher who was trying to save unborn babies, then I conned that same preacher and his flock in order to screw over an ex-governor for a bill that might just wreck the Kansas economy, for all I know. Plus, I did it all behind the back of the second best man I ever knew after my father, and it was the culmination of a career that was always a grave disappointment to my father. I'm telling you, Dan, if I didn't do the right thing, I'm going so deep into Hell that the Devil himself won't drop by to say, 'Howdy.' "

Dorsey waved his beer bottle, and opined that one pays one's money and takes one's chances.

"Yeah, what the hell," Livengood said. "How's everything back in Topeka? Any word of my few remaining friends?"

"Governor Harley says 'howdy,' " Dorsey reported. "That was a close call in the primary, but it doesn't look like he'll have much of a problem in the general. Your pal Stark—who also says, 'Howdy,' by the way—did a fine job running that campaign."

Livengood was only slightly surprised to learn that Dorsey knew that, and grateful it hadn't been printed.

"Who gives a damn who runs the campaigns?" Dorsey said. "I thought about writing a story, what with Mark being such a sinner and all, but I never wrote one about you running the first campaign, and it seemed kind of inconsistent."

Livengood asked for any other news.

"Your ex says, 'Hi.' She's the one who gave me the directions to get out here, but she said she wasn't sure they were right, that she had to get them from your dad. After Harley won the primary, she gave up her secure post and took a job with him."

"How's she liking it?"

"She hates it."

"Serves her right," Livengood said.

"That Darla Morland kid would probably want me to say, 'Howdy,' too. She's having a baby any day now, you know."

Livengood seemed relieved by the news.

"Her old man wanted her to get rid of it," Dorsey said. "But she talked him into paying for a nanny and a place she can keep the brat while she goes to school."

"She told you all this?"

"Go figure," Dorsey said. "I stopped befriending kids after I met you, but we got to talking one day around the rail, and she just started telling me all this. She kept saying it was because I'd 'done stuff.' "

"I understand," Livengood said. "She figured that with you being a reporter, you were in no position to judge her."

"I asked her what she would have done without the rich daddy, and she said she didn't know," Dorsey said. "Nice kid, though. Still has the great ass."

"I read your interview with Ellie Whimple," Livengood said. "She seems to be doing well."

"Prison life agrees with her," Dorsey said. "Not much chance for baby-saving in there, but at least there's always somebody to tell you what to do. She also asked me to say, 'Howdy.' "

With obvious reluctance, Livengood asked about Rebecca Reynolds.

"She's still running around the capitol, searching for Democrats. I hear she's dating some professional student type back in Lawrence. A Marxist or some such shit."

"Serves her right, too," Livengood said. "How about Kathy, Wilbur, Ed, Greg, all those guys?"

"They're all very happy about keeping their jobs. They all say, 'Howdy,' and, 'Thanks.' You can bet your sweet ass that they think you did the right thing."

Livengood said he certainly hoped so.

"By the way," Dorsey said. "What made you pull a crazy stunt like that, anyway?"

"I don't know. I guess it's like you say, it was the only thing I could do. At any rate, it was the only thing I could think of."

"It had to have been something," Dorsey said, walking to the refrigerator and helping himself to another beer. "I figured it must have had something to do with almost getting blown up by Edna and Will. Some kind of near-death thing."

"Naw," Livengood said. "I'd already been hit by a tornado, and I knew that all that realization of mortality crap wears off. Facing death isn't nearly so scary as facing the rest of it. I sure as hell wasn't going to pull a stunt like that just because I almost got blown up by a couple of crazy people."

"So then," Dorsey said, "what happened?"

Flipping the burgers again, Livengood poured some salt and pepper and Worcestershire sauce on them, then got another beer for himself. He leaned across the counter, scratching his chin and looking out on the empty prairie. "I think it started with that thing with Darla," he said. "She told me about the kid, because I'd 'done stuff,' and she asked me what I thought she should do."

Dorsey asked what Livengood told her.

"I didn't know what the hell to tell her. I just kept saying 'damn.' What do you tell a girl like that in a situation like that?"

Dorsey admitted he did not know.

"Well, neither did I," Livengood said. "That got me to thinking that I didn't have any business telling her what to do, and maybe nobody else did, either. If God wants to do me in for failing the unborn babies, well, that's His right. I still say that Edna Dimschmidt didn't have any damn jurisdiction, though."

Dorsey expressed surprise that Livengood and Darla were such close friends.

"We weren't," Livengood said. "Half the time she just drove me nuts. But she always did her job, she was always square with me, and I was supposed to watch out for her. Obviously I didn't get her knocked up by introducing her to fags or feminists, but I can't say I set the best example, smoking dope and guzzling booze and eating pussy in coatrooms that she might walk into."

Dorsey said that he hadn't heard that story.

"Never you mind about that," Livengood said. "The point is, I shouldn't have been doing it. Like it says in the Good Book, 'whosoever shall offend one of these little ones which believe in Me, it were better for him that a millstone were hanged about his neck, and that he were drowned in the depth of the sea.' "

"Wow," Dorsey said. "You can never completely shake that stuff from being a preacher's kid, can you?"

"Thank God for that," Livengood said. "I shudder to think how big an assole I'd be without it. Of course, all that damn religion was partly what got me in that mess. That's why I had to get Harley's river bill through, no matter what."

"What?" Dorsey said, skeptically. "You thought it was God's will or something?"

"I didn't, but Harley did, sort of. Harley'd been praying on it, praying on it real hard, and he'd had this dream. Harley being the kind of guy that he is, I figured that if he believed it, I'd better get on with it. I figured it's better that Harley should be the governor than me."

Dorsey asked if Livengood's newfound conscience was troubled by the methods he employed.

Before answering, Livengood placed the burgers on two sets of buns, then heaped on tomatoes, lettuce, onions and a generous amount of mustard. He put the burgers on plates, added large piles of French fries, and moved the meals to the counter. He then sat down across from Dorsey.

"It's like you say, Dan, that was the only way I could do it. Besides, it was bothering me enough already, to the point that I decided to get the hell out of the game. I figured that if bullshitting people was the only way I could make things work, even if I did do it well and occasionally for a good cause, then I ought to get out and let someone like Harley make things work. Politics takes brains, but leadership takes character. Of course, I had to arrange it so I would leave with things in good enough shape for the idiot to win a second term."

Dorsey chewed on his buffalo burger, then asked if Livengood were trying to save his soul or something like that.

"Yeah, something like that," Livengood said.

"How's it going?"

"So far, so good," Livengood said. "I'm going to church now and then, a non-sectarian one, because there aren't enough people left around here for sects. I'm down to one pack of cigarettes a day, I only toke now and then, and these beers I've been drinking in your honor are the first I've had in a week."

Dorsey was duly impressed.

"That's nothing," Livengood said. "What I'm most pleased about is that I haven't laid any bullshit on anyone since I left the capitol."

More than impressed, Dorsey was flabbergasted.

"Henceforth, I bullshit no one," Livengood said. "I'll offer a good burger for a fair price, and anyone who doesn't want the deal doesn't have to take it."

Dorsey conceded that the burger was quite tasty.

"And so it shall be in the rest of my life," Livengood said. "I'll be honest with people, and I won't tell them what to do, or let them tell me what to do. If they don't want me, they don't have to take me, and I won't blame them a bit."

Dorsey raised his beer in a toast to the truth.

"But not the whole truth," Livengood said. "I'll still tell an ugly lady that she's looking lovely, and I'll even tell people that I hope they have a nice day. I'm trying to be nicer. I'm going to live in my house by the side of the road and be a friend to man, and less of an asshole. I want to be more like Harley, only not so much of a dumbshit."

The two men ate their burgers, drank their beers, swapped jokes and spoke of the old days. A pink, purple and orange sunset formed over the flat horizon, and Dorsey explained that his failing night vision required him to begin the long journey to the nearest motel. Livengood offered a bed, but Dorsey declined. They shook hands at the door, then figured what the hell and gave each other a hug.

"Good luck with your soul," Dorsey said.

"You, too," Livengood said. "You'll need it."

After starting the Buick, Dorsey reached through the opened window to give Livengood a final handshake. Looking at the rearview mirror as he drove away, Dorsey chuckled. Through the flying dust, Dorsey could see Livengood holding his arms oustretched in farewell, a cigarette in one soft hand, a beer in the other, a rare smile on his face.

Frankie Livengood stood defiant on the Kansas plains.